"Katherine Kingsley has once again told a unique story with elegance and sensitivity. . . . a tribute to the strength of hope and the miracle of love. A powerful book not to be missed."
—Connie Rinehold, author
of *More than Just a Night*

"Warm, loving, highly original. I just couldn't stop reading. Tender, touching; this is a true garden of delights. *No Sweeter Heaven* is a very satisfying read."
—Edith Layton, author of
A Love For All Seasons

"If you haven't discovered Katherine Kingsley, you don't know what you're missing. She's a writer who never disappoints, and in *No Sweeter Heaven*, she's at the top of her form."
—Lindsay Chase, bestselling
author of *The Oath*

"An incredible reading experience; an irresistible love story every reader will cherish."
—*Romantic Times*

Buy Two Topaz Books and Get One Free Romance Novel!

With just two purchases of Topaz books, you'll be able to receive one romance novel free from the list below. Just send us two proofs of purchase* along with the coupon below, and the romance of your choice will be on its way to you! (subject to availability)

Check title you wish to receive:

*Send in coupons, proof of purchase (register receipt & photocopy of UPC code from books) plus $1.50 postage and handling to:

TOPAZ 🔱 GIVEAWAY
Penguin USA, 375 Hudson Street, New York, NY 10014

NAME_____

ADDRESS_____ APT. #_____

CITY_____STATE_____ZIP_____

No Sweeter Heaven

by

Katherine Kingsley

A TOPAZ BOOK

To my husband, Bruce,
who first gave Pascal into my safekeeping.
All my love.

TOPAZ
Published by the Penguin Group
Penguin Books USA Inc., 375 Hudson Street,
New York, New York 10014, U.S.A.
Penguin Books Ltd, 27 Wrights Lane,
London W8 5TZ, England
Penguin Books Australia Ltd, Ringwood,
Victoria, Australia
Penguin Books Canada Ltd, 10 Alcorn Avenue,
Toronto, Ontario, Canada M4V 3B2
Penguin Books (N.Z.) Ltd, 182–190 Wairau Road,
Auckland 10, New Zealand

Penguin Books Ltd, Registered Offices:
Harmondsworth, Middlesex, England

First published by Topaz, an imprint of New American Library,
a division of Penguin Books USA Inc.

First Printing, August, 1993
10 9 8 7 6 5 4 3 2 1

 Topaz is a trademark of New American Library,
a division of Penguin Books USA Inc.

Printed in the United States of America

Acknowledgments

THE abbey of St. Christophe de Montebon is loosely based on the history of L'Abbaye Saint-Pierre de Solesmes. I thank Rory Graham, Philippa Lawrence-Jones, Pat Kendall, and Elinor Sinclair for pointing me in the right direction. For various details of monastic life, I thank Jacques Couturier, who took the time to set me straight on how it *really* is.

George Bursick, Michael Mondavi, Gerard Yvernault, Christian and Luc Joly, and Jean-Pierre Chaminade were most gracious in giving their time and advice concerning viniculture. The Chaminades were also of great help in describing the Périgord of the last century.

Thanks to Susie Schneider and Doug Foster of the Vail Valley Medical Center, who provided me with various essential details and descriptions of a medical nature.

For unflagging support and a careful eye to detail, I thank Jan Hiland and Connie Rinehold, who went far beyond the call of friendship to get me through the final stage of this book.

Finally, my heartfelt thanks to all the readers who took the time to write me with their thoughts and feelings about *No Greater Love.* I was delighted by how many of you wanted a story about Pascal. The last third of the trilogy will be out in the summer of 1994. Please continue to write with your opinions, suggestions and comments. They are a wonderful source of inspiration and encouragement and are much appreciated.

You can write me at P.O. Box 37, Wolcott, Colorado, 81655.

Happy reading!

For He shall give His angels charge over thee,
to keep thee in all thy ways.

Prayer Book, 91:11

Prologue

THEY said it all began the night that the duke succumbed to the typhoid epidemic that swept through Saint-Simon like the last of the ten plagues of Egypt. It took his infant son hours later, then claimed his wife the next morning.

The bodies were laid to eternal rest in the château's chapel, where all of the Ducs de Saint-Simon and their progeny had been buried, with the one notable exception of the duke who had been martyred in the Wars of Religion. It was a terrible thing—the sixth duke and his wife had been seen kissing under the walnut tree below the south vineyard only three weeks before, his dark head bent over her bright one, both healthy and happy and deeply in love. And now they were gone and their only child with them.

The mood of the villagers was decidedly grim, for not only had they lost many of their own, but the duke's brother was the next in line. He was rumored to be a cruel and ambitious man, fond of his pleasures and careless where he took them. As it turned out, rumor was correct, and all of Saint-Simon suffered as a result. The vines withered from neglect. The people swore there was a curse on them as the crop failed year after year, and the village grew poor.

The seventh duke died only two years after his brother, and his wife took their son back to England. The estate was left without guidance, and the vineyards continued to fail. Over time the legend took hold: until the heir to Saint-Simon came back to the land, it would not thrive.

But the heir had been back three years now, a man full grown, and still the vines suffered. The people began to despair whether there would ever be another harvest.

1

"**T**HIS is absurd," Lily murmured, gingerly shifting her weight on the branch beneath her feet. "It might . . . just possibly . . . even be preposterous," she added, wondering whether she'd finally managed to fulfill all the dire things said about her character. She adjusted her grip, then hitched herself up onto the natural fork joining two sturdy branches, pushed down the annoying bulk of her skirts, and peered through the leaves to watch the cloisters and any monks that might be gliding about below.

After an hour her bottom grew numb and her leg hurt where she'd scratched it during her climb. Lily began to wonder if she would ever achieve her objective. It was just her luck that her quarry had to be a religious recluse. Her heart had sunk the moment she'd rung the bell on the great abbey door and a wizened old man appeared, dressed from head to toe in black. It took all of two minutes for the monk to dismiss her.

"I am sorry, mademoiselle," the porter said, not looking particularly interested in her or her dilemma. "We do not allow the world inside these walls. Perhaps you might write to the abbot, Dom Benetard, with your questions."

The door closed in her face.

Dejected, Lily turned to leave, then spotted the large elm tree that towered well over the forbidding wall of the abbey. An idea began to take hold. She had to do something or her beloved half brother was sure to lose everything.

So now, for better or for worse, here she was, sitting in the elm's higher limbs, admiring a particularly fine view of the Abbey of St. Christophe de Montebon.

Lily knew it was very wicked to spy. She knew she would probably burn in hell if God happened to be watching His servant, the wayward Elizabeth Mary Bowes, at that particular moment. But as God had more than likely given up on her long ago, and Jean-Jacques needed her services far more than God did, she felt her loyalties really ought to go to her brother. Anyway, from the look of those black-garbed monks drifting about below, God had more than enough servants enlisted in His cause. He could afford a stray sheep or two.

She shuddered to think that she might well have ended up consigned to a convent—indeed, if she hadn't been her father's only child, he would have dispatched her to the sisters at the very first opportunity. But instead of marrying her to Christ, he was determined to see her married to a mortal. Lily was equally determined not to oblige him. At each refusal, Father Mallet presided over the raging argument, his fixed mask of spiritual piety no doubt covering a very sincere desire to wring her neck.

He would wring her neck too, he and her father both, if they *ever* discovered what she was doing at that moment. She would never be allowed to see Jean-Jacques again, for they'd blame it all on him. Still, it was worth the risk.

"Oh, Jean-Jacques," she whispered, "I love you more than anything or anyone on the face of the earth. I swear, somehow I'll find a way to fix things. Papa will never know about your troubles; I swear that too, for I couldn't bear to see you humiliated. I'll find this stupid monk, somehow I will, and he'll know just what to do for your crops."

A long stream of monks emerged from the cloisters and crossed the courtyard to the church for midday prayers. She waited impatiently, wishing they would get on with it. Not that she had any firm plan as to how to locate her particular monk. It all seemed quite hopeless, really. But maybe if this monk had such a special way with miracles, as the village priest had insisted, he'd be obliging enough to sport a halo.

Lily remembered Father Chabot standing in the château's shadow, looking down at her poor brother's barren vineyards.

"It will take a miracle, Lady Elizabeth," he had said doubtfully. "Hmm. A miracle. A miracle . . . now what does that remind me of?" He scratched his balding head as if he'd just jostled a thought and it was rattling around in a fog. And then he smiled brightly as the memory finally emerged into the light. "Ah, yes! I remember now. A friend of mine, a priest, wrote me a letter a few months back. He lives farther north, you see.''

''No, I don't see,'' Lily said impatiently. ''What does your friend up north have to do with anything?''

''There is a man at a monastery in Montebon . . . apparently he has become something of a legend in the Loire Valley for his ability to work wonders with living things. 'A maker of miracles,' they call him.''

Lily, who had no use for old wives' tales, or for so-called miracles, had scoffed until Father Chabot added that the monk was a botanist, which naturally explained his ability to Lily. She had a healthy respect for science, far more than she had for religion. It had taken her no time at all to make her way directly to Montebon.

The monks streamed out again from the church and crossed the quadrant toward what she imagined was the refectory, for by now it was lunchtime. She wondered what would happen if she called down to them: *Excuse me, but I'm looking for one of your brothers, although I don't know his name. Does one of you happen to be a botanist?*

But that was an absurd strategy, she knew, with no likelihood of success. There'd be monks littered everywhere. Still, there had to be a way. . . .

Her heart skipped a beat as a solitary figure exited through the rear of the refectory. Unlike the monks, this man was dressed in a simple white shirt, jacket, and trousers, and his dark head was bare.

His back to her, he walked across the park, past the large, sunny clearing where the working gardens for the abbey kitchens stood, and finally stopped in a smaller, partially enclosed area that looked as if it contained seedlings.

Lily watched as he fetched a basket of tools from a large shed, took off his jacket and rolled up his sleeves, and settled down to work in a tilled patch among the young plants, weeding and watering, working the soil with his fingers and a trowel, his back turned away from her.

''Perfect,'' she murmured. ''A gardener.''

Here was someone who might actually be willing to speak to her, might even know of the monk she was seeking. If her luck held, the gardener might even be willing to carry a message. Her heart pounding with excitement, she started to climb down toward the top of the wall. And then she froze as two monks followed the first man's path over to the kitchen gardens. To Lily's dismay, they set to work, hoeing and weeding only a few feet from her quarry.

Suppressing a very strong desire to scream with frustration, she rearranged herself in the tree and prepared to wait some more. Maybe the monks would suddenly feel a pressing urge to return to the church and she'd have her gardener to herself again.

Restlessly she shifted, and shifted again. A dead branch fell to the ground with a thud loud enough to make one of the monks look up, but after a moment he went back to his work. Lily released a long sigh of relief and, for lack of anything better to do, focused her attention on the gardener.

He moved rhythmically, with the easy grace of a person long used to physical activity, a man comfortable with himself and the outdoors. It was a pleasant and compelling sight to Lily. Simplicity was in short supply in her life at the moment, and there was something comforting about observing this man going about his chores, something soothing about the way in which he blended into the peaceful surroundings of the monastery.

For one fleeting moment Lily wished that she had nothing more to worry about than working a small plot of land, perhaps going home at the end of the day to a small family who demanded nothing greater than food on the table and some pleasant conversation.

Yes—that was probably how it was. No doubt there were a few small children running about and a homely but welcoming wife who greeted him cheerfully, as the smell of baking bread drifted out the door of their little cottage. Lily could just see it. And at night, when the children had all been tenderly tucked up in their beds, he would turn to his wife and enfold her with those strong arms, bend that dark head of his to hers, and do wonderful, passionate things with her. . . .

Lily shook her head, dispelling the mists of fantasy. The man probably looked like her father's favorite hound, despite the broad back and powerful legs. They usually did. In any case, what did she know about passion? Absolutely nothing, at least not since she'd been eight and was smitten with the new butler. For a full three months she'd decided that all she wanted in life was to be a footman so that she could serve under her beloved. She had followed devotedly in Robert's footsteps until one day the passion of her life had mysteriously disappeared, to be replaced by a stiff old martinet.

Ever since, all the male staff at Sutherby had been extraordinarily unattractive.

Her gaze returned to the gardener, and she sighed with pleasure. There was a certain appeal in a strong, well-made figure, even if it wasn't proper for her to admire it. But who was to object, given that she was hidden in a tree, with no one to see? And it *was* only his back she was admiring.

The gardener suddenly glanced up over his shoulder as if to check the position of the sun, and Lily nearly fell off her perch.

The first shattering image that came to mind was that of an angel—a fallen angel. His eyes, a deep, clear brown, held something that she'd never seen before. She couldn't even define it to herself beyond the impression that he didn't quite belong to this world, as if he possessed a knowledge that humans ought not to possess. She saw something else too, something dangerous and unsettling, like looking directly into the eye of a hurricane.

Lily swallowed hard. What was a man that extraordinarily handsome doing working in a monastery? Gone was the vision of the homely wife, the sweet young children. This was a man more suited to running about the brothels of Paris, disporting himself with loose women.

She imagined that he had sinned terribly, perhaps ruined some poor innocent—maybe even killed someone in a duel—and was now paying his penance, which would explain that . . . well, that *haunted* look in his eyes. The man was a repentant rake, an exile from society.

Lily had always wanted to meet a proper rake. Her father had drilled into her head the terrible dangers such men presented, their complete lack of ethics, their unconscionable desires. She wasn't exactly sure what an unconscionable desire was, but she did know that it led to ruin and worse.

The rake's eyes returned to earth and Lily shivered. She felt as if she had just been turned inside out, turned right side back again, and a piece of her, somewhere in the region of her stomach, hadn't gone back into its proper place. Lily wasn't at all sure she liked the feeling.

At last the two monks drifted back to the building, and the rake continued his work, as Lily had hoped. She was just wondering how best to get his attention when he stood and put his tools away. For a moment she was afraid that he might follow the monks, but her luck continued, for instead of heading toward the abbey he walked directly toward her.

It appeared he might actually pass under her tree, and her heart began to beat faster with anticipation.

To her intense irritation, he stopped before he reached her and sat down on a stone bench that was a good twenty feet short of the elm, his back to her. But instead of behaving like a normal person and sitting there enjoying the view, he pulled his legs up, crossed his ankles so that his thighs rested flat on the stone, placed his hands in his lap, and closed his eyes.

At first Lily didn't know what to make of this extraordinary performance, but then she realized that he must have gone to sleep, for the rise and fall of his chest changed almost instantly and became slow and deep. It was beyond her how anyone could sleep in such an uncomfortable position, but she didn't have time to worry about it. She would have to return to the inn soon, for Coffey would begin to worry, and she had taxed her old nurse's patience enough as it was.

She bit her lip. The rake really was too far away to be hailed, certainly not without shouting. There was only one thing to be done. Lily cautiously lowered herself onto the wall.

Pascal drifted, lost somewhere between the stars and heaven. Meditation was as natural and essential to him as breathing, but this evening something tugged at the back of his mind, an annoyance, like an insect buzzing too close to him. He resettled himself on the bench, trying to concentrate on inner peace. But peace continued to elude him. In its place there was a hiss, not unlike that of a distressed toad, he thought, opening his eyes just a fraction and peering around. There was nothing to be seen, at least nothing immediately apparent, and, in any case, he was certain that toads did not reside in this particular part of the world. Perhaps it was a demented frog.

Pascal closed his eyes again and took a deep breath, concentrating on clearing his mind completely, but this evening he was finding it difficult to focus; the annoying hiss just would not go away. His eyes snapped open in frustration and he looked about him, searching the ground for the intruding reptile. He realized that the noise was coming not from the ground but from higher above, and he turned around, his gaze wandering slowly upward. It traveled over the coarse stone of the wall that formed the west boundary of the monastery—and stopped in disbelief.

There was a young woman—a woman, of all things—creeping precariously along the top of the wall, her hair, a burnished bronze in color, tumbling over one ear in a lopsided loop. Her skirts were hitched up about her knees in a most unseemly fashion, and there was a tear in the stocking on one exposed calf.

Perhaps she was an escapee from an insane asylum, he decided in alarm as the creature stopped, closed her eyes, and hissed again for all she was worth, then bowed her head, breathing hard.

As aggravating as it was to have his meditation interrupted, Pascal had never turned away a person in need, most certainly not a sick one. He quickly rose from his bench and went to a spot directly underneath her.

"Madame," he said, squinting up at her through the sun's lowering light, "are you in need of aid? Is there something I might do for you?"

The creature's eyes flew open and she lurched upright from a crouch like a praying mantis preparing to do battle. Her mouth moved as if to speak, but nothing came out save for a long sigh, and her eyes closed again. She leaned to one side and slowly toppled off the wall, her body landing with a thud at his feet.

Pascal instantly dropped to his knees. She was alarmingly pale, and he quickly unfastened her cloak, opened the bodice of her dress, and loosened her corset. He felt for a pulse, which he was reassured to find, and he ran his practiced hands along the contours of her body, checking for broken bones and slipping his hands under her skirts to examine her legs. She seemed to have survived the long fall in one piece, but whether she had sustained any internal injuries was another question.

He was about to pick her up and carry her to the infirmary when stars exploded inside his head, and he lurched forward and fell on top of her, his hands clasping his temples as a shrill scream reverberated in his ears.

"God above . . ." he moaned, his head feeling as if it had just been caught in a vise.

"You depraved beast!" the lunatic cried from under his prostrate body. "You filthy excuse for a penitent!" She pushed him off her and rolled to her knees, glaring at him, her eyes snapping with rage. "How could you take advantage of a woman's insensibility? How—how could you even think of mauling someone inside the walls of a monastery? Have you no shame?"

"Madame," Pascal said weakly, his head still reeling from the blow she'd given it, "who are you? What are you?"

He was doing his very best to be compassionate and turn the other cheek, but as he'd never had any experience in dealing with madwomen, and since she had already lambasted both sides of his head between her fists, he didn't think there was much room left in which to negotiate. He struggled to sit up, his head pounding painfully.

"What I am is a person not accustomed to being attacked! And do not think that I shan't tell your superiors that, either, for I shall! I am sure they will be deeply disappointed that you have returned to your immoral ways!"

Pascal stared at her. "My . . . Woman, *what* are you going on about? Have you mistaken me for someone else, perhaps? Or is it your habit to beat men about the head when they are attempting to see to your welfare?"

"Ha!" she said, turning away and struggling with the strings of her corset, her hands shaking. "My welfare, you say? You have obviously been too long without the company of women if you feel you must strip one the moment you have the chance!"

"I was not attempting to strip you. I was merely attempting to ascertain whether you had injured yourself," Pascal said as patiently as he could manage.

"Which is why your hands were wandering about under my petticoats?"

"Madame, you have an exceedingly high opinion of yourself if you think you are so irresistible that a man cannot help but grope at you the instant you happen to be unconscious."

Lily, stung, glared at him. "I should not add insult to injury, you horrible man. You are in enough trouble as it is."

"Oh, and what sort of trouble do you imagine that is?"

Pascal retorted, his usually even temper stretched to its limit.

She pointed a shaking finger behind him while she hastily attempted to pull the bodice of her dress together with the other hand.

Pascal looked over his shoulder and saw young Julien and the abbot, Dom Benetard, hurrying toward them. "Oh, no," he muttered under his breath. "Oh, please, dear Lord, have mercy."

He slowly rose to his feet and turned to face them, a cold chill taking hold of his heart. The expressions of dismay on both faces were a clear indication of their thoughts. The madwoman's next words only served to add to their consternation.

"Thank goodness you have come—your gardener attempted to assault me!"

Julien looked at her in horror, but the abbot had more self-control. He turned to Pascal and spoke in a calm, gentle voice. "Is this true, my son?"

"No, it is not true, Father. I was attempting to help the woman after she fell from the wall. I loosened her clothing and examined her for injuries." He lowered his voice. "I fear she might be unbalanced in her mind."

"Unbalanced?" Lily said indignantly. "I am no more unbalanced than I am deaf, so it is no good using that tactic to try to excuse yourself."

"Then if you're not unbalanced, you might explain why you were crawling along the top of the monastery wall hissing like a lunatic," Pascal snapped, thoroughly out of patience and extremely annoyed to have been put in this ludicrous situation. "Such behavior is hardly normal."

"I don't have to explain myself to you," she said, glaring at him. "You seem to forget that I am the person with a grievance, not you." She turned her attention back to the abbot. "If you please, lock this man away, for I do not wish to look at him anymore."

"I am afraid it is not that simple, my child," the abbot said. "We cannot lock a person away when there is some doubt as to what actually occurred. Is it not possible that you might have been mistaken, and Monsieur LaMartine was attempting to see to your well-being?"

"By pawing at my . . ." She blushed furiously. "Under my . . . *you* know. At least I think you do." She glanced at the slight monk, who was blushing even more fiercely than she. "And if you won't lock him away, I think you should dismiss him from the abbey immediately. I can't imagine what my father would have to say if I told him that you let such a thing go unpunished! I am sure you would be very sorry."

"And who is your father?" the abbot asked.

"Oh. He is . . . he is no one," Lily said, catching her lip between her teeth, her eyes dropping from the abbot's.

"One's father is always of significance, my child, and furthermore, by your manner, bearing, and speech, I suspect your father is not an insignificant man. It would be best, I think, if you tell us his name, and yours, and where you have come from." Dom Benetard's words, though gently spoken, brooked no argument.

"He is the Duke of Montcrieff," Lily said, staring at the ground. "In England," she added unnecessarily.

The abbot paled, and poor Julien swayed as if he might faint. Pascal felt a little queasy himself. The Duke of Montcrieff had been more than generous to the abbey. In fact, the abbey and its lands might not have been acquired at all eight years before if the duke had not offered his patronage and considerable funds.

Dom Benetard cleared his throat. "I see. And your name, my child?"

"Elizabeth Bowes."

"Yes, of course. Your father has spoken of you to me."

"Has he?" she asked, her eyes flashing up to meet his defiantly.

"Indeed he has," Dom Benetard said equitably. "It is a natural thing, is it not, for a loving father to speak of his daughter?"

"It is kind of you to say so." The defiance in her face fled as she saw that there was no judgment there, and Pascal wondered what had been behind that particular sortie. He felt slightly disoriented, as if they were suddenly having a pleasant social exchange, rather than being involved in a volatile situation with potentially far-reaching consequences. But Pascal knew that anything might be transpiring in the abbot's head.

Dom Benetard was silent for a long moment, considering the problem. "Yes, indeed, Elizabeth," he finally said, "I can understand your alarm under the circumstances. After all, you have been very carefully brought up. Although I can assure you that Monsieur LaMartine's character is above reproach, we appear to be in a dilemma. I think it would be best if we discussed the matter at length. Brother Julien," he said to his alarmed companion, "perhaps you would be so good as to escort Lady Elizabeth to the gate. Vespers is about to begin, and I do not think she will be seen exiting. Where do you stay, my child?"

"I have put up at the Lion D'Or, Father."

"Very well. I will attend you there before Compline this evening." He turned to Pascal. "My son, you will come to my lodging after Vespers. I feel confident that we can come to a satisfactory solution."

Julien couldn't leave fast enough, his legs taking him off at a pace that threatened to leave Elizabeth Bowes behind. Elizabeth Bowes, whom Pascal still thought completely unbalanced despite—or perhaps because of—her rarefied parentage, cast one scathing last look in his direction, then hurried after Julien. The sight of the two of them side by side created a complete contrast in both body and soul: one small, slight, and silent, the other tall, lithe, and lunatic.

Pascal sighed heavily and turned to face the abbot, but before he could speak, Dom Benetard held up his hand to forestall him.

"We will go into Vespers now. Use the time of prayer wisely, Pascal. I too have much to meditate upon. We will talk after."

Doing as he'd been told, Pascal went directly to the church. It was not that Dom Benetard hadn't believed him, he thought as he knelt and began the ritual of evening prayer. It was not even that he had betrayed the abbot's trust and confidence. It was simply that this was a matter too inflammatory for the recently confirmed abbey to deal with without serious repercussions.

Scandal threatened if the right thing was not done. It mattered not why the woman had been on the wall, nor that she had accidentally fallen. Since she believed Pascal had been about to defile her, then the right thing would have to be done regardless.

Pascal's blood ran cold when he contemplated what interpretation the abbot might put on "the right thing." He closed his eyes and prayed in earnest.

"Oh, Coffey, I've gone and done it now," Lily wailed, falling into the arms of her faithful old companion, who had been waiting at the inn for Lily's return as calmly as she could manage, her anxiety turning to panic as the hours had gone by with no sign of the girl. Now here Lily finally was, but badly disheveled, with streaks of dirt on her face and hands. Coffey shivered with a sense of foreboding.

"What have you done, pet?" she asked, patting Lily's back uncertainly. "Did you not find your monk, then?"

"It's far worse than that—there was a dreadful man who I thought could help me, and then when I fell, he attempted to—oh, Coffey . . . he attempted to ravish me!" Lily burst into tears, caused more by hunger and exhaustion than anything else.

"No!" Coffey gasped, deeply shocked. "He didn't take . . . take *advantage*, did he?"

"No, he didn't, because two monks arrived just in time, but I cannot think what might have happened if they hadn't. I knew he was a rake, just by looking at his face, but then I never thought to fall."

"No, of course you didn't," Coffey said soothingly.

"It was only because I hadn't eaten since breakfast, and my head spun."

"Oh, dear heaven, child! How dreadful for you!"

Lily nodded in vigorous agreement. "It was. I never meant to get so close to him, I promise, for I know what you've always said about the wickedness of men, but I was at least ten or fifteen feet above his head, so what could he have done? And anyway, he was inside a monastery, for heaven's sake, so being ravished was the very last thing I expected!"

Miss Mary Matilda McCofferty, nurse to Lily from the time Lily had been an infant, and a good Scots Catholic, released her charge suddenly and crossed herself in horror. "You didn't actually fall *into* the monastery, Lily? You don't mean to say you were climbing about on the abbey wall?"

"Well . . . there really wasn't any other way to find my monk except to go looking for him from above."

Coffey paled. The deep sockets of her eyes seemed to have sunk even further, but her little button eyes blazed black against her white skin. "You are telling me that a monk tried to ravish you? And you expect me to believe you? A Benedictine monk, my girl, a man of God? Surely you must have misunderstood?"

"But he wasn't a monk," Lily said, desperate to have someone believe her after the terrible experience she had just been through. "He was only a layman, a gardener who works for the abbey. Oh, Coffey, don't be cross—I know I ought not to have been on the wall to begin with, and I don't know exactly why I was, but it was all for Jean-Jacques, and anyway, you agreed to come along."

Coffey sat down on the one chair in the sparsely furnished

bedchamber and folded her hands tightly together in her lap. "I agreed to come with you, my lady, because I would not see you chasing off across the French countryside on your own. Now look at what has happened. What did I tell you when you came up with this scheme of yours?"

Lily swallowed. "It's worse than you think. The abbot is coming to see me. He knows Papa, of course, for I made the terrible mistake of blurting Papa's name out before I thought of the consequences . . ."

Coffey passed a hand over her eyes and whispered a quick prayer to the Blessed Mother for help.

"I know," Lily said miserably, knowing exactly what her old nurse must be thinking. "Papa is bound to be told everything. I shall just have to think of a way to soften the blow."

Coffey glared at Lily. "You don't intend to compound your sins by lying to an *abbot,* my lady?"

"Oh, please don't call me that, for then I know you are truly put out with me. No, I don't intend to lie, but then I don't think the abbot really needs to know about Jean-Jacques and his troubles, do you?" Lily tapped her mouth with her finger. "I'll have to think of something milder by way of an explanation. Something harmless."

"You'll only make more trouble for yourself, Elizabeth, by not telling the truth," Coffey said sternly. "It is bound to come back to you. Take my word for it."

"Nonsense," Lily said impatiently. "Anyway, I can't think at all unless I have something to eat. Do you think you could ask the innkeeper to send up a supper tray, and perhaps some hot water so that I might wash? I ought at least to look respectable for the abbot when he comes."

Moving astonishingly quickly for a woman who needed a cane to get about, Coffey disappeared through the door.

Having successfully distracted Coffey from the tongue-lashing she knew was forthcoming, Lily breathed a sigh of relief and began to undress, looking ruefully at her ruined stocking. It was extraordinarily lucky that her stocking was the only thing that had been ruined.

"But, oh, how is it that I am always getting myself into trouble?" she moaned and threw herself onto the bed, arms flung over her head.

Why couldn't life just be simple?

2

LILY washed, changed, and managed to eat a good dinner before Dom Benetard was scheduled to arrive at the inn, and she felt much better for all three. Not much could put Lily off her food, which she always approached with relish. That was why her usual punishment of bread and water for a week was so aggravating. Father Mallet's philosophy held that starving her greedy body would feed her needy soul—but then Father Mallet never looked as if he enjoyed anything.

Lily arranged a private parlor for the meeting, the innkeeper suitably impressed that she was receiving Dom Benetard. She gathered that the townspeople were in great awe of the man. Well, that was all well and fine, as it secured her the parlor with no trouble, but Lily was not nearly as impressed as the innkeeper. Dom Benetard was merely an elevated priest, and she knew from bitter experience how to deal with that breed. Keep one's eyes down, pretend humility, agree with everything, say a penance or two, then go one's own way.

She settled herself in a chair by the fire, pulled her dress down to be sure it covered her ankles, and placed her hands demurely in her lap. She hoped she looked the picture of innocence, although the picture would be destroyed if her father had said anything to Dom Benetard regarding what he considered to be her impossible behavior.

Coffey had brushed her hair until it shone and arranged it primly atop her head as the old nurse felt befitted a young lady. Lily could only hope that Dom Benetard would not be put off by the fiery color that Father Mallet called the taint of the devil, for she needed the abbot to think her beyond reproach. Satisfied that she had done all she could to deflect the repercussions of the plan that had so badly gone awry, she took a deep breath and prepared to receive the monk.

* * *

In the end, it felt more as if it were Dom Benetard who received her. He arrived in his simple black habit, politely refusing her offer of fruit and wine, instead focusing his clear, tranquil gaze upon her. Lily realized instantly, and with strong confusion, that this was no Father Mallet. This was a man the likes of whom she had never met, whose very presence seemed to wrap her in a cloak of peace.

He sat opposite her and she focused on the large but simple wooden cross that hung on his chest. Her eyes crept up again to his strongly boned face. His features were even and pleasantly arranged; she judged him to be somewhere in his early forties, young for the weighty position of abbot. But there was something about Dom Benetard that defied age. His face held a wisdom and a serenity that made one want to gaze upon it, to find stillness and safety there.

Her belligerence fled as it had in the monastery when she had been prepared to lie through her teeth about her father's identity. Lily would never have believed it of herself, having fought her entire life against authority, but she found she longed to tell the abbot everything. And yet she knew she could not. She'd sworn to protect Jean-Jacques.

"Tell me, my child," the abbot began in his deep, lyrical voice. "How did you come to be inside the monastery walls? It was as Monsieur LaMartine said? You fell?"

Lily nodded and prepared to tell the tale she'd constructed, feeling terribly guilty. "I did. I know I should not have been there, but I could not help myself. My father has spoken so often of his devotion to the Abbey of St. Christophe and I was curious."

"Curious?" the abbot asked calmly.

"Well, yes. I wanted to see its beauty with my own eyes and being a woman, I knew I would never have the opportunity." She smiled sweetly, hoping she looked positively angelic.

"Go on, my child," the abbot said.

"Well, um . . . my companion and I were traveling through Montebon and I did not think there would be any harm in looking, if no one saw me. So I climbed the elm tree just outside the wall."

"I see." Dom Benetard folded his hands into a steeple.

"Once I was on the wall, I overbalanced and fell," Lily said, unnerved by his complete lack of expression, "and when I did, your gardener took advantage of me. But if you are prepared to forget the incident, then I am also. I am sure you would wish to avoid scandal. You need not put him in your jail," she added generously, "although I do not think he is suited to life inside a monastery, not if he is inclined to temptations of the flesh."

Dom Benetard actually smiled, and in his eyes she was astonished to see a natural joy that radiated from within his being and lit up his entire face.

"I can say with all honesty that I had not considered incarcerating our good brother. I cannot help but doubt that he was succumbing to temptation." His smile faded, and Lily felt as if the sun had just disappeared. "Still, the facts themselves do create a problem."

"But they don't have to," Lily persisted. "I really am prepared to forget all about it. And I am deeply regretful that I climbed onto your wall," she added for good measure.

"It is beyond dispute that you ought not to have been observing the abbey from its own walls. I believe you have some forgiveness to ask of God for that. However, that is another matter. What weighs on my mind is the responsibility I have to your father."

"Oh—but you have no responsibility to my father at all! I won't say a word, and it is not as if you knew I was on your wall in the first place."

"Yes, child, but your claim that Pascal LaMartine assaulted you cannot be ignored."

Lily deeply regretted having ever opened her mouth—not an uncommon regret, as her mouth was her usual downfall. "I don't see why not," she said in a small voice.

"Elizabeth. You have brought a serious charge against Monsieur LaMartine. Your father must be informed, and Monsieur LaMartine must be given a chance to clear his name. It is up to your father to judge the truth of the matter. I can think of no other way."

"But—but surely it is your job to discipline the man," Lily said, faltering. "My father really has nothing to do with the running of the abbey, has he?"

"No, he has no authority, only our gratitude. But you must also understand that although Monsieur LaMartine has been with us for two years, I have no ecclesiastical authority over him, as he has not taken any vows. Do you understand?''

Lily swallowed. "Yes. I—I do.''

"That is good. So you understand that this must be left to your father. I've decided that the most sensible thing to do is to send one of our brothers to escort you to Sutherby Park along with Monsieur LaMartine.''

"You—you will send me home in the company of the man who attempted to *defile* me?'' Lily asked incredulously.

"As I said, one of the brothers will go with you. Brother Julien has offered his services. I shall entrust a letter to him, describing the events that have transpired today.''

The fire snapped and crackled in the grate, and Lily stared into it, contemplating the full repercussions of this appalling announcement. Her gaze slid back to Dom Benetard as she struggled for speech. "That man—Monsieur LaMartine, I mean—surely he will not agree to go, knowing what my father will do to him?''

"Monsieur LaMartine has already agreed. Your father, having contemplated the matter, will then determine what must be done. We must all agree to abide by his decision.''

"What . . . what sort of decision?'' Lily asked nervously, not entirely sure she was grasping the point.

"It is not for me to say, child.'' The abbot tucked his hands securely within the sleeves of his habit. "It would be best if you remained in these quarters until you hear from me regarding arrangement for your travel to England.''

He stood, said a blessing over her bowed head, and quietly departed, leaving Lily in a state of shock.

Pascal spent the entire night in the church in prayer and contemplation, but his last hours at St. Christophe de Montebon passed in anything but peace. The outcome of his talk with Dom Benetard had come as no surprise. His disquiet stemmed more from his lack of understanding of why such an unwarranted situation should have befallen him. It seemed an odd conclusion to a spiritual quest, a quest that had taken him halfway around the world and ended up in St. Christophe.

Pascal rose as the chill of dawn spread through his bones. He took one last look around the long, narrow church, topped by a gracefully vaulted ceiling that gave it such balance, gazed one last time at the extraordinary sculptures of

the saints, their stone faces so lifelike. The scent of frank-
incense from last night's Compline still lingered in the air,
rich and dark.

Pascal turned and walked out into the daylight.

He went wearily to the bare room in which he had lived for
the last two years. There was not much to collect, only a
few items of clothing, some books, and a small, well-
executed painting. It had been done five years before, and
although Nicholas and Georgia would look much the same,
the children would have changed considerably since he had
last been home.

He'd missed them—Charlie would be nearly a man now
at eighteen, and Ghislaine, at sixteen, would soon be ready
to trade her braids for the finery of a young woman. As for
Willy and Kate, they were still bound to be trouble, racing
about, looking for mischief in every corner. If there was
one small measure of comfort to be found in being forcibly
sent to England, it was the thought of seeing them all again.

He carefully placed the painting in his satchel with the
rest of his possessions, covering it with a cloth to protect
the surface. He fastened the straps, his fingers struggling
with the leather that had become stiff from lack of use. He
then left to find Dom Benetard.

Pascal knelt before the abbot, accepting the Benediction
being said over his head. He rose from his knees, feeling
quite sick.

"It is not such a bad thing, my son," the abbot said,
placing his hand on Pascal's shoulder. "You have benefited
by your studies, and our gardens have benefited from your
devoted work, as have the people. But this is perhaps an
answer from God to the question that has been troubling
you, no?"

Pascal regarded Dom Benetard's serene face, his familiar,
beneficent smile, and he wondered how his mentor could
be feeling quite so calm at consigning him to such an unwanted, unexpected, and uninvited fate.

"Father . . ." he said haltingly, "I do not know. In all
truth, I cannot say. Why would God throw a deranged no-
blewoman off a wall at my feet as an answer to my question?"

"I cannot speak for God," the abbot said with a slight
twinkle in his eye, "but should it come to that, marriage is

not such a bad thing. There are many whom it suits very well, and it is an esteemed state in God's eyes."

"But I don't even know the woman! It makes no sense." Pascal clamped down hard on his anger, fighting for self-control.

"Perhaps it makes no sense just now, but God has a hand in everything. You have long prayed for resolution, and perhaps it has been given to you."

"This has nothing whatsoever to do with marriage as I understand it," Pascal said tightly. "As you know, I had not thought to marry at all. I have none of the usual things to offer a wife."

"But it is not a finished thing. The duke might decide no harm has been done." Dom Benetard hesitated for a moment, one hand moving on his cross as if he were looking for guidance. "I think I must tell you," he continued, "that Montcrieff has spoken of his daughter to me, but not as lovingly as I implied to Elizabeth."

"Oh?" Pascal said, raising an eyebrow. "Why am I not surprised?"

"He is a forceful man, Pascal, and Elizabeth has lived a life of rebellion. There has not been peace between them, although I am not sure that the duke has handled the matter as well as he might have. Nevertheless, he knows his daughter is prone to impulsive behavior. I do not think he will lay any blame at your door, especially given your curative skills, which I have mentioned in my letter."

Pascal gave the abbot a look of real alarm. "Father—"

Dom Benetard held up his hand. "It is only natural that a man with medical training should examine someone who has taken a fall," he said.

Pascal exhaled.

"Still," Dom Benetard said, "there are other factors to be considered. Whatever Montcrieff decides, I know I can trust you to accede to his wishes."

Pascal dutifully bowed his head in submission, although what he really felt like doing was throwing something across the room. "I shall do your bidding, and make the best of a bad situation, if that's what is required. I would never think to bring disgrace upon you or St. Christophe."

"No. I know you would not, but as I told you last night, this is not so much about disgrace as it is about finding your way. You are nearly thirty years of age. It is time for you to discover where God means you to be.''

"Father," he said desperately, his control slipping for one unguarded moment, "if I knew where God meant me to be, I would have been there a long time ago! At least I have found a measure of peace at St. Christophe.''

"I understand. But it would be wrong for you to stay at St. Christophe if you have not truly been called to an ascetic life. Go, my son, and find the life that the Good Lord has in mind for you. Go out to where you do belong.''

Fighting bitterness and anger, Pascal, followed by Julien, walked out through the great arch of the Abbey of St. Christophe du Montebon. His heart twisting painfully, he rested his satchel on the dry earth and stopped for a last look at the honey-colored stone of the abbey, bathed in soft, early-morning light. Julien waited patiently, as if he knew Pascal needed to fix the image in his mind, a memory he could draw upon in the years to come.

"Go out to where you belong," the abbot had said to him. But the truth was that he didn't belong anywhere. He never had, and he had a terrible feeling that he never would. Nevertheless, despite his confusion, one thing was clear: he most certainly did not belong with Lady Elizabeth Bowes.

Pascal picked up his satchel, nodded to Julien that he was ready, and walked away.

3

"WE leave on the first tide," Pascal said. He stood just inside the threshold of the private parlor where Lily was eating her evening meal alone, as she had taken all of her meals in the two interminably long days that they had traveled toward the coast.

Brother Julien stood just behind him, his hood pulled up, his hands tucked inside the sleeves of his habit, looking, Lily thought, as if the devil himself might leap out from the corner at any moment. Indeed, Pascal LaMartine made no move without him. They ate together, they walked together, they even slept in the same room. Lily was not sure if Brother Julien was supposed to be protecting her from the rake, or whether it was the other way around.

Brother Julien never met her eyes, nor spoke to her, but behaved as if she did not exist at all. As Pascal LaMartine behaved in nearly the same fashion, speaking to her only when absolutely necessary, it had been a silent and thoroughly unpleasant journey so far. It was not that she had anything to say to him, or any wish to listen to him. It was just that she was not accustomed to being so completely ignored, and she found his attitude extremely annoying.

"Did you hear me, Lady Elizabeth? I repeat. We leave for England on the morning tide."

Lily waited for a moment, then glanced up casually enough from her dinner of a most superb confit of duck. "I heard you perfectly well the first time. We leave on the first tide. However, if you insist on playing a mute, there is no reason why I should not play equally deaf."

He did not bother to respond to that sally. Instead, he merely looked at her in that unnerving fashion she was coming to know, the one that made her feel as if he had just unclothed her, somehow found her wanting, and clothed her again. It had a tendency to undo her, that look of his, to make her feel as if someone else entirely lived inside her skin, someone not the least bit likable.

Well, what did she care? She didn't want him to like her. She wanted him to despise her to the point that he would shrivel up with loathing and disappear. She knew how to play that game, had played it successfully on all the miserable suitors her father had been throwing at her for years.

"Was there anything else?" she asked coldly, in her most imperious manner.

"No. Be prepared to sail first thing in the morning. And then be prepared to travel directly to Sutherby upon disembarking. We will not stop. This matter needs to be resolved as soon as possible for the abbey's sake."

"It cannot be resolved soon enough for me," she said. "And when my father hears the full story, you shall be thrown off the premises and I will never have to look at you again."

A small flash of anger sparked in those dark eyes, and she saw with immense satisfaction that she'd finally managed to goad him out of that infuriatingly cool, remote demeanor of his.

"No," he said, "you won't, for no doubt your father will have you instantly placed in an asylum when he hears you have been climbing about on walls, spying on monks."

"I think chances are far better that he will want to see you instantly placed in a jail cell."

"One cell or another, what difference? I am accustomed to solitude."

"Good. Then leave me here, for I cannot be rid of you soon enough. I am more than capable of making my own way home."

Pascal gave her another of his impenetrable looks. "Believe me, if I could, I would not hesitate. But as I have given my word to Dom Benetard that I will behave honorably, so I shall."

"Honorably?" Lily said. "Honorably? I don't think you even know the meaning of the word! You are nothing more than an unprincipled French—French *defiler,* hiding behind a mask of hypocritical piety!"

This barb actually elicited a small gasp from Brother Julien, but Pascal ignored it. "I do not think you are one to judge, Lady Elizabeth," he said softly. "Fortunately, it is not you but your father who will be passing judgment on me."

"Believe me," Lily said, "he will. And you shall live to regret your actions for the rest of your life."

Pascal nodded, and it seemed that again the insult had slid right off his shoulders. "I can only pray that will not be the case. Good night, Lady Elizabeth."

He turned abruptly and walked out of the parlor, Brother Julien scurrying behind.

Lily let out a long breath, suddenly feeling very tired. Tomorrow would be a very long and trying day, and she needed to sleep if she was to keep her wits about her. Her confit of duck had lost its appeal, and she pushed back her chair and mounted the stairs to her room, wishing for quick oblivion.

Pascal shoved his hands through his hair, then lifted his head and looked out over the pounding sea as if that might somehow drown out the clamor of his thoughts. The wind cut sharply through the material of his coat, but he didn't notice the chill. He was so cold on the inside that a blizzard wouldn't have made an impression on him.

It had been all he could do over the last three days to keep a grip on himself. Every time he looked at Elizabeth Bowes he wanted to put his hands around her throat and choke her until those full lips turned blue and her gray-green eyes bulged out of her head. It was not the sort of thought that someone like himself ought to have, but he didn't give a damn. He didn't feel like himself. He didn't feel like much of anything other than a pawn in someone else's game.

He thought of one of the books in his satchel, *De Materia Medica*, and all those herbal formulas Dioscorides had written down for posterity nearly two thousand years before, among them how poisons might best be used for assassinations. Hemlock—but he didn't have any on hand. Deadly mushrooms—oh, what a wonderful thought. Easy to find, although unfortunately it was a bit early in the year for them.

"Foxglove, henbane, laburnum," he recited softly, naming poisonous plants methodically and in alphabetical order. "Larkspur, monkshood, petty spurge . . ."

And then he gave a snort of disgust. Little comfort it was to think about assassinating the girl. She'd gotten there first, having already assassinated his name, his character, his reputation. Now she was about to throw him to the wolves and let her father finish the job. A fine way God had of paying back Pascal's years of service in His cause—not that Pascal had had any choice in that, either.

He looked down at his hands, turning them over and then back again. They appeared perfectly ordinary to him, normal bones and tendons, flesh and blood like everyone else's. And yet people looked at them as if they were made of something entirely different—as if *he* were made of something entirely different, as if he were not quite human. It didn't seem to occur to people that he bled just as they did, that he hurt just as they did, and ate and slept and laughed and cried just as they did. He was set apart, as surely as if there were an invisible fence around him.

He hadn't asked for such a gift. There were many times when he wished that it would just go away, that it had never been given to him in the first place. But it was useless wishing. God had had other things in mind for him when He'd sent Nicholas to fetch him out of the heaving sea, as drowned as one could be, and God had put Georgia there to breathe life back into him.

Pascal sighed heavily. Who was he to question God's will? His Heavenly Father had always done with him precisely as He pleased, with no care to what Pascal might wish in the matter. And now the Lord was sending him back to England with the most selfish, shrewish, arrogant woman he'd ever had the misfortune to meet. How was he supposed to understand that?

His fingers wrapped around a hard rock, the rough edges biting into his cold palm. He barely felt it. He'd schooled himself not to feel anything—he couldn't afford to feel, knowing what might be coming. He grasped the rock tightly and threw it as hard as he could, watching it hit the swell of a wave and sink without a sound.

"Just like you, my friend," he whispered. "Just like you."

"Lily? Elizabeth? Come, child, you must wake up now. It is time to rise, and for once in your life I think you should do as you're told."

Lily felt her shoulder being shaken in a not-very-gentle fashion by a bony claw, and she blearily opened her eyes.

She had hardly slept at all, tossing and turning throughout the small hours, finally falling into an exhausted slumber what seemed only moments ago. A faint gray light seeped in through the windows, and she could just make out Coffey's anxious face bending over her. "Oh. What time is it?" she asked the old woman, pushing herself up in bed and shivering in the cold air.

"Gone half-past four now."

"Half-past four? Oh, Coffey," Lily groaned. "You can't possibly make me get up at this ungodly hour. It must be ages before the boat sets sail." She flopped back down onto the pillows.

"The monk and Monsieur LaMartine have risen and already eaten, pet."

"Yes, but that's because they're always up before dawn," Lily said patiently. "It's like Father Mallet. I don't think he ever sleeps."

"The ship is in the harbor, and they have gone down to it along with your trunk," Coffey said equally patiently. "I know you don't like rising early, Lily, but you're just going to have to get out of bed now, that's all there is to it."

Lily pushed her fingers into her eyes. "Oh, all right. But I know he only arranged this horrible hour to make my life even more miserable."

She threw back the covers and went to the window to see for herself. Sure enough, there was a ketch, the tall masts rising toward heavy skies that looked as if they might open and weep at any moment. There, too, moving about on the pier, were the unmistakable figures of Brother Julien and the wretch, one distinguished by his slightness, his habit, and his cowl, the other by his height and his dark, uncovered head. She felt a strong rush of loathing for them both, and turned abruptly from the window, wishing the pier would open up so that they both might drop to the bottom of the ocean, never to be seen again.

She allowed Coffey to help her dress, but that was the extent of her goodwill. Lily refused to eat more than a piece of bread. There was a knot of dread in her stomach, for unless something extraordinary happened today, such as the ketch going down in a storm, or perhaps a convenient accident on the road to Winchester, she would be facing her father's certain wrath that evening. The only solace she had was the absolute certainty that punishment for her attacker would be swift and furious. However, her own punishment for what her father and his priest would consider an unforgivable act against God on her part was also sure to be equally swift and perfectly horrible. She deliberately lingered over her piece of bread, picking it into small pieces, partly to delay the inevitable, and partly to annoy the wretch, who was no doubt waiting impatiently.

There was nothing to do during the long journey aboard ship except sit below in the cabin. It was not much different than waiting out the long hours in a carriage, except that mercifully the French wretch and his shadow were above on the deck where Lily did not have to look at them.

"Now, Lily, pet," Coffey said, glancing up at the hatch as if to ensure that her words would not travel up and directly into the ears of the enemy, "you and I need to have a little chat."

Lily managed a smile. "A little chat? Oh, dear, Coffey. Those are far too familiar words coming from you. Do I sense a lecture coming?"

"Not a lecture, child. Simply a few words of advice. There is bound to be a fuss when we arrive, and . . ."

"Well, naturally there is going to be a fuss," Lily said, cutting her off. "Whatever that wicked man has coming he deserves in every way."

"No doubt he does, but it is not Monsieur LaMartine whom I am concerned for," Coffey said. "It would do you well to remember that it was your exploits that put you into this stew to begin with."

"Well . . . I don't expect to escape completely unpunished for my part in everything, but as I am far too old for one of Father Mallet's thrashings, thank goodness, I think a good tongue-lashing is more like it." She flashed a brave grin at Coffey. "Well . . . perhaps I'll get the usual bread and water for a week—maybe even two—and I'm sure there will be a book full of penances too, from Father Mallet, but what else can they do to me? You must not worry for your own sake, Coffey. I shall make it very clear that it was all my idea, and I demanded that you stay behind when I went for my walk."

"After this, your father might not let you go anywhere ever again, most especially Saint-Simon," the older woman said tartly. "And whose fault would that be? Look how long it took you to persuade his grace to let you visit your brother at all, and what did you do? At the first opportunity you ran wild with one of your crazy schemes.''

Lily managed to look remorseful. ''Perhaps I didn't think it through as well as I might have. But Papa will never connect my visit to the abbey with Jean-Jacques. Why should he?''

Coffey shook her head, the bunch of cherries on her bonnet swaying crazily about. ''I should never have let you talk me into this one. I should have insisted that we stay at Saint-Simon, instead of sneaking off in the dead of night like two thieves, with no explanation of why you were chasing off on your own—and in a foreign country too.''

Lily bristled with indignation. ''But I did tell Jean-Jacques, Coffey. I left him a note explaining everything.''

''What, that you were off to find a solution for his land? That is no kind of explanation. Further, I do not think that listening to fairy tales and fantasies about magic gifts is any way for a sensible, well-bred girl to behave, certainly not one of two and twenty, and a duke's daughter to boot.''

''I wasn't,'' Lily said with exasperation. ''I was looking for a botanist. It was Father Chabot who came up with all that other nonsense.''

''Still, you should be married and settled with a husband and children,'' Coffey persisted. ''Instead, you are in a scrape unlike any you have managed yet, and this time you might truly have ruined yourself. Only you, Lily, could manage to be compromised within the walls of a monastery.''

Lily gave her nurse an amused look. ''Oh, does that make being compromised somehow holier?''

''Sacrilege, my girl, will get you nowhere, and you watch your tongue in front of your father.'' Coffey sniffed.

''Why, may I ask, have you held your own tongue for the last few days only to vent it on me now?''

''Because this is the last opportunity I have to speak in private without those two men above to hear.''

''Don't be silly, Coffey; neither one understands a word of English.''

''Yes, and it's a good thing they don't, given some of the scathing comments you've made to me about Monsieur LaMartine—and before a monk, no less.''

Lily grinned. "Oh, do you mean what I said about the brute's probable parentage—or lack of it?"

"It is not nice to imply that anyone is born outside the sanctity of marriage, dear," Coffey said reprovingly. "We are all the same in the eyes of God, whatever the circumstances of our birth."

"Not according to Father Mallet we're not. As for my father, he thinks the only people who are truly equal in the eyes of God are other peers, preferably ranked earl or higher."

"Nevertheless, it is unkind to imply that any living creature is born unwanted, which is what you said about the man in those very words."

"Well, I certainly don't want him, or anything to do with him," Lily replied acidly.

"Naturally you don't, and it will all be finished soon. But Lily, child, you really must watch your tongue, for even if the man couldn't understand, I don't think it was quite nice to say that you wished he would go back to the sewers of Paris."

"Well, his accent *is* Parisian."

"Nevertheless, you mustn't mock those less fortunate than yourself—and in any case, his speech is perfectly educated. I was quite surprised with you."

"But Coffey—you forget that he tried to ravish me. How can you defend him like that?"

"I am not defending him. I am saying that your manners could use some improving. Furthermore, it is not for you to judge what the monks of St. Christophe might be feeling at his departure. Really, Lily, where you have learned some of your language, I don't know. I was shocked."

"Mr. Smith, the gardener," Lily said with a grin. "He can be quite colorful when he doesn't know you're about. I've learned all sorts of things listening to him."

Coffey covered her mouth. "Elizabeth, you should be ashamed of yourself!"

"Why? You have always said we should have open and curious minds."

"I was speaking in terms of a higher education, not meaning that you should go lurking about bushes, spying on gardeners—not to mention monks. Now I want you to stop this nonsense."

"I have tried to be civil in their own language, despite the violence of my feelings. Surely that is enough?"

"You are a lady and should behave as one at all times, whether you are understood or not. I have told you a hundred times that gentleness of manner, no matter the circumstances, is a sure sign of breeding. The way you have been carrying on, Elizabeth, one would think you were the daughter of a dustman rather than a duke."

Lily stuck her little chin forward belligerently. "I never asked to be a duke's daughter. I'd have been just as happy, if not happier, with a dustman for a father."

"Absolute nonsense, my girl, and I won't have you speaking with such disrespect. You have responsibilities to your name and birthright, Lily, and as an only child you also have a responsibility to provide an heir for your father, a duty which you have nicely managed to sidestep for five years. It is no wonder his grace despairs."

Lily shrugged. "If I am ever fool enough to marry, what difference would any of it make? I wouldn't be allowed to govern what is mine any more than I am now. I'd far prefer to wait until my father dies and I inherit."

"Child! Bite your tongue!"

"How do you expect me to feel? I am a person who has no freedom, treated as if I had no mind of my own. I have suitors thrown at me as if I should be grateful for their sniveling attentions, and I am chastised for being disgusted by their lack of appeal and intelligence and spirit."

"Now, now, Lily, you exaggerate."

"I do not exaggerate," Lily said furiously. "I am nothing more than something to be exchanged in barter and then taken to bed in order to produce sons to continue the same dreary tradition. What about *me*? I am an educated woman with a mind and a heart and, as I've been told so very often, a soul. My eternal soul and my mortal womb seem to be the only two things that matter to anyone other than myself, and I begin to think my womb is top on that list. Look what happened to my mother."

Lily paled and snapped her mouth shut, clasping her hands together so hard that her knuckles turned white. She hadn't meant to say that. She hadn't spoken of her mother at all, not since that awful day fourteen years ago. She would never forget sitting in the window, numb with shock and disbelief, watching as her mother climbed into the waiting carriage, not looking back. The footman put up the steps and closed the door, and the carriage drove away, taking Lily's heart with it. She had not seen or heard from her mother since.

On that day Lily realized that she was completely unlovable. The last fourteen years had proved her right.

Coffey patted her clenched hands. "Don't worry yourself, child, over what can't be changed. Your mother was a good woman."

"My father didn't think so," Lily said bitterly. "He never forgave her for having produced Jean-Jacques for her first husband and then managing nothing for him but me and a number of disappointing stillbirths. Do you understand now why he resents Jean-Jacques so much? As for me, I am nothing more to him than my mother was—his final hope for a male successor."

"Lily, you mustn't upset yourself like this. I am sure it is not so. . . ."

"Oh, it is so. Believe me, it is so. He has as much as told me so. Do you see why I would rather be the daughter of a dustman, who might love me just for myself?"

"Your father is a good man," Coffey said. "Your father is also a pious man, which is why I want you to listen to me now, and listen very carefully. I want my words to stick in that stubborn brain of yours and not go chasing out the other side as they usually do."

Lily dropped her eyes, and the fury drained from her face as quickly as it had come. "Forgive me. I did not mean to speak so harshly."

Coffey reached over and squeezed her hand. "You are distraught and tired and hungry. It has been a bad few days, I know. You have been very brave, being forced to travel in the company of the man who tried to defile you."

Lily attempted a smile. "And just think, he tried to defile me without even knowing at the time that there was a huge dowry to be had. Of course, he was probably desperate, being locked up in a monastery."

"You are good-looking enough, my lady, and that is more than enough," Coffey said darkly. "Men are at the mercy of their bodies. All it takes is being in the vicinity of a female and they lose the little sense God gave them."

"Exactly my point," Lily said triumphantly, "for that is exactly what happened to the wretch, and my father will see that immediately. After all, he never ceases to talk about the sins of the flesh and men's disgracefully base urges—''

"That is quite enough on the subject," Coffey said firmly. "I will return to my original point, which is your father. Despite the violation done to your sensibilities, you had best deal with his grace with the utmost humility. It probably wouldn't go amiss for you to get down on your knees and beg your father's forgiveness.''

"I most certainly will not," Lily said indignantly. "I will ask his forgiveness for accidentally falling into St. Christophe, but I will never go down on my knees to him or any other man.''

"Then let your pride be on your own head, my lady, and I will pray that it does not bring you down in the end.''

"Oh, Coffey, don't be such a prig now. Don't worry, I'll be humble enough. It will all turn out, you'll see. It always does.''

"Just you remember your place, Lily," Coffey said sternly.

"You've made it nearly impossible for me to forget. Come now, Coffey dear, stop looking so disapproving and be my friend again?''

Coffey merely pursed her mouth as if she'd just bitten into a particularly sour lemon and refused to say another word on the subject. The old nurse wasn't about to tell Lily, but she had a terrible feeling that she was not going to be able to protect her charge from this latest escapade, nor any escapade in the future. Coffey was certain that his grace was going to terminate her employment and send her packing, and the thought was breaking her heart.

The hired carriage pulled through the great gates of Sutherby at ten that same evening. Lily wondered what the Frenchman was thinking when the house itself came into view, for it was huge and extremely impressive if one wasn't accustomed to such grandeur. She hoped that he was feeling cowed. She stole a glimpse at him through the deep gloom, but much to her annoyance, he wasn't even looking at the house. Instead, he seemed to be staring at the floor. The monk was asleep.

Lily swallowed hard, summoning up her nerve as the door opened and two footmen instantly appeared, letting down the steps and opening the carriage door. They bowed deferentially as Lily emerged from the interior, followed by Coffey, and finally the two Frenchmen.

She gathered herself up. "Good evening, Phillpotts," she said to the startled butler who had appeared at the door. "If you please, fetch my father at once. Tell him I have returned, and there is an emissary from St. Christophe de Montebon with me. He has an urgent message from Dom Benetard."

"Yes, my lady. May I say welcome home?"

"Thank you, Phillpotts. We will await my father in his study. Coffey, bring the gentlemen, please." She marched across the huge marble hallway and waited for a footman to open the massive double doors, then marched through as if she had not a care in the world. Lily would rather die than admit that her heart was pounding so hard it threatened to leap directly out of her throat.

She took a seat but offered no invitation to the others. If there was one time that Lily needed to look every inch a future duchess, it was now. But then, her father had been hammering the role into her since the day he'd realized he would have no sons, so she had it perfected.

Five minutes later the door opened again and Lily's father appeared.

The Fifth Duke of Montcrieff, Eighth Marquess of Banesbury, and Tenth Baron of Northrup and Milton stood in the doorway, regarding the unexpected and odd assembly with a terrible eye, every moment of the past seven hundred years of his impeccable breeding apparent in his stance.

"Elizabeth?" he said in glacial tones. "What is the meaning of this?"

Lily stood. "Papa, there has been a slight problem—a mishap of sorts. Brother Julien has come directly from Dom Benetard with a letter addressed to you, explaining everything."

"And the other man? Who is this person with you?" Her father scowled darkly at Pascal.

"He is a man who has caused me great personal distress. But the letter will explain everything."

She shot a quick glance over at Brother Julien, who had developed a faint sheen on his upper lip.

"The letter, Brother Julien," her father commanded in flawless French, and with fumbling fingers the little monk withdrew it from the pouch at his waist, handing it to the duke.

Lily couldn't help noticing that Pascal looked impervious to the proceedings, as if he weren't affected in the least. No one stood in her father's presence without quaking, but there was nothing, absolutely nothing on the wretch's face to indicate fear, or much of anything else save an abstract interest.

"Thank you, brother." The duke took the missive, and without wasting another minute he opened it, scanned the pages, first quickly, then with more care, and finally, with disbelief. "I find this quite extraordinary, to say the least."

He directed his attention at Brother Julien. "I thank you for your devotion and sacrifice in escorting my daughter here. You are welcome at Sutherby for as long as necessary to see this matter through."

The monk bowed his head.

"Miss McCofferty, please escort the brother to a footman and request a bedroom for his use. I will see you, Miss McCofferty, at precisely eight o'clock tomorrow morning, when I shall expect a full explanation of your part in this absurdity."

"Yes, your grace," Coffey said, managing a stiff curtsy before doing as she was bid, leaving Lily, Pascal, and the duke alone in the room.

"As for you, Elizabeth," the duke said, riveting his eyes on his daughter, "you are to go to your room. You are not to leave it until I summon you."

"But, Papa," Lily protested. "Can I not tell my side of the story? This man has done very badly by me, and I know I ought not to have been where I was, and, oh, Papa, forgive me, but—"

"*Elizabeth Mary Bowes*! That is enough! You will leave us now—and on your way out you will instruct Phillpotts to summon Father Mallet immediately."

Confused and deeply hurt, Lily shot one last pleading look at her father, only to see it was in vain. She leveled a scathing look at Pascal, and then with head held high she left the room.

4

LILY paced her room, gripped by fear. She had no idea what was transpiring downstairs, but she had not liked the expression on her father's face, not one bit. She had the dreadful feeling that whatever Father Benetard had written in the letter had not painted her in the best possible light. There had not been one glimmer of sympathy in her father's eyes or his voice.

She sat down on the edge of a chair and smoothed her skirts over her knees. She had long before dismissed the maid, as she had no wish to have anyone hover about her when she was in such an unsettled state. In any case, it did not seem worth the trouble to undress, for there was no way of telling when her father might call her to give her accounting. Her father was unpredictable, and she suspected that he deliberately drew out her apprehension for effect. Lily had always preferred a swift sentencing, so that she knew what she was dealing with. It was the fear of the unknown that made her sick.

The clock ticked the minutes away, the steady, hollow noise grating on her nerves. Eleven o'clock passed, then midnight, and the small hand was creeping toward one when a light tap came at the door.

Lily nearly jumped out of her skin, then ran to the door and jerked it open. "Yes? Oh, it's you, Phillpotts." She swallowed hard.

"His grace will see you now," Phillpotts said, his ugly face drawn into lines that might almost be interpreted as sympathy.

Lily swallowed again. "Does it look very bad, Phillpotts?"

Phillpotts considered. "I cannot say exactly, my lady. But judging from the lateness of the hour and the length of time your father has been closeted away with Father Mallet and the other gentleman, I would say that this time you have been involved in some very serious mischief.''

"I was perhaps . . . imprudent.''

"Indeed, my lady? Well, in that case I shouldn't dally.''

Lily nodded, then followed Phillpotts along the long corridor, down the enormous and ornate staircase, across the marble hall, and over to the doors of her father's study, which Phillpotts now pulled open. Lily wanted to dig her heels in and refuse to enter, but she knew from past experience that it would be unwise.

"Lady Elizabeth is here, your grace,'' Phillpotts intoned and stood back.

Lily walked in, made a deep curtsy to her father and another to Father Mallet, who stood behind her father's shoulder, his gaunt face stiff with icy disapproval—in fact, he looked almost blue around his thin lips.

"Good evening, Father Mallet,'' she said sweetly. "I trust you are well?'' She heard the doors close behind her with an echoing click of finality.

"I am deeply disturbed, Elizabeth, as is your father.''

"Oh . . . yes, I can imagine. It was a very upsetting incident. Have you decided what to do with that—that *brute*?''

Lily's father tapped his finger hard against his desk, then raised it and pointed it somewhere over her left shoulder. Lily followed its direction and turned, then frowned when she saw Pascal standing by the fireplace. He met her eyes evenly, but said nothing.

"Oh,'' Lily said and turned back again.

"Sit down, Elizabeth,'' her father commanded.

Lily sat.

"You will start at the beginning. You left your brother's house long before you were meant to and without permission. Why?'' He regarded her like a hawk—not a good sign at all.

"Well, Papa, I decided to cut my stay at Saint-Simon short, as I felt homesick and Jean-Jacques was far too busy with business to look after me. I thought I might surprise you, which is why I didn't write.''

"Surprise me?'' the duke said dryly. "Oh, yes, Elizabeth, you have managed to surprise me—and just when I thought there were no surprises left. Go on.''

"Coffey and I left, and as we were passing near Montebon on the way home, I thought it would be interesting to see the abbey to which you have devoted so much of your time and energies. I went for a little stroll in the morning to stretch my legs before embarking, and I was so taken by the beauty of the abbey that I simply could not resist having a peek at the inside.''

The duke passed a hand over his forehead. ''You could not resist having a 'peek' at the cloisters of a monastery? Cloisters that you *know* very well are forbidden to those of the world, most especially *females*?'' His voice had risen to a roar, and Lily winced.

''Yes, I know, Papa, but you had so often spoken of their beauty—''

''And how, may I inquire, did you manage to get yourself up onto a fifteen-foot wall?''

''I climbed a tree,'' she said.

A muffled choke came from behind her, and she glanced over her shoulder to see that the wretch had turned away. No doubt he was having a severe attack of nerves about his imminent punishment.

''And then I fell off the wall,'' she said, looking back to her father, ''and in a matter of seconds, when I was senseless, he—'' she turned and pointed her finger at the wretch accusingly—''assaulted me.''

''What exactly did Mr. LaMartine do, Elizabeth, that would constitute assault?''

Lily flushed. ''You can't mean you wish for me to describe the details?''

''Yes, I do wish for you to describe the details. Every detail, if you please.''

''Could I do it privately, Papa?'' she pleaded, overcome with embarrassment.

''No. You may not. You have brought serious charges against this young man. I will have your story, and then Father Mallet and I will decide the next course of action.''

Lily wanted to die on the spot, anything rather than having to enumerate in front of Father Mallet the intimacies taken with her person. Her chest tightened with true hatred for the man who had brought her to this.

She squeezed her hands tightly together in her lap and spoke without inflection, as if she were reciting by rote.

''He opened my bodice and my corset. He put his hands

under my skirt. He felt my—he felt my limbs . . . and then he fell upon me and covered my body with his own.''

Father Mallet moaned, and Lily saw that he had gone quite pink in the cheeks, which made her own cheeks blaze even more brightly.

''But that is as far as it went,'' she said quickly, for she didn't want either of them to think she had actually been ravished. ''I fought him off, and then Dom Benetard and Brother Julien came. I was terribly ashamed, but I tried to make myself modest, and then I told them what had happened to me. Dom Benetard was very kind. You know the rest.''

There was a long silence, and then the duke drew in a deep breath and released it heavily. ''You swear to all of this, Elizabeth?''

''Yes, I do, Papa. I have told you just how it happened. I am deeply sorry for my own actions, and I truly am ashamed that I climbed the wall, but I cannot be held responsible for what . . . what that man did to me.''

''I see. Well, perhaps Mr. LaMartine would like to answer your charges, even though he has already given us his version of events. Mr. LaMartine?''

The wretch came forward, not looking at Lily. ''I will tell you again what I told your daughter at the time, that I was attempting to see to her welfare. She had taken a bad fall and knocked herself senseless; she might have sustained any manner of injury. I did what was necessary under the circumstances.''

Lily's head jerked up and her eyes snapped with fury. She stared at him, not quite able to believe her ears. He had just spoken in English—perfect, fluent English, with only the very slightest trace of a French accent.

''You *hypocrite*!'' she cried. ''You deliberately misled me!''

He flicked her a glance. ''I have led you nowhere at all, Lady Elizabeth. You have believed whatever you have chosen to believe in several matters without any encouragement or discouragement from me.''

Lily averted her gaze, knowing exactly what he was referring to, all those dreadful things she'd said about him to Coffey in the carriage, thinking he couldn't understand a word.

Her father frowned. "Are you saying this man is lying, Elizabeth?"

"But of course he is lying! Why would he tell you the truth and incriminate himself? He has come up with a cleverly constructed excuse for his monstrous behavior."

"Your grace, I have no doubt that your daughter truly believes I tried to attack her. The story she has told you is accurate in every detail with the exception of my intent toward her."

"You mentioned nothing about pinning her beneath you," the duke said severely. "That does not sound like the act of a man concerned with bodily injury."

Lily breathed a sigh of relief, but it was short-lived when the wretch nodded in agreement.

"Indeed, your grace, at that moment the only bodily injury I was concerned with was my own. I had forgotten to mention it, but when your daughter regained consciousness she boxed my ears and practically concussed me in the process. That is why I landed on top of her."

The duke chuckled. "I see. Well, that explains it then."

"Papa, you cannot believe this man's story over mine?" Lily said desperately.

"It is the same story from everything I have heard. Mr. LaMartine is right, it is now only a matter of interpretation, for his account matches yours exactly."

"Of course it does, Papa. The man may be wicked, but I don't believe he is stupid. He'd be an idiot to tell an entirely different story."

"That is quite enough, Elizabeth," the duke snapped. "I have heard everything that I wish to hear from you. I believe Mr. LaMartine is an honest man and has told the truth. Further, Dom Benetard sent an excellent character reference along with his endorsement of Mr. LaMartine's account of the incident."

Lily wanted to scream with frustration. She had been there—it had happened to her, not to Dom Benetard, or to her papa, or to Father Mallet. She knew the truth, and so did the lying, manipulating brute next to her chair.

"Thank you, your grace," the wretch said, as if butter wouldn't melt in his mouth, and Lily glared up at him.

He stood there, regarding her father with a look of complete innocence on that disgracefully handsome face. Well, at least that was one blessing, since her father thoroughly disapproved of handsome faces. No doubt her father would now toss him out into the street, even if he chose to do nothing else.

The duke tapped his finger on the desk for a moment, then glanced up at Father Mallet, who gave an abrupt nod of his head. "Very well," the duke said. "I have reached my decision."

"I am prepared to abide by your wishes, your grace."

"I appreciate your willingness to do so, Mr. LaMartine. I am distressed that my daughter's foolishness has caused you this trouble and forced you to leave St. Christophe." He frowned heavily. "I am afraid, however, that in order to protect the abbey's newly elevated status, we must do everything possible to avoid even a breath of scandal. A layman seen rolling about on the ground with an unmarried woman . . ."

"I have accepted the fact that I shall not be returning to St. Christophe," Pascal said.

"It is a weighty thing to ask a man to forsake a vocation in favor of marriage, my son," Father Mallet intoned heavily, and Lily stared at the priest with horror.

Marriage?

"Is that your desire, your grace?" Pascal said quietly. "Do you ask me to marry your daughter?"

The duke inclined his head. "I can see no other solution."

"No!" Lily's entire body recoiled in shock. "You cannot mean it . . . you would never be so cruel!"

"I am sorry, Elizabeth, but you have no voice here. You have brought this marriage upon yourself by your own foolishness."

"Oh, Papa—please. Please do not force me to marry this man!" She covered her mouth with trembling hands, trying to force back the tears burning at her eyes. The world had just upended itself and she felt as if nothing was quite real. This couldn't be happening to her, it just couldn't. "Please, Papa," she whispered. "I'll do anything . . . a thousand penances, I'll go to a convent, whatever you wish—please, *please* don't do this to me . . ."

"I have made my decision. I shall not change my mind."

"Father Mallet, please speak to my father—it can't be right to force someone into an unwanted marriage? Surely that goes against God's wishes?"

"I do not believe you are one to speak of what God might wish, Elizabeth," the priest said harshly. "You have already violated His wishes by violating the privacy of those called by Him."

Seeing no help there, Lily finally turned her face up to the man her father had just chosen as her husband, the man she despised more than any person in the world. "You," she said, trying to keep her voice steady. His face swam through her blurred vision, and she wiped her eyes with the back of her hand. "You cannot want this any more than I? Please, won't you tell them?"

"I gave my word to Dom Benetard that I would accept your father's decision," he said. "I will not dishonor him or myself by breaking that promise."

She looked down at the floor and mutely shook her head.

"Mr. LaMartine, a room has been made ready for you. Attend me here at ten o'clock tomorrow morning, and we will negotiate the marriage settlement."

"I want no settlement, your grace."

"Nevertheless, one shall be made. Elizabeth has an extensive dowry."

Pascal bowed his head for a moment, then looked directly into the duke's eyes. "In the matter of your daughter, I will do exactly as you ask until the day she and I are wed. After that time I must insist that, as her husband, I am allowed to act according to my own wishes."

"You will be her master in all things," the duke agreed quickly. "It is only fitting."

A little moan escaped from Lily's lips, and the duke's gaze jerked back to her. "As for you, Elizabeth, you will be an obedient wife in every way. Father Mallet will instruct you in your duties. He will also instruct you as to your punishment."

White-lipped, Lily looked at her father defiantly, her chin thrust forward, her eyes swollen but dry. "Nothing can be more punishment than what you have just decreed. Nothing."

"Silence!" he roared. "Your rebellious, disobedient nature will be tamed, I promise you this."

"You may break me in body, and possibly even in spirit, but you cannot touch my soul. That is mine alone."

"And it is in mortal danger." Father Mallet stalked forward to tower over her chair, and Lily did her best not to shrink back. "You will pass what remains of the night in prayer and beg forgiveness," he announced. "Until the day you are married, you will spend every waking hour in the chapel saying penance for your sins. You will fast from dawn until dusk and take only bread and water in the evening. You will sleep in the chapel's antechamber." He paused only to draw breath. "You will not speak to anyone but myself or your father, should he wish it. You will purify yourself in body and spirit in the hope that you go to your husband a docile, respectful wife."

Lily listened to this pronouncement silently, but the taste of copper filled her mouth where she had bitten the inside of her cheek and drawn blood.

"You may go now, Elizabeth," her father said, dismissing her with a wave of his hand.

Lily stood, her legs feeling as weak as an infant's. She managed a curtsy, knowing it would be foolish to show any sign of dissent now. What good would it do? "Good night, Papa, Father Mallet." She turned to leave.

"Elizabeth!"

She looked at her father in surprise. "Yes, Papa?"

"You will be respectful to Mr. LaMartine!"

Lily, who had in truth forgotten all about his presence, winced internally. "I beg your pardon."

She met the wretch's eyes, and naturally there was nothing remotely readable in them, although they did look even darker than usual. "Good night, Mr. LaMartine," she said dutifully, although she almost choked on the words. She dropped a final curtsy and walked quickly toward the door.

"Good night, Lady Elizabeth," came his deep voice after her, in that maddening, nearly perfect English accent.

Lily suppressed a desire to pick up her skirts and run.

The minute Pascal left the room, quietly closing the doors after himself, the duke thumped his hands on his desk in complete glee. "Can you believe it, Harold? Can you believe it? How did such a stroke of good fortune fall into my lap?" He smoothed out Dom Benetard's letter and beamed down at it. "A devout Catholic male from a good British family! What more could one ask?"

"Yet it says here that he is French by birth, your grace." The priest bent down and pointed to the exact line.

"Yes, yes—but has lived in England since he was a child, Harold. I shall discover all the details tomorrow."

"Excellent, your grace."

"A humble man," the duke pointed out. "He wasn't the least interested in Elizabeth's dowry, even though he said earlier that he has nothing of his own to bring to the marriage."

"He is a man of God," the priest said modestly.

"Yes. A man of God." The duke sighed happily. "And straight from St. Christophe. God must be rewarding me for my work. Dom Benetard thinks highly of him as well. Look at this glowing testimony to his character."

"Yes, your grace. I have read it," Father Mallet said, disguising his annoyance. "Well. Elizabeth is to be married at last. It is indeed the grace of God at work." He touched the tips of his long fingers together. "Perhaps Elizabeth will finally learn humility and piety."

"Yes—one can only hope. Ah . . . Harold, do you not think Elizabeth's punishment is perhaps slightly severe?"

"Severe? It is nothing next to what she deserves. If she is to go to her husband as a good wife should, she must be cleansed of sin. Prayer, fasting, and solitude—that is the only way."

"Yes, I suppose so . . . ah, well. Never mind, then. We must write immediately for a special license. The sooner this marriage can be performed, the better. Just think, if Elizabeth does her duty properly, I might have a grandson within the year. I was beginning to despair that I had wasted all that time petitioning the Crown for the succession to pass through my daughter." He peered up at Father Mallet. "Ah—be sure you instruct Elizabeth as to her marital duties."

The priest jerked back in alarm. "Me, your grace?"

"Indeed. Who else?"

"Miss McCofferty, perhaps? Although I do not think she is a suitable influence. It is not the first time I have said as much, but after this latest incident—"

"I agree, and I intend to dismiss Miss McCofferty first thing in the morning. Elizabeth no longer needs her nurse."

Father Mallet's eyes lit up. He despised Miss McCofferty almost as much as he had despised the duchess, but he had not had the same success in driving the nurse away. "A wise decision, your grace. Leniency is no way to subdue a disobedient spirit."

"So you have often said. But as you know, I kept her about so that Elizabeth would have a woman's companionship. Well. Enough of this for now. This has been a fine night's work, Harold. I shall sleep like a babe."

He marched off to bed, thinking of grandsons.

The priest went just as happily to his own bed, thinking of a house with no females in it to disturb his peace.

Pascal sat quite still in his chair, trying to bear the endless interrogation with grace, but he was having trouble excusing the insufferable intrusion on his privacy.

". . . I was born on the ninth of June, 1809, your grace, just outside of Paris.

". . . My father was a bookkeeper, your grace. No, my mother was British. She moved to France in her youth. I beg your pardon? Oh. She came from Bath, I believe.

". . . Yes, that is correct, your grace. I did receive an education, Father Mallet. I was initially tutored at home, and from there I went up to Oxford.

". . . I have traveled extensively, your grace. Where? All over the East, India, China and Japan, Europe, of course . . . no, I have never served in the military. . . ."

It went on like this for all of the morning and most of the afternoon. The minute Pascal was released from the duke's study, he escaped into the sunshine to clear his aching head.

He had borne the insulting questions as best as he could, hoping he had given nothing of his feelings away. That would have been the final violation, knowing that they had seen either his humiliation or his disgust.

He had been required to give a review of his entire life, and he hadn't enjoyed the process at all, most especially talking about the less stellar moments, such as the death of his parents, his year on the streets of Paris, and his rather grim arrival on the shores of England. But whatever the duke and his priest had been looking for, Pascal's account must have satisfied them, for then had followed the tedious discussion of the marriage settlement, Lily's unusual claim to succession, and the future of their possible offspring.

Pascal shook his head. In some ways it was little wonder that Elizabeth Bowes had become what she had, if this was the atmosphere in which she'd been raised. The duke excelled at arrogance. He was gifted at insensitivity. But his true genius was in the complete, utter presumption that his judgment was infallible. One would think that he and God played billiards together every Thursday by appointment, deciding the fate of the world and its inhabitants over a glass of port. His daughter had inherited his attitude just as surely as she had inherited his gray-green eyes.

Pascal rubbed a hand over his eyes, dismissing the duke, his daughter, and his priest in favor of the pleasures of the outdoors. He drew in a deep breath of fresh air. There was something distinctive about the smell of England in the springtime, when everything was coming to life. It made him think of his childhood at Raven's Close, of happy hours spent digging and planting, of the mix of certain fragrances prevalent only at this time of year.

He quickly headed down the steps, toward what appeared to be a man-made lake with some fine gardens bordering it, stopping briefly to examine an interesting clump of evergreens on his way. "Hmm," he murmured, then strolled on, passing the chapel, which sat off to one side of the path, its leaded-glass windows high and narrow. It was a good example of fifteenth-century architecture, although he very much doubted that Lady Elizabeth Bowes was engaged in admiring the construction of the nave.

His gaze fell on a weathered old gardener setting out some young plants in the far beds, and Pascal instantly set off in that direction, pulling off his jacket as a plan formed in his mind. Here was a perfect source of information, and he intended to take every advantage of it.

The gardener was muttering to himself under his breath as Pascal approached, and he couldn't help smiling at what he overheard.

"Blasted papists," the gardener grumbled, digging his trowel ferociously into the soil. "Locking a body away in a church with naught but bread and water and a bunch of rotting relatives—heathen, that's what I'd call it."

"I couldn't agree with you more," Pascal said, and the old man started, then glowered up at him, the lines drawn deep in his weather-beaten face.

"And who might you be?"

"Pascal LaMartine. I'm afraid I'm a blasted papist, too."

"That comes as no surprise," the old man said sourly. "I'm about the only one around here who isn't, and that's only because his grace likes his flowers and I know my gardens.''

"Yes, I can see that," Pascal said. "I noticed the magnolias on my way down. It's the hybrid *Magnolia soulangiana,* from the Chinese stock, isn't it?''

"Good heavens," the gardener said, giving Pascal a sharper look, taking in the shirt that was slightly frayed at the collar and the old trousers, and jumping immediately to the conclusion Pascal had hoped for. "How would you be knowing that, my boy?''

"I'm a gardener myself," Pascal said. He dropped to his heels and picked up a spare trowel. "An extra pair of hands never hurts, does it?''

"And Albert Smith isn't one to turn down an offer of help. It's about time I had another pair of hands. Just arrived, have you?''

"Yesterday. Tell me," Pascal asked, gently picking up one of the seedlings and examining it. "How do pelargoniums fare in this chalky soil? The Cape of Good Hope is a long way from southern England.''

"Well," the gardener said, giving him an approving look, "it's the first time I've set them out, mind you. I've grown them in pots before this. But it looks to be a warm May, so they're safe enough, I reckon. Now the hollyhocks over there against the chapel wall, they've come along nicely.''

"Yes, they look as if they've naturalized well, and they must be enjoying the southern exposure. But then I've found *Althaea rosea* to be quite hardy. I wonder, do you alternate their wet-dry cycles?''

"I do . . .'' The old gardener happily settled in to the conversation, and they chatted companionably for a while. Pascal took his time, gaining the gardener's confidence and waiting for the right moment, and then he carefully brought the conversation around to the subject really on his mind.

"I suppose you must know the family well, having been here for so long.''

"Aye, that I do, and all I can say is sometimes I wish I didn't, not with them and their—begging your pardon—their papist ways.''

"You needn't beg my pardon in the least. A man's entitled to his opinion, although speaking of papist ways, I think Father Mallet's opinions might be a little on the extreme side.''

"That's right, my lad—you have it exactly! Just look at that poor Lady Lily, dragged into the chapel at first light by that—that zealot, locking the door on her white face. I saw it with my own eyes, I did. Home one night, and she's already in trouble. Lady Lily, I said to myself, must have really gone and done it this time if they've started locking her up in the chapel.''

Pascal leaned back on his knees. "Is Lady Elizabeth forever getting into trouble, then?''

"Trouble? The girl was born for trouble. Too much curiosity and spunk for her own good, that's what it is. The trouble with Lady Lily is she hasn't enough to do with herself, especially with her older brother gone these past few years.''

"Lady Elizabeth has a brother?'' Pascal said, astonished, wondering why he wasn't in line to succeed.

"A half-brother, anyway. Lady Lily dotes on him, not that he has much common sense either. They both take after their mother in that.''

"Oh, yes,'' Pascal said casually. "I'd wondered. There doesn't appear to be a duchess about the place.''

"Convent,'' Mr. Smith said with a snort. "She took herself away when Lady Lily was all of eight.''

"Really?'' Pascal said, trying to disguise his surprise. "The duchess took vows?''

"No, she's no nun. She just lives at the convent. I told you it was a papist family, and that priest is right in the middle. Nothing happens without his say-so.''

Pascal absorbed this piece of information, which marched along very well with the conclusion he'd already reached. "It is an interesting situation, isn't it?'' He gathered the earth into a mound around the last seedling and reached for the watering can.

"He has his hands in every last thing that goes on around here,'' Mr. Smith said, warming to his tale. "You watch your step, my boy, or you'll be out the door.''

"No hope of that, I'm afraid,'' Pascal said with a wry smile.

"You don't think so? Look at what happened to poor Mary McCofferty, here for twenty-two years and out the door this morning, bags packed and crying her eyes out.''

Pascal's head snapped around and he looked hard at the gardener. "Mary McCofferty?''

"That's right, Lady Lily's nurse, and a dear-hearted soul. Gone to her sister's on the public coach, George—he's one of the footmen—told me. Now who does Lady Lily have to comfort her? No one. It's all something to do with that monk and the man who came with him last night. No one knows what happened, but you can depend on one thing—that priest had something to do with it."

"Not really," Pascal said. "He may have pushed his grace in the direction he wanted him to go, but Father Mallet didn't actually say very much."

"How do you know that?" Albert Smith asked eagerly. "Did you hear something about it, then?"

"Every word. Lady Elizabeth is to be married."

"Go on!" the gardener said, and it was his turn to look astonished. "How do you know that?"

"Because she's to be married to me."

Albert Smith dropped his trowel.

5

LILY shifted on her sore, bruised knees and shivered in the dreadful damp of the chapel. She was amazed she hadn't caught her death, although she almost wished she had, for after seven nightmarish days and nights she'd decided that she really might prefer oblivion to any more of this punishment.

She'd said every penance known to God or man, she'd said confession every single day, she hadn't once complained of her sore back and aching legs, nor of the pain in her empty stomach. She'd said nothing of her night terrors, of the times she'd been so frightened that she'd pounded on the locked door, pleading to be let out, knowing there was no one there to hear.

She'd listened to Father Mallet drone on and on about humility and piety and obedience, her head bowed, her hands clasped together. Lily thought she'd behaved like a saint, but it had made no difference. She was still to be locked away in the chapel.

She heard the key turn in the chapel door, and she quickly bowed her head, knowing that it was Father Mallet by the rustle of his cassock and the thin voice behind her.

"Stand up, Elizabeth."

She obeyed, nearly stumbling, for her legs had gone numb. "Good afternoon, Father."

He looked at her pale face with satisfaction. "I can see that your penance is doing some good. Now, this afternoon I have a very important matter to discuss with you. Sit down."

She sat.

"I have just come from your father. He wishes me to inform you that you shall be married on Sunday."

Three more days, Lily thought with a rush of relief. Three more days, and she would be freed from this prison. An image of the wretch flashed into her mind, but she instantly dismissed it. After she had had time to regain her senses, she realized that her father was trying to frighten her. He would never, ever marry her to a person of no consequence—and certainly not to a lowly gardener. The idea was ludicrous, and she was embarrassed that she had let them see her fear.

"Are you attending me, Elizabeth?"

"Yes, Father," she said obediently.

"Very good. Then it is—hahum. It is time to instruct you in your marital duties. Your husband will expect certain, hahum . . . certain things from you, which you are obliged in the eyes of God to offer him."

Lily felt the heat creep into her cheeks as she realized what he was about to say. "I am sure that Coffey will tell me everything when the time comes. But thank you for your concern," she added for good measure.

Father Mallet looked down his long beaked nose at her. "Miss McCofferty is no longer at Sutherby," he said with a satisfied sniff.

Lily stared at him. "Oh . . . oh, no! But it wasn't her fault, none of it was, it was all my doing!"

"Miss McCofferty was dispatched the morning after your return, and high time. Your father and I felt that she has long been a poor influence on you."

Lily bent her head, trying not to let Father Mallet see her distress. She felt utterly helpless, as if the last person in the world who cared anything at all about her had gone away. Coffey had at least tried to protect her from Father Mallet. But now there was no one between Father Mallet and herself, and Lily couldn't help cringing at the thought.

"Now," he said, his voice dry as dust, "I shall begin your instruction."

At first Lily tried to shut out Father Mallet's monotone, for she wasn't sure that she could bear the mortification, but for the first time ever she ended up listening to the priest with true fascination. It was impossible to understand half of what he was saying, for he spoke in an extraordinary combination of biblical references and euphemisms. When he started talking about rods and staffs and mighty fortresses she had an almost irresistible urge to burst into horrified laughter. She had long before grasped the basic essentials of human anatomy, but she wasn't at all sure that

Father Mallet had, given the way he was going about explaining things.

". . . And so your husband sows his seed upon your fertile soil, the, hahum . . . the earth that bears his fruit." He cleared his throat again, looking flushed and agitated. "The seed—should God will it—produces a child. Not always, which is why your husband might often wish to, to . . . to sow with you. Do you understand?"

She nodded mutely, not trusting herself to speak for fear of collapsing in hysteria. She wondered if she was not beginning to lose her mind.

"That is good," he said quickly. "Just remember to surrender to your husband in all things, and I am sure it will become very clear. I will leave you to ponder my words. You will say the Hail Mary one hundred times before dinner."

"Father," she said hesitantly, throwing her pride to the wind, for after dinner came the dark, and she really wasn't sure if she could bear another night locked away. "I am truly sorry, I am, Father. Do you suppose I might sleep in my own room, if I come to the chapel at first light?"

"Certainly not. You will serve your full punishment, alone where there is no one but God to see you in your shame."

He turned abruptly and left, and the key grated in the lock. Lily shuddered and squeezed her eyes shut, trying hard not to cry. She began saying her Hail Marys in earnest, just on the highly improbable chance that someone might be listening.

Pascal sealed his letter to Dom Benetard, then put the writing materials away. He stood and handed the letter to the monk, who tucked it carefully into his leather scrip. "Thank you, Julien, for all your help," he said, smiling down at the young man. "I wish you a safe journey home." Pascal swallowed against the hoarseness in his throat.

His eyes full of sympathy, Julien patted his arm.

"I know," Pascal said. "I wish myself luck as well. This was not the outcome I had hoped for, but as the abbot says, it is not our job to understand God's will, only to follow it. I wish I felt that confidence in my heart, but I have tried to take comfort from the words."

Julien nodded vigorously, then pointed out the window toward the chapel with a questioning look on his face.

"Lady Elizabeth? I don't know if even a year of solid prayer would do any good, not if the prayers don't come from her heart. But I must confess that I am appalled at the severity of the punishment."

Pascal watched carefully as Julien's hands quickly and cleverly sketched in the air in his silent language. Pascal nodded. "Yes, you're right. Father Mallet is a dangerous man. At times I find his theological opinions alarming. It's a good thing you've managed to miss them, for I am sure you would have been horrified."

Julien smiled happily.

"You're a crafty one, aren't you? You know that both the duke and his priest are under the impression that you've taken a vow of silence, although why it hasn't occurred to them that Dom Benetard would never send someone under that vow out into the world is beyond me. Never mind, you played a good game, having your meals sent up to your room under the pretext of seclusion. I wish I'd been able to get away with that."

Julien's grin grew even wider, then he shook his head and touched his heart.

"Thank you for your sympathy, my friend. It is appreciated. Do you know, I still cannot believe any of this? And it's all because that lunatic girl climbed onto the abbey wall, just to have a look inside."

More of the silent language, this time expressing bewilderment mixed with real disapproval.

"I know. As I said, lunatic. Furthermore, I've never seen anyone so unpenitent in my life," Pascal said, gazing out the window. "You should have seen the look on her face when she was sentenced. Oh, not to marriage—that genuinely distressed her—I would have burst into tears myself if I hadn't gone into severe shock. No, I meant when Father Mallet gave her his list of punishments. Her head went up and her chin went out, and she would have taken on her father, Father Mallet, and the Good Lord Himself if she'd thought she had a fighting chance." He shrugged. "Apparently, not only am I to be married, I'm to be married to an unbroken, unwilling, unholy child."

Julien raised both his eyebrows.

"What, do you object to my calling her unholy?" Pascal asked with a curt laugh.

Julien slowly shook his head, then raised his hand above his head.

"Oh, I see. Well, she may be two-and-twenty, but she behaves like a ten-year-old. My sister Kate behaved with more maturity when last I was home, and she was only nine." He gave Julien a rueful look. "I wish I could find something in Elizabeth to like, but I'm afraid that the most I can summon up is a sense of distaste. It would have been better to have had a few days to try to know her before being married to her, not that I expect anything more than what I've already seen and heard."

The monk touched his heart again.

"Thanks. I'll manage somehow. But I will tell you this— if I'm to keep my sanity, that girl will need some serious rearranging."

That earned an enthusiastic nod, and Pascal laughed and clasped Julien's slim shoulders. "Take care, my good friend. I shall miss you, I really shall. Keep an eye on the gardens for me. The camellias should be beautiful this year, shouldn't they?"

Julien nodded sadly, tears sparkling on his eyelashes.

"You'd best go now," Pascal said, releasing him. "You don't want to miss your boat. May God bless you. And say a special prayer for me tomorrow."

Reaching back, Julien pulled his hood over his short blond hair, and his face fell into shadow. Gone was the boy Pascal had known, transformed back into the monk he'd become. He picked up one of Pascal's hands and pressed a kiss to its back, his eyes filled with pain.

"Save your homage for God," Pascal said. "He is fortunate to have you in His service, Julien. Be happy at St. Christophe."

Julien nodded and managed a smile.

Pascal saw Julien into the duke's carriage and waved his hand as the carriage rolled down the drive. He watched it until it had turned through the gates. He was happy for Julien. The boy had taken to monastic life as if it had been water poured down a parched throat, water that had soothed and helped to heal the deep scars on Julien's soul. But he really would miss him. There were a lot of things he was going to miss.

He closed his eyes for a moment, forcing away the ache of parting, then headed out to the gardens to find old Albert Smith, who was the only person at Sutherby who seemed to have any sense.

Lily blinked as she emerged from the chapel, then raised her face to the morning sun, drinking in the light and the blessed warmth. She looked about her. The grass was a vibrant green, and the apple trees were in full, glorious bloom. All the color hurt her eyes, but she reveled in it. She would have sent up a prayer of thanks to God, but she had lost all faith in His existence long before.

"Elizabeth, hurry along, please," Father Mallet commanded, waiting impatiently on the path. "We do not have all morning."

Lily obeyed instantly, but the short distance from the chapel to the house seemed to stretch ten miles, for each step she took shot knives of pain through her knees. She couldn't wait to go to bed and fall into a long, dreamless sleep.

But two hours later she was being led back again along the same path. She'd been dressed in white silk and lace, her head covered with a lace veil that trailed to her shoulders. Her father's hand rested under her elbow as if she might bolt if he let her go.

"Father Mallet explained everything to you?" he asked uncomfortably.

Lily nodded, thinking that the game really had gone on long enough. It was becoming frightening.

"I hope your time spent in penance impressed itself on you."

"Oh, yes, Papa, it did. Very much so. I am so terribly sorry, and I shall never do such a thing again." She looked up at him hopefully, sure that he would see he had scared her badly and would now give her the expected reprieve.

The duke looked down at his daughter. "From this day on," he said, "it is nothing to do with me. You are your husband's charge. Be a good wife and treat your husband with respect. Obey him in all things. Do not repeat your mother's mistakes."

They had reached the chapel, and for the first time Lily understood that this terrible thing was truly going to happen. "Oh, Papa—oh, Papa . . . please?" she said desperately. "I will marry anyone else you choose, I swear it. Please do not force me to marry this man, I beg you. I will be the model daughter from now on!"

"You will marry Pascal LaMartine, and you will do it now." He looked down at her, his eyes snapping. "Do not think to disobey me, or it shall go very badly for you."

He tugged on her arm and literally forced her over the threshold. She felt light-headed, disassociated from her surroundings, and wondered if this was how people felt when they were being led to the gallows.

He was there, of course. He stood to one side of the altar, dressed in a black coat and trousers, his waistcoat gray satin, his white shirt and neckcloth crisp, his dark hair shining. Lily couldn't help but blink. Pascal LaMartine, rake, rogue, wretch that he was, looked every inch the correct gentleman, as if he'd been born to the position. Lily's stomach turned over.

It took an hour. Mass had to be said. Vows had to be made. The wretch's hand took hers, slid a wedding ring onto her finger, and his mouth briefly touched her cold lips. She hardly felt it. Lily moved through it all with a sense of distance, as if it were someone else who spoke the words, someone else who took that hard masculine arm and walked out of the chapel. She sat through the small wedding breakfast in silence, unable to eat the rich food, speaking only when spoken to, smiling at the handful of guests and hoping they took her silence for nerves.

And then she found herself being led to the carriage that had been given to them as a wedding present, her trunk strapped to the back, her traveling dress appropriate for a newly married woman—she'd discovered earlier that morning that a quick trousseau had been made for her while she had been locked away.

She suffered her father's kiss on her cheek, the good wishes of the guests, the curtsies and bows of the staff, who had lined up in the driveway to see her off. The only people she really noticed were Phillpotts, who bowed to her, his eyes full of pity, and Albert Smith, who tugged his cap, then winked. As Albert Smith had never winked at her in her life, she was slightly startled, but touched nonetheless.

Her husband climbed into the carriage beside her, and they started off.

Despite all the days that Lily had had to contemplate the

future and, worse, the nights when she had lain awake on her hard cot, her eyes fixed on the ceiling, her hands clutching the thin blanket, she had not gone so far as to imagine this. She had worked out, of course, why the wretch had gone so quietly to his fate. No doubt he was congratulating himself on his good fortune—a duke's daughter and an enormous dowry, as well as husband to a future duchess or potential father to a duke.

Oh, yes, Lily had made sense out of everything. But she had never, ever believed that her father would be so heartless as to force her into a marriage with the very man who had attempted to defile her.

Everything that Lily had assumed about her world, everything that involved trust and honesty and truth had been wrenched away from her. The entire fabric of her life had been altered so that she no longer recognized it, or even herself. She watched Sutherby disappear, and she felt nothing at all.

"Elizabeth?"

It had been an hour since they had begun traveling. Lily had no idea where they were going, as the wretch had not seen fit to tell her.

Lily turned her head to look at the man who was now, by law, her husband.

"It's been a long day," he said. "I thought we would stop at an inn this evening."

"Whatever you wish. I have been instructed to obey you."

He considered that. "Have you? How fortunate for me. In that case, we'll stop."

Lily looked back out the window.

There was a momentary silence, and then he gently touched her elbow. "Elizabeth, look at me. This will not do. I no more asked to be married to you than you did to me, but by a series of profoundly unfortunate circumstances we are permanently joined. Conversation would be a useful device, don't you think?"

Lily pulled her arm away. "You don't *have* any conversation that I've ever noticed. It seems you simply use force or wiles to get your way."

"And you have a tongue in your head that will bring you to grief," he said. "It's already brought you to grief, not to mention myself. Haven't you learned anything?"

"I have learned a very great deal, Mr. LaMartine, most of which I wish I hadn't. You, on the other hand, have taken a very fine advantage of the situation."

He frowned. "I can't help but wonder what you mean by that."

"I mean that you are a scheming devil. From the moment you discovered my identity, you realized the possibilities in it for you."

"I did, yes, although why you should construe that as scheming, I can't imagine."

"And furthermore, you pretended no knowledge of English in the hope of gleaning even more facts about the benefits you might gain by marriage to me."

"I see. Yes, I think I finally see where this is leading."

"That's good, for I'm tired of these games. Tell me, to which of my estates are we driving? When is it that you plan to take over my affairs? Tomorrow, the day after? You will be a man of very great consequence—surely you'll wish to impress that fact upon the world as quickly as possible, given your humble beginnings."

He gave her a hard look but said nothing.

"I expect you will give me a small allowance from my marriage portion; that would only be fair. Even my father gave me an allowance. I suppose then you'll go directly to London for the remainder of the Season."

She stared out of the window, but all she saw was what her life was about to become—she, helpless and alone, locked away in the country somewhere, while the wretch went happily about the business of whoring and whatever other pleasures dissolute men usually indulged in.

"Oh, yes," she said, turning to look at his handsome face, her heart filled with bitterness. "Once the marriage announcement appears in the paper you will be an instant curiosity—a celebrity, the man who managed to steal the hand of the Catholic heiress. I am sure you will have a fine time squandering all my money in the brothels and gaming hells of London."

The wretch leaned back against the cushions and folded his arms across his chest. "You're quite unbelievable. You truly are beyond anything I have ever come across before."

"And you are the most self-serving, despicable man I have ever, ever met, and I have met many!"

"No doubt. You have a tendency to bring out the very worst in people."

Lily's hand flew out to strike him, but she found it caught in a tight grip. "Impertinent brute! Wretch!" she cried, struggling to pull away.

"Elizabeth. Listen to me carefully."

He released her, and she rubbed her wrist, thinking she'd forgotten to add physical abuse to the list of things he would subject her to. "I'm not interested in anything you have to say," she said coldly.

"Why? Because you had the incredible foolishness to fling yourself off an extremely private wall and land virtually at my feet?"

"Because you're a liar and a reprobate," she shot back. "Because you may have fooled everyone else with your glib tongue, but you haven't fooled me, even if I am unfortunate enough to be married to you—and against my will, no matter what I said in that dreadful chapel, for I didn't mean a word of it. I will not honor you, nor any of those other things, even if I am forced by law to obey. And I probably won't do that very well either, so it's no good trying to force me—or beat me. It won't make any difference."

He looked her up and down with that cool look, the one that made her feel objectionable and somehow inferior. "At first I thought you completely deranged, but I quickly came to realize that it's not your sanity that's in question. However, I'm not sure that I can go through the rest of my life dealing with a spoiled child."

"A—a spoiled *child*?" she said, staring at him. "How dare you speak to me like that, you . . . you disgraceful lout!"

"A spoiled child," he repeated. "And until the day you're prepared to behave as a mature person, I refuse to treat you as one. Think it over."

"I'm not the least interested in what you think of me. In fact, you're extremely presumptuous to think anything at all." She turned her head away.

"I can see you gave the matter a great deal of consideration," he said dryly. "Very well, Elizabeth, be stubborn. It's your choice, although you might let me know should you change your mind."

"I will *never* change my mind," she said, turning back

to glare at him. "I *hate* you! I will hate you for all eternity—
I swear it on my soul!"

"You've more than proved my point," he said, appearing
not the least distressed by her heated vow. "Very well, so
be it. It's a shame that you don't have more sense, though.
There are certain advantages to behaving one's age, such as
being treated with respect."

"You're not my father," she said, stung. "I'm not obliged
to listen to this."

"You're right, I am not your father, nor anything like
him. Nor have I anything in common with Father Mallet,
save for a religion, and that commonality is questionable.
Don't make the mistake of comparing me to either of them."

"*Comparing* you?" Lily said with contempt. "You're not
only a rake, you're a conceited jackass. You think I would
ever compare *you* to a duke? Or to a priest, for that matter?
You're insane."

He rubbed a finger over his full lower lip, back and forth,
back and forth, his thumb resting on his square chin.

Lily found the gesture extremely unnerving. She pulled
her gaze away, looking at the floor, the ceiling, the window—anywhere but his mouth.

"Elizabeth," he finally said, "I want to make something
very clear. I'm neither the rake nor the molester you've made
me out to be, and now that we're married I would appreciate
your giving up the fiction, for it has no further use."

Lily gave a most unladylike snort. "You can't be serious.
The only thing that has changed is that now when you molest me it's acceptable. According to Father Mallet, you may
do whatever you wish to me, and God will applaud."

Two spots of color flamed high in his cheeks, and Lily
saw that she had hit her mark—perhaps too accurately, for
he reached out and grabbed her arms none too gently,
abruptly pulling her around to face him.

"I've tried to be tolerant in the face of what has happened, and I've tried to be sympathetic toward you, but you
push me too far! Has it once occurred to you that you're not
the only one trapped in a miserable situation?" He gave her
a hard shake. "Has it ever occurred in that spoiled, stubborn
little head that because of your misguided actions and accusations my life has also been irrevocably turned upside
down? You're so certain of my lecherous past that you haven't
taken the time to consider any other possibilities!"

Lily, truly frightened by the rage she saw on his face, tried to pull away, but he held her in a viselike grip.

"Did you hear me say I wished to do anything at all to you?" he continued furiously. "It may come as a surprise, but that's the last thing in the world I wish. Why would I want to go to bed with someone I don't even know, let alone like?" He let her go as abruptly as he'd seized her, as if he were shaking off something disgusting. "It's a blasted duty, Elizabeth, and one I would just as soon forgo."

"Then forgo it," she cried, wanting to curl up into a little ball, but refusing to show him that he'd humiliated her. "I wish nothing to do with you—ever!"

"Good," he snapped. "Because I have no intention of coming anywhere near your bed. But make no mistake. I will be your husband in every way but that—there will be no annulment, if that is what you were hoping. You will not put either of us, or our respective families, through that scandal, not when the sole reason I married you was to avoid one."

He took a deep, shuddering breath, rubbing his palms back and forth on his thighs, his head bent.

Lily stared at him, so taken aback she did not know what to say at first. A mass of conflicting emotions—relief, anger, confusion—raged through her. "You can't be serious," she finally choked.

"I'm very serious," he said more calmly, but his eyes still flamed. "I would have been prepared to consummate this marriage had I been dealing with a willing, cooperative adult. But since I no more molest children than I do women, that's out of the question."

"But—but what about heirs?" she stammered.

"Let some other poor fool beget your blasted heirs," he said coldly. "I want no part of it. You've made it clear that you have no wish to listen to me, nor to make any sort of peace between us. There seems little point for me to continue to try."

"Try? *Try?* Are you completely deluded? You've been nothing but foul and despicable to me from the first miserable moment we met, intent on ruining my life! Well, you've succeeded, and now you have what you want, haven't you?"

"I have the very last thing I want," he said flatly. "You have no idea how little I want this. You're too damned selfish to see anything but your own misery."

"I don't believe you," she said. "I don't believe you for a moment. You gained every advantage by this marriage. Money, land, social distinction. You may not want me, but don't try to tell me that you don't want what came along with me."

He shook his head, then rubbed his eyes with one hand. "Very well," he said, looking over at her. "Insist on misjudging me; that's your prerogative. But let me set you straight on one vital point. Your money, and your estates, and the London Season can go hang for all I care."

Lily looked at him in disbelief. "What?"

"As I said. I'll appoint someone to look after your business concerns, since I have no interest in them, and you are certainly too immature to be trusted with anything." He regarded her with those dark eyes, his face coldly set in such a way that she could no longer decipher anything from his expression.

"You don't want my money?" Lily felt as if she'd just been submerged in a tub of cold water.

"I don't want anything that belongs to you, no."

"I—but . . ." Lily blinked rapidly. "But then where are we going to live? *How* are we going to live?"

"We'll live on what I can afford. As for where, I don't know yet. We're going to my home until I decide what to do next. Obviously I'll have to find employment."

"Home? What kind of home?" she asked with true alarm.

"It's not Sutherby, but it's certainly livable. Don't worry, Elizabeth, I'm not taking you to live in the sewers of Paris."

Lily flushed. "I didn't know at the time that you understood," she muttered, hot with embarrassment.

"No doubt. I'm sure you thought Brother Julien didn't understand either, although he understands English very well even if he can't speak it—that, by the way, is because of a brutal injury to his tongue five years ago. But that's another story. Suffice it to say he is a mute."

"Oh," she said, feeling very small.

Pascal looked down at his hands. "In any case, he's a good and worthy man, and I can only hope that his English didn't extend to some of your more colorful vocabulary, for whatever you might think of me, Brother Julien wasn't deserving of it." He flicked her a cool glance.

"Oh . . ." Lily said again, even more mortified. "I hadn't realized."

"It was not my impression that you were giving much thought to anything but your own aggrieved self."

Lily very much wanted to go for his throat in that moment, but instead she clenched her hands together, vowing vengeance. "Where is it that you live?" she asked, thinking that once in France she could run away from the wretch, straight to Saint-Simon. Jean-Jacques would protect her, she was sure of it. It was just a matter of getting there.

"In Sussex," he answered, dashing the small shred of hope that had arisen. "It's not so far from here."

"Sussex? You are from Sussex? But you cannot be—you're French!"

"Did no one tell you anything at all about me?"

"They told me only that I had to marry you and go away with you."

He ran a hand through his dark hair, then released a deep breath. "This is absurd. I explained it all to your father and his priest in exhaustive detail."

"Well, neither said a word to me about you. Not that I care," she hastened to add, even though curiosity burned in her, "but I think I should know something about the man I've been forced to marry."

He gave her a long look. "I am originally from France," he finally said, his tone neutral. "However, my home is in Sussex."

"Oh. I see."

"I doubt very much that you do, and I'm not inclined to explain just now. I imagine much will be made clear tomorrow."

Lily couldn't imagine anything being made clear, but she was too tired and overwrought to argue. She turned her head away, and before too long the rocking of the carriage and her own exhaustion sent her to sleep.

6

LILY glanced over at her husband, who was successfully ignoring her, his attention fully on a thick book
that he held in front of him. He had not bothered making
polite conversation since the afternoon before. Their evening meal had passed in almost complete silence, and she
had breakfasted alone. But he had kept his word and stayed
away from her room, and for that she was grateful.

She glanced at him again, completely baffled, trying to
work out what he might be playing at, for she knew there
was definitely some sort of game afoot. She was certain that
he was bluffing about her money. No one chose to live in
poverty, so his statement to the contrary did not concern
her overmuch. But not to insist on his marital rights?

A thick lock of hair had fallen over his brow, and he
absently reached up and brushed it away. She noticed his
hands for the first time. They were well made, the fingers
long and squared, and although they were clean, she could
see that the skin just under the base of the fingers was cal-
lused from work. The backs of his hands were bronzed from
the outdoors, as bronzed as his neck and face.

She couldn't see his eyes, only the sweep of his long
lashes, the profile of high cheekbone, and the long, high-
bridged, slightly arched nose typical of the French. Jean-
Jacques had a nose that was not dissimilar, but her brother
had none of the other features that were arranged in such a
way as to make this man so terrifyingly handsome. Her gaze
dropped to his mouth, intriguingly wide, yet finely etched,
the lower lip full and beautifully shaped, with a small square
indentation in the middle. He was freshly shaven, but a faint
shadow of beard surrounded his mouth and ran over his lean
cheeks and strong, square chin.

A sudden chill took hold of her and she shuddered, then
dragged her gaze away, quickly looking out the window at

the distant line of the shore. The countryside had begun to change, and she could almost taste the salt in the air. And then the carriage swung slightly north, and the coastline with its plunging cliffs disappeared as meadow and forest came into view. Not too much later they approached an impressive pair of gates, and Pascal closed his book and put it away in his satchel.

"We're here," he said.

Lily looked about her for a cottage, but there was nothing to be seen. The carriage swung through the gates, then continued down a long drive bordered on one side by a broad sweep of lawn and on the other by a thick wood. They were obviously traveling through someone's estate, although she had no idea whose. She swallowed nervously, hoping they were not trespassing.

An enormous house finally came into view, and with a jolt of surprise Lily suddenly realized where they were, for she had seen drawings of Ravenswalk, seat of the Earl of Raven and considered to be one of the finest examples of Baroque architecture in the country. But what they were doing on the property she could not imagine. She hoped to heaven they would not encounter either Lord or Lady Raven, for Lily knew they would not be pleased to see her. She licked her lips.

"Um, Mr. LaMartine, don't you think it's a little rude to be using Lord Raven's front drive?"

"Why? It's the most direct way."

"Nevertheless, the back entrance would be more fitting."

"Oh, you know the estate then?"

"No, I have only heard of it. Where do you live? On one of the tenant farms?"

"No. I live here," he said as the carriage pulled up in front of the house.

Lily stared at him. "Here?" she repeated in a strangled whisper. Servants did not approach a house by its front door, ever. The nerve of the man! Just then a footman opened the door and put down the steps, and the wretch put his hand out to bar her.

"Stay here," he said and climbed out.

"Mister Pascal!" the delighted footman exclaimed the moment he saw him. "We were not expecting you. Welcome home, sir. It has been far too long."

Lily watched incredulously as her husband smiled—actually smiled—and shook the footman's hand. "Thank you, James. It's nice to be back. How is your wife?"

"Thriving now, Mister Pascal. Her spirits will soar when she hears you are home. She's never forgotten what you did for her."

"It was nothing. Is either Lord or Lady Raven at home?"

"His lordship is in his study and her ladyship is out gardening. Oh, they will be pleased . . ."

"Pascal!" A fair-haired woman of about forty dropped the basket of flowers she'd been carrying and ran across the driveway, and with a sinking heart Lily saw that it was Georgia, Countess of Raven. "Pascal!"

"Madame." He held his arms out to her and she ran directly into them, holding him as tightly as he was holding her.

"I don't believe it." She looked up at him with a huge smile, brushing away the tears in her eyes. "I simply don't believe it."

"Madame," he said, smiling tenderly. "It is good to see you.

"And you, *chéri*, you have no idea—this is the most wonderful surprise. It's been over two years, you beast. I was beginning to think you were never coming back. The children are going to be so happy—you won't believe how they've grown. Charlie has taken the others on a fishing expedition, so you'll have to wait until later to see for yourself. James, you must fetch my husband immediately!"

"No . . ." Pascal said, staying the footman. "No, madame, I'll go to him. I must speak to you both, and it's better to do it privately."

The smile faded from her face. "Trouble?" she asked softly, examining his face more closely.

"That is a matter of interpretation. I have another surprise for you." He walked over to the carriage, where Lily was still sitting, and he held out his hand. She took it, her stomach sinking, and climbed out of the carriage.

"Allow me to introduce my wife to you. Elizabeth, Lady Raven."

Georgia's face reflected her shock as her eyes flew to Lily. "Your wife? Why—why, it's Elizabeth Bowes, of all people. My dear, how nice to see you again." She didn't sound at all sure that she meant it, and Lily colored, for she knew just what Georgia must be thinking. Lily had not created a favorable impression among London society. She knew; she'd heard the talk behind her back. Still, she was embarrassed for Georgia to see the level to which she had sunk.

"Thank you, Lady Raven," Lily said and stared at the ground.

Georgia turned back to Pascal. "But when did this happen? Never mind . . ." she said, taking in the tight expression on Pascal's face. "Perhaps you had better both come inside." She patted Pascal's arm, then turned and led the way up the front steps.

Lily followed, still in a state of shock, wondering why the wretch had received such a warm welcome.

Pascal sent Lily off to wait in the conservatory, as he didn't feel there was any point in having her present while he spoke with Nicholas and Georgia. She would only make a fool out of herself in front of them.

Nicholas was as delighted to see him as he was to see Nicholas, although he had no way of knowing how Nicholas was going to react to his news.

". . . And so," Pascal said, "there we were, looking extremely foolish. There was only one thing to be done."

"Wait," Nicholas said, rubbing his nose and looking as if he were going to burst into laughter. "Do I have this right? You are trying to tell me that you were accused of attempting to ravish Elizabeth Bowes?"

"I was."

"And you are also telling me that someone actually believed it? Really, Pascal. I find that hard to credit."

The shadow of a smile touched Pascal's face. "Do you insult me, good monsieur?"

"I would never think to insult you, dear boy, but given everything, it surprises me that anyone who knows you, most especially Dom Benetard, would think anything other than the obvious."

"He didn't think it, once I'd explained the real reason that I'd been discovered lying on top of a disheveled female."

Nicholas suppressed a choke of laughter. "I—I'm sorry. Forgive me. It is only that the entire situation seems so ludicrous. I am not sure how you have ended up here. Did

Elizabeth not disabuse Dom Benetard of this absurd notion?'' He tried very hard to keep a straight face.

''No. She was the one who made the accusation, believing it to be true.''

''Oh, dear,'' Georgia murmured, her own amusement vanishing. ''How unfortunate.''

''Yes. In any case, I thought it would be best if I brought Elizabeth here. To be honest, I had no other idea what to do.''

''Goodness,'' Georgia said. ''Yes, I can imagine, and we are very glad you did, Pascal.''

''I can see what a dilemma you have on your hands.'' Nicholas folded his fingers together and rested his chin on them.

''No, monsieur. There's no dilemma. We've been married. We'll remain married. It's only that I felt I owed you both the complete truth. If in any way this brings disgrace upon you, then naturally I shall remove myself from the family.''

''You will do no such thing,'' Nicholas said with exasperation. ''I wish you would stop being so blasted noble all the time, Pascal, for it becomes exceedingly tedious. When Georgia and I took you into this family it was a permanent arrangement. I'm afraid you can't back out now or at any other time.''

''Thank you,'' Pascal said with a slight smile. ''I had thought that was what you would say, but I felt obliged to offer.''

Nicholas inclined his head. ''Naturally you did. I am sure if I insisted, you would throw yourself off a bridge.''

''Only if I felt you had good reason. You may consider me overly noble, but I'm not suicidal,'' Pascal said dryly.

''It is a relief to hear. Now, as to your accommodations. Why do you not move back into the Close? It's stood empty since you last left, and I'm sure it would be better off for being inhabited.''

''Please do, Pascal,'' Georgia pressed. ''There is more than enough room here, of course, but the Close is really your home.''

''But I cannot—as I have told you before, it wouldn't be right. Charlie must have it, and then Willy when the time comes. It's not for me.''

Nicholas gave Pascal an amused look. ''As I do not plan

to die for some time, and as Charlie is planning to go to India to be trained in the family business, and Willy is all of twelve, the Close will continue to stand empty. I don't insist that you move into it for all time, only while you have need of it, for however long that might be. In any case, as I have told *you* before, you are by all rights, save for the tedious laws of birth and inheritance, my eldest son. Surely I may dictate to my son as I please?''

Pascal shook his head. ''You, monsieur, are as impossible as ever.''

''And you are as stubborn as ever. However, I insist, and you are obliged to obey me.''

''Very well, if you insist, then yes, we will stay at the Close—it is less damaging than flinging myself off a bridge,'' Pascal said. ''But we'll stay at the Close with the understanding that it's only until I have my feet more firmly on the ground.''

''An interesting place for them to be,'' Nicholas murmured. He put an arm around Pascal's shoulder. ''Welcome home—we're mightily glad you're back. Now that you're here, do try to leave behind these habits of raping and plundering that you learned at the monastery, will you? We don't want to have you influencing Charlie adversely. He's already wild enough as it is.''

''Thank you for your understanding, monsieur,'' Pascal said. ''And you also, madame, for I know this news must have been upsetting for you.''

''I can't think as upsetting as it has been for you,'' Georgia answered quietly.

''I've accepted my fate,'' he said with a little shrug, closing the subject. ''You've both been very kind. By the way, the monk who came with me?''

They both looked at him.

''It was Julien.''

Georgia gave a little gasp. Nicholas simply nodded. ''I would understand his loyalty. Naturally he would have seen you through to the end of this.''

''He is well?'' Georgia asked with concern.

''He is well. Now, if you'll excuse me, I'll fetch my wife and install her at the Close.''

''I'll send some of the servants over immediately to open the house and help you unpack,'' Georgia said.

''No, please,'' Pascal said quickly, ''don't send any servants over just yet. I know where the key is, and I need some time alone. Elizabeth surely can do without a maid for an hour or two? After all, she has managed for one night already. I can air the linens and carry water.''

''As you wish,'' Georgia said with a little smile. ''I can easily understand your desire to be private.'' Pascal didn't reply, and Georgia quickly changed direction. ''We dine at eight. You will join us, won't you? The children will want to see you, and they'll be anxious to meet your wife. In any case, Nicholas should welcome her properly to the family.''

''You are right,'' Pascal said. ''Elizabeth should meet her new family. Trust me, it is far superior to the one she has come from.''

Nicholas nodded. ''I have met her father. It was enough. I don't envy you the last two weeks.''

''I thought you might understand.'' Pascal went out, softly shutting the door after him.

Georgia turned to Nicholas the instant they were alone. ''Imagine. Pascal, married. I never thought I'd see the day, although I'm sorry it had to be to Elizabeth Bowes. Poor Pascal.''

Nicholas grinned. ''Poor Pascal, indeed. The girl's a hellion.''

''Hellion only half covers it. You were not there last year at the Amesleys' ball when she embarrassed poor James Knighthorn in front of half of London by telling him he wasn't fit to kiss her boots, let alone her hand.''

''Oh? Well, she wasn't far off. I can't abide James Knighthorn. Further, he has no chin.''

''Nicholas, you are missing the point.''

''Not in the least. As it happens, I am feeling rather pleased with Elizabeth Bowes.'' Nicholas came around his desk to slip his arms around his wife's waist.

''*Pleased?*'' Georgia said, pulling back to give him a hard look. ''How could you possibly be pleased with the girl? She's a disaster!''

''Maybe, but thank God something saved Pascal from himself. I think we should crown Elizabeth for her unbelievable idiocy—and thinking of that, do you realize that Pascal has gone and married one of the richest women in England? It's a damned comedy, Georgia.'' He released her and idly picked up a quill, turning it round in his fingers, then brushed it under her chin. ''Just think of it—all those greedy fools chasing after the untouchable Elizabeth Bowes—James Knighthorn included. And look what comes of it: she marries the last man in the world who would care about any of it. She marries a would-be *monk*, for God's sake.''

"I only hope she can make him happy," Georgia said, her brow furrowed with worry.

"Happy? Who knows? But if she can bring him back to earth where he belongs, I will be exceedingly grateful to her. You have to admit, being around Pascal is like being around a blasted angel."

"Nicholas. How can you be so awful?"

"You know *exactly* what I mean." He gestured toward the window. "Look at the way he walks around, charming the birds out of the trees and the fish out of the water— never mind the rest of the extraordinary things he does. There's nothing normal about Pascal—not in the way we understand it."

"Exactly," Georgia said. "I'm sure that's why he has tried so hard to find refuge—not that I ever thought him suited to monastic life . . .''

Nicholas snorted. "Good God, no. What a waste that would have been. He had me worried there—first that Buddhist place in Tibet, then the last two years in St. Christophe. Thinking about it, I don't know how he's managed those interminable stretches of celibacy."

"You wouldn't," Georgia said wryly.

"That I will take up with you later, madam," Nicholas replied with a grin. "Well, all I can say is he will find no refuge in this marriage, and thank God for it. Trying to keep Elizabeth Bowes in line should keep him firmly rooted to the ground. Although I must admit, if anyone can tame Elizabeth, it will be Pascal."

Georgia regarded her husband thoughtfully. "You might be right about that," she conceded. "But that still doesn't make a marriage, Nicholas. Pascal deserves some happiness. He's suffered enough."

Nicholas walked over to the window and stood there in silence for a minute or two, looking out over the lawn. Then he turned, and Georgia could see the shadow of pain in his eyes. She knew how deeply Nicholas loved Pascal—they shared a special bond, forged by mutual experience and deep anguish, and it had bound them together as tightly as blood.

"You're right, of course," Nicholas said, rubbing the back of his neck. "You're right. He deserves every bloody bit of happiness he can get. It must be damned lonely out there for him, given everything, no matter how much he's loved by all and sundry. But I wasn't being facetious, Georgia, not really."

"Oh?" she said with a half-smile, moving to his side and wrapping her arms around his back, laying her cheek on his broad chest. "How is that?"

"Well . . . it's an odd thing, but in a way you have one person who's halfway to heaven and another who's halfway to hell. Maybe, just maybe, each could use a touch of the other."

"You, my darling, are secretly an optimist." She looked up him, her eyes bright with amusement.

"It's only common sense," he retorted. "I reckon that they'll either kill each other or fall head over heels in love. I very much doubt there will be indifference."

"I sincerely hope it ends up the latter, although looking at Pascal right now you'd think it was the end of the world. Did you see the desolation in his eyes?"

"Yes, I saw it, and the anger as well, despite how well he thought he was hiding it from us. I'm sure I would feel the same way if I'd been forced into a loveless marriage."

"You were," she said, smiling broadly.

"Oh, no I wasn't. If I had been, I'd have run fast and furiously in the opposite direction. Believe me, Georgia, I was no lamb to the slaughter. I knew exactly what I was doing."

"You did, didn't you?" she said happily.

"Yes. But this is different. Pascal truly did have his hand forced, and being Pascal, he did what he saw as his duty." Nicholas shook his head with sympathy. "Still, we must let him make the best of this on his own, with no interference. He wouldn't thank us. The only thing we can offer at this point is support."

"And love," Georgia said.

"Oh, always love," Nicholas replied and proceeded to kiss her thoroughly, so as to make his point very clear.

* * *

"This is Raven's Close," Pascal said, bending down and pulling a key from under a flowerpot that stood next to the front door. "It's part of the Ravenswalk estate."

Lily looked up at the house. It had three wings and a gabled roof; the largest wing, where they were standing now, was covered in ivy. It was a pretty place, warm and welcoming, and Lily breathed a sigh of relief, for she had not known what to expect when the wretch had put her back in the carriage without a word of explanation and started down the carriageway. They had turned off before reaching the gates, and it had taken only a few minutes to arrive. Obviously her husband was a favored employee of the family, and he hadn't let the opportunity pass by for her to see his standing with them.

"Don't make yourself too much at home," he said, opening the front door. "The house is only on loan to us. As soon as I find a position we'll be moving away. Please, go in."

"Um, what exactly do you plan to do?" Lily said, entering a square, airy hallway. A flight of wide wooden steps led to the upstairs, and off to the left Lily saw a dining room through an open door. The doors to the right were all shut. It was simple, but would be adequate, she decided.

"As you saw at the abbey, I work with plants," he said, bringing her trunk in and easing it onto the floor. "I will continue to do so."

"Oh, yes, of course, how silly of me. Can you not stay on here?"

"No. I can't. In this new set of circumstances such a thing would be impossible."

"Yes, I can see that it would be awkward, given everything. But surely I could recommend you to people who would be willing to help find you work in a more—a more *elevated* position?"

"I think not, Elizabeth. I will find my own work."

"You are so proud that you will refuse to take advantage of my many contacts? You wish to continue just as you were? Do you really expect me to believe that?"

"That I wish to continue the work in which I was trained? Yes. I do."

"So. You are telling me that I am to be married to a gardener. That is how the world is to see you?"

"Yes. In essence, that is what I am."

"And me? I am now to become a gardener's wife?" Lily

tried to sound nonchalant, but inside she was quaking with panic, thinking of that little cottage she'd so fondly conjured up when she'd been sitting high above the abbey wall, the cottage with the smell of baking bread drifting out the door—and the welcoming wife in the portal. Lily could no more bake bread than she could boil water, and she was as far from a welcoming wife as could be found.

Suddenly the entire charming picture changed in her mind. The door hung off its hinges, there were holes in the windows (the few windows that there were), and she was dressed in rags, looking tired and bruised around the eyes, her hair stringy, her hands reddened. Lily had seen such people before on her father's own estates.

She shuddered at the thought of what was likely to become of her.

"Do you find the idea of having a husband who works repulsive? It is what most men do, those of us who were not born to dukedoms, that is."

Lily put her chin up. "I know that some men have to work, and as for dukedoms, your jibe misses its mark. My father works hard at keeping his estates—and his employees—in order. It is the idea of physical labor that I find repellent." She cast a pointed look at his hands.

Pascal followed her gaze and held his hands up, turning them so the palms faced her. "You find these offensive?" he asked softly, his voice heavy with irony.

"I find them coarse," she replied smugly. "No doubt you wish to coarsen my hands as well, and as soon as you possibly can. You would have been better off marrying a fish-wife—she at least would have had some idea how to go about seeing to your humble needs."

He folded his arms across his broad chest and leaned one shoulder against the wall, looking steadily down at her, and Lily swallowed, for he suddenly appeared formidable, even though his face registered nothing but indifference. "It is true. My needs are humble," he said. "Does that worry you?"

"I suppose you'll expect me to take in washing to help support us?"

"Take in wash—" He bit off the word and paused, then continued smoothly. "No. I do not expect you to hire yourself out, but yes, naturally I expect you to do the washing."

Lily stared at him. "I suppose you will also expect me to cook and clean for you?" she asked, her temper rising.

"Of course," he said. "Who else do you think is going to do it? I'll be out working all day. You are my wife. Certain things are expected of you. You are not thinking of shirking your duties, are you?"

"I cannot believe you! I have more money than you have ever dreamed of in your life, and it is now by law entirely at your disposal. Why would you refuse to avail yourself of that and at least provide me with the comforts to which I was born?"

"You are married to me now, Elizabeth. My comforts will be your comforts, and those comforts will be determined by what I can afford."

"I don't understand you. Do you wish to live in poverty because that is what *you* are accustomed to? Or do you just mean to humiliate me, to punish me for my birth?"

"Why would I want to punish you for your birth? I have no interest in it. I thought I'd made that very clear yesterday, as I did my feelings about your dowry. I'm perfectly happy living a simple existence."

"Then—then what are you doing at a place like Ravenswalk?" she said irrationally. "Why are we here?"

"I thought I had made that clear as well. This is my home, my family."

"Then where is this precious family, and why have you not introduced me to them? Are you ashamed? Did you think to impress me by taking me first to Ravenswalk so that I could see you would be received inside?" She gestured around her. "And now you have brought me to this place so I can see that Lord Raven thinks highly enough of you to lend it to you? Well, it makes no difference," she said with a toss of her head. "There is nothing you can do to impress me, nothing at all."

"I have no intention of impressing you with anything," he said coldly.

"Oh? Well, in that case you might as well take me straight to your family and let me see how it really is, what you really come from. As your wife I have a right to know what it is I have married into."

He looked at her with incredulity. "My God, you really are unbelievable. I thought I had heard it all yesterday, but I was mistaken." He unfolded his arms and straightened to his full height. "Well, Elizabeth. I hate to disappoint you, but you are also sadly mistaken on a number of counts. As it happens, you have already met one member of my family."

"Who? James, the footman?" she said, pushing her chin out even further in an effort not to cry.

"No, not James the footman, although I would be proud enough to call him family. I was referring to Georgia."

"She cannot be of your family," Lily said, furious at this bald-faced lie, "and it is no good trying to pretend to me, for I, of all people, would know, you idiot. How could you even think to claim such a thing and get away with it? Lord Raven is a peer of the British realm. And you . . . you are . . . are nothing more than a low-born French guttersnipe!"

Pascal nodded. "As you say. But this low-born French guttersnipe was nevertheless adopted by that particular peer of the realm and his wife. This is the house where I spent the second half of my childhood, which is why it has been loaned to us."

Lily paled. The image of Lady Raven hugging Pascal as if he were a long-lost son came rushing back to her, and she suddenly had a terrible feeling that he might be speaking the truth. "Adopted?" she whispered. "You? But why?"

"Do you mean why would they adopt such an ill-born, uncivilized, unwanted creature as myself? Perhaps they felt it was their civic duty. Or perhaps they simply wanted an unpaid servant to black their boots." He shrugged. "Why don't you ask them at dinner? We are expected. Oh, and it would be wise to change your dress. They may have had the poor taste to adopt me, but they are reasonably correct in all other ways."

He bent and easily hoisted Lily's trunk onto one broad shoulder, starting up the stairs without another word. Lily followed at his heels, feeling like one of her father's misbehaved hounds that had just been severely chastised without knowing why.

Pascal went to the kitchen and lit the stove, then filled a kettle with water for washing and slammed it onto the stove to heat.

"Damn you, Elizabeth Bowes," he muttered from between clenched teeth, pulling out a chair from the table and throwing himself into it. He crossed his arms over his chest and glared out the window.

He had never before in his life come across someone with such an attitude—with the exception of her father, but Montcrieff at least kept his tongue between his teeth when it came to outright insults. Oh, he had been called a guttersnipe before, and it had been true enough. That didn't bother him so much as her unbelievable haughtiness. She had no idea how the rest of the world went on, nor did she have any interest in knowing. Take in washing, indeed. He ought to force her to it just so she would know what it was like . . . in fact, that wasn't such a bad idea. She could damned well learn to cook and clean and dress herself, and there was no time like the present.

He'd take Georgia aside after dinner and ask her not to send any servants over, not a single one. Georgia would naturally leap to all the wrong conclusions, which was as he would have it. He wouldn't want her to think he was displeased with his wife, especially when they had been married only two days. He certainly would not want her thinking he was avoiding his wife's bed, for Georgia would not understand that at all, not with the relationship that she and Nicholas shared.

Pascal smiled faintly as he remembered all the times over the years that he had come across the two of them in an embrace, unaware that they'd been spotted. It was a great joke among the children, the wanton behavior of their parents. He sighed heavily, then poured the water into pitchers.

He delivered the first pitcher at Lily's door, gave a cursory knock, then took the remaining pitcher across the hall to his old room, where he'd already tossed his satchel onto the bed. The satchel sat there, a grim reminder of his recent journey. He remembered when Nicholas had given it to him, just before he departed for Oxford, nervous, feeling like a fish out of water. Nicholas had come into his room while he was packing and sat down on the bed, casually tossing the satchel over to Pascal with a few lightly reassuring words and a joke or two.

It had made all the difference at the time. Unfortunately there was nothing Nicholas could do or say now that would make any difference at all.

Pascal walked to the window and leaned on the sill, looking down over the gardens that he and Georgia had worked so hard to bring back after they had been allowed to go to ruin by the previous Lady Raven. The shrubs he had brought Georgia from the Himalayas on his last trip home had taken hold and were thriving, their vivid colors cheerfully bright, caught in the setting rays of the sun. He let out a shaky breath. It was all so familiar, exactly as he remembered it, and yet his life had changed beyond recognition.

Suddenly desperate to be outside, he quickly washed and changed, then went downstairs and out the back door into the walled garden.

The absolute peace of the garden at dusk was only heightened by the gentle call of doves, the low hoot of an owl, the treble songs of wren and robin above, the swift whir of a random bird on the wing. Subtle shifts of wind brought individual fragrances to him, each unique, each delightful. The collaboration of color and smell had been designed to calm the senses rather than to excite, to soothe the soul and offer comfort. Comfort? Where was that to be had? It seemed that everything even vaguely resembling comfort had vanished from his world.

Pascal shut his eyes tightly. *Don't think. For God's sake don't think or you'll fall apart.* He stood very still for a moment, then walked past the stone statue of a young boy, to the bench set beneath the willow tree. He leaned over and put his head in his hands, breathing deeply in an effort to quiet the terrible pain in his chest. He felt as if it might rend him in two.

Seeing Nicholas and Georgia had nearly undone him. The numbness that had wrapped itself around him from the moment Elizabeth Bowes had made her ridiculous accusation had instantly been stripped away when he saw Georgia running across the lawn toward him, her face wreathed in unquestioning welcome. Georgia, his friend, his teacher, and Nicholas, the man whom he loved more than any other man alive—both of them, always there for him, his only family, everything that he had in this world. His beloved monsieur and madame, names he had given them in childhood, which had somehow stuck. He had missed them even more than he'd realized.

And yet he knew as clearly as he knew anything that he could not stay. To stay would be to be reminded every minute of every day what marriage really meant, to see what love was and to know that it would never be possible for him. To stay would be to make a travesty of everything he held dear.

The thought of leaving wrenched a groan from his chest, and he dropped his hands to his sides, clenching them into fists, struggling for control. He needed to draw on all his strength, for the last thing in the world he wanted was for Georgia and Nicholas to see what he was feeling and be upset by his misery.

Tomorrow he would make inquiries. Anything, anywhere, to leave this raw, agonizing pain behind.

He rose to his feet, feeling far older than his twenty-nine years, and returned inside to take his high-born fishwife to dinner.

"Pascal, Pascal—no, let me tell, Willy! It was my catch, after all."

Lily watched the young, dark-haired girl grab her brother's arm—Ghislaine was her name, she thought, trying to sort them all out. But Lord Raven, or Nicholas, as she was supposed to call him, inadvertently corrected her, and Lily realized that it was Ghislaine, the blond older girl, who was laughing about something with her mother at the other end of the table.

"Kate," Nicholas said, "do go ahead, will you, before we have all-out war at the dinner table? Willy, let your sister speak."

"Well, it was my line that tugged. So I pulled at it gently, just as you showed me, Pascal, and then I gave it a slight jerk, and the fish was hooked. But it wasn't so easy as all that. You remember the place, beyond the stand of oaks where it's so shaded?"

"Yes, of course," he said. "Tell me, what did you do next? You were subtle, I think?"

Lily listened in silence. She did not know how to respond to this enthusiastic family, where the conversation leaped from one thing to the next and everyone seemed to talk at once. Lily didn't understand, not any of it. She felt like an outsider. Worse, she felt like a fool, for the wretch had obviously told her the truth about his place in the family.

She frowned, watching as he quietly conversed with the youngest girl, the one who had caught the fish. All the children had vied for his attention throughout the evening. He was clearly popular with them, and she was amazed by the difference in his manner. She'd never seen him behave like this before, attentive, congenial. He even *appeared* agreeable instead of cold and forbidding, and she found it oddly disconcerting.

She looked away and studied Nicholas instead. He was so similar in looks to the wretch that he might have been his natural father. The wretch was tall and well built, as was Nicholas. They shared the same dark hair and full mouths, the same dark eyebrows, although where Nicholas's were winged, the wretch's were nearly straight.

They had something else in common too, although she couldn't quite place it; it was more of a natural affinity they shared, as if there was a deep, unspoken understanding between them. Lily instantly dismissed that thought. The wretch was incapable of understanding. No, she decided, it was just that Nicholas was a generous man who made an effort to make people feel comfortable, unlike his adopted son. He and Georgia had been nothing but kind and welcoming to her. Their easy warmth had wrapped her in acceptance, though she didn't really know what to do with it.

She was trying her best to fit in, but she wasn't any good at this sort of thing. She was accustomed to a house where any display of affection was considered wicked, where joking and laughing were reason for punishment. She and Jean-Jacques had been conspirators, players in a daring game of consequence. But here no one was silenced.

Charlie, who had his father's gray eyes but his mother's fair hair, turned to her with a wicked smile. "So, Elizabeth. How does it feel to be introduced to Bedlam?"

"I—it is different. I am not used to large families."

"Never mind. It won't take long. Those who consider themselves well brought up are generally appalled—children at the dinner table? *Quelle horreur!* We do make rather a lot of noise, don't we?"

Lily nodded. "We always had a priest at our table. We weren't meant to speak except about religious things."

"God forbid! Oh, sorry. So, out of habit—oops, never mind—I meant out of practicality you went and married Pascal. It's about time someone did. I suppose it makes sense, both of you being Catholic. What I'd like to know is how you got him out of that monastery he'd shut himself away in. What a victory. You must have made quick work of it, too."

Lily flushed a horrible red and, surprisingly, her husband came to her rescue.

"Charlie, enough of your questions, if you please. You are embarrassing my wife, and in any case, it's none of your business. So. What's this I hear about your going to India? Monsieur tells me you are entering into the business. What, no university?"

Charlie shrugged. "I'd rather apply myself to practical things, like wine, women, and song."

"Charlie," Nicholas said on a note of warning. "You shan't be going anywhere if you carry on like this."

"Sorry," Charlie said cheerfully. "Anyway, I thought I'd make my way down to Italy and catch one of Papa's ships from there. You've done it. And you loved India—and the Himalayas. You made them sound like magic. Just think, all those teachers of yours might have a beneficial influence on me. Maybe you'll give me some introductions. What do you think?"

"Tomorrow, Charlie. It's too long a subject to go into now. Anyway, I doubt I could give you the sort of introductions that you might be seeking." He turned toward Nicholas. "Which branch do you plan to start Charlie in? Bombay?"

"No, I think not. Bombay would not bring out the best of Charlie's character."

Pascal nodded, his face serious. "No," he said, "I think perhaps you're correct. Bombay isn't the place for Charlie. So, what shall it be—what's the most staid office you have in all of India? This is where Charlie must go."

"Papa!" Charlie launched instantly on a line of defense, and the two were on him, teasing unmercifully.

Lily was left alone to think her own thoughts. She wasn't sure she could make sense out of what she observed. She knew that her husband was a wretch and a scoundrel. He was also an opportunist. He had not been brought up in the common sort of family she had originally thought, and it was clear that these people were extremely fond of him. They were mistaken in their fondness, for how were they to know what sort of life he had led away from the confines of their home? It was far from what he had led them to believe. In fact, she found it extremely irritating that they were so adoring, so loving to him.

And yet . . . there was something about him tonight,

something different, that belied her experience. Look at the way the little girl leaned toward him, took his hand in hers, so trusting, the way he bent his dark head and gravely listened to her.

But no. She refused to be taken in by such chicanery. It was obviously the method he used to fool people. That was always how it was—she knew well. People behaved one way and intended something else entirely. People lied and manipulated, anything to obtain their own ends. Her own father was a perfect example—charming in public, brutal in private.

Typical.

Lily had ended up with a younger version of her father. Next would come the priest at the dinner table. She shuddered.

Life was just not fair.

7

LILY woke at first light to the sound of some very noisy birds scrapping outside of her window. She rolled over and tried to go back to sleep, but it would not come. Between the birds, the growing light, and her own unhappiness, she could see that she was to have no peace that morning. Thinking about it, she realized she hadn't had a peaceful morning since she'd encountered the wretch.

She dressed, her fingers still unaccustomed to doing everything for herself, although she'd had plenty of practice in the chapel. She hadn't bothered to ask why there were no servants in the house—she could just imagine what sort of reply she would be given. No doubt the wretch would tell her she was spoiled just for inquiring. Oh, she really did loathe him.

Lily crept down the stairs. There was not a sound in the house, no other presence. There had always been someone about at Sutherby, if only a parlormaid lighting the fires. In an odd way it felt nice, knowing she was completely alone—with the exception of the wretch, but he was upstairs fast asleep.

She looked around the ground floor curiously, strolling through the drawing room, the library, then the kitchen and dining room. But what truly drew her eye was a garden outside the window. A thick silver mist floated and shifted delicately among magnificent shrubs and flowering plants. The moon had not yet finished its course and hung a more fragile, fading silver in the gray sky. She found the door and let herself out.

The garden was enclosed by thick stone walls beaded with moisture, and a vine she'd never seen before, a buttery yellow in color, tumbled heavily off the end of the wall nearest to her. She walked down a few steps, her shoulder brushed by the purple flowers of clematis that cascaded over an arched hoop. Her feet immediately became soaked by the dew, but she didn't mind. She found herself drawn into the sense of the garden.

She'd never seen anything like it in her life. A long bed of roses, just beginning to open with delicate, pale petals, lined a path that curved off to the left; on the right was a low border filled with what Lily thought must be medicinal herbs, for she recognized rosemary, sage, lavender, and foxglove. There were a great many other things that she did not recognize, but she could at least appreciate the color and the groupings. She wandered down the path, drinking in the smell of honeysuckle, the sight of primrose, alium, pansies, forget-me-nots—wherever she looked there was something different and wonderful. There was order but no order. Unlike her father's idea of creating a carefully controlled and rigid landscape, here there was a freedom, an imagination that had been allowed to run unfettered.

Beehives sat along the edge of one wall where iris and tulips grew. In the center of the garden was a statue of a child, with more bulbs pushing up about its feet, and a silver carpet of lamium ran over the ground beyond. Lily bent down and ran her fingers over the moist, springy stuff, gently touching the tiny pink flowers that danced among the leaves.

All of this was counterbalanced by a variety of trees and shrubs, some in flower, some evergreen. There was even something that looked like a blackberry bush, covered in lovely white blooms. It was magic, pure unadulterated magic. Even though Lily had never taken much interest in gardens, she felt as if she were a child again, safe in a place where nobody could hurt her, where the world couldn't find her. Yet she couldn't resist the temptation to reach out and push on the great wooden door to the outside, to see if it would open, and also to see what was out there.

The door creaked, but it swung open easily enough. Lily gasped, and her hand crept to her mouth in wonderment. Directly in front of her the sun was climbing over the horizon, a huge blood-red circle pushing through the mist to hover over the valley as if reluctant to leave it. She looked and looked, trying to drink in the sight, for she couldn't believe that the sun could look quite so—so enormous, so very beautiful. "Oh . . ." she whispered.

"It's not bad, is it? I hadn't realized that you enjoyed this sort of thing."

Lily squeaked and jumped around. He stood there, one hand resting on top of the door, the other hanging easily at his side. His shirtsleeves were rolled up and his collar was open. He wore no jacket. "I don't," she said out of sheer contrariness.

"Oh?"

"I—I couldn't sleep. There was nothing better to do."

"I see. So to alleviate your boredom, you decided to come outside for the sunrise, even though you don't enjoy watching?"

"There's no need to be rude," Lily said indignantly.

"I beg your pardon. I was merely perplexed. The last time I saw you up at this hour you were extremely disgruntled."

"It's not a crime to enjoy one's sleep," Lily informed him, "and I see no reason for you to be so argumentative."

He looked at her, and there was a faint gleam of amusement in his eyes. "Coming from you, that is laughable."

Not quite sure how to respond to that, Lily said, "How long were you standing there?"

"Long enough to know you've just told me one enormous lie. Really, Elizabeth, where is the shame in admitting to enjoying one of God's miracles?"

"It was just there," she said. "And anyway, I don't believe in God." She waited for him to explode, but, oddly, it didn't happen.

"Really?" he said equitably. "Somehow I'm not surprised. Do you suppose He believes in you?"

"What sort of a question is that?" she demanded. "Of course He does—or He would if He existed, which He doesn't."

"Do you know, when I was a very young child," Pascal said, looking at the huge sun, "I used to worry that we were all just one of God's dreams. I thought that when He woke up from His night's sleep we would vanish as if we had never existed at all."

"You are a very strange man."

"Probably. But at least I've moved beyond that particular piece of theology—well, more or less. In the very simplest of terms, I accept that we are a part of God's dream, but I no longer worry that we're in danger of vanishing. It seems to me that what's happened to you is you have woken up from the most beautiful dream possible, and it is you who has made God vanish. That's quite a clever trick.''

Lily stared at him. He really was the oddest man she had ever come across. ''I have no idea what you are talking about, but I think you are extremely foolish.''

He shrugged, then lifted his arm. Elizabeth followed the direction of his wave and saw Charlie coming toward them, two fishing poles in one hand and a saddlebag in the other.

''Good morning,'' Charlie said cheerfully as he reached them. ''Are you coming along with us, Elizabeth? How nice.''

She rubbed her toe in the grass. ''No—I'm not. I wasn't invited, and in any case, I don't know how to fish.''

''What?'' Charlie looked at her in astonishment. ''How can anyone not know how to fish? It's a sin! I mean—it's a shame. Well, you're certainly invited, isn't that right, Pascal?'' he said, grinning broadly. ''It won't do, your having a wife who can't fish, not with you being one of the world's great fishermen. Look here, you can have my pole, Elizabeth. Together we should be able to teach you to catch a fish or two.'' He started to turn. ''Come on, we should get started before the sun gets any higher.''

''No,'' Pascal said suddenly. ''You take Elizabeth. You and I will fish together another time. There's something else I really should do, if I might borrow your horse?''

''Yes, of course, but I confess I am deeply disappointed— I have a thing or two to show you. I've been waiting to impress you for two whole years.''

''I'm sure I'll be awed by your wizardry, but this is also important, and now you have Elizabeth to concentrate on impressing. I'll see you a little later, yes?''

''Yes, all right. Later—and watch my horse. He's skittish.'' Charlie turned to Elizabeth and smiled. ''Ready?''

A refusal was on her lips, but then she couldn't help herself. Charlie was too charming to resist, and besides, it would be pleasant to be with someone who seemed disposed to be nice to her. Anyway, it sounded like fun, especially without the wretch there to ruin her pleasure. ''Oh—all right,'' she said, and picked up her skirts, hastily following Charlie over the wet grass.

* * *

Pascal mounted Charlie's gelding and urged him toward the woods. It took him only ten minutes on horseback to reach his objective, a beautiful little grace-and-favor cottage that sat behind Ravenswalk. He tied the gelding to the mounting post and swung down, pushing open the gate and walking past the lush front garden, which he was pleased to see was flourishing.

He knocked and waited, confident that Binkley would be up at this hour, as was his habit. After a minute, he heard footsteps, and then the scrape of the latch. The door opened slightly, and Binkley's bald head peered out. He looked sleepy and surprised to be having a visitor so early, but his eyes shot open when he saw who it was. The door flew wide.

"Master Pascal! Oh, good heavens—you're home!"

Pascal laughed with pleasure at seeing his old friend again. "I am."

"Fancy that," Binkley said. "I thought you'd forgotten all about us, but here you are, and it's a fine day indeed."

"I'm happy to see you also. Do you think I might come in?"

"Of course, of course, my boy. How delightful, to be sure. When did you return?" He stood aside, and Pascal ducked his head to pass through the door.

"Last night."

"You have seen his lordship?" Binkley asked severely.

"Yes, it was the very first thing I did. Don't worry, Binkley, Nicholas and Georgia were not unduly disturbed by my sudden appearance."

"Very good. And the reason for this abrupt return?"

"I don't suppose you have a kettle on the stove? I'd love a cup of tea."

"Naturally I have. What a foolish question. Come and sit down and I will bring tea out directly."

"Binkley, there's no need to wait on me. I'm happy to do it."

Binkley looked insulted. "I may be an old man, but I have not lost my abilities nor my senses. Do as you are told and sit down."

"You are supposed to be retired, my friend."

"Once a butler, always a butler, and proud of it too. Don't you go trying to take away my pleasures, young man. I have few enough of them left." He shuffled away, and Pascal shook his head in amusement. There had never been a more loyal servant, nor a more loyal friend than Binkley, and Pascal valued him as much for his crustiness, which had only increased over the years, as for anything else.

When Binkley came back, he had not only a teapot but a tray laden with fresh scones, sweet butter, and his own homemade blackberry jam, and he laid it all out on the little dining room table that overlooked the back garden.

"Now," Binkley said, when they had finished the satisfactory meal, "what brings you to my door, other than the obvious? My eyes might not be as keen as they once were, but you look troubled to me."

Pascal hesitated, and Binkley scowled at him. "Come, come, get it off your chest. I'm not going to live forever and my time is precious."

"Your pardon," Pascal said, trying to keep a straight face. "I had forgotten you have been at death's door these last ten years."

"No need for impertinence. I have enough of it from Charles and the others. A disrespectful lot, those Daventry children, and both his lordship and her ladyship should be paddled for allowing it. I don't know what happened to good manners. It is all these modern ideas, no doubt."

"Why, Binkley!" Pascal said, leaning back in his chair and assuming an incredulous expression. "Are you saying that the Daventry children are anything less than perfect?"

"Perfect!" Binkley pursed his lips. "Perfect indeed. I cannot think what the dear queen, God bless her soul, would say if she saw how things went on at Ravenswalk—children running wild, shouting all day long, into scrape after scrape, playing practical jokes on me, and at my age. Why, just last week William and Katherine left a basket of frogs on my doorstep. Why they thought that amusing I do not know, but I had the devil of a time chasing those blighted things out of the garden, I can tell you."

"The children?"

"Certainly not. I refuse to chase children, but I absolutely will not abide reptiles among my periwinkles. Weeding is bad enough on an old man's back, but let me say that crawling about on one's hands and knees after leaping frogs is quite beyond reason, not to mention dignity." He grunted. "So. You have decided to return to the world. Why?"

"It was not a matter of choice, exactly." Pascal was touched that Binkley had made such an effort to put him at his ease. Binkley had always been like that, though, as Pascal remembered from the very first day of his arrival, or at least from the day that he had recovered enough from his fever to find himself not only alive but safe and warm and dry as well.

"It must have been a matter of something. People do not generally hop about between countries, let alone in and out of monasteries, without reason."

Pascal, thoroughly sick of the story, nevertheless explained. Binkley's round face registered nothing during the telling, nor did he interrupt. But as soon as Pascal had finished, Binkley laced his fingers together and looked at Pascal over them in a gesture that unconsciously imitated Nicholas—or who knew? Perhaps it was the other way around. Master and servant had been so close for so many years that one hardly knew where one began and the other left off.

"Well?" Pascal asked, uncomfortable with the scrutiny.

"What sort of idiotic comment is that? Do you expect an analysis of the situation, or even my sympathy? You will get neither, young man. So what did you really come for?" He unlaced his fingers and started drumming them on the table, his bushy eyebrows wiggling up and down in time to the beat.

Pascal swallowed a laugh. Binkley's eyebrows looked like two beetles facing off against each other. He'd always been fond of Binkley's eyebrows.

"Well?" Binkley demanded. "I haven't all day."

"I—I didn't expect your sympathy, Binkley," Pascal said contritely. "Actually, I was looking for some advice."

"Good. And here it is. You are, whether you like it or not, a married man with a wife to look after. Get to it, and stop feeling sorry for yourself."

"But I never intended to marry—"

"Nonsense," Binkley said, cutting off his objection. "God obviously didn't want you in His monastery, He wanted you practicing your talents out here with the rest of us. I can't see what difference it makes how He went about it—you're here now and you can't change a thing."

"In a very odd sort of way, you sound like Father Benetard," Pascal said dryly, pushing a stray bread crumb about the table with his finger.

"Well, I don't know any Father Benetard, and I'm sure

it's a good thing, for I'd tell him a thing or two about keeping you in a place you didn't belong and for much too long.''

''I was not being kept there, I was working for the abbot, Binkley, as you know perfectly well. The gardens had been burned during the Revolution and serious damage had been done to the stock; I was inclined to bring the garden back and stay to see the job through. I must confess I did think about taking vows, but somehow I never quite felt called.''

''I should think not,'' Binkley said indignantly. ''If God wanted you for Himself, He'd have taken you sure enough, and from the way you were spat out of the sea and onto our doorstep all those years ago, I'd say He wasn't the least bit interested in you just yet, at least not in that way.'' He started drumming on the table again. ''Someone needs to set you straight, and his lordship is too respectful of your privacy to do it himself.''

''Oh?'' Pascal said, slightly taken aback.

''You might very well say 'oh,' for I sometimes think that when God gave you those other things He forgot to include sense. Here is his lordship good enough to legally adopt you, and you are too stubborn to take his name, or a farthing of his money, or his permanent offer of the Close—oh, yes, I know all about it.''

Pascal opened his mouth and shut it again.

''I can understand your reasons for all of that, and his lordship does too, but this is something else again. Now you say you're not going to take a farthing of what your wife brought to the marriage—your marriage.''

''That's right, Binkley,'' Pascal said, his jaw set. ''So what is your point?''

''My point, which even a blind man could see, is that you're behaving like an idiot and standing on your pride. And stop pushing that crumb about,'' he added irritably. ''You're going to grind it into the table and I'll be days getting it out again.''

Pascal obediently picked the crumb up and put it on a plate.

''What do you think you're going to do with a rebellious duke's daughter if you don't have the first idea of where you're going to go and what you're going to do, with no money to do it with, and you say that you cannot stay here? That sounds like the talk of a fool to me.''

Pascal nodded. ''I know, and therein lies my predicament. I am a fool indeed, but perhaps not *quite* so much of a fool as you might think, for there is a degree of reason behind my decision. If there is to be any hope for Elizabeth—or for me—it's only going to be found somewhere as far away as possible from the drawing rooms of English society."

"Where do you plan to take her, may I ask? Tibet? Or maybe you were thinking of Siberia this time?"

"Umm—no. Not exactly. I need to find a place where we can live simply but with purpose, where such things as money and rank are secondary, if not meaningless."

"That will be no easy task," Binkley said, rubbing his ear thoughtfully. "But I believe I begin to see your point."

"My reasoning is sound, I think." Pascal leaned forward earnestly. "Look, Binkley, if I use Elizabeth's money, it will only prove to her that I married her out of greed. I need to work, and Elizabeth needs to see that I'm supporting her, not using her." He thought for a moment. "I suppose that I also want Elizabeth to learn the value of life—real life. Do you know what I mean?"

"I'm not sure *you* know what you mean. You've just come out of a monastery, boy. You can't call that real life, now can you?"

Pascal smiled. "You do have a way of putting things in perspective, even though I don't think you know the first thing about life inside a monastery. It's the sort of thing you have to experience firsthand."

Binkley grunted, which was as much of a concession as Pascal was likely to get.

"What I mean," Pascal continued, "is that Elizabeth has a lot to learn about people, about ordinary people who don't live in castles or stately homes. She's never been given a sense of anything more than her own status and empty importance. You may think Charlie and the others wild and full of mischief, but you will never find one of them throwing his position up at anyone, and if he did, you can be sure he'd have his ears boxed." He shook his head. "Elizabeth is something else again. I don't know how I'm going to manage a lifetime with the woman—not the way she is now." He scraped his chair back and started to put the plates on the tray.

"Leave it, if you please," Binkley commanded. "You'll break something with the angry way you're going about it.

What exactly are you referring to? Your wife is throwing her position up at you?''

"My God, Binkley, she's called me things even you wouldn't believe. She thinks I'm a—oh, never mind.''

"Do you feel inferior in some way to your wife?'' Binkley asked, and Pascal nearly choked.

"Good Lord, no,'' he said. "I'm answerable to no one but God, and I don't think that He has any interest in rank—despite what some might like to think,'' he added caustically. "No, it's Elizabeth who thinks herself superior. I may be stubborn, but I have never considered myself a proud sort of person. Still, I confess that she pricks at me, Binkley. In truth she does.''

"Oh?'' Binkley asked neutrally. "How is that?''

Pascal sighed. "I can't seem to hold my temper for more than two minutes when I'm near her, and it's growing shorter by the moment. I dislike myself even more for responding to her with anger, but I can't help it. And that is no excuse at all.'' He looked down at the table, then up at Binkley, feeling ashamed.

Binkley was smiling with a satisfaction that Pascal could not even begin to understand. "None,'' the old man said. "But then no one has ever needed an excuse for being human.''

"Well, Charlie,'' Lily called down from her branch, where she had climbed in order to better observe the movement of the river, "I can't say that I understand why you have caught two fish and I haven't had even a nibble, but I suppose you must be doing something right.'' She peered into the dark depths of the river, wondering how Charlie could possibly see when a fish was coming and know where to cast his line.

"You'll never catch a fish by swishing your rod back and forth like that, Elizabeth,'' he said, looking up at her.

"Oh, do call me Lily, won't you? It would make me so much more comfortable, and there's no one else to do it.''

"Not even Pascal?'' he teased.

"*Especially* not him,'' she said with disgust.

Charlie's winged eyebrows rose. "What do you mean by that?''

"He calls me 'Elizabeth' as if the word were poison in

his mouth. Personally, I think that poison would be too good for him.''

''Could we possibly be talking about the same person?'' Charlie asked, lowering his pole to the ground, his eyes sharpening in interest.

Lily swung one bare foot back and forth. ''How many Pascal LaMartines do you know?''

''Only one, and he's one of the finest people I could hope to know.''

''Then you don't know him at all,'' Lily said, her voice suddenly thick with misery.

''Oh, dear. This doesn't sound like a marriage made in heaven,'' Charlie said with real concern.

''Hell is more like it,'' Lily replied over the knot in her throat.

Charlie walked over to the tree and held out his hand. ''Here, give me your pole and come down from there. It seems to me as if you need a friend.''

The very words brought tears to Lily's eyes. She'd never had a friend—other than Jean-Jacques and Coffey, of course. Her father hadn't approved of such things. He had always said people were opportunists and would only befriend her for her status and wealth, and in any case she ought not mingle with anyone beneath her. The hitch to that had been that there weren't too many Catholic dukes' daughters running about for her to mingle with. And now, when she felt more alone than she ever had, to have this nice boy offer his hand in friendship for no reason other than he thought she needed it—it was almost too much.

She blinked her tears away and carefully climbed down.

He gave her a reassuring smile, then picked up the fishing tackle and the fish he'd caught. ''Come, let's go back to the house and have some breakfast. I'm starving, and I can't possibly talk about serious matters on an empty stomach.''

''But I don't know if there is anything to eat,'' Lily said, picking up her wet shoes and stockings, but not bothering to put them on. ''There doesn't seem to be any staff, and I have no idea if there is even any food in the house.''

Charlie held up the fish. ''These will do brilliantly. And if I know anything about it, by now word has gotten around that Pascal is home. There are bound to be offerings outside the kitchen door.''

''Oh,'' Lily said, wondering if people left offerings because they knew how impoverished her husband was—although if he was the adopted son of the Earl of Raven, surely he would have money of his own? In which case, why did he need to be a gardener? Her head spinning with unanswered questions, she followed Charlie back to the Close, wondering most of all how she was going to manage to cook Charlie's fish.

"Now," he said, dropping the fish on the kitchen table, "you start cleaning them, and I'll make up the stove."

"What do you mean, *clean* them?" Lily asked, recoiling from the two very dead trout. "They must be clean enough, having just come from the river?"

Charlie gave a hoot of laughter. "You really are an innocent, aren't you? No, Lily, I mean you have to take a knife and split them down the middle, then take out their innards." He grinned wickedly at her look of dismay.

"I . . . I don't think I can," she said, paling.

"Oh, very well, do you think you can start a fire?"

"I—I don't think so. I mean, I've seen the parlormaid do it, but I've never paid any attention."

"Then sit down and watch carefully. Now that you're married to my brother, you're going to need some basic skills. Pascal has a habit of taking off to the back of beyond, and you had better be prepared to go with him."

Charlie lit the fire, then went to the back door and opened it. "Aha!" he said triumphantly, coming back in with a basket of eggs, a jug of milk, a loaf of bread, and a wrapped ball of cold butter in his arms. "As I thought. We will have a feast this morning. Here, at least you must be able to slice bread." He put the loaf in front of her, along with a knife he found in a drawer.

"Do you really know how to cook?" Lily asked curiously, watching him throw butter into two pans.

He looked over his shoulder. "Naturally. My mother is a brilliant cook—she learned from her mother, who was French. Look. You let the butter melt, like this, then in go the fish."

Lily managed to look, now that Charlie had done the necessaries to them. Into the pan they went, spluttering in the hot butter, and she watched as he salted and peppered them, then turned his attention to the eggs.

"You break them carefully in half and slide them into the butter. Then all you have to do is watch until the whites are

set and the yolks are still soft. Lily, come now, the bread.''
He turned to the table. "What in the name of God—oh,
sorry—but it does look hacked to death. Oh, well, never
mind. Just run it under the fire in that thing there for a
moment to brown it.''

"Ouch!" Lily cried, instantly managing to burn herself,
and Charlie laughed and took the griddle from her.

"Never mind," he said, as she sucked her palm. "Next
time. All right. You'll find plates in the cupboard to the far
left, glasses next one over, and knives and forks directly
underneath in the drawer. Surely you can't do any harm to
them, and I feel confident that you can pour milk.''

Lily did as she was told and soon enough had the table
laid. Charlie expertly dished everything out and they sat
down to a meal that Lily thought delicious and felt vaguely
proud about, even though she hadn't had very much to do
with it.

"I'm impressed," she said, wiping her mouth.

"How gratifying. You'll have the hang of it soon
enough." He pushed his plate to one side. "Now. To you
and Pascal. I gather this was not a love match?''

"Anything but. In fact, I don't know why everyone thinks
he is such an angel. He's a black-hearted devil. I am sorry
to speak so about your brother, Charlie, but it is the truth.''

"*Is* it? How interesting that you should think so.''

"Well, I do. I've lived with him for three days and two
nights and he hasn't had a kind word to say to me." She
brushed away a tear. "I don't think he knows how to be
kind.''

Charlie scratched his blond head, looking uncomfortable.
"I wonder if you ought not to be having this conversation
with my mother.''

"Oh, no," Lily said. "I couldn't possibly. It's obvious
that she adores Pascal.''

"That is true enough, and that's the crux of the matter,
for I've never known anyone who didn't. Ah—it occurs to
me that this might be one of those things that happens to
young brides.''

"Whatever do you mean?" Lily asked.

"Oh, dear. How to be delicate. Well. To be perfectly
blunt, I mean because of the necessary marital chores involved.''

Lily frowned. "I can't think that every bride in the world

is forced to cook and clean for her husband. *Most* people have servants to do it for them, you know.''

Charlie grinned. ''That wasn't exactly what I meant. I meant the other side of marital duties, the ones conducted after the lights go out.''

Lily suddenly realized what he was talking about, and her grin matched his. ''Does everyone talk in euphemisms, I wonder? You sound precisely like Father Mallet, and you're the furthest thing from a Catholic priest that I can think of.''

''Thank God for that. I mean—I don't think it's my calling. Anyway, who is Father Mallet to be talking to you about such a delicate matter? It doesn't sound in the realm of priestly things to me.''

''He was forced to it, but I don't think he knew what he was talking about any more than I understood. He made the whole thing sound like the storming of a castle, complete with impregnable walls and battering rams.''

Charlie burst into laughter. ''No . . .'' he choked. ''He didn't really, did he? Oh, God, how awful! No wonder you've been having problems with the thing. Battering rams?'' He dissolved again.

Lily, wondering just why Charlie was so amused, but pleased to have made him laugh, nodded. ''But you're wrong,'' she said in clarification, ''for that's not the problem at all. Quite the opposite, for that shall *never* happen.''

Charlie's amusement immediately vanished. ''It hasn't? I mean . . . it shan't? Isn't that why people usually marry each other?''

''Not in this instance. The plain fact of the matter is that your brother assaulted me, and as a result, I was forced to marry him.''

Charlie stared at her in complete, openmouthed fascination.

''It is the truth,'' Lily said defensively.

''My brother assaulted you?'' he repeated slowly. ''Pascal?''

''Yes. Your brother Pascal.''

''My brother Pascal.''

''Yes, and I don't know why you find that so hard to believe. My father insisted that your brother pay the consequences, as much as marriage went against my wishes.''

''I see. Would it interest you to know that Pascal has never assaulted so much as a fly? He even throws the fish back in the water after he catches them, a practice which has always caused my father to tear his hair out, since Pascal never fails to catch more than anyone else.'' Charlie smiled with amusement. ''My father says that Pascal calls them over, they are foolish enough to come, and Pascal cannot help but feel guilty, so he sets them loose.''

''Don't be ridiculous,'' Lily said with annoyance. ''And don't try to change the subject, for it is exactly what happened.''

''No,'' Charlie said, clearly trying not to laugh.

''Yes,'' Lily said, goaded despite her embarrassment. ''I fell off the wall at St. Christophe quite by mistake, and your brother instantly tore my clothing off and leaped atop me.''

It was too much for Charlie. He burst into great howls of laughter, wiping his streaming eyes with his napkin. ''P— Pascal? Oh, God, this is incredible. Lily, you—oh, Lord— you really must have gotten hold of the wrong end of the stick. Oh—oh, sorry.'' He bent over, clutching his sides.

''I cannot see why you think this is cause for such hilarity,'' Lily said, frowning. ''It has been no fun for me, I assure you.''

Charlie lifted his head and sobered with great effort. ''No. No, I can imagine not, and even less for Pascal, if I know anything about it. No wonder he looked so strained last night. I thought it must have been—been lack of sleep. But I gather that's not the problem. Oh, dear. Ha!''

''Charlie, you make no sort of friend at all. I thought you might at least be sympathetic to my plight. I am forced by my father to marry a completely cold-hearted, cold-blooded degenerate, and you can do nothing but laugh?''

''I'm sorry,'' Charlie said more gently. ''You have absolutely no idea, have you?''

''Idea of what?''

''Of whom you have married. Didn't you wonder about the food that appeared outside of the back door this morning as if by magic?''

''I assumed it was put there because Pascal could not manage to buy it for himself.''

Charlie shook his head. ''No. It was put there as a gift, as it will be every day he is here.''

''What do you mean by 'a gift'?'' Lily asked scoffingly. ''Is that another word for charity? It's the same thing, isn't it?''

Charlie's eyes sparked with sudden anger. "My brother has no need for charity. Nor has he need for a wife who scorns him."

Lily looked down at her plate. "I apologize," she whispered to her newfound friend. "I understand your loyalty and should not have trespassed upon it. I'm sure I would feel the same if you spoke badly of my brother."

"Your apology is accepted. I didn't know you had a brother. Is it just the two of you?"

"Yes . . ." Lily couldn't help herself. She needed a reminder of her beloved Jean-Jacques, whom she feared she might never see again if left to the dictates of her horrible husband. Her worry about Jean-Jacques had not once left her mind.

"He lives in France," she said in a rush, "and I've missed him dreadfully ever since he left home. I finally pestered my father into allowing me to visit him last February, even though he despises Jean-Jacques."

"How unfortunate," Charlie observed dryly.

"It is. It's awful. Jean-Jacques is having a very difficult time of it, trying to run his estate. It won't produce—the crops keep failing—and if he doesn't have success soon, I don't know what will happen. He is nearly out of money. Saint-Simon is his only inheritance."

"Oh, dear. Drastic circumstances," Charlie said sympathetically.

"They are, Charlie, they truly are! Just before I got into all this trouble I was trying to find someone who could work out what was wrong with the land and put it to rights."

"Why don't you ask Pascal?" he said simply, pulling the plates toward him and stacking them.

"Why would I ask him? He doesn't have a farthing to his name except for my dowry, and he won't touch that, nor let me touch it. He's said as much, and in no uncertain terms. And you wonder why I'm bitter?"

"Have you told him of your brother's plight?" Charlie asked reasonably, carrying the dishes to the sink.

"No, but why should I? He wouldn't listen. He hasn't listened to anything I've said. I'm stuck in the most hopeless situation with no way out. There's no way to help Jean-Jacques, and I don't know if I'll ever see him again." She leaned her elbow on the table and bowed her head. "And now I'm married to someone who simply doesn't care. What would be the point in bringing it up? Your brother would only find a way to be angry with me for loving my brother, just as my father did.''

"You know, you are badly mistaken when it comes to Pascal. Do you know anything about him, anything at all?'' He leaned back against the counter and regarded her curiously.

"No,'' she admitted. "Only that he was adopted by your family, and also that he was the gardener at St. Christophe for two years.''

"The gardener? Well, I suppose you could call him that if you liked.''

"He was no monk,'' Lily said darkly.

"No, thank God it didn't come to that, although it wouldn't have surprised me in the least.''

"Why? And if he wasn't a monk, then why was he at St. Christophe in the first place? Was he a penitent?''

"A penitent?'' Charlie laughed. "No. He was not a penitent. Pascal is a very special man, Lily. I suppose since we have all grown up around him, it's obvious to us. Perhaps it isn't to you.''

"I would expect you to love your brother, even if he isn't your flesh and blood,'' Lily said, granting what she considered to be an enormous concession.

"Yes, of course, but that isn't what I meant at all. Let me tell you a little story, and maybe you'll understand better.'' Charlie pulled out a chair and sat down. "One day, when I was a small boy, all of four, Pascal and I were out riding. I trusted him absolutely, of course. I had always been his shadow, and he never begrudged me a moment of his time, despite how annoying I must have been.''

"I don't think you're the least bit annoying,'' Lily said loyally.

"Oh, well, thank you very much for the testimonial, but I assure you I can be—very much so. Anyway, we were riding through the forest, Pascal slightly ahead of me. I was on a pony, steady as the day is long. But on this particular day a wild boar came crashing through the bushes from behind me.'' He shuddered in memory.

"And?'' Lily demanded, fascinated. "What happened?''

"What do you think? The pony spooked and reared, and I was thrown off, directly into the path of the boar. I swear to you, Lily, I've never been so frightened in my life. It had its head lowered, and I could see its little red eyes and wet snout and those huge white tusks. I thought I was going to die.'' He smiled. ''I did the only sensible thing and wet my britches.''

Lily burst into laughter. ''I can imagine you did!''

''Yes. Well, anyway, the next thing I knew, Pascal was there—not on his horse, mind you, but standing directly in line between me and that boar. In that quiet voice of his, the one that can send chills up your spine, he told me to roll out of the way into the brush.''

Charlie's eyes went soft and distant as he spoke, and Lily saw in them the deep affection he held for his brother, poor misguided boy. She could just see the wretch facing off against a boar—it was a pity it hadn't gored him. ''And then?'' she prompted.

''And then—and then he damn well talked to the thing, looking it straight in the eye. I can't remember for the life of me what he said, but the boar must have listened, for it turned around like the tamest of farm pigs and trotted away. I've never seen anything like it.''

''I don't believe you,'' Lily said. ''Things like that don't happen. The boar must have just eaten and decided it wasn't interested in either of you. It was nothing more than coincidence.''

''Coincidence? Maybe. I don't think so, knowing what I do of my brother. But even if you choose to believe that it was coincidence, Pascal risked his life for me that day. I know without a shadow of a doubt that if the same thing happened tomorrow, he'd do it again, and the boar would trot off exactly as he bid it.''

''What is that supposed to prove?'' Lily asked. ''That your brother can talk to pigs? Or perhaps you want me to think that he is strong and brave.''

''You are a little cynic, aren't you? It's not meant to prove anything, only to point out that you haven't married the usual fop.''

''That much I did realize, as I know the breed quite well,'' Lily said with a tight smile.

''Oh, good. Then we are making progress.''

''Telling pig stories again, are we, Charlie?'' Pascal walked into the kitchen, and to Lily's surprise, Charlie colored slightly.

''I'm not telling tales out of school, if that's what you

mean." Charlie looked uncomfortable and Lily wondered why.

"I didn't mean anything at all. Hello, Elizabeth. I trust the fishing went well?"

"Charlie caught two fish. We had them for breakfast."

"Ah. Did you? And did Elizabeth do your fish proud, Charlie?"

Lily wanted to kill him. "Your brother cooked them," she said belligerently.

"In that case, I am sure they were delicious."

Lily eyed the bread knife.

"They were delicious," Charlie said diplomatically, looking back and forth between them. "As were the eggs and bread and milk and butter. I hope you don't mind that I helped myself." He leaned back in his chair, rubbing his stomach. "I really ought to breakfast with you more often when you're home. I'll swear that you're given the cream of everything by your adoring public."

"The grass is always greener, Charlie, and if I know you, you'll return home to eat a second breakfast immediately you depart, so my heart is not breaking with sympathy for you."

"Pascal! Of course your heart is breaking with sympathy for me. It's always breaking with sympathy for me, or have you forgotten? I'm incorrigible and will probably never change."

Charlie flashed his brother a particularly charming grin, and Pascal ruffled his hair. "How could I forget such an obvious thing? You've been incorrigible since the moment you first drew breath. Speaking of which, I've been to see Binkley." He swung into a chair. "He told me that you are all just as disgracefully behaved as ever, gave a brief ode to the young queen, and mentioned an incident involving some frogs. And thank you for the horse. He is very sweet-natured, very sedate."

"Sedate!" Charlie said, insulted. "He's a handful!"

"Ah, yes. Of course he is," Pascal said, nodding, but his gaze wandered with fascination to the mangled remains of the bread loaf. He pulled his attention back to his brother with an effort.

"Let me tell you something about your horse, Charlie. He's trying very hard to be exactly what you wish, but I think he'd be happier if you'd let him be the peaceful beast he is by nature. It grows very tiring having to snort and paw and roll one's eyes all the time, especially if the heart's not in it.''

Charlie leaned over and punched Pascal's shoulder. ''Do you have any idea how aggravating you can be?''

''Oh, yes,'' Pascal said, looking at Lily. ''I do. I've been told all about it.''

Charlie licked his bottom lip, a gleam of calculation and mischief in his eyes. He cleared his throat. ''Pascal,'' he said casually, ''did you know Lily has a brother?''

Pascal raised one eyebrow. ''Yes. I did know that. Why?''

''Because Lily's been telling me all about him. She loves him very much, and she's terribly worried about him.''

''Oh? Why is that?''

''Apparently he's in trouble. It sounds to me as if you might be able to help him out.''

''In what way?'' Pascal asked suspiciously. ''Is he over his head in gambling debts?''

''Oh—oh, no, it's nothing like that,'' Lily said quickly, reluctant to have the wretch involved in any way with her beloved brother. ''It's really nothing at all.''

''Good. Then we shall leave the subject alone.''

''He has an estate in France,'' Charlie persisted. ''Apparently it's in a bad way. Failing crops and failing money as a result, so I gather that the land stands little chance of recovering.''

Pascal looked at Lily, and this time his eyes were keen with genuine interest. ''What sort of failing crops?''

''None. Everything is just fine,'' Lily said. She was not about to give the wretch a chance to belittle her brother. ''I exaggerated.''

Pascal looked over at his brother. ''Leave us, Charlie,'' he said quietly. ''Your horse is tethered out front.''

Charlie instantly rose, and Lily shot him a desperate look as he turned to go. Charlie only smiled. She wanted to murder him and string him up next to his brother.

''What sort of failing crops?'' Pascal repeated, once Charlie had gone out the door. The look in his eyes demanded an answer.

''Grapes,'' she said reluctantly. ''He can't seem to make the land produce.''

''Why not?'' Pascal absently picked up a spoon and ran it through his fingers, his gaze fixed on her. She suddenly felt as she had when Dom Benetard fixed her with a similar look.

"Because . . . because Jean-Jacques can't afford a steward who knows how to deal with the problem, and because the villagers are all against him, so they won't work properly, and because . . ." She let out a long breath and looked down at the table. "Because he hasn't a clue what he is doing, and no one else knows what is wrong," she said helplessly. "I would do anything in the world to help him, and I don't know how."

"Do you know," Pascal said softly, "those might be the first honest words you have spoken to me? It makes a nice change."

Lily's gaze flew back to his, and she colored.

"So," Pascal said, putting the spoon down and folding his hands together. "Your brother is in trouble. Why don't we go and see what we can do to help him?"

"What?" Lily stared at him, unable to believe her ears. There had to be a trick in it somewhere, but she couldn't see it. "You're serious?"

"Perfectly. It seems an answer to many problems. I need a job. Your brother needs help. You will be happy for your brother's company, I think, and I happen to speak French. Therefore I will offer myself as your brother's steward for a reasonable salary."

"You? But you're a gardener—what would you know about vineyards?"

"Not a very great deal, but I did live in the Loire Valley long enough to get a vague idea."

"A vague idea?" Lily said, torn between her desperation to be returned to her brother and her worry at presenting Jean-Jacques with a steward who knew not much more than how to grow a petunia. Her desire to return to her brother won. "I suppose a vague idea is better than no idea at all. Do you think you can run an estate?"

"I'm sure your brother will find my credentials adequate," he said. "But for practicality's sake, tell me—who is your brother and where is his estate? It would be difficult to grow one grape, never mind entire vineyards, on top of the Pyrénées, even under the best of circumstances."

"No—oh, no, it's nothing like that." Lily was so intent on getting to Saint-Simon that she didn't notice Pascal was smiling. "The estate is in the heart of the Périgord. Jean-

Jacques is the Duc de Saint-Simon, and Saint-Simon itself is not so very far from Beaulieu.''

"Oh, dear God, not another blasted duke," Pascal murmured under his breath. "Your brother was raised in England?" he asked in a more audible voice.

"Yes, at Sutherby. He has been at Saint-Simon only three years. It was an estate once well known for its wines, but the vines have failed year after year, and he hasn't been able to bring them back to health." She stared at the table. "Jean-Jacques lives in a most beautiful château, but even that is falling to bits, since it was neglected for nearly thirty years, and Jean-Jacques hasn't the funds to put into it. I'd give him my money—''

"I think not," Pascal said.

She looked at him imploringly, batting her eyelashes the way she'd seen women do in London. "Oh, but just think, it could make all the difference to him. Why can't I? You don't want it.''

"Elizabeth. It's not a matter open for discussion, and fluttering your eyelashes is a waste of time. Feminine wiles are entirely lost on me.''

Lily slumped back in her chair, unable to think of a proper retort.

"So. We'll go, and we'll go immediately, for it's already the middle of May and there's no time to be lost. Under normal circumstances I would write to your brother and wait for a reply, but that would lose too many valuable days. We'll leave tomorrow.''

"We will? Tomorrow?''

"Yes.''

"Oh—oh!" Lily's entire body froze with happiness. "Y-you have no idea what this means to me," she managed to stammer. "Truly, you—you do not.''

"Perhaps not, although it's clear to me that you have a great fondness for your brother, which is how it should be.'' A shadow crossed his face. "There's one condition. When we arrive I would thank you to leave out your version of why we were married. If I'm going to help your brother I'll need his trust. Do you understand me?''

Lily nodded. All that was in her mind was Jean-Jacques and Saint-Simon, and that she would be with them both soon. Nothing else mattered. Nothing.

"I take it by your silence that you understand me well

enough. That's good, for I warn you not to cross me in this, Elizabeth.''

"I—I shan't,'' she promised. "I'll come up with an acceptable explanation.''

"Thank you. Now if you'll excuse me, I'm going to find Nicholas and Georgia and tell them of our plans.''

Lily was left alone in the kitchen, her head spinning. Never in a million years would she have thought getting back to Saint-Simon would be so easy. She could kiss Charlie for his brilliance, she really could, for somehow he had known that the wretch would jump at the chance. Maybe Charlie thought it was his brother's only hope for a job.

Lily shrugged, dismissing Pascal. Now she had to work out a way to put her hands on her money so that Jean-Jacques would have funds again. Pascal seemed adamant about keeping it away from her—hardly surprising since he was not a man to see reason.

But she couldn't stand on her pride in this matter. She would have to find a way to persuade him, that was all there was to it. How did one go about persuading a man like Pascal LaMartine? He'd said he wasn't interested in feminine wiles, which was just as well, since she wasn't very good at them.

Lily propped her chin on her fist and thought hard. A slow smile crept across her mouth as she hit upon a plan. Her wretched husband might not know a grape from a grape-press, but she knew he approved of humility in a person.

She frowned, trying to remember all the horrible things he had said to her in the three days they'd been married.

He thought her a spoiled child. He thought her selfish and uncaring. Very well. She would kill him with sweetness. Sweetness and kindness and—and total, absolute humility. She would have thrown in piety, but unfortunately she'd already told him that she didn't believe in God. Oh, well. Maybe she could pretend to have changed her mind about that, too, if she did it carefully.

The very idea of pretending all of those things to a man she detested made her stomach turn, but for Jean-Jacques she'd do anything. Anything at all.

8

"**B**INKLEY, thank you for your hospitality yesterday morning," Pascal said, shaking the old butler's hand. The family and staff were gathered outside of Ravenswalk, and Pascal was not having an easy time saying good-bye, although he hoped it didn't show.

"Just you remember what words I put into your ear," Binkley said in an undertone, but gruffly nonetheless. "I think you're doing the right thing, Pascal, just so you know. I applaud your decision. Very sensible. Very sensible indeed." He shot another curious look Lily's way.

"Oh, I don't know about that," Pascal said with a wry smile. "But it does seem that God responded very quickly to my plea by dropping this challenge in front of me, and, I confess, I couldn't resist picking up His gauntlet."

Binkley nodded, then raised his voice. "I wish you all luck in your marriage, Master Pascal."

"Thank you," he said solemnly. He then shook the hands of all the gathered staff, hugged the children, speaking softly to each one in turn, and gently wiped away Ghislaine's tears with his thumb. "It won't be so long until the next time, I promise," he said to her. He gave Charlie a great thump on the back. "Behave yourself. Come visit us in France if your travels ever bring you our way. I'll write to give you the direction."

Charlie nodded and flashed a grin at Elizabeth. "I'll do that. It will be nice to see you both."

"Where has the monsieur gone? He was here just a minute ago," Pascal asked Georgia, looking around him.

"I believe he has gone off to get a present for you and Elizabeth," Georgia said. "It is something to remember us by."

"Madame, you have given me too much already. I can't

tell you how much I appreciate your replenishing my supplies.''

"You couldn't very well have taken supplies away from the monastery,'' Georgia said. "Losing you must have been enough of a blow.''

"Nevertheless, I need nothing more.''

"Typical,'' Nicholas said dryly, appearing with a small struggling bundle of rough white fur that sported a brown circle over one eye and a matching one above the base of a frantically wagging tail. Its little ears quivered with delight at the sight of Pascal.

"It's one of the Raleigh pups,'' Pascal said with pleasure.

"She's a great-great-granddaughter of Raleigh's,'' Nicholas amended, "and the line is growing stronger with each generation. I'm succeeding in breeding a brilliant line of ground hunters, Pascal, all out of Raleigh's stock.''

"Then she's bound to be exceptional. Raleigh was the finest of dogs.''

"Indeed he was, and you will find this little bitch equaled by none, I am confident of it. Not that you'll want to hunt her, I know,'' Nicholas said with an exasperated smile, "but a better companion you could not ask for. She is my wedding present to you both.''

"Thank you,'' Lily said quietly. "You are very thoughtful.''

"I hope she gives you pleasure, Elizabeth. And you will not be stubborn and refuse her, Pascal, or I shall be extremely annoyed with you.''

"Thank you, monsieur. You're very kind.'' He took the puppy into his arms, where she proceeded to thoroughly wet his ear. "I think I shall name her . . .'' He held the pup up and looked at her closely. "I think I shall name her Bean,'' he pronounced.

"Bean?'' Nicholas asked with a laugh. "Why ever Bean?''

"Because she looks exactly like one, a little spotted bean. Thank you so much, monsieur. We will treasure her.''

"You might not treasure her so much by the time you have arrived at Saint-Simon. She's young yet at twelve weeks and not completely trained.''

Pascal rubbed the puppy's head. "I'll have a serious word with her. I'm sure that one way or another we'll come to terms. Thank you both for understanding. I know it's been a very short visit after such a long absence.''

''Oh, but it's a good thing to settle in a place Elizabeth loves and with people who love her,'' Georgia said cheerfully, trying to hold back her tears. ''I hope you'll both be very happy in Saint-Simon. Look after Pascal, Elizabeth. He is precious to us.''

''Thank you both for welcoming me so warmly to your family,'' Lily said shyly. ''It means more than I can say.''

Pascal looked at her with surprise. Her small speech was the last thing he'd expected, and he realized that she actually looked quite pretty when she wasn't being sullen.

''Good-bye,'' Nicholas said, taking her hand. ''Be well and happy. And please, write to us and let us know how you are getting on.''

''I'll do that,'' she said. ''Or at least I'll try. I've never been very good at writing letters.''

Pascal gave her another thoughtful look. It occurred to him that maybe she'd never had anyone to write letters to. But he pulled his attention back to the immediate necessity of saying the most painful farewell of all.

''Monsieur. Madame.'' Pascal embraced each in turn. ''Thank you. You'll be in my thoughts and prayers, as ever.''

''And you in ours,'' Nicholas said. Georgia was beyond words. Nicholas rubbed the squirming puppy's head. ''Look after them, Bean,'' he said. ''Safe journey to you both.''

And then they were off, and Pascal had to force himself not to look back as the carriage barreled down the long drive and out through the gates toward the coast.

''Mr., um, Mr. LaMartine . . .'' Lily tugged at the back of his jacket to get his attention, for her words were blown away by the wind.

Pascal pulled his weight from the railing and turned around. ''Yes?'' he asked pleasantly enough. ''Are you feeling ill? You're looking slightly green.''

''No! I am perfectly well. It is the puppy who is unwell— I do not know what to do for it. For her,'' Lily amended miserably. ''She's been sick everywhere!''

Pascal's brow furrowed. ''What do you mean by everywhere? I thought you had her confined in your cabin.''

''I did, but she escaped. The first mate, or whoever he

is—the one dressed in the uniform—tried to catch her, and she was sick on him, and he dropped her, and then I chased her, and one of the other passengers caught her and she was sick on him, and now she is back in the cabin being sick on the bed." Lily held out her hands helplessly. "I apologized to the two men, but I don't know what else to do, and really, she can't possibly carry on like this."

Pascal quickly moved past Lily and down to the cabin he'd reserved for his wife's comfort. He found the puppy lying on the floor, her nose resting miserably on her paws, the latest result of her intestinal turmoil beside her. He immediately scooped her up, whispering soothing words to her. Bean opened her eyes and looked at him imploringly, then shut them again and shuddered, and Pascal gave a smothered laugh.

"Here. Take the poor infant up onto the deck," he ordered Lily, who had come in just behind him, looking nearly as helpless as the puppy.

"But I can't," Lily protested. "She'll only get away from me again!"

"Bean is by now far too weak to be thinking of bolting anywhere," Pascal said, handing her the pup and surveying the damage done to the cabin. "And someone has to clean this mess up. I hardly think it is going to be you. In any case, the fresh air will help her stomach." He glanced back at Lily, who was holding the puppy at arm's length in front of her. "You might try talking to her and giving her some sympathetic attention. Holding her like that isn't going to give her confidence, nor make her feel any better. Surely you must have some idea of what a puppy needs?"

Lily slowly shook her head, trying to find a comfortable position for the animal in her arms. "I've never had a pet before," she confessed. "It wasn't for lack of asking, it was just that my father didn't tolerate them. He kept a kennel of hounds for hunting, but thought pets an unnecessary indulgence." Lily looked back down at the miserable, limp bundle of fur in her hands. "I'm sorry. I've always wanted a dog. I just don't know what is required, and I think she knows that I don't know. Please, Mr. LaMartine, tell me what to do?"

Pascal ran a hand through his hair, then dropped it to his side. "Very well. We'll start at the beginning. You have to realize she's only a baby and needs what every baby needs.

Cuddle her against you. She needs to know she's safe and cared for.''

Lily nodded, her expression grave.

''She also needs to know she's not in trouble for having been sick. Go on, Elizabeth, cradle her in your arms as if she were an infant. It won't hurt either of you. If it's any reassurance, she most likely has nothing left in her stomach to be sick with, so you're quite safe.''

''Oh, I don't mind that so much. It's more that I don't think she likes me.''

Pascal halted in the midst of dampening a cloth in the water bowl. ''Doesn't *like* you? What in God's name gives you that idea?''

Lily looked up at him, surprised at his incredulous tone. ''Well,'' she said, attempting to sound practical, ''why would she? People generally don't like me, so why should a puppy?'' She hunched a shoulder. ''Bean was much more interested in being with you from the start, and when you left, she scratched frantically at the door. And then she was sick. I thought it was because she didn't like being left with me—and she didn't, because as soon as I opened the door, she ran away.''

Pascal slowly put the cloth down, then leaned a hip against the table where the basin stood and folded his arms across his chest. He gave Lily a very long, assessing look, and she wondered what she'd said wrong now. She had been trying so hard to do everything right, but it seemed to be getting her nowhere at all.

''Tell me something,'' he finally said. ''What sort of life did you have at Sutherby? You said your brother was there with you?''

Lily wondered what this had to do with anything, but she nodded. The puppy had now found a comfortable position, her little head pushed hard into the crook of Lily's shoulder. Lily held her gingerly, secretly thrilled at her trust and liking the feel of the soft nose pressed against her dress.

''Jean-Jacques came to Sutherby with my mother when she married my father,'' she said, stroking the puppy's back. ''Jean-Jacques was only seven. I don't think my father liked him—they fought like cats and dogs from the time I can remember. Poor Jean-Jacques had to live under my father's authority until he gained his majority. Once he had, though, he was gone like a shot.''

"He went directly to Saint-Simon?" Pascal asked.

"N-no . . . he went to Paris to live. But eventually he ran out of funds, and so he had to close up the house and move to Saint-Simon. It's a great hardship for him, living in near poverty, Mr. LaMartine, for he is not accustomed to such things." She looked at him with what she hoped was distress, but he didn't seem particularly moved.

"I see," he said. "So you were without your brother's company at Sutherby for some time?"

Lily nodded again. "I missed him terribly. My father finally relented and let me visit Jean-Jacques this year, although it went against his grain, feeling as he does about my brother. I think he let me go because he hoped that Jean-Jacques would introduce me to eligible Frenchmen. He'd run out of British suitors and he was at his wits' end."

"In an odd sort of way his strategy worked, didn't it? I doubt even your father would have thought to go looking inside a monastery for a husband, but in the end he did manage to marry you to a Frenchman—although I wouldn't have described myself as eligible, exactly."

Lily colored hotly, but then she realized that there had been no sting in his voice. She was beginning to wonder if the wretch actually had a sense of humor, but that seemed impossible, so she dismissed the idea.

"I think I'll take the puppy up above now," she said, and started out of the cabin, Bean clutched to her chest. But as she went down the corridor she could have sworn she heard a snort of laughter from behind the closed door.

So much for humility, Lily thought bitterly and clutched Bean even more tightly to her, taking comfort in the puppy's warmth.

Pascal shifted his position against the oak tree, watching Lily walk Bean in the haphazard fashion she'd developed since leaving the boat three days earlier. The pup bounded off in every direction at once, and instead of bringing her into line with the leash that Pascal had made out of some spare rein, Lily chased in all directions after her.

It occurred to Pascal that Nicholas had been extremely clever in his choice of wedding present, for the puppy had created a new, if fragile, link between Lily and himself. He wondered if Nicholas had not understood a great deal more about the state of affairs between himself and his wife than he had realized. Knowing Nicholas, Pascal thought surely he had. And, typical of Nicholas, he had chosen subtlety over any more obvious approach.

He was distracted by a yelp, not from the puppy but from her mistress, and Pascal saw that they had both somehow managed to wrap themselves around a tree.

"Oh, help!" Lily cried again, for now the leash was twined not only around the tree but also around her legs, and the white whirling dervish on the other end was intent on complicating the situation even further with a nice big bush.

Amused, Pascal removed himself from his post and ambled over to the scene of disaster, first picking up the scrabbling Bean and detaching her from her leash, and then unwinding his wife.

"Madame. You may have your legs back." They had slipped naturally into speaking French as soon as they'd landed in that country, and he was grateful for Lily's fluency, even if there was nothing else he could find to be grateful about.

"Thank you," she breathed, pushing the hair out of her flushed face. "I—I don't think I quite have the way of this yet."

"No, but it will come. You and Bean will learn together. You need to be firmer with her, Elizabeth, for she'll test you on every point. Nicholas has bred these terriers carefully, and they're as keenly intelligent as they are curious. The combination is a sure recipe for trouble, unless you quickly establish who is master."

"Oh," Lily said uncertainly. "But I don't want to hurt her. She always squeaks so pitifully and trembles when I scold her."

Pascal shook his head, and Lily gave him a puzzled look.

"You won't hurt her," he said. "I promise. She's been playing you for all you are worth; I've never seen a dog wrap a person so quickly around its paw, never mind every tree in sight. Watch this."

Pascal put the puppy down on the ground, first taking the precaution of attaching her leash to her collar. "Sit," he told her, and the puppy reluctantly parked her bottom on the ground, tongue lolling out of mouth, tail wagging furiously. "Good Bean," he said. "Now, let us go for a dignified walk. Forward." He let out a little leash and

immediately pulled it back when she attempted to dive into
a ditch after a squirrel. Bean had the good sense to realize
she was defeated, and obediently pulled back her pace and
trotted in front of Pascal, ears held alertly forward, tail high.
"Good girl," he said, bringing her alongside his heel.
"Now sit." The puppy sat, looking enormously pleased
with herself.

"I don't know how you do it," Lily wailed. "You make
it look so easy, and it's not at all."

"Elizabeth, it hasn't escaped my attention that you have
a strong will. If you use that will to a positive end, you'll
have a well-behaved animal who will also be eternally loyal
to you. Be kind but firm. All right? Here, you try." He
handed her the leash, and Bean instantly bounded forward,
dragging Lily along behind her.

"Hold her in!" Pascal shouted.

Lily put both hands on the leash, leaned back and dug
her heels in, and after flying up in the air in surprise, Bean
obligingly stopped. But the sudden release of tension took
Lily by surprise too, and she toppled over backward. Bean
took this as great good fun and pounced, giving Lily's face
a thorough, good-natured victory wash.

The sight of the would-be duchess lying pinned to the
ground by a small ball of fur, leaves in her hair and dirt on
her face, was too much for Pascal. He laughed until his
sides ached and tears rolled down his cheeks. "Oh . . . oh,
no," he said, making a valiant attempt to recover. "B-Bean,
stop it now. D-down."

Bean paused only for an instant, and then, seeing that her
master's heart wasn't in the command, she went back to
showering her struggling mistress with enthusiastic affection. Pascal burst into laughter again, dropping to his knees
in helpless hilarity.

Lily finally managed to extricate herself from Bean and
sat up. "You're laughing at me," she said accusingly.

Pascal looked up at her, still gasping for breath. "S-sorry
. . . it's just that—it's so . . . ah—"

"Funny?" Lily asked indignantly.

"Yes. Funny." He wiped his eyes. "I—I'm sorry, I'm
not laughing at you, just at the—the situation."

"I've never seen you laugh before." She tried to stand
up, but her skirts were caught under her legs and she had
only one hand free; the other one was full of Bean. "Oh!"

she said, falling back down. She let out a startled laugh, then bit her lip as if embarrassed.

Grinning, Pascal walked over to her and took the puppy, then offered her his hand and easily pulled her to her feet. "I suppose I haven't had much reason to laugh recently," he said. "Just as you haven't had much reason to smile. Smiling suits you." He reached out and disentangled a twig from her hair.

"It does?" Lily said, blushing fiercely. "No one has ever told me so before."

"No? Perhaps there hasn't been reason," he said gently. "One needs to do it for people to comment." He gazed down at her, and what he saw surprised him.

She looked open, vulnerable, suddenly very young, certainly pretty, her cheeks and lips rosy. Her eyes locked with his, the green soft as smoke. He had a sudden, absurd desire to brush the dirt off her cheek with his fingers, to kiss that rosy mouth back into a smile. But he quickly pushed that thought to the back of his mind, not able to believe he'd thought it at all. She spoke, surprising him again.

"Maybe you're right," she said, looking down at the ground. "I don't know, really. I don't think I've ever made anyone laugh before, except for Jean-Jacques—oh, and Charlie, but he seems to think nearly everything is funny."

"Charlie has a highly developed sense of humor, yes. You and he got along well, didn't you? Bean, *sit.*"

"I've never known anyone like Charlie. He doesn't seem to expect anything of a person, good or bad. He just accepts what is there." She raised her eyes to his again. "I suppose that must be the mark of a friend."

"Yes, I suppose so," Pascal said slowly, wondering what had brought on this sudden and remarkable transformation in his wife. She looked sad, and he wondered just how lonely Lily had been in the years of her growing-up. His heart suddenly ached for her, for from the little she'd said, and from much he'd observed for himself, he was beginning to think that the situation must have been truly dreadful.

For the first time he saw the young child she'd been, suffering at the hands of Mallet and her father, with no mother to protect her or offer comfort, only a brother caught in an equally helpless situation. Had she been brought up at Ravenswalk with all of the laughter and love that abounded there, she might have turned out to be a very different person.

Maybe beneath that prickly, self-serving surface there was a sweet young woman lurking. He was well aware of the game Lily had been playing ever since she'd decided to try to win him over to her brother's cause. Her performance had been so transparent that it was ridiculous. But in this moment he sensed truth, although he didn't think she was aware that she'd let her guard down. Lily reminded him of a mistreated animal, desperately in need of love but terrified of taking it for fear of being beaten down again.

"The mark of a friend," she had said. Charlie had done a far better job than he, her husband, had. He had been indulging himself in anger rather than looking for a way to make things better for her, seeing only her obstinacy and his misery, and he was suddenly ashamed. What Lily needed was not anger and coldness—she'd had enough of that already. She needed fresh air and laughter and a sense of being cared for, like any living creature. Lily needed a friend.

But now was not the time to ponder any of that at length, for it was growing late, and if they were to reach Bergerac by nightfall they would have to hurry. He'd have time enough to think while he was driving.

He picked up the puppy. "Come, Elizabeth—we only have another three hours of daylight, and we should put them to best use."

She nodded and turned abruptly toward the carriage.

Pascal looked after her, then glanced down at Bean, who had begun to wriggle. "So," he said softly, scratching the puppy's ears, "there is a chink in your mistress's armor after all, little Bean. I wonder . . . I just wonder. Maybe what the girl needs more than anything is a chance to heal, and maybe what I ought to do is give it to her. What do you think?"

The pup vigorously washed his neck in reply. Pascal started after his wife, mulling over the possibilities.

Lily glanced once more at Pascal. Something was different tonight and it puzzled her. Her gaze traveled over his dark head, down to those long, square fingers, which at the moment were employed in cutting a piece of meat. She frowned. What had changed? He seemed more approachable to her, less forbidding, but he hadn't said or done anything in particular that should make her think so.

A picture of the forest that afternoon flashed into her mind, and Lily flushed as she remembered the sight of Pascal on his knees in helpless mirth. It had completely transformed his face, drawing laugh lines about his eyes and little grooves around his mouth. She realized that he must have laughed often to have put them there. He had pulled her to her feet and looked down at her almost—almost tenderly, then taken a twig from her hair. His touch had been as gentle as his voice, and it had made her feel most peculiar, almost like crying. No one had ever touched her like that before. It was the last thing she had expected, and from the wretch, of all people.

Lily tore her gaze away from him, terribly confused. She hated him—she *detested* him.

His eyes unexpectedly lifted and met hers full on, and Lily's stomach turned over with that strange, unnerving sensation she had first experienced at the monastery and had been trying to avoid, as she had him, ever since.

"Elizabeth? You're not eating. Doesn't the meal agree with you?"

"I—it was very nice. I've had my fill. But perhaps you would . . . you would care for more mutton, Mr. LaMartine?" Lily gestured feebly toward the platter on the table. "There are still a few appetizing pieces."

"Thank you, but I've also eaten my fill. And please, call me by my given name. I'd find it much more comfortable. After all, we are married. There's no need to stand on formality."

"As you wish," Lily said tentatively, remembering that she was meant to be acquiescent.

"Thank you. It's a relief to have you give in to the matter without a fight."

"I have no desire to fight. Why should I?"

Pascal cocked an eyebrow. "Do you really wish me to answer that?"

"I . . . no." Lily forced herself to meet his eyes, and wished she hadn't, for that *look* was in them. "I mean, no thank you. It's not necessary."

"I thought not. I don't suppose this means you're willing to bury the hatchet?"

"The hatchet?" she said in confusion, nervously chewing on her bottom lip.

Pascal leaned his chin on his hand, watching her steadily. "Yes. The hatchet. The one that you first swung at me at St. Christophe. The one that you were probably planning to bury in my back while I was sleeping. But I must confess, ever since we left Ravenswalk I've felt more confident about surviving the night."

"I don't understand," she stammered.

" 'To bury the hatchet' is just an expression," he said. "It's derived from the habits of North American Indians and means 'to make peace.' I've had the feeling that you've been trying to make peace and wondered to what I might attribute this change of attitude."

Lily froze for a moment. "My change of attitude?" she repeated, wondering if he had realized what she was up to.

"Yes," he said, putting his knife and fork together on his plate. He tossed his napkin onto the table and pushed back his chair with a slight scrape on the bare floor.

They were not staying at a stylish inn, and although it was clean enough, it was short on luxury, including rugs. He'd sold the carriage and horses they'd been given by her father, buying something more simple and using the rest of the money to pay their way to Saint-Simon.

"I don't suppose it has something to do with my taking you to your brother?" he asked as he warmed himself by the fire that burned in the small grate.

She wound her fingers together in her lap and stared down at them, thinking how best to deflect his question. "You have shown every kindness by agreeing to help my brother," she said after a long pause. "The least I can do is try to be pleasant. As you said, you don't wish my brother to see that we're at odds, so we should try to be civil to each other. I have no wish to distress Jean-Jacques. He has enough troubles."

Pascal nodded and examined the toe of his boot. "That's fair enough, and it's an eminently sensible attitude."

"I thought it through and realized that I have reason to be . . ." The word stuck in Lily's throat. "To be grateful to you." She was damned if she was going to mention her right to her own money.

"I see." He propped his shoulder against the mantelpiece, looking down at her. "I shouldn't be too grateful,

Elizabeth. You might find yourself choking on the sentiment.''

She looked at him hard, but instead of his usual cold and
unreadable expression, Lily saw amusement. ''Do you make
fun of me?'' she asked hotly.

''Yes, I do, and it's no good working yourself up over the
matter. You must learn to laugh. There's more than enough
unhappiness and pain in the world, and I see no need to
compound it, do you? Scowling seems a terrible waste of
time.''

Lily forgot all of her resolutions to be sweet and humble.
''You're no one to talk—you do nothing but scowl, and almost all of the time.''

''Do I?'' he said, not the least troubled. ''I assure you,
it's not my usual habit. You don't suppose it's the natural
arrangement God gave my features, do you? That would be
distressing. Have you a mirror by any chance?''

Lily stared at him, thrown off balance.

''What's wrong? Are you afraid it might shatter? I can't
be that unfortunate in my face, can I?''

''I don't—I don't think that is your problem,'' she managed to say. ''And furthermore I think you know it.''

One corner of Pascal's mouth lifted. ''Oh? Are you now
accusing me of extraordinarily *good* looks? I find you a very
contradictory person, Elizabeth. I can't work out whether I
strike you with horror or with awe. Up until now I could
have sworn it was horror.''

''You strike me with neither,'' she said tartly, ''and I
think you are very conceited. Did Dom Benetard never tell
you that vanity is a sin?''

''I don't remember his mentioning it, no. I think he was
more concerned with other aspects of my character.''

''Such as?'' Lily asked smugly.

''Well . . . let me think. I'm only a simple gardener, so
it's hard for me to retain things. Yes, that's it. I believe he
said that he thought me prone to forgetfulness.''

Lily's eyes sparkled with reluctant amusement. ''Really.
What else did he tell you? If you can possibly bring yourself
to recall, that is.''

Pascal cocked his head back and regarded the ceiling.
''He told me that I was better suited to growing vegetables
than to cooking them, for when I did a shift in the kitchen
the infirmary ended up full. I believe it was the cabbage that

did it. But I don't suppose you could consider that a character flaw, could you? It's more a case of incompetence. Let me see. Character flaws. Gracious me. Do you know, I cannot think of a one.''

"Vanity," Lily said helpfully. "And arrogance."

"Well, really, they are one and the same," Pascal said. "Surely you can do better than that?"

"Avarice?" Lily supplied.

"Come, Elizabeth. I think that's unfair, given everything." Pascal gave her a wounded look.

"Oh, very well. You do seem to thrive on pauperism." She ran through Father Mallet's standard list. "I have it—false humility."

"Hmm. Perhaps. That's a tricky one, isn't it? I'll have to think it over, for I can never tell if I'm being humble or merely stupid."

That earned a choked laugh from Lily. Father Mallet would have gone very red in the face if he'd heard that particular remark. "Sacrilege," she said with a grin.

"Quite possibly. Dom Benetard did remark on my language on occasion, but how could I help myself? I learned it at Nicholas's knee—well, perhaps at his chest, as we didn't meet until I was half grown. Still, it was influence enough. I'm afraid the monks thought me blasphemous. Fortunately Dom Benetard was more understanding. I was only occasionally sent to my cell."

Lily touched her finger to her mouth, curiosity burning through her. "How did the two of you actually meet?"

"Dom Benetard and I? Unlike you, I walked in through the front door." His laugh lines showed around his eyes.

"No. I—actually, I meant Nicholas."

Pascal's expression abruptly sobered. "That is a long story and one for another time. Suffice it to say that I owe him my life."

"Oh." Lily felt as if she'd just been chastised, and her cheeks flushed with angry embarrassment. "I apologize for asking. I didn't mean to pry."

"You didn't pry. It's only that there are certain things that are difficult to discuss. Maybe one day when we know each other better and there is trust between us I'll be able to speak of it with you. But that time is not now."

Lily's heart gave an unfamiliar twist as she realized that she had touched a raw nerve in him. It made her even more ashamed that he didn't bother to pretend she hadn't—he was being completely honest with her at his own expense. Lily bowed her head. "I'm sorry," she whispered, and this time she was truly contrite. "I won't ask again."

"Elizabeth," he said, walking over to her and taking her chin, gently lifting her face up to his. "Don't ever be afraid to ask anything of me. All I ask of you in return is that you accept the times when I cannot answer, or cannot give you the answer that you want. I'd far rather have honesty between us with that understanding than foolish games that lead nowhere." He dropped his hand. "I'm going to take Bean out before bed. We have an early start in the morning if we're to reach Saint-Simon before sundown. Good night. Sleep well."

He left the parlor, quietly shutting the door after him. Lily sat very still. She felt as if her world had shifted yet again, but she didn't understand how or why. For the first time since she'd been summarily handed over to Pascal LaMartine, she didn't feel defensive or angry or afraid. For the first time in as long as she could remember, there was the faintest thread of hope that everything would be somehow all right. Lily lifted a hand to find that tears were running down her cheeks. She didn't understand that either.

It didn't occur to her that for the first time in her life someone had treated her with compassion.

9

THE following morning Lily was invited up onto the driver's box by her husband, who had never before made such a suggestion. She hesitated, surprised, then gamely climbed up. She'd always liked being up high, and besides, the countryside looked more immediate from that vantage than it did from behind a closed window. If truth be told, although she hated to admit it, she was happy for the company. Anyway, she had never sat in the driver's box before, and it seemed an interesting thing to do.

Row after row of straight-backed poplars passed by, lining the road that wound past gently rolling hills and fertile valleys. Villages were scattered here and there, some perched on hilltops, others pocketed cozily away in their folds, the dark tiled roofs and pale stone walls of the houses forming a natural part of the landscape. They passed through a forest thick with oak and chestnut, the mossy smell of wet earth and fresh leaves richly fragrant, and then, as they emerged on the other side, the scent of sunshine surrounded them, beating down on fields ripe with newly burgeoning crops.

Lily loved the feel of the sun on her skin and the wind in her hair, the warmth of Bean's soft little body tucked securely against her. She knew it was sinful to take pleasure in sensual things, but she didn't care.

Pascal didn't speak much, keeping his eyes fixed on the road and his hands loosely holding the reins, but that suited Lily well enough. She was still feeling unsure of herself after her peculiar reaction the night before. If anything, she felt shy and a bit ridiculous. She didn't know what to say to him, how to react, even what to feel. She'd spent so much time convincing herself that he was an immoral, degenerate wretch—no, *knowing* that he was an immoral, degenerate wretch, that it was disconcerting to realize there might be

another side to him, a side that laughed and teased and even
. . . even hurt.

She stole another glance at him. His silky hair shifted
lightly about the nape of his neck where the breeze caught
it. He might have been a gypsy, with that dark hair and
those dark eyes and bronzed skin.

Lily wondered if this was what it was like to be a gypsy,
wild and free, riding down endless roads, a puppy snuggled
against you, sharing a lunch on your lap, nothing between
you and the sun but the sky. Nothing before you mattered
but the road, nothing behind you mattered but the last camp.
It was wonderful.

Pascal had bought a loaf of bread and a slab of cheese at
the inn before they'd left, along with a bottle of wine. Lily's
job was to divide it up and serve it out, and suddenly the
gypsy life lost its charm. Lily struggled with the bread,
mutilating it even more horribly than she had the loaf at
Raven's Close, although eventually she managed two ragged
chunks. As for the cheese, a mouse would have done a better job, for every time she attempted to cut it, the cheese
crumbled until she had only tiny bits.

She peeked over at the wretch to see if he'd noticed, but
his eyes were still on the road, so she quickly attempted to
press the crumbs of cheese down on the bread with her
thumbs.

He took his portion and put it on the seat next to him—
safely on the other side of Bean, who immediately leaped
up with attention the instant the food was produced. "Thank
you," he said.

Lily looked at him sharply. She thought she saw laughter
lurking in the back of his eyes, but he returned her gaze
innocently enough. "Shall I open the wine?" he asked.

Lily hesitated. "No," she said decisively. "I'll do it. I
have the corkscrew right here." She bent to her task. It was
only when she had pushed the cork halfway into the neck
for the third time that Pascal finally reached for the bottle
and handed her the reins—yet another new experience. She
shot him a look of panic, forgetting to be offended.

"Just hold them loosely—no, loosely, Elizabeth. You
don't want to mangle the poor horses' mouths. That's it."
He smiled reassuringly. "They'll go along nicely if you
don't manhandle them. Here, hand me the corkscrew, or

we'll die of thirst. No, don't watch me, watch the road. That's it. Good.''

In another minute or two, the wretch had somehow managed to retrieve the errant cork and pull it out. He poured the wine into two mugs he produced from the satchel next to him and handed her one, then took back the reins.

"Have you never driven before?" he asked conversationally.

"No. I was never given the opportunity." Lily bent to her piece of squashed bread and cheese.

Pascal suddenly took a great interest in the hay field off to the left. "I suppose your father didn't consider it ladylike for you to drive a carriage," he said after a moment.

"It wasn't that so much," Lily replied, taking a sip of wine to wash down the dry bread. "It was because he thought things like that were frivolous and unnecessary when there were more important things to be done."

"Such as?" He fed a piece of bread and cheese to Bean, then looked at her curiously.

"Studying, reading, praying."

"What, no embroidery?" Pascal asked dryly.

"Oh—yes, embroidery. I forgot. But only passages from the Bible. It took me four years to finish the First Epistle to the Corinthians." The memory was enough to make her brain numb.

Pascal stared at her. "You're *serious*?"

"Yes. Of course, you must like that sort of thing excessively, having lived in a monastery."

"What, embroidery?" he asked, tongue in cheek. "Not really. Gardening is more in my line."

"You know what I meant," she said, annoyed. "I was talking about praying and all of that. I realize that you just worked there, but still, surely you had to go to church fifteen times a day?"

Pascal chuckled. "Not quite fifteen. And yes, I found it enjoyable enough."

"*Enjoyable?*" Lily said, shocked. "You're not supposed to enjoy it."

"You're not? What are you supposed to be doing then, if you're not enjoying it?" Pascal asked curiously.

"You're supposed to be enumerating all of your sins and asking forgiveness of God."

"Really?" he asked with a straight face. "The entire time?"

"Yes—surely the monks taught you that much?" Lily said impatiently.

Pascal slowly shook his head. "No. They didn't."

"Well, they ought to have done, but I suppose they didn't think it was their job. Of course, they don't talk much, do they?" Lily got out two apples and picked up the knife, but Pascal quickly took his apple from her before she could start cutting it.

"I prefer mine just as God designed it," he said, that hint of laughter back in his eyes. "Do you know, you have me worried now. Perhaps I ought to write to Dom Benetard and inform him that he's been going about the thing all wrong. Can you imagine, the monks actually go to prayer in joy? They have no idea they're meant to be miserable."

Lily looked at him suspiciously. "You're teasing again, aren't you?"

"Yes, I'm teasing, and it's no damned wonder you don't believe in God, not if that's what you think He is all about. I wouldn't believe in Him either. Who wants to be miserable the whole time? Tell me. Have you ever seen anything born?"

She shook her head.

"Have you ever seen anything die?"

Lily shuddered. "No. Oh—I once saw a frog squashed beneath the wheel of a carriage. It was revolting."

"Yes, I can imagine, but the point is, faith isn't something that can be explained. Either it's there or it isn't. It helps, though, to have seen God's hand at immediate work. I've found that birth and death have a way of putting things into perspective."

"I don't think I would care to see either," Lily said, wrinkling her nose. "They sound equally unattractive."

Pascal gazed at her with fascination. "You do have an interesting way of looking at things," he said. "I can see that we have a way to go."

"If you think to convert me to your point of view, you are wasting your time," Lily said tartly. "Father Mallet tried all this time and failed miserably. I won't change my mind. I have a scientific view of life and don't believe in anything other than clinical explanations."

Pascal bit into his apple. "I agree with you about a scientific approach," he said when he'd swallowed.

"You do?" She narrowed her eyes, looking for the trick.

"Yes, of course," he said easily. "It's important to have knowledge and skill in order to deal with various aspects of life." He took another bite and chewed it thoughtfully. "I think . . . I think that where you and I differ is that I believe we're not here on this earth merely as a result of a biological process. We're here because of a biological process, and a brilliant one at that." He gestured at her with the apple. "But as far as I'm concerned, all a body does is provide us with a temporary house. It is transient. We are not." He looked back at the road.

Lily chewed on her lip. She'd never heard anyone talk like this before, and it was alarming, yet intriguing at the same time. "What about sin?" she asked, knowing she'd catch him up on that one, sinner that he was. He'd never admit to it.

"Sin? What about it? If you're asking about human fallibility, the only answer is that we're all fallible."

"No," she said impatiently. "I mean true sin, the kind that's supposed to make you burn in hell for all eternity."

Pascal rubbed his lower lip, then slanted a look at her. "I have a confession to make. I don't believe in hell."

"I knew it," she crowed. "So how can you call yourself a Christian? Do you believe in heaven?"

"Oh, yes," he said quietly. "I believe in heaven."

"You can't believe in one and not the other," she informed him. "It's not consistent."

"Perhaps I should explain," he said, amused.

"Yes, I think you should," she replied, wishing he wouldn't look at her in that way of his that reminded her of just how masculine and dangerous he was. If anyone should worry about hell, it was the wretch.

"I believe God loves all of His creatures, no matter where they've gone wrong," he said, gazing off into the distance. "So instead of sending those of us who have strayed to a burning inferno, which seems pointless, I think He gives us a chance to come back time and time again until we get it right."

"But you can't possibly be a Catholic," Lily said, staring incredulously at him. "That's not even Christian! How could they have let you into a monastery?"

Pascal chuckled. "There wasn't much of a problem. You may think me a terrible Catholic, but I'm a very good gardener. And if you recall, I wasn't at St. Christophe in the capacity of a monk. Besides, God is God, Elizabeth, no matter what slant you choose to put on the matter.''

"There is only one slant," she crisply informed him.

"Oh, really? What do you suppose God did before creeds were developed? Scorned His own creations for lack of a proper theology?''

Lily's brow furrowed. She'd never really thought of it like that. "Aren't you supposed to believe that Christ is the Son of God and died to save us from our sins, and that's why we have life eternal? In theory,'' she hastened to add.

"Yes, and I do believe that, although not exactly the way the Church has put it down. Someday ask me about the councils of Nicaea and Constantinople. They shed an interesting light on certain theological dictums.''

Lily rolled her eyes. "325 and 381 A.D., respectively. And the council of Constantinople was formed to deal with troublesome heretics like you.''

"I know, and I'll wager that my version of what really happened at both those councils differs greatly from the one you were spoon-fed. The Church had a way of distorting certain details for its own end. Still, I know that you've had enough theological dictums shoved down your throat to last you the rest of your life, so I can hardly blame you for feeling the way you do.''

"You haven't answered my question," Lily said smugly. "The one about what happens to non-Christians, since God took the trouble to send Christ with His word.''

"I thought I had," he said. "Heaven is heaven, Elizabeth, no matter what you believe. Do you think God would turn away any of His creatures, simply because they didn't adhere to a particular religion? Where's the sense in that?''

Lily had no answer. "I still think you're a heretic," she said.

"And you're an atheist. We're a fine pair, aren't we? What do you suppose Father Mallet would make of us? He'd probably wish the Spanish Inquisition back.''

Lily couldn't help grinning. "He *is* the Spanish Inquisition.''

"I somehow got that idea. Never mind. Father Mallet is no longer a part of your life.''

No, but you are, Lily thought. *And I wonder just what that is going to mean.*

* * *

She knew they were growing close when the cliffs appeared, towering stretches of limestone, some with houses built into their sides, others with shrines perched on their tops or deep grottoes carved into their foundation. Lily held her breath as they approached the final corner that would bring Saint-Simon into sight. For some reason she loved it more than she had ever loved Sutherby or any of her father's other estates, including the ones that now belonged to her—or rather, unfortunately, to her husband. There was something about Saint-Simon, about its position high atop a hill, about its entire feel, that drew her to it, despite its shabbiness, despite the failing crops. She felt toward it as she imagined she might feel toward an infant. It needed protecting, it needed nurturing—as did Jean-Jacques. Perhaps that was why the two of them were linked so closely in her mind.

The small river Cère, a tributary of the much larger Dordogne, over which they'd just passed, glittered in the near distance, and Lily's heart quickened. "Look! Look, there," she said, touching Pascal's arm in her excitement. She pointed up.

The Château de Saint-Simon stood on its hilltop like a jewel caught in the setting sun. Its square towers and steep roofs rose high over the trees that surrounded it, a brilliant display against the gold and rose of the sky.

Pascal slowly brought the horses to a halt, silently looking up. He took in the gray and yellow limestone, the crenellated ramparts, the pepperpot towers, the balustrades and turrets, and then his gaze traveled to the hills that descended around it. They were planted with vines, but the vines did not appear to be thriving. He closed his eyes and took in a deep breath, trying to absorb the feel of the place. It had hit him with an unexpected impact—the beauty of the château itself had nearly knocked him over. But far more important was the land. To his eye it looked sickly; to his heart it felt thirsty and abandoned. It was an odd thing. Virtually all of the land they had been traveling through had been healthy enough. Why was this one area so barren? His eyes narrowed as they swept over the hills and then down about the surrounding countryside. He saw no apparent difference in topography; perhaps there was a specialized climate, but it would be impossible to tell without a detailed examination.

He turned to Lily. "Take me to your brother. There is much to be done."

Lily instantly complied.

10

J EAN-JACQUES appeared at the library window that looked out over the château's courtyard, surprised to hear the sound of a carriage coming across the drawbridge. He had not had many visitors since departing Paris three years before; the word had gone around quickly that he was out of funds and out of fun as a result. Life had grown unbearably dreary, and he was excited that one of his old friends might have decided to stop by to give him a little pleasure.

But the carriage that pulled up was not familiar to him. There was nothing to distinguish it, no coat of arms, no livery, the two horses not showy. With a start of surprise he heard his sister's unmistakable voice coming to him, and he peered harder out of the window. It *was* his sister, and she was sitting on the driver's box, of all things.

He couldn't believe it. He had half a mind to bolt the front door and hide in one of the turrets, for Lily and her ambitious schemes were more than he felt prepared to deal with at the moment. He'd been secretly relieved when she had disappeared late one night and hadn't returned, and he imagined from the note she'd left that she must have gone back to England for her "solution." He hadn't heard a word, but that was typical of Lily, and he thought it meant that her father had gotten his hands on her and she wouldn't be back anytime soon.

Yet here she was. Furthermore, she was in the company of a man he'd never laid eyes on before—and unchaperoned. Jean-Jacques closed his eyes and groaned. Wherever his sister went, trouble was sure to follow, and he shuddered to think what might result from this latest escapade. He had no desire to tangle with Lily's father ever again.

The knock inevitably came and Jean-Jacques sighed and went to open the front door, for Olivier, who acted as but-

ler, valet, footman, and general dogsbody, was nowhere to
be seen. Hardly surprising. He was probably upstairs in bed
with the chambermaid. It was the usual state of affairs. He
cautiously pulled the enormous door open, having no idea
what to expect on the other side.

"Jean-Jacques!" Lily flung herself at him, her arms flying about his neck as she rained kisses upon his face. "Oh,
Jean-Jacques, how wonderful to see you—it hasn't even been
a month yet, but it feels like at least a year. How are you?
Are you well? Have there been any changes, any good
news?"

Jean-Jacques's gaze traveled over his sister's head to the
tall man standing quietly behind her. "Nothing new, Lily,"
he said, detaching himself from her. "And you? Where have
you been? What have you been doing? And who, may I ask,
is this gentleman you have arrived with alone?"

"This is Pascal LaMartine—my husband—and he's come
to be your steward," she said brightly.

Jean-Jacques didn't move for a moment, and then he bent
his head and rubbed his eyes. He finally looked up at her
again. "Your husband?"

"Yes."

"I don't suppose your father knows anything about this,
Elizabeth?"

"Oh, yes, he does. He gave the marriage his full ap-
proval. You see, Monsieur LaMartine is a Catholic."

"Oh, of course he is. Naturally that explains everything."

"Well . . . not everything, but don't worry, for Papa gave
me away with complete enthusiasm, then washed his hands
of me, so there's no trouble from that quarter. The good
news is that we've come here to live, and my husband is a
gardener, and he has offered to be your steward, and isn't
it marvelous?"

"*This* was your solution?" Jean-Jacques asked, raking a
hand over his face in exasperation. "You went and married
a gardener so that I could have a bloody steward? Are you
out of your mind?" His voice had risen to a shout.

"No, I'm not out of my mind, and that's not what happened at all. It is mere coincidence that Monsieur La-
Martine is a gardener. He was kind enough to offer to help
when he discovered your troubles."

"I don't understand any of this." Jean-Jacques shoved his hands onto his hips.

"I'm hardly surprised," Pascal said, speaking for the first time. "I've found that your sister has an interesting approach to telling a story. Perhaps we could sit down together? I might be better able to explain the situation to you, and there are things I need to know about your situation here to determine what can be done, if anything."

Jean-Jacques nodded abruptly, then stood back and gestured inside. "Please. Do come in. Lily, I will speak to Monsieur LaMartine alone. Take a walk or something."

Pascal turned to her. "Bean could use a good exercise. Take her on her leash, and don't forget what I told you yesterday. Be firm. And Elizabeth," he added as an afterthought, "don't worry. I'll get everything sorted out with your brother. Have a nice time; there's a beautiful sunset to be enjoyed this evening. Surely you have a partiality for sunsets?"

He smiled at her, his eyes teasing, then disappeared into the depths of the château with Jean-Jacques.

Lily was left looking at a closed door, and for the first time in her life she decided to leave well enough alone. She went to fetch Bean, whose little face was anxiously pressed against the window of the carriage, where she'd been safely shut away.

"Never mind, Bean," Lily whispered against one velvet ear, holding her tight. "You heard what Pascal said. Somehow it will all work out. Somehow. Now let's go for that walk. Down, Bean." She slipped the leash on. "No, sit. Sit!"

But the command didn't work the same as when the wretch gave it. Bean took it as an immediate invitation to run, and Lily was forced to run after her, the leash and Lily jerking about in every direction.

Pascal noted the almost empty great hall, the places where paintings and tapestries must have hung at some point fairly recently, given the disparate coloration of the stone. The place was not falling down anywhere to the degree that his wife had implied, but it was obvious that money was being funneled out of, rather than into it.

Jean-Jacques showed him into a library that was comfortable, and the furniture there, at least, had not been depleted.

"So," Jean-Jacques said, pouring them both cognac and handing Pascal a glass, "you have married my sister. Why?"

"Because her father desired the match. It was my impression that he felt your sister had tarried long enough. He wants heirs, if I am not mistaken."

Jean-Jacques smiled bitterly. "He wants nothing else in life save what he perceives as his deserved award in heaven. I sincerely hope he is refused it, if he even gets that far. Why were you picked for the heir-giver?"

"Because I was convenient." Pascal met Jean-Jacques's eyes squarely.

"Convenient? I find that extraordinarily easy to believe, but I confess, this is the first I have heard of you. La-Martine? I do not believe I know any family of that name."

"I'm not surprised. My parents didn't travel in elevated circles."

"Ah, the bourgeoisie, is it?"

Pascal didn't bother gracing that with a reply.

Jean-Jacques scratched his cheek. "I am surprised that my stepfather consented, then. Do you claim to love my sister?"

"No," Pascal said bluntly. "I hardly know her. I no more desired the match than she did, but there was no way to avoid it. Montcrieff had made up his mind."

"He does that, doesn't he?" Jean-Jacques said snidely. "And for what reason did he make up his mind?"

"As I said, it was convenient to him. He used a promise I'd made to a dear and trusted friend to force my hand. I'd rather say nothing more on that subject. As for your sister, she had no choice but to obey him. He—or rather Father Mallet—locked her in the chapel for ten days to ensure her obedience."

Jean-Jacques turned a slow red, remembering his own imprisonment—and the methodical beatings that had gone along with it. "Did he? Damn his eyes! Damn both of them to hell! My God, the two of them—they deserve each other."

"Regardless, Lily survived her incarceration and we are now married."

"Yes. And you are here, which seems ridiculous, given all of Lily's estates and the money that came along with her dowry. You did well for yourself, monsieur. So. Did my sister cry on your shoulder and beg you to come and rescue me?''

"Actually, I heard about your predicament from my brother, in whom Elizabeth had confided." Pascal put his untouched cognac down on the table next to him. "By virtue of marrying your sister, I was displaced from my last job. Your situation seemed an interesting challenge, so I offered to come and see what could be done."

"I can't think you can do anything, Monsieur LaMartine, unless you are here to offer me money at Lily's urging."

"No, I'm not," Pascal said. "Quite the opposite, for I will require a salary."

Jean-Jacques gave a harsh laugh. "A salary? With my sister's entire fortune at your disposal? You must be joking."

"Not in the least. I refuse to touch your sister's money, and I must work for a living."

Jean-Jacques met this announcement with stunned silence.

"I must also make it clear that I cannot take the position until I have had a chance to examine the vines," Pascal continued. "Should you and I come to an agreement that I will work for you, then you must—and this is without question—you must commit yourself to doing whatever is necessary. I insist on your promise, or we can go no further."

Jean-Jacques stared at him. "I—I beg your pardon? You *insist*? Do you know to whom you are speaking, monsieur?''

"Oh, yes. I'm aware that you're the Duc de Saint-Simon. It doesn't matter to me who you are, other than my wife's brother and the keeper of this land, of dying vineyards."

"I know what I am keeper of, monsieur. There is no need for you to remind me," Jean-Jacques said, his color flaring.

"But there is," Pascal replied evenly. "Because if your vineyards can be saved, not only will they save you and your pockets but they will also save the village that depends on you. It does, does it not? I looked carefully as we drove past. What I saw was brave poverty. I also saw despair. The people have the look of those who live from hand to mouth and have for years."

"That is no doing of my own," Jean-Jacques snapped. "It was like that long before I came."

"Nevertheless, if I can find a way to make your crops produce," Pascal said calmly, "then a great many people will be enriched. You need the faith and goodwill of the villagers as much as you need anything else. Are we clear on the matter, then?"

Jean-Jacques blinked several times. He had never been spoken to in such a way before, at least not by anyone other than his stepfather and Mallet, and he'd been more than happy to escape them both. But this man was different. He looked at one with a pleasant enough expression, yet Jean-Jacques felt as if he had just been run over by an army battalion. This Pascal LaMartine obviously had no respect for rank, nor for money, nor for any of the other things his betters took for granted. He swallowed and drew himself up. He would not be intimidated by a mere commoner.

"As you say," he intoned imperiously. "Examine the vines. See what you think. Should you feel you can do something, then by all means, take over. I have no one else. But I warn you, I can afford almost nothing in pay."

"We will work out an arrangement that pays a minimum salary for now, but should the crop come in as I hope, then I would like a small piece of the profits from it—let us say fifteen percent. That seems equitable to us both. Should I fail, you are not required to pay me anything more."

"I hope you don't expect to live here?" Jean-Jacques said, nervously fidgeting with his glass.

"No. Actually, I would prefer to live elsewhere, although I must be close to the fields. If you have any outlying houses that are empty, I would be very grateful. We need nothing elaborate."

Jean-Jacques stared at him again. "You mean to say that you don't *want* to live here?"

"I don't think it would be wise."

Jean-Jacques couldn't believe his good luck—he couldn't get the man out of his house fast enough. "Very well. There is a cottage," he said with alacrity. "It is just down the hill before the final approach into the town. Take the small road that leads off to the right. You cannot miss it. It has a barn attached on the west side and a patch of garden on the south. It is nothing grand, and not in the best of repair, and I'm not sure how much furniture there is . . ."

"We will manage."

"You, perhaps. But Lily?"

"Your sister will live wherever I live."

Jean-Jacques's face broke into a grin. "Ah . . . *The Taming of the Shrew,* is it? I see. Good luck. Many have tried before and failed, her father and his familiar most particularly."

Anger sparked in Pascal's eyes. "It's nothing of the sort, and please do not refer to my wife in such a manner. She's been ill-used enough by her family, as you've just pointed out."

Jean-Jacques shrugged one shoulder uncomfortably. "Yes, of course she has. I meant nothing by it."

"I'm pleased to hear it. I'll meet with you tomorrow morning, after I have had a chance to walk the land. Shall we say ten o'clock?"

"Ten?" Jean-Jacques said, thinking that sounded hellishly early. "Ah, yes. I can make myself available at ten."

"Very good. I shall see you then." He reached out his hand and Jean-Jacques shook it.

"I—I, ah, well . . . this is all quite unexpected."

"Yes, I understand. Tell me, is there anyone, anyone at all, who might be able to give me details on the history of the vineyards?"

"Oh. Well, I suppose old Monsieur Jamard, for he's always going on. I'll warn you right now, you're only going to hear the most absurd tales from the peasants about lost heirs and grieving land."

"I beg your pardon?" Pascal said, frowning. "Your sister mentioned nothing of this to me."

"Because it's a load of rubbish, and Lily believes it no more than I do. They have this absurd legend that the reason the vineyards have failed all these years is because the heir left the land, and the land wouldn't come back until the heir did. Well, the heir has returned, and they're still not satisfied. I don't know what the hell they think I'm supposed to do—wave a magic wand about and make them all suddenly thrive, and the vines too?" He shook his head in disgust. "Ignorant, lazy fools, the lot of them. If you ask me, the typhoid epidemic that decimated the village all those years ago wiped out the manpower needed to keep the vineyards going. That's what did it, nothing else."

"A typhoid epidemic? How very tragic for these people. Has there been sickness since?"

"Not that I know of, but then I've only been in residence

three years and no one tells me anything. I don't think so, though. Why?''

"I was only wondering. It's interesting. Sometimes the two things go hand in hand. But of course it's impossible to say.''

"What two things? Superstition and sickness?''

"No, although when desperation of any sort comes, it does tend to bring superstition in its wake. I meant the land and the people. Very often one type of health is dependent on the other. It only makes sense.'' Pascal shrugged. "Never mind that now. The light is fading, and I should find your sister and take her to our quarters. Have you extra candles, some bread and cheese, perhaps some cold meat that we might take with us? Oh, and some linens and blankets would be useful. I may be taking your sister to a cottage, but I'd like her to be comfortable.''

"Yes, of course. My man will pack some things up for you and bring them down. There should be firewood stacked inside the barn if I remember correctly.'' Jean-Jacques hadn't been inside the cottage for three years, but he was fairly sure the wood was still there.

"I will look for it,'' Pascal said. "Thank you.'' He left swiftly and silently.

Jean-Jacques let out an enormous exhalation. Lily was one thing, but Pascal LaMartine made him feel decidedly peculiar, even uncomfortable. He gave orders with extraordinary ease and with no care about to whom he was giving them. Jean-Jacques didn't like it one bit, but he was in no position to argue. He knew he ought to be grateful to Lily for having brought her gardener along. He also knew he ought to feel guilty for Lily's having married a gardener in the first place, for there was no doubt in his mind that she had made an enormous, if foolish, sacrifice on his behalf. It was typical of Lily and her loyalty.

He did feel bad about consigning his sister to that crofter's cottage, but he did not want LaMartine living in his house, and there hadn't been anywhere else to put them. It might even do Lily some good, he rationalized.

Anyway, he didn't believe that LaMartine intended to keep his hands off Lily's fortune. He'd probably decided to put the fear of God into the girl, teach her some sort of lesson—and who was Jean-Jacques to interfere between a man and his wife? Let him scare her for a few days, then use her money to arrange for decent lodging.

For the moment, Jean-Jacques had a cheap steward who seemed to think he might know something about vineyards. If perhaps by some miracle things went very well, he would be able to return to his former lifestyle.

After all, there was the lovely Violette to be considered, and she wasn't strong on patience at the moment. He'd do anything for Violette. She was such a saucy devil, and she did need her indulgences, as she was so fond of pointing out.

Jean-Jacques smiled nostalgically and raised his glass to that rarefied beauty. *To you,* mignon. *To you and a delicious future.* He drained the contents and tossed the glass into the hearth as if to seal his silent pledge.

Then he regretted the gesture, for he really couldn't afford to waste good crystal at the moment. He got another glass, then settled down with the cognac bottle and happily began to plan his comeback.

"What do you mean, we're not staying?" Lily put her hands on her hips and glared at Pascal. "You and Jean-Jacques can't have had a fight already! And anyway, I'm not going anywhere. I'm not. You said we'd come and help my brother—you promised. You can't go back on your word— it's not . . . it's not honorable. Not that you've ever shown yourself to have a shred of honor in you, but I was trying to give you the benefit of the doubt, and what do you do? You prove yourself to be the filthy, beastly cad I've always known you to be!" She stamped her foot.

"Elizabeth," Pascal said on a warning note. "Stop this tirade and listen to me."

"I won't! Why should I? You'll just come up with some flimsy excuse and drag me off God knows where."

"The only place I am taking you is down the hill to a cottage your brother is providing for us, and I damned well *will* drag you if you don't cease this nonsense. Now get back up on the box."

Lily halted in mid-breath. "We're staying?"

"Yes, we're staying—at least until I can have a look at the vineyards."

"Oh. But why aren't we staying with Jean-Jacques—and what do you mean by 'a cottage'?" Her eyes narrowed suspiciously. "Surely you don't really mean a cottage? What you must mean is that Jean-Jacques has loaned us a house somewhere close by. How very obliging of him. He is a very nice man, is he not?"

"I meant a cottage, and you might as well prepare yourself, for your brother doesn't think it's in the finest of repair. And as we're staying only so long as I think there is something I can do, you had better pray that the vines aren't as hopelessly impaired as they looked from a distance." He pointed at the carriage. "Now get on the box, or ride inside, but get on with it, for we need the last of the light to find our way."

Lily, refusing to give him satisfaction by riding inside, sullenly climbed on the box, Bean clutched to her chest as if she might offer protection from the heartless wretch and his imperious demands. She was not concerned, however, for she knew that Jean-Jacques would see to her comfort. He probably wished her to begin her married life in an establishment of her own and had so arranged it.

Lily's brow furrowed, for she did not remember her brother's mentioning any attached properties, but he was so absentminded about his affairs that it was hardly surprising.

She kept her silence as the carriage clattered back over the drawbridge that spanned a grass-filled moat, kept her silence as they went back down the hill, kept her silence all the way to the turning that led down a rocky path. It was the sight of the tumbledown cottage that finally opened her mouth, and only then to force a long, jerky gasp of disbelief from her throat.

"We're home," the wretch said, jumping easily down from the carriage and holding out a hand to her.

"N-no. No, this cannot b-be," she stammered. "It cannot. It is a joke."

"It is no joke, and if you don't come down off your perch this instant, you shall be spending what I judge is going to be a chilly night outdoors." He held out his arms. "Here, hand me Bean. She might as well have a run, and I doubt she'll go far." He put the puppy on the ground, then held out his hand again.

She ignored it.

"Elizabeth," he said dangerously, *"give me your hand."*

Lily obeyed out of shock more than any sense of obedience. It was her nightmare come true. It was the hovel, complete with shutters hanging off their hinges and filthy windows and—and cobwebs in the outer corners.

"Good girl. Now let's go and see what sort of home we have. Your brother's man is coming shortly with a few essentials, but we might as well make a start at things." He detached Lily's trunk from the back and lifted it up onto his shoulder, then walked over to what appeared to be the front door. She trailed after him, feeling quite sick.

"Locked," he said, trying the handle. "I should have thought to ask for a key. Never mind, I'll try the barn. There's bound to be a way in." He disappeared around the corner, and sure enough, a few minutes later he appeared from inside the door. Lily had to duck her head to get under the portal, swatting more cobwebs as she went.

She looked around her, trying to absorb the reality of the place she was actually to live in.

It was filthy. That came as no surprise. The walls were fashioned of coarse stone, chunks of it scattered about the floor of the small room along with a thick layer of white dust. There was a fireplace in one corner, smoke-blackened above the hearth, the ingrained soot extending over the heavy and roughly hewn beam that served as a mantelpiece.

Beyond, there was another, larger room, fashioned of the same rough stone. A huge wooden table, slightly warped in the middle, stood in the exact center. A basin with a hand pump that fed into it took up the middle of one wall. Opposite it was a fireplace, this one much larger than the one next door, with an old kettle resting on a grill. An open staircase ran along the east side, and when Lily cocked her head back she saw that there was a large gallery above, containing a low, wide mattress and very little else. Yes, indeed. It was a hovel.

Pascal fed wood into the fireplace of the larger room, unconcerned with what she might be thinking or feeling. In fact, he was on his knees stuffing wood and paper into the thing as if he might actually be enjoying himself. Lily drew herself up to her full height, which was considered quite statuesque for a female, and took a deep breath.

"Monsieur LaMartine," she said in her grandest tones, "do you think you might consider offering me one of these— these excuses for a chair?"

He looked over his shoulder. "No. If you want a chair,

pull one out for yourself. I am trying to provide us with some warmth, as surely you can see for yourself. You might look around and see if there are any rags to start cleaning with. It doesn't look as if anyone has lived here for years.''

''I couldn't agree with you more. I think I will go back to the château now. I refuse to stay here even one night.''

Pascal stood, and Lily instantly felt dwarfed. She swallowed hard, not liking the forbidding expression on his face.

''Elizabeth. Let me make something perfectly clear before you throw any more of your airs about. This is our home. This is where we are to live. You are not going anywhere, most certainly not back to your brother's house. If you attempt it, you shall be sorry, I promise you. He will not thank you for your misguided efforts and neither will I.''

''My brother would never have meant this for me. You must have misunderstood the direction.''

''He was explicit about the direction. Listen to me, for it is important that you understand the point.'' He took her by the shoulders, his touch firm. ''You are my wife. You will therefore behave accordingly and obey me. Your brother will live his life in his house. We will live our life in our house, which is this, and I am sorry that it is in such a shabby state, but there is nothing I can do about it at this moment.''

''You don't even care! You want to keep me from my brother, which is why you have done this terrible thing!'' Lily put her face in her hands in total misery.

''No.'' He took her chin in his fingers and pulled it up, forcing her to meet his eyes. ''Should you wish to see your brother, I will not stand in your way, as long as you are not unreasonable about the matter.''

''Unreasonable?'' she said on a sob. ''How could I be unreasonable? Jean-Jacques is the only person who understands me—I love him and wish to be with him. What is unreasonable about that?''

''Nothing, although you're going to have a great deal to keep you busy here. I shouldn't put too much emphasis on spending time up at the château. As long as your chores are done and there are no more pressing matters, you may do as you please, but only then.''

Lily bit her lip. ''You truly are a wretch and I loathe you!

I thought today that you were trying to be my friend, but you were obviously only wanting to ingratiate yourself with my brother so that he would give you a job!''

Pascal looked at her as if she'd lost her mind. ''So he would give me a *job*?'' he said. ''That's what you think?''

''Yes. And it worked, didn't it? You must have told him appalling stories to have him behave so toward me.''

''Actually, I told him very little. He understands the marriage was made against both our wills. That is all he knows, and please, leave it there, Elizabeth.''

Lily ground the toe of her shoe into the floor, staring down at the filthy wood. ''Why? Why should I? He is my brother. I have a right to know what you talked about, haven't I?''

Pascal shoved his hair off his brow impatiently. ''Yes, of course. The rest of our conversation regarded your brother's situation. It concerned the vineyards.''

''I don't believe you. There must have been more to it than that. You must have done something or said something to make him put me in a place like this.''

''I only said that we needed our own quarters. Put what interpretation you will on that—he clearly didn't want us with him, any more than I wanted it. This is what your brother has given us, and this is where we will live. You might as well make the best of it, starting now. So please, see if you can find some candles. Night is drawing in, and there is no way of knowing when or if your brother's man will arrive.''

As it happened, he did not arrive until noon the next day. Lily was forced to sleep upstairs on the bare mattress, wrapped in an opera cloak from her trousseau trunk—obviously the best use the cloak would have, given her distressing change of circumstances. The wretch had chosen to sleep on a smaller straw pallet that he'd found in the barn and put next to the fireplace. He had probably been wonderfully warm the entire night while she had tossed and turned and shivered. Even Bean had abandoned her in favor of the wretch and the fire.

Lily woke, her nose cold, her limbs stiff. She pulled the velvet over her face, not wanting to wake at all and face such a dismal reality. She might as well have been locked back in the chapel—although at least here she had the free-

dom to walk out the door. She peered blearily over the edge
of the platform. All that was visible was the empty pallet,
a tossed-aside jacket, and Bean, who had snuggled straight
into the middle of that jacket, her nose to the dying embers,
her body curled up against itself in an effort to keep warm.

Lily was envious of the physical warmth Bean had shared
during the night. She rose, shivering, and splashed cold
water on her face, then dressed and went quickly downstairs. She thought darkly of the wretch, who had abandoned them both to cold and hunger, who cared so little
about either of them.

Bean jumped up when she heard Lily coming down the
stairs and ran over to her, nudging her cold nose into Lily's
ankle.

"What do you want?" Lily asked crossly. "Oh. I suppose you're hungry. Very well. Just take your nose away.
I'm cold enough." She went to the cupboard and pulled out
what was left of yesterday's loaf and pointed it at Bean.
"Here."

The puppy looked at her in bafflement.

"You're supposed to eat it," she said as patiently as
she could manage. "It's food. What were you expecting,
beef?"

"She might take it a bit more easily if you didn't thrust
the entire stale loaf at her."

Lily swung around to see the wretch standing in the doorway that led from the barn. He was holding an armful of
wood and wearing an infuriating smile on his face. Worse,
he didn't even look exhausted.

"I—I was trying to feed her. She's being difficult."

"If you go outside, you'll find a pail with some milk that
I took from an obliging cow. Tear up the bread into pieces,
then find a bowl and soak the bread in the milk for a few
minutes and put it outside the door. Bean is too little to be
able to manage the bread like that."

"Oh," Lily said.

"But in the meantime," he continued, carrying the wood
over to the fireplace, "I think what she really wants is to
be let outside to relieve herself. She's probably desperate."

"Oh," Lily said again, embarrassed that she hadn't
thought of that herself.

"It's fairly simple, Elizabeth. Think of what you need,
then apply the same criterion to Bean and see to her needs

first. As you remember, the privy is out back. Isn't Bean fortunate? She has the entire outdoors."

"You might have let her out yourself," Lily said grumpily.

"At five in the morning? Bean had no intention of leaving her bed. She ignored my suggestion and went straight back to sleep. Like her mistress, I don't think Bean is an early riser."

He turned back to light the fire. Lily would have liked to take that proverbial hatchet to his head, but Bean's imploring look propelled her toward the door.

When Lily came back inside, Pascal was laying out a breakfast of eggs and fresh bread. He'd even managed coffee. Lily looked at the table, then at her husband, then back at the table again, her mouth watering despite herself.

"How—how did you do that?"

"I went into the village earlier," he said nonchalantly, handing her a bowl of bread and milk and gesturing to the door.

"Thank you," she said stiffly.

"You can make it tomorrow. Sit down and eat your breakfast before it grows cold; we didn't have much of a supper last night, and you must be hungry. I have to be off to look at the vineyards. Will you be all right alone here?"

Lily desperately wanted to tell him that she wouldn't, but her pride prevented her. "Of course I will."

"Good. There's much to be done and you can make a start. If I were you I should concentrate on cleaning up the inside. I found a broom and some rags in the barn. Ah— you do know how to clean, don't you?"

Lily glared at him, wanting to scream with anger and humiliation, but she managed to hold it in. "I'm not helpless, you know. Go to the fields, but don't expect a meal when you get back."

"I wouldn't think of it. Have a pleasant morning. I'll give you a full report when I return."

Lily waited until he'd closed the door, then threw a tin cup after him. She looked at the chipped dishes and the greasy pan to be washed. She looked at the filthy room, the filthy windows, the ceilings and walls hung with cobwebs. She thought of the shining, magnificent life she was supposed to have had, of all the dreadful suitors she might have accepted who would have given it to her. And she had been reduced to this.

But worst of all, Jean-Jacques hadn't even lifted a finger to help her. Lily put her head in her hands and she cried.

Pascal walked every field he could find. It didn't take all that long, for he saw the same thing in each one. At least someone had seen that the vines had been pruned midwinter, but now many of them appeared to be suffering from a form of fungus. It wasn't erysiphe, from what he could tell, nor botrytis, the "noble rot" that was useful only when it attacked certain varieties of ripe white grapes. He wasn't exactly sure what it was, for he found oily patches on some of the leaves, and he'd never seen such a thing before.

But it was still a form of mildew, and the vines would have to be treated immediately or the mildew would destroy the leaves and later shrivel the grapes. Fortunately, he thought he knew of an effective remedy, for he'd had a long discussion with a notable oenologist in Vouvray on the subject of fungoid diseases and the very latest strides made in their treatment.

He doubted the mildew was the only problem; it seemed merely an opportunistic attack on a weak stock. Lily had said that this failure had been going on for some time, so there had to be other factors involved. He was fairly sure that the soil was depleted, which explained the sickly, almost yellowish hue of the leaves.

He bent over and picked up a clump of earth, first smelling it, then sifting it through his fingers, once again analyzing the contents. It was consistent throughout the fields: clay, chalk, and silica, an adequate—even desirable—combination for growing good grapes, but it had been overused and the minerals not correctly replenished. Ideally the earth should have been fertilized after the last harvest—but in this case, who knew when the last harvest had been? Still, the leaves were young, the vines not yet in flower, and there was a thread of hope.

Pascal looked up at the château, then drew in a deep breath. Lily's brother. It had not been difficult to assess that particular situation. What might be done to change it was the challenge. Jean-Jacques suffered from what Pascal was coming to think of as the Sutherby syndrome, a disorder brought on by a combination of lack of love, religious fanaticism, and constant drivel about the importance of money, station, and oneself. It was as debilitating to human nature as mildew and soil depletion were to vines.

However, whereas Lily had a natural fire to her spirit, Jean-Jacques struck him as weak. Pascal still could not believe that a supposedly loving brother had consigned his own sister to a cottage in such a state of disrepair and had forgotten to send his man with food and blankets to ease her first night. Sutherby training, he was sure. Jean-Jacques probably thought that someone else would take care of it and put the entire idea out of his head.

Pascal shook his head. In an odd way, the situation was exactly what he had prayed for, although he hadn't been quite so explicit about the dirt and cobwebs. God's idea of a joke, he imagined—but poor Lily. The look on her face had torn him between laughter and tears. Nevertheless, they would make the best of it, and if it meant Lily had to experience the sharp edge of poverty for a time, so be it. He would see to it that they didn't starve, or freeze, and she would be kept so busy that she wouldn't have time to think about anything else.

Jean-Jacques was another matter. He would have to be persuaded to some severe measures, and Pascal would have to see that he took them.

". . . In order to correct the situation you'll need large amounts of copper sulfate and slaked lime—*Bouillie Bordelaise* is the name of the mixture. Then sulfate of iron, among other minerals, liberally applied to the soil to cure the chlorosis of the vines—"

Jean-Jacques waved his hand impatiently, nearly knocking over his ale. "Never mind the details, man. How much will it cost?"

Pascal calculated the materials, adding a generous portion for the laborers into it, for they would need a good incentive to work as hard as they would have to. He added an extra margin, then named what he considered to be a reasonable price.

"I cannot possibly afford such a sum of money. Surely Lily has told you I am nearly penniless?"

"You have assets all about you," Pascal said. "There are things that can be sold. There are banks from which you can borrow; a mortgage can be taken against the estate if need be. It is really not so large an amount that I am asking for.''

''Are you mad? You are asking for a small fortune, you fool! How do you think I am going to raise money against vineyards that have done nothing but wither for thirty years? Tell me that.''

Pascal waited a moment before speaking, for it was obvious to him that Jean-Jacques was not listening as he paced about the room, pulling at his hair, and generally acting like an overgrown child, a tendency he shared with his sister.

''If you don't heed my advice,'' Pascal said as patiently as he could manage, when the man had finally flung himself into the chair behind his desk, ''I can guarantee that you will not have a crop this year, or in the years to come. Your problem is serious, but it is mendable. You should count yourself fortunate that you don't have to tear up all your stock and cleanse the soil, as sometimes happens.''

''I cannot see what difference that makes, given what I have now.'' Jean-Jacques drained his ale and scowled into his empty glass.

''It is simple. If you carry on as you are, you'll only continue to drain the estate. This is an investment in the future and one that has a chance of succeeding.''

''Why should I believe you? No one else has been able to offer me a solution, and you are nothing but a gardener.''

''Ah, but you can afford me, for I have asked no more pay of you than a gardener would. I have also been studying viticulture in my spare time. What I don't know about the subject, which is considerable, I do have access to.''

''Oh?'' Jean-Jacques asked sarcastically. ''You actually confess to ignorance, then?''

Pascal summoned every last drop of forbearance he had left. ''To a certain amount, yes. I plan on writing letters to some specialists today. However, I won't waste my time unless you are personally prepared to take on this project. You already know what sort of financial commitment you must make. Everything now rests on your decision.''

Jean-Jacques's eyes flickered. ''How much of a profit do you think I can make this year?''

Pascal shrugged. ''It's impossible to say. You may make none at all—it depends on whether there is time to turn this year's crop around. I think there is hope for it, but I can make no guarantees. I can't guarantee the weather either, which, as you must know, is critical.''

''Yes, of course I know that,'' Jean-Jacques said with annoyance.

''Good. Then you know that the weather has to hold reasonably well. But even if you have no profit this year, you'll be making a start on next year's crop. You won't have any good wines to sell for a few years, but you ought to be able to sell a portion of your crop to other vintners, should it be healthy and of fine quality. If not, you have less than nothing anyway. What's another painting or two against what you know will otherwise be a loss?''

''Then why won't you make me a loan yourself if you are so confident, Monsieur LaMartine?'' he said testily. ''It seems the easiest of solutions, doesn't it?''

It was not as if this hadn't occurred to Pascal, and he'd wondered how long it would take Jean-Jacques to bring the subject up. But although it would probably be the quickest way to get the necessary funds, the idea went against his grain. Jean-Jacques needed to commit himself to the land, and Pascal suspected that money out of Jean-Jacques's own pocket was the best way to ensure that he followed through with his commitment.

''I can't do that,'' Pascal said levelly. ''I'm sorry, for I can see that it would solve many of your problems. I'm here to offer my services, not to act as your banker. You must decide if you are willing to trust me. If you are not, your sister and I will leave this afternoon.''

He watched Jean-Jacques struggle, his long face pinched. It was interesting, the family resemblance, or lack of it, for though Lily and her brother shared the same thick auburn hair and strong cheekbones, they had little else in common save for a slim frame. Jean-Jacques's eyes were brown, and his nose was long and high-bridged, unlike Lily's, which Pascal could only describe as pert. Jean-Jacques's mouth thinned when he was angry or worried, whereas Lily's mouth did something else entirely. If rosebuds could be angry, that was Lily's mouth in a full-fledged pout. Then there was that sharp little chin that thrust forward, as obvious a sign of incipient rage as a red flag.

''Very well,'' Jean-Jacques said abruptly, breaking into Pascal's thoughts, ''I'll do it. Go ahead, order the necessary ingredients on my credit. I'll find the money somewhere.

Just get me a crop. And don't bother me with any of the rest, for I understand nothing about it, nor do I care to.''

"As you wish," Pascal replied. "I'll report to you only when necessary—but I will need to know when you have the funding, so that I can continue with the various things that need doing. I can't order on credit forever, and I have to keep the books updated. You also need to think past the crop to the tasks beyond. It we are successful, then we must be prepared for the *vendange*.''

"Oh, yes, of course," Jean-Jacques said, sounding bored.

"I haven't yet had a chance to see the winery, and naturally, should it come to that, you will need a properly trained wine-maker. It's imperative that the winery is in good order, for when the picking is complete, the vats have to be ready. Agreed?''

Jean-Jacques rubbed his eyes. "Yes. Agreed. Whatever.''

"Good. Oh, and would you send that man of yours with the things you promised last evening? Your sister is not accustomed to such spartan conditions as currently exist at the cottage.''

Jean-Jacques colored. "Oh. Yes, of course. How is Lily?''

"Coping, thank you, although she would be grateful for linens and candles and some warm blankets. Good day, then. Please, don't trouble yourself. I'll let myself out.''

Pascal left him standing by the crackling hearth looking like a sulky schoolboy. He reached the outdoors, drinking in deep breaths, for his encounter with Jean-Jacques had left him feeling airless.

The next order of business was to find the Monsieur Jamard whom Jean-Jacques had mentioned the evening before. Luckily enough, he was alive and well and sitting in the village square enjoying a café-cognac.

"Monsieur, may I?" Pascal asked, approaching the table in the sun that the *patron* had pointed to.

The old man glanced up, narrowed his eyes, then nodded at the chair opposite.

Pascal sat down and ordered a coffee from the hovering waiter, who appeared very interested in his business with Monsieur Jamard.

He waited until the disappointed waiter had disappeared before speaking. "Monsieur, I am newly arrived in your

village. My name is Pascal LaMartine, and my wife and I
have taken the old cottage up on the hill after the turning.''

"Baumerd's cottage? That is all very interesting, monsieur, but what has that to do with me?'' The old man eyed
him warily.

"I am to manage the Saint-Simon estate, including the
vineyards, and Monsieur le Duc told me that you are the
man to whom I should speak regarding their history.''

Monsieur Jamard's hand jerked in surprise and his coffee
splashed over the side of the saucer. "Monsieur le Duc, you
say? And you his wine-maker? No—this cannot be possible.''

"I'm no wine-maker, monsieur. I'm merely a man who
knows a little about the earth. This earth is sick, I believe
more from benign neglect than anything else.''

"What makes you think this?'' Jamard asked, regarding
Pascal with deep suspicion.

"I've studied the way of the earth for some time. I don't
pretend to know everything, but I do have a feel for the
land, and in order to make it well again, I need to know
about the past. Can you tell me?''

Monsieur Jamard took a sip of cognac and considered
this, muttering under his breath for a moment or two, shaking his head back and forth as if he were having a private
conversation. Finally he nodded. "LaMartine. LaMartine.
It is not an uncommon name in these parts, but we lost the
last of them some years ago. We lost so many in the great
sickness.

"I'm sorry,'' Pascal said. "It must have been hard.''

Monsieur Jamard sighed. "Ah, well,'' he said. "God's
will.'' He peered at Pascal closely. "I do not see as well as
I used to, but you have a familiar look about you. Where
are your people from, boy?''

"From Paris, monsieur.''

"Ah. It must be a distant branch of the family. The
LaMartines were good people, honest and hardworking, a
cut above us peasants.''

"I'm happy that you held them in esteem.''

The old man nodded slowly. "Yes, those were good days
before the sixth duke and his family died. He cared for the
land, the people. We were prosperous then, with fine har-
vests—some years better than others, of course. Then the
typhoid came and took him away, and his brother came.

Bah! For Saint-Simon, seven was an unlucky number.'' He spat into the dirt.

"I gather you didn't think much of the duke's brother?'' Pascal asked mildly.

"A wastrel, monsieur. He was careless, that one. Bad to his wife—English, she was, and a good friend to the dear duchess. But after, she was on her own; the duke was never here, leaving her all alone with the child. It was just as well the seventh duke was killed in that hunting accident. No, nothing has been the same since his brother died—and now we have this one, the nephew, who throws the land away.''

"Not anymore. With luck and a great deal of work the land will come back—of this I am certain.''

"Well, maybe the old story was right, then, and the heir's return will finally make things grow. Better late than never. You have come to the right man, monsieur.'' He took a long sip of his cognac, then carefully set the glass back down on the table and excused himself, going to take relief around the corner.

Pascal waited.

Monsieur Jamard ambled back. "Between you, me, and the wall, this new duke, he is a fool,'' he said, sitting back down. "It surprises me that he even bothered to mention my name, for he has never listened to anything before. Why should he listen now?''

"It's not he who is listening, monsieur. I've been hired to listen for him. Monsieur le Duc realizes that he has no talent for this sort of thing, and he sees the sorry state that the vines have come to. So, understanding that, and also realizing that the village suffers as a result, he wishes to make things better.''

"About time too, after all these years. God be praised, but even God will have a difficult time with these blighted fields. What do you know about it, anyway, boy? What's your training? No point wasting my time if you don't know what you're talking about.''

Pascal pulled his chair a little closer and began the delicate process of eliciting trust from one who had long ago forsaken the practice.

11

LILY was ready to drop from exhaustion. The windows were—well, they weren't exactly clean, more smudged—but the floors were swept, and she had managed to eliminate most of the spiderwebs. That had been a horrific task in itself. She slumped in one of the chairs at the table, her head on her arms. She barely managed to raise it when she heard the front door open.

"Elizabeth . . . you look tired," Pascal said, entering the room with a large canvas sack that he dropped on the table. "I see you've been working hard. I'm very impressed."

"Go hang," Lily said succinctly.

"Not just yet. It's been a fruitful day. Here, we actually have dinner, and I have a decent pot in which to cook it. Where's Bean?"

Lily raised her head. "She's tied up in the barn. I spent a good hour trying to get her to leave some godforsaken burrow she'd found."

"Did you try picking her up and carting her away?"

Lily dragged the back of one hand across her aching forehead. "I wish you'd stop trying to make me feel like an idiot. If I'd been able to get to her I would have done just that, but she was on the other side of the stream and there was no crossing. So I called and called and she finally came. Are you satisfied?"

"Very, and I'm sorry if you've had a miserable time." He began to take all manner of things out of his sack and within minutes good smells wafted through the air.

She sat up and looked with more attention. He'd sliced bacon, carrots, onion, and garlic and thrown them all into the pot that sat simmering over the fire she'd miraculously kept going out of sheer desperation. He was now cutting up some kind of raw meat.

"What is that?" Lily asked, not sure she really wanted to know.

"Rabbit. A farmer gave it to me when I stopped to help him mend his wheel."

"Was it dead?"

"Oh, yes." Pascal looked up with a grin. "I wouldn't have risked bringing it home in any other condition." He tossed the pieces in the pot as well, and in another moment the smell of braising meat joined the other odors. Lily's mouth began to water.

"Will it be ready soon?" she asked longingly, watching him pour wine into the pot along with some wild herbs he'd pulled from a jacket pocket.

"In about an hour and a half," he said, putting the lid on. "I thought I'd build a fire next door and heat some bathing water. Would you like that?"

Lily nodded fervently. "Yes. Oh, yes, please." She could have kicked herself for sounding so desperate, but in truth she was, and nothing was going to keep her from a bath and a hot meal, not even pride.

He was as good as his word. He stoked the fire until the room had a lovely glowing warmth to it. He had found a small tub somewhere and filled it with hot water. It wasn't large enough to actually climb into, but it was large enough to be able to dip various parts of herself into one at a time, and oh, it felt so wonderful. When she finally emerged with a clean body, clean hair, and a clean dress, she almost felt like Elizabeth Bowes again, although the heat had made her so sleepy that she could have lain down in front of the fire and never opened her eyes again—if she hadn't been so hungry. The smell coming from the hearth was incredible. The wretch definitely had a useful side.

He glanced up from a stack of writing paper as she emerged. "Better?"

"Yes, thank you. What are you doing?"

"Writing letters, although I'm about to have a thorough wash."

"Oh. But won't it take forever for you to heat more water? Surely the stew will be ready soon?"

"Yes, but I'll use the extra water I left on the hearth. I won't be long." He pushed back his chair and started toward the other room.

Lily colored hotly. "I—I didn't realize. I used it myself," she finally said.

Pascal halted midstride and turned to look at her. "You used it *all*?"

"Yes. I washed my hair."

"It didn't occur to you that I might be in need of a wash as well?" he asked.

"N-no. It didn't."

Pascal sighed. "Never mind. I suppose you think that people like myself naturally gravitate outside to bathe in freezing streams, or perhaps you think we don't bathe at all. You must be worried about when the stench is going to set in. How good of you not to have mentioned it, but I'm sure you were trying to spare my feelings."

"I'm sorry," Lily said. She thought that he was teasing again, but she wasn't entirely sure.

"It's all right, Elizabeth. I'll survive."

"I'm not accustomed to this sort of thing." Hot tears began to slide down her cheeks and she turned away, even more mortified.

Unexpectedly, Pascal walked over to her and turned her around to face him. "I know you're not. I realize this is difficult for you, and you're doing a valiant job. Just look at the windows—why they're—they're . . ." Pascal fought for the right words for the smeared panes.

"They're horrible," Lily said, hanging her head in misery. "I don't know what went wrong, but everything seemed to get worse instead of better."

"Never mind. Vinegar, water, and newsprint will work wonders. I learned that trick from the monks, not that we have the necessary ingredients on hand. And look, you've managed to clean years of dust away." He said nothing about the great pile of dirt he'd stumbled on when he tried to cross the threshold. "Forget about the bath water—it's not worth upsetting yourself over. Just try to keep in mind the next time that there are two of us."

Lily furiously brushed at her cheeks. "I will try. This is very new to me."

Pascal gently chucked her chin. "I know. It will become easier, I promise."

"It would have been much easier if you had let my brother help us. It would have been even easier than that if you were not so stubborn about my money."

"Your brother didn't offer to help. In fact, he seemed pleased to have us here rather than at the château. I'm sure he prizes his privacy."

"Jean-Jacques isn't like that," she insisted. "He is kind, and generous, and caring. You just don't know him, and you're predisposed to think badly of him because he is my brother."

"I'm not predisposed to anything but restoring the vineyards—and this place," he said.

"I am sure that Jean-Jacques had no idea what a terrible state this cottage was in, for he would never have put me here had he known."

"I'm sure you're right," Pascal said, lying because he didn't think Lily could take more disillusionment. He could only hope that with time she would see the brother she idolized in a more realistic light.

"Can't we use a little of my money to make it better?" Lily asked hopefully.

"No. We will live on what I can afford. I don't believe that your money would be of any help to your brother, and it certainly would be no help to us."

"Money is always of help," Lily said, sniffing miserably.

"That depends on whom it is helping."

"I—I don't know if I can survive another night here, Pascal. There are lumps in the mattress. And spiders in the walls, even though I tried to sweep their webs away."

"You'll feel better once you've eaten, and I think you'll sleep so soundly that you won't notice your bed or the lumps, or even the spiders, whom you probably put the fear of God into today. They must have felt as if a typhoon had just blown through, after years of blissfully uninterrupted peace."

Lily gave him an uncertain smile. "Yes. I suppose so. I'm not particularly fond of spiders."

"I doubt they're very fond of you either. But all that aside, I'm going to wash, then we'll have a nice dinner and some good local wine. Why don't you fetch Bean from the barn and give her some dinner from the pot, then let her out for a few minutes? I won't be very long. And Elizabeth?"

"Yes?"

"If it's any consolation, I think you're being very brave."

"You do?" Her eyes widened, for this was an enormous compliment coming from the wretch.

"I do. It's not easy taking on a complete change of life-style, and under such difficult circumstances, but you rolled up your sleeves and tackled it. You should feel proud of yourself."

"Thank you," she whispered, absurdly pleased.

"You earned every word. Will you set the table? I've cleared my papers away."

"Yes, of course," Lily said, forgetting her resentment. She put out two plates, two glasses, and knives and forks. Then she nervously eyed the wooden board where the baguette of bread sat on what passed for a kitchen counter. She figured that it had to be easier to slice bread on an unmoving board than on her lap in a bumping carriage, so she took the knife to it, this time careful to saw in extra-wide slices. For some odd reason they came out fat on top and thin on bottom, but that was better than having holes everywhere.

Feeling pleased about that, she filled a bowl for Bean, taking the precaution of wrapping her hand in a clean rag before approaching the pot. The bulk made it a little awkward to take the lid off, but she managed.

A delectable smell burst from the pot in a cloud of mouth-watering steam. She didn't think she'd ever smelled anything quite so wonderful before, and it made her stomach churn in painful hunger. Having to feed a dog first went entirely against her grain, and she considered eating the whole thing herself, but then she remembered that little Bean would be just as hungry as she was, and she was supposed to be a civilized person. Eating the dog's dinner was just not done. Life in a hovel was already affecting her.

Lily sighed heavily and put the bowl on the floor, watching enviously as Bean wolfed her meal down; then she took the puppy outside and watched her play foolishly about, finally getting around to business only as an afterthought. She brought Bean back in and sat down to wait for Pascal to emerge so that she could finally eat.

He appeared only minutes later, his hair damp, his face freshly shaved, for she noticed the nick on one cheek.

"If you had a valet," she said pointedly, "that sort of accident wouldn't happen."

"If I had a valet," he said wryly, "I'd have been shaved with hot water, which generally helps prevent such things."

"Have you ever had a valet?" Lily asked, not wanting to get back onto the subject of hot water.

"When I lived at Raven's Close, Binkley served in all capacities. He would not have thanked any intrusion onto his terrain. In later years, I sometimes had someone who looked after things, but not in the role of a valet, for he would have had to be quite an unusual man."

"Why?" Lily asked. "And what could possibly take the place of a valet?"

"I had a bearer, or a porter, or any of the equivalent, depending on where I happened to be. Most valets are not taken with climbing over mountain passes with one's belongings strapped to them."

"Really? You've climbed over mountain passes? I suppose I'm not surprised. Charlie said you had a way of disappearing into the back of beyond."

"Did he?" Pascal ladled the rabbit stew out onto the plates, and Lily couldn't help but notice the strands of damp hair that curled over the nape of his neck and the pull of the linen shirt across the muscles of his back. She blushed and looked away.

"Yes, he did. As far as I'm concerned, this is more than far enough in the back of beyond."

Pascal straightened, his eyes sparkling with amusement as he put the plates down. "Is it? I consider this quite civilized."

"You would," Lily said, annoyed, for all that bravery he'd complimented her for seemed diminished by the thought that he'd experienced much worse.

Pascal uncorked the dark wine and poured it into the glasses. "Do let's eat. I'm famished." He pushed the lopsided bread toward her.

Lily didn't need an invitation. She dived into her meal as if she would never eat again. "How did you do this?" she asked when her hunger was sated enough to allow her to speak.

"You watched most of it. Take whatever is available, cut it up, add some herbs and some spices if you have them, then some wine or stock or even water, and let it all cook together." He made a stirring motion. "When the meat is tender enough to fall off the bone, it's done. But you might be overestimating my culinary abilities. It's said that appetite is the best sauce, and from the way you've been eating, I'd say you have a very healthy appetite.''

"I've never had anything like this," she said, mopping up the sauce with her bread.

"How much time did you spend in the vast kitchens of Sutherby?" he asked, watching her with amusement. "I doubt you wandered in that direction at all.''

"Only to escape my tutor," Lily admitted, "and I only went through the pantries.'' She took another deep swallow of the wine, enjoying the earthy flavor and savoring the warmth it spread through her body.

"You've made my point. It's a shame, because there's an art to food.'' He smiled at her over his glass.

"I suppose I've never thought about it before," Lily said. "Food just appeared on the table. I didn't wonder about how it was prepared, or from what.''

"Why should you? Your ears were probably being filled with religious tracts and opinions, if my experience with Father Mallet is anything to go by. He's enough to make anyone lose his appetite.''

She nodded vigorously, cleaning up the very last morsel of stew. "That's true enough. I hadn't realized you were subjected to Father Mallet at the table.''

Pascal held out his hand for her plate. "What a load of drivel. I would have escaped to the kitchen if I'd had the chance—you would have benefited by escaping to the kitchens too.''

"We weren't supposed to mingle with the servants," Lily said, her eyes fixed on the ladle he was using to dole out a second helping.

"Pity," he said, handing her plate back with more stew on it. "There's a lot you might have learned from them.''

"I can't think what," Lily said, frowning. "I received a perfectly good education.''

He laughed. "A little less education and a little more attention to the realities of life would have done wonders for you. It's useful to know how to feed oneself, don't you think?''

"I suppose so," she said, taking another piece of bread, waiting while he refilled her glass.

"One of the best places to learn is in a peasant kitchen, because the people have learned to make the best of the simplest foods.'' He pointed at her plate with his fork.

"Like tonight's dinner. This was no plump and pampered rabbit kept in a cage and fed on table scraps. This rabbit was the reason for the broken wheel and his own broken neck."

"Oh. I wouldn't have thought that a rabbit would be large enough to break a wheel." She dug into her second helping, feeling no sympathy for the rabbit, too happy to eat it.

"It wasn't," he replied, serving himself. "The farmer was annoyed that he'd allowed his wheel to become so loose. I wasn't about to argue when he handed the poor thing over, along with the sack of vegetables, since I wasn't sure what we were going to have for dinner." He smiled apologetically. "I have to confess, I'm not the best provider when it comes to meat. I'm willing to eat it if it's already dead, but I'm hopeless when it comes to the act itself."

"No? What about fish?" she asked, remembering what Charlie had said.

"Only marginally easier."

"Birds?"

Pascal winced. "No, I can't eat anything that flies. Chickens are all right for some reason, but nothing with proper wings. I must sound like a lunatic."

No, you sound like a very sweet and dear person, Lily thought, and then brought herself up short. A sweet and dear person was nothing that meshed in any way with her understanding of this man. The wine and her own exhaustion were causing her mind to play tricks on her. She refused to have tender feelings for the wretch who had caused her such misery to begin with.

"I am sure you have your reasons," she said instead.

"Actually, I do, but they're not worth enumerating. I'm pleased you enjoyed the stew." He turned his attention back to his meal, and Lily felt as if he'd just shut a door in her face. It bothered her, although she didn't understand why. She'd had doors slammed in her face all of her life.

"Pascal," she said tentatively, after a few minutes of silence had passed, "did I say something to make you angry?"

He looked up at her, his eyes puzzled. "Why would you think I was angry? Because of what I said earlier about the water? I was only joking."

"I know," she said, a flush creeping into her cheeks at the reminder of her thoughtlessness.

"Thank God you do," he replied, leaning back in his chair. "I was beginning to think your sense of humor had been misplaced. But you didn't answer my question—why did you ask if I was angry?"

"Because your expression turned aloof."

"Really?" Pascal said, gazing at her with fascination. "What do I look like the rest of the time—other than when I'm scowling? I've never had such an analysis of my face as I've had in the last few days. It's quite an education."

"You look—I don't know. You don't look so forbidding."

Pascal thought this over. "Forbidding. That sounds exactly like Father Mallet. How depressing."

"Oh, no—it's nothing like Father Mallet," she said quickly. "It's just as if you've gone away and I can't tell what you're thinking."

"Does what I'm thinking matter to you?" he asked softly, turning his glass around on the table.

Lily shifted uneasily. "No, of course not."

There was a small silence. "I see," he said and looked away.

Something in Lily's chest rolled over as she sensed she had touched another nerve. "That's not true," she amended. "It does matter. It's difficult to know where one stands with you."

The firelight flickered across his face, highlighting the strong bones, casting parts of his skin into shadow. She realized he had a slight touch of sunburn on the tip of his nose.

He brushed away the lock of hair that kept falling onto his forehead and regarded her steadily, his cheek resting on his palm, his fingers curved into his hand. "Not *everything* you say has a negative effect, you know."

"Are you teasing again?" she asked uncertainly.

"No, I'm not," he said quietly. "I'm quite serious."

Lily pulled her eyes away from his, suddenly uncomfortable under his scrutiny. When he looked at her like that, she felt vulnerable, exposed, as if he could see straight through her. "I suppose I'm accustomed to having a negative effect, so that's what I expect," she mumbled.

"I know," he answered gently. "I think in a perverse way you use that as armor, so that no one can get near."

A shock ran directly through her, and she sat bolt upright. "What a presumptuous thing to say!"

Pascal, instead of taking offense, smiled. "Case in point." He abruptly changed the subject. "I think it's time for you to go to bed. Don't worry, I'll do the dishes."

Lily, who had not even considered washing the dishes, stood. "Very well," she said glacially. The last thing she wanted was for the wretch to see he'd shaken her.

"I'm going out with Bean," he said, with a catch of laughter in his voice. "I doubt I'll see you in the morning, but I'll bring some bread and milk and cheese back from the village and leave them on the table."

"Oh—I don't know what I could have been thinking. I forgot to ask you about the vineyards. Are you going to be able to fix them?"

"I don't know. I hope so, and I intend to try, but you might say a prayer or two."

"I don't pray," Lily said curtly, starting up the stairs.

"I know that too. But it's never too late to start—you might be amazed by the results."

She tossed her head, but all that accomplished was to make her wince. Every muscle in her body ached. "You can do the praying. I'm going to sleep."

"Good night, duchess," he said softly.

"Good night, gardener," she replied, and went the rest of the way up the stairs. But as she readied herself for bed, she couldn't help but wonder why his last words had felt like the gentlest of touches on her soul.

12

SHE hated the house, she hated the backbreaking work, she hated her life.

For the next three weeks Pascal disappeared after dinner and returned after sunset with something for the pot. Lily was usually too tired to care what it was, though she was always grateful to eat it. They would talk a little about the day as Pascal painted her some colorful portraits of the villagers. Why he found them so interesting was beyond her. Her previous contact, although limited, had caused her to despise them, just as much as they despised her and her brother. She imagined it was how all peasants felt about their betters.

For the first few days she had been sure that Jean-Jacques was playing one of his silly tricks on her and would come and rescue her from her misery. Instead, he didn't come at all. After nearly a week she had swallowed her pride and trudged up the hill for an explanation of his desertion.

"I am sorry," the servant who opened the door said. "Monsieur le Duc left for Paris five days ago."

"Paris? Without telling me?"

The woman only shrugged. "I am sorry. I know nothing more."

Lily trudged back to her hovel, her spirits lower than she would have thought possible. Pascal later informed her that Jean-Jacques had gone to finance a loan for the vineyards. They'd had a raging argument over that—or rather, she raged and the wretch simply did not listen. He didn't back down from his ridiculous position either.

"Jean-Jacques has to take responsibility for his own property, Elizabeth. It won't be any good to him or anyone else unless he does. Think about it for a minute—he wouldn't have come to Saint-Simon at all unless he'd been forced to when he ran out of funds in Paris. What do you suppose he'd been doing with that part of his inheritance?''

"I won't have you talking about my brother in such a way!''

"I'm not trying to insult him, I'm only pointing out the obvious. What did you see when you came to visit your brother earlier in the year? Did you see him doing anything to improve his situation?''

"He was despondent,'' she said defensively. "He didn't know what to do. That is why I went . . . never mind.''

"That is why you went where?'' he asked, looking up from his papers.

"Why, I . . . why I was going back to my father,'' she improvised, not about to disgrace herself by offering him the truth. "I intended to ask him for his help, or at least to release some of my dowry to me so that I could help Jean-Jacques.''

"You can't be serious! You don't really expect me to believe that? You yourself told me that your father and Jean-Jacques fought constantly, that there was no love lost between them.''

"No. There wasn't. But I couldn't think of anything else to do, or anyone else to turn to.''

"No. I suppose you couldn't. But really, Elizabeth, you must let your brother fend for himself.''

"Why? Why should I? We have only each other in this world. Why should I not want to see to his welfare?''

"As he has seen to yours?''

Lily tilted her chin forward. "It is only because he can afford nothing else.''

"And neither can we, so let us leave the subject alone.'' He bent his head back to the accounts, effectively dismissing her. Lily seethed for the rest of the evening, banging pots and pans and generally being as disruptive as possible, but it had no effect aside from eliciting a few irritated shakes of the wretch's head as he tried to concentrate.

She furiously wrung out his wet trousers, pretending she was wringing his neck. She felt utterly deserted, left to her fate in the hands of a mule-headed man who had no sympathy for her or her brother, or what should have been their proper positions in life. What did he care? What did he even know about it? He had not been born to wealth or privilege. His miserable blood did not carry the generations of breeding that would enable him to understand the finer points of life.

He went off every day into the fields like the laborer he was, mingling happily with the peasants, coming home with filthy clothes that she had to wash—which was exactly what she had to do at this time every morning so that the sun would have a chance to dry them before the blasted evening dew made them wet all over again.

Lily stood up, her back aching, her knuckles raw. She threw the wet clothes into a basket and heaved it up, going to the washing line and hanging the clothes out in neat rows. And hadn't *he* thought it was funny, the first time he'd seen the results of her labor.

"Oh, dear, duchess," he said. "I think you have some learning to do. Look, if you hang shirts by their ends rather than their cuffs, they'll look better when all is said and done, and it's much less ironing for you to do." He showed her, rearranging her painstaking work. "It goes the same for skirts and petticoats. And look here, one peg will work as well to hold two pieces together if you put them side by side like this."

She'd felt like pinning him onto the washing line by his ears. Then there had been the time that he found her on her hands and knees, trying to figure out how to cut up the chicken he'd brought home. He'd plucked it for her, thank God, but still, she couldn't make out how to turn it into small, neat pieces. She finally took the ax to it, which was not very successful. The wretch laughed until he cried.

She really did not see the amusement.

When it came to crying, Lily was too tired at night to indulge herself. But every morning when she opened her eyes she was forced to face her miserable destiny. Every morning the tears streamed down her face as she washed it, as she went out to the dreadful privy, as she faced the prospect of the day ahead, the never-ending chores, knowing that there was no end in sight to any of it.

Bean was the only comfort she had, and she talked to the puppy all day long. Bean seemed to like it, though, for she stayed nearby, sunning herself while Lily slaved in the vegetable garden that the wretch had insisted on laying out, and finding a comfortable place near the hearth when Lily slaved inside. At least Bean was there for her, even if no one else cared about her misery.

"A person needs someone to talk to, doesn't she, Bean?"
Lily said, drying her hands. "Do you know, even Father
Mallet's droning would be preferable to all this silence.
Well, maybe not. Come on, the laundry is done. It's time
to do the weeding—and this time stay out of the lettuce."

At least the weather was warming and the wretch had
given up his constant worrying about frosts hurting the vines
before they flowered. One would have thought they were his
children, the way he fussed over them. Lily knew she should
be happy that he did, but she was jealous, for not only did
he spend all day with the vines but when he came home at
night he did nothing but read about them, trying to educate
himself, and then he went back out to sleep in them. Vines,
grapes, diseases were the wretch's world. Weeding, washing, crying were hers. Oh, *what* she would give to escape,
if she could only think of a way.

Lily thought about the small chest again. It had come
with the wretch from Raven's Close and sat in the corner of
the room.

"I wish I knew what was in that chest, Bean. What deep,
dark secret could the wretch have that would necessitate
keeping something locked and the key hidden? Money? No,
I don't think so, do you? If he'd wanted money he could
have helped himself to mine. It's obviously something that
he doesn't want me to know about." She yanked out another weed and put it into her basket.

"Maybe he has compromising love letters hidden away
. . . that would be typical, wouldn't it? Or maybe there's
some evidence of a terrible crime he committed." She sat
back on her heels. "Wouldn't it be wonderful if there were
something as awful as a body in there? I realize that the
chest's too small for a body. Well, I suppose one would fit
if it had been hacked into small pieces, but still, there would
be the smell."

Bean wagged her tail vigorously.

"Anyway, if I could find something, some sort of incrim-
inating evidence, then I could annul this terrible marriage
and regain my life."

Lily closed her eyes. Visions of servants and soft beds
and suitors vying to kiss her white hands danced before her
eyes. She would never scoff at another suitor as long as she
lived, she swore it. There would be constant banquets—oh,
lots of lovely food. She could see it now, tables and tables

of food. Sweets and savories and great joints of meat . . . and no wretch anywhere in sight.

"Whatever it is must be enthralling," a deep voice said above her head, and Lily started, jerked out of her fantasy.

Her gaze fell on a pair of boots and traveled all the way up to her husband's face. Her hand crept to her mouth, wondering how long he'd been standing there and whether she'd been talking to herself or not.

"I—what are you doing home at this hour?" she demanded, badly flustered.

"What, is that all the welcome I get? Actually, I thought I'd work on the house. You've been very patient about waiting, and now that we've nearly finished the last of the pruning, I'm going to take an afternoon off." He squinted up at the cottage. "I'm going to start on the shutters. Some nails, a few bolts, and a fresh coat of paint ought to do wonders."

Lily nodded.

"Why in God's name are you looking so guilty? Do you have a lover hidden under your skirts, or were you thinking of various diabolic ways to dispatch me? There has to be some reason for that beatific smile I saw on your face."

Lily gave a horrified laugh, thinking he was far too close to the truth on the latter guess. "Actually, I was thinking of soft beds," she said.

"Oh, well that explains everything—I think."

"I can't think it means anything to you, since you seem happiest sleeping on the ground."

"I like sleeping under the stars. Well, to be honest, I like sleeping under the stars when the weather is fine. It's actually not so bad, duchess. You ought to try it sometime."

"Not on your life. I'll take lumps in my mattress any day."

"You would, being too stubborn to try something different. I brought home a treat to have for a midday meal. I thought we could eat outside since the weather's so nice."

"What did you bring, Pascal?" she asked with a surge of excitement.

"Go inside and see for yourself," he said, holding out his hand to help her up from her knees. She pointedly refused it and he shrugged.

"It's no feast, but it's better than the usual fare of bread and cheese."

Lily wanted to cry when she saw the nice fat pâté he'd

somehow managed to produce. Wrapped in another bundle
were a pickled *tête de veau* and a shiny head of lettuce. A
luncheon. They were actually going to have a luncheon. It
was too good to be true.

She quickly laid the table that sat outside under the walnut tree and spread the food out, opened the bottle of cold
white wine, then stood back to admire her efforts.

Perfect. It almost looked civilized. Well, perhaps not civilized, since there was no cloth to cover the warped wood
of the table and only the usual stubby glasses for the wine
instead of fine crystal, but as the wretch had said, it was
better than the usual. At least it was a warm day, and the
sun was shining, and Pascal was finally going to mend the
shutters.

She followed the banging of a hammer, intending to call
him for lunch. But as she rounded the corner, she came to
a sudden halt, her hand creeping to her mouth.

He was up on a ladder, nailing two of the long shutter
boards together, his shirt casually looped over one of the
middle rungs of the ladder. The sun beat down on his
bronzed back, a faint sheen running over his powerful
shoulders and the long, smooth muscles that divided his
spine and ran across his shoulder blades, shifting beneath
his skin as he rhythmically drove the nails home.

Lily had never seen anyone's naked back before, save for
glimpses of her own when she'd craned her neck over her
shoulder to look in the mirror, and it certainly hadn't looked
like *that*. He was magnificent, a perfect balance of grace
and power. He looked like the Da Vinci sketch of a nude
male she'd found in a portfolio in her father's library. She'd
taken it out and hidden it in her room to study in private—
until Coffey discovered it and took it away, reading her a
stern and alarmed lecture about the sins of the flesh. Everyone forever lectured her about the sins of the flesh, as if she
were in constant mortal danger.

Lily could see why. Something hot and unfamiliar radiated outward from deep in her belly, making her feel disoriented and breathless, heavy with a nameless wanting.

She swallowed, thinking she was fortunate that Father
Mallet wasn't anywhere around to read her thoughts or he'd
have flailed her alive. It was no wonder he and her father
had filled the house with ugly men. They must have realized
that she was prone to these fits of lust.

She shut her eyes for a moment, hoping the terrifying feeling would go away as quickly as it had come, but when she opened her eyes again, it was still there, the wretch's back was still bare, and she still wanted nothing more than to run her hands down over the muscles, to feel those hard curves under her fingers, to put those mouth to his warm skin and taste the salt with her tongue. . . .

He turned and looked down, as if he'd felt her scrutiny.

"Is it time for . . . what is it, duchess?" he asked. "You look as if the sky just fell in."

"*It did,* she thought miserably, noting that his front side was just as magnificent as the back, a beautiful, solid wall of sculpted muscle. And she had thought Leonardo da Vinci had been idealizing the male form.

"You didn't drop the pâté, did you?" he asked with a grin. "I can't think what else would make you look so shaken."

"No. The pâté is on the table. I came to tell you that everything is ready. You should come before the wine grows warm."

He nodded, giving her a puzzled look, but obligingly descended the ladder, picking up his shirt on the way and shrugging it on. Lily averted her eyes, then turned away, quickly heading back to the table.

He appeared a few minutes later, his hands and face still damp from washing, and sat down opposite her.

He picked up the bottle to pour the wine, and Lily stared at the fine, dark hair that was lightly scattered over the back of his hand. She knew now that the same fine, dark hair grew on his forearms too, and she couldn't help but admire the shape of his fingers as he took a piece of bread from the basket.

They ate in silence, Lily keeping her eyes fixed on her plate. Her stomach felt hollow, but not with hunger, despite her eager anticipation of the treat. All she could think of was the large and very masculine body in front of her, the powerful musculature that lay beneath his clothes.

"All right," he said, wiping his mouth when he'd finished and examining her speculatively. "What is it? You've been behaving in a very odd fashion since I appeared unexpectedly."

"I—I'm not used to having company during the day." She stood and began to gather the dishes.

"I know, and I'm sorry for that. But until the vineyards are under control, I won't have much time to spend here." He reached over to take the dishes from her.

"No! I mean, it's really not necessary."

"Oh? And why is that? Are you telling me that you'd prefer me not to help you?"

Lily fidgeted. "No, I'd just rather have you do other things around the house. I know nothing about carpentry or masonry or that sort of thing."

"I wouldn't expect you to, but that doesn't explain why you're behaving as if you have a guilty secret. For the life of me, I can't think what it is, unless you really do have one of the farmer's sons hidden away somewhere." He regarded her curiously.

Lily blushed crimson. "I certainly do not! I would *never* do such a thing!"

"Why, because it would be adultery, or because the poor man would be merely a farmer's son?"

Lily exploded. "What do you think of me?" she said furiously. "I've done nothing but clean and wash and weed and—and wait on you hand and foot, and all with no choice in the matter." The anger and resentment that she'd been building up for weeks came pouring out in a single furious rush.

"First you try to ravish me, then you take me away from everything I've ever known, drop me among strangers, force me to live like an—an animal, and all because you're too proud to accept my dowry. Now, on top of that, you accuse me of being an adulteress? How dare you!"

"I was only joking. And I have to confess, I'm surprised by this tantrum you're having. I thought you'd given up the habit."

"I am not having a tantrum," she said, struggling for control. "I am justifiably angry. You seem to think it's fine for you to go off all day and most of the night and do whatever you please, while I am supposed to stay here and do your chores for you."

"I expect you to carry your weight," he said levelly, but his color was as high as hers.

"Oh, and I do, every last ounce of it, and don't you dare accuse me of shirking!"

"I didn't—" he started to say, but she cut him off.

"Well, now that I'm a gardener's wife, a farmer's son

might be suitable company—certainly better company than none at all—and how do *I* know you're not bedding some farmer's buxom daughter? It would be in character, wouldn't it? I'm sure you've been having a fine time out in the fields late at night. No wonder you like to sleep outside—vines must be truly appealing when viewed from ground level.''

Pascal's eyes snapped in sudden anger. "That's absurd, and you know it. I'm sorry if you've been lonely, but I've been busy trying to rescue your precious brother's vineyards. And why, Elizabeth? Because you damn well asked!''

"I've never asked a thing of you. Nothing except to give my own money to my brother, and that one thing you refused.''

"I may have refused you that, but I brought you here, didn't I?'' he replied tightly, his jaw clenching.

"You brought me here because you wanted a job and probably couldn't find one anywhere else.'' She was about to poke him on his chest with her finger, but thought better of it. "Then you further humiliated me by dragging me to this hovel and forcing me to be your personal slave.''

"My personal slave?'' he said, glaring down at her. "Are you out of your mind? What in the name of God do you expect, that I come home after working all day and do your chores as well? You live here too and you can damn well contribute—and you can damn well stop complaining about it, because it's not going to change.''

Lily glared back at him. "Well, I hope you're happy. I hope you're truly satisfied, because I'm miserable. I hate this, and I hate you for bringing me to it. Even my own brother was too embarrassed to visit me here before he left, knowing what I have come to.''

Pascal, who had been about to take her head off, was stopped short by this unbelievable incongruity, stopped short by Lily herself. She looked like an avenging angel, her eyes blazing, her hair falling about her shoulders, the sun lighting it from behind like a fiery halo. But there was something different about this Lily.

He'd been so distracted with the vineyards over the last three weeks that he hadn't paid attention to the changes in her, other than that she'd stopped her constant needling. Yet here she was, her face lightly touched with sun beneath the angry pink of her cheeks, a delicate scattering of freckles across her nose.

Her body had a new ease to it, as if daily work had relaxed her rigid posture, and her muscles were becoming sleek and well conditioned. This Lily was human, touchable—far too touchable, he thought with disbelief, feeling his groin tighten with unexpected arousal.

He tore his gaze away from her and stared at the ground.

"Don't you have anything to say?" she demanded.

"I'm sorry," he said, rubbing his eyebrow.

"What?" Her hands dropped from her slim waist in complete surprise.

"I said, I'm sorry." He looked up at her. "You're right, you are justified in your anger, but it has never been my intention to make you feel demeaned or insulted."

"Do you expect me to believe that?"

"Yes," he said simply.

"Well, I don't."

"I wish you would," he said softly. "It would mean a great deal to me if you learned to believe me—and not just about this."

Lily's eyes narrowed. "I think you have a bad case of sunstroke."

"Yes, that must be it. In which case I'm going back to mending the shutters so that you won't have to listen to any more of my madness. Do you know, duchess, you're actually becoming a nice person. I think I rather like you. Or do you think the sun really has affected my brain?"

He turned and disappeared back around the corner.

Lily stared after him, wondering if it wasn't she who had been struck by the sun.

"More chicken?" Lily asked later that night, about to get up from the table.

"No, thank you," he said, only half hearing her, his mind on her lips. So full, so soft. So very, very rosy. And so eminently kissable. He idly toyed with his fork. He was not accustomed to dwelling on women's lips, but there was something about Lily's that captured the imagination—far too much so, for he'd been thinking about them all afternoon and evening.

"Are you sure?"

"Hmm?" And then there was Lily's throat, all that smooth, soft skin just asking to be caressed—first with the tips of his fingers, and then . . .

"Pascal, where have you gone?"

To bed with you. "I'm sorry. My mind was wandering. You have the rest of the chicken."

"I'm not hungry," she said, sitting back down.

"You?" Pascal said, looking at her flushed cheeks—the very color of desire. He quickly looked away and pushed his knife and fork together neatly, as if that might restore order to his senses. Feeling a little more under control, he risked a glance at her, genuinely concerned about her high color. "You're not feeling ill, are you? You'd tell me if you were, wouldn't you?"

"Don't be ridiculous," she snapped. "Not that you'd know anything about it if I were, but as it happens I'm merely hot and tired from working in the sun all day."

Pascal gave her a skeptical look, then rose from his chair and approached her, putting the back of his hand against the juncture of her throat and ear in as professional a manner as he could manage. Still, he couldn't help savoring the softness of her skin and the silky wisps of hair brushing his knuckles.

Lily jerked away as if she'd been burned. "What do you think you're doing?" she demanded, her hand covering the delicate patch of skin that he'd touched.

"I was attempting to see if perhaps you'd had too much sun after all, in which case you might have a fever," he replied evenly, a minor miracle, given that his heart threatened to choke him.

"Well, I haven't, have I, and the next time you can take me at my word and keep your hands to yourself."

"I beg your most humble pardon, duchess, but I was only seeing to your blasted welfare."

"Oh," she said sarcastically. "Again? Well, we both know where that leads, don't we?"

"Elizabeth!" he roared, pushed to the end of his rope. "That's enough! How much of this do you think I can take?"

"How much of what? I'm not responsible for your sins, and it isn't my problem that you don't like being reminded of them."

"You are the most impossible woman God ever put on this earth," he said, ready to tear his hair out—and hers, while he was at it. "*When* are you finally going to get it through your head that I never intended you any harm?"

"Oh? Is that why you force me out into the sun all day to do your washing and weed your stupid garden? You're worried about your back breaking. Did you ever give any thought to mine?"

"Actually, I think the sunshine has done you some good, and your back looks fine to me. I haven't noticed you hobbling about, or moaning and groaning, until now."

"That's because you're never home, and when you are, you never notice anything anyway."

Pascal took two steps toward her, a very strong desire to

throttle her sweeping through him. "Sometimes I cannot believe you're real. You can be a living nightmare!"

"Do you think you're my idea of a pleasant dream?" Lily retorted, desperately wishing he was short and fat and his face covered with disgusting warts, for it was difficult to keep her concentration with that solid wall of masculinity towering over her, those beautiful dark eyes flashing into hers. "In fact," she said less certainly, "the only time I *can* escape you is in my sleep."

"And you were just complaining that I'm never home," he said tightly. "Make up your mind, Elizabeth."

"You really are a wretch, you know."

"So you keep telling me, and dear God, but you tempt me into behaving like one."

"Tempt you?" she said with disbelief. "It's second nature to you."

He shook his head, staring down at the floor. "Does nothing I say or do make any impression on you?"

"Everything you say and do makes an impression on me. What I don't understand is why you think that impression should be favorable. You may have fooled many a woman in your time, but I am not so stupid or naive to be taken in by your—your masculine charms."

"My—my *what*?" He stared at her as if he hadn't heard her correctly. "My masculine *charms*?"

"As I said, and you can keep them to yourself." Lily, seeing that she'd hit some sort of mark, although she wasn't quite sure what it was, smiled smugly. "I'm going to bed now," she announced.

"Already?" His eyes slanted down at her, measuring, assessing. "Are these masculine charms of mine scaring you away?"

"Don't be ridiculous. "I'm tired." *And terrified,* she added to herself. In that moment he looked thoroughly dangerous.

"Good night, then, Elizabeth," he said smoothly. "I'll be outside should you need anything."

She nodded without meeting his eyes and fled upstairs.

Pascal raked both hands through his hair in frustration, damped down the fire, and spent the night tossing and turning beneath the stars.

It had been a hell of a way to spend his thirtieth birthday.

13

OVER the next fortnight Pascal almost began to thank God for the unceasing work that forced him to spend long hours in the vineyards and away from Lily. Though it had initially seemed that Lily was softening, she now resembled a hedgehog that had rolled itself into a ball, spines fully extended.

He could say little to her without getting a sharp rebuff—either that or she was impossibly distant. He couldn't get anywhere near her, no matter what strategy he employed. And yet there was something different about her. This was not the obnoxious behavior of the girl he had married but something else. It was as if she were afraid of something, but of what? She seemed to have settled into her new life, although she still refused to leave the immediate vicinity of the cottage. But that would come with time—no doubt when her brother returned.

Her prickly behavior had started the day he'd brought her the picnic as a surprise. Yet he'd said and done nothing he could think of to upset her, save for his stupid joke about the farmer's son—but she'd been rattled before that, rattled when he arrived unexpectedly.

He'd been over and over it, and he couldn't help but wonder if Lily hadn't been up to some mischief, perhaps something to do with her brother, although he couldn't think what. He wished to God that it didn't matter to him, but it did. For some insane reason it did. Lily did. And he wanted to matter to her.

As if that weren't enough to trouble him, there was the other matter. He realized that he had been shut away from women for a very long time, but he hadn't been bothered by that. Then again, he had never lived in such close quarters with a woman, other than those in his family—not the same thing at all. Lily was . . . Lily. She was with him day and night, an integral part of his life, and their quarters were so small that there was no escaping her.

He couldn't seem to control his baser nature, the one that made his eyes stray to the soft breasts that strained against her dress in the flickering light of the fire as she sat sewing of an evening. Images of Lily invaded his dreams at night, waking him stiff with desire, his mind full of rosy lips, soft caressing arms, even softer thighs, yielding, opening to him, taking him into her. Woman. The ultimate mystery.

Although it hadn't been necessary to watch for frost for some time now, he nevertheless made a habit of sleeping outside at night, for he felt exactly like the lustful beast she had accused him of being, and he didn't dare risk giving in to foolish impulse. He wished he could take back his vow that he wouldn't take her to bed, the vow that condemned him to the living hell of never-ending, unsated desire.

Still, even if he could take those words back, it would make little difference, since Lily definitely did not want him. Oddly enough, it hurt.

He finished trimming the row of vines and straightened, his back sore from bending over for so long. What was he going to do come winter? Sleep with the cows?

"Eh, LaMartine! What are you looking so pained over?"

Startled, Pascal looked up. Pierre Marchand grinned at him, his cap pushed back on his head, his red, round, good-natured face as streaked with sweat and dirt as his shabby clothes.

"Lost, were you, monsieur? Come, forget your troubles and share some bread and wine with us. It doesn't do for a man to go hungry." He slapped Pascal's shoulder with one beefy hand. "Why do you never bring a meal along, eh? Your wife does not like to feed you? Look what Claubert's wife put in his pail as a fond memento." He waved a skinny *saucisson* in the air, to the delight and guffaws of his fellow workers.

Pascal grinned. "Thank you. I am sure Madame Claubert has a fine touch with a *saucisson*."

That remark earned great howls from the men.

"Ah, maybe, but you should see what my wife can do with a nice fat sausage," Marchand said, his belly shaking with laughter as he poured out a glass of wine and passed it over to Pascal. "She's a genius! I'm a genius!"

"You may be a genius," said young Alain Lascard, who

had just finished his own meal and pushed himself to his feet, "but Claubert's wife is eight months gone with child, which says much for the spice of a *saucisson*."

"Bah," Pierre said. "What do you know about it, Alain? You're all of sixteen—a baby! You probably haven't even had your first woman."

Alain blushed to the roots of his hair, and Pascal felt instant sympathy. "I shouldn't pay the slightest attention to this lot, Alain. They're envious of your youth and stamina. Go on, back to unloading the barrels." He scrubbed Alain's dark hair with one hand and gave him a companionable push on the shoulder toward the road, then accepted his glass.

"It's no wonder the grapes are coming along so nicely," he said to the men. "You're feeding them more manure than I could ever have hoped to procure."

"Ah, *merde*!" Claubert said crudely. "There's nothing like it."

Fresh waves of laughter rolled over the vineyards. Pascal settled down among the men and fell into their chat, easily absorbing the bawdiness, grateful for the acceptance and camaraderie, and most grateful of all for the distraction from his own restless thoughts.

Lily practically burst when the mail came that day, for as well as the usual slew of letters for the wretch from various people and places, there was a letter for her from Jean-Jacques. She opened it with fumbling fingers and read so quickly that she could barely take in the words—but she instantly grasped the essentials. He was coming home. He'd managed to get his money, far more money than he'd expected, and he was feeling pleased with the world.

Lily smiled and hugged the letter to her chest. Jean-Jacques, she suspected, was pleased with the world not only because he had managed his money but also because he'd been in Paris and had seen a number of his friends. She knew how much his friends meant to him. Jean-Jacques loved people and they loved him back. But then he was lovable, unlike herself.

She had always had sharp edges to her character and a tongue that far too readily spoke what was on her mind, whereas Jean-Jacques was easygoing and affable. She was happy enough on her own, whereas Jean-Jacques needed equally affable people around him, or he was miserable.

Oh, how her poor brother had suffered during those long years at Sutherby, for he had been born to bask in deserved admiration. She didn't need or expect anyone's admiration, so Sutherby had not been quite so dreadful for her. Anyway, she despised false praise, for she knew it was only given to gain a private end.

Lily sighed as she pulled off her apron and put Bean safely away in the barn. The wretch had also received a letter from Jean-Jacques, and she knew he would want it immediately. He'd been concerned that he had heard nothing in the five weeks that her brother had been gone. He would eat his words when he saw that Jean-Jacques had succeeded so brilliantly.

A moment's hesitation stopped her. Did she really want to take the chance of finding Pascal without his shirt once again and be plunged into that miasma of misguided desire? She thought about it and then decided that it would make little difference.

Desire had been plaguing her ever since it had first struck, as if a candle had been lit and would not be extinguished. She could only pray that this particular candle would shortly burn itself out—it was a most uncomfortable and embarrassing thing to live with. She hated the way his touch burned at her skin and started her heart pounding. He was her sworn enemy, and yet her bones turned to water when he smiled down at her. She woke in the night craving his touch, betrayed by her own body. She was a true disgrace.

The only solution was to keep well out of his way. Still, she couldn't resist taking him Jean-Jacques's letter. Even though they stayed well off the subject, she knew his opinion of her brother was not what it should be. Well, this would put him straight once and for all.

Pascal had said he would be working on the southern slopes of the vineyard that day, and Lily noticed with surprise that the climb was far easier than it had been three months ago when she had marched into the village to fetch the priest, seeking his opinion about the crop.

Men were spread out in the fields with pitchforks, working something into the soil from large buckets. It smelled like the same disgusting stuff Pascal had dug into their own garden. She wrinkled her nose in memory of that less-than-auspicious day and its accompanying odors.

A few of the men tipped their caps as she went by and

she nodded. She imagined she looked so different now from her first visit to Saint-Simon that they were unlikely to recognize her. She scarcely recognized herself on the rare occasions that she bothered to look in her little vanity mirror.

She spotted Pascal instantly—his height distinguished him from the others. He was engaged in conversation, or, more succinctly, he was saying something that the other man seemed to find vastly amusing.

No doubt he'd been telling his companion about yesterday's episode with the mouse, as if she could have helped screaming when it had fallen through a hole in the ceiling and onto her head, where it had entangled itself in her hair. To add insult to injury, he had gently removed the creature and placed it outside. The wretch had laughed just as hard then as his companion was laughing now.

Pascal glanced over and saw her, then said something quickly that she couldn't hear and detached himself. He walked toward her, clearly surprised, a smile still on his face, his hair windblown and his shirt mercifully undone only partway down his chest.

"Elizabeth. What brings you out this way? I don't suppose you've brought me lunch, have you?" His eyes were filled with bright amusement.

"I've brought you something much better than a lunch," she said and thrust out the letter. "Here. It's from Jean-Jacques. Go on, open it."

He shot her a look of curiosity, then took it from her and unsealed it, reading the contents. His expression changed from anxiety to amazement. "Good *God*," he said, shoving his hand through his hair. "But why? Why on earth would he have borrowed such an enormous sum when I told him we only needed . . ." And then he stopped. "Well, not for me to wonder. This is the most remarkable news."

"It is, isn't it? But didn't I tell you? Oh, Pascal, I am so pleased."

"I am equally pleased," he said, grasping her hands between his. "Best of all, I think we might have a harvest to make it all worthwhile. Look at this vine. Do you see the color? It's not yet what it should be, but it is coming back."

Lily examined the leaf. "Are those grapes?" she asked, pointing to a tiny green cluster.

"Those are indeed grapes, or the beginnings of them, anyway. If the rain continues to hold off, they're going to do well enough. We have to continue to put nutrients into the soil and keep guarding against diseases, but I have hope that we'll succeed."

Lily beamed. "Jean-Jacques will be so happy."

Pascal nodded. "I am sure he will be, and so will the merchants who have given us the necessary materials on nothing more than a promise that they'll be paid. Let us also not forget how pleased the villagers will be when their pockets and their bellies are full."

"But haven't you been paying them?"

"Yes, but not very much, as you can't pay people on promises. Jean-Jacques left nothing for their wages, so I had some money transferred from England."

"You said you wouldn't touch it." Lily looked at him in bewilderment.

"I haven't. Not yours, anyway. I had some money of my own put away from various jobs I've done over the years. It's not much, but it's enough to pay the wages until Jean-Jacques returns with the necessary funds. When he does, I can repay myself, and we'll have more to eat."

"How splendid," Lily said happily.

Pascal laughed, then took her face between both his hands and kissed her cheek. "Have you really been that hungry? Accept my apologies for starving you."

Lily almost fell over in shock. Her cheek burned where his warm lips had touched, and her heart hammered against her rib cage like something desperate to escape.

"What—what did you do that for?" she asked shakily.

"Why not? It's a beautiful day, you came up here to give me a letter that could have waited, and you look adorable when you blush. Reasons enough?"

Bemused, she nodded. "I—people don't usually kiss me. And I am *not* adorable."

"You are when you're standing in the middle of a vineyard with your eyes aglow and your cheeks rosy and your hair tumbling down your back. You look positively approachable."

Lily was about to make a retort to that absurd statement when a warning cry rang out.

"Alain! Fait attention!"

Pascal instantly turned and Lily turned in the same moment. What she saw stopped her heart. Below them on the road a horse attached to a wagon had gone berserk. Alain lay on his back, having fallen in his haste to get out of the way, and the horse was out of control, snorting and wildly pawing, pushing the huge wagon backward.

Pascal didn't waste an instant—he was already halfway to the road. But he wasn't fast enough to stop the wagon. It continued to roll backward, and Alain wasn't fast enough either.

It all happened in a split second. Alain scrambled desperately to push himself away as one back wheel caught him on his midriff and kept revolving, dragging him along with it. His mouth opened in a terrible scream and his hands flailed outward, his fingers clutching desperately at the ground as if he might somehow be able to pull himself free. But the wheel continued to roll over him, relentlessly twisting at his flesh. He screamed one last time, a sound of horrible agony as the wheel finally rolled off him.

Alain's hands flew to his stomach, catching at loops of something gray and glistening. Lily thought she was going to be sick as she realized that the loops were his intestines and he was literally trying to keep them from spilling onto the ground. In that last dreadful instant the wheel had split his abdomen wide open.

Pascal didn't stop to see to the injured boy. He ran directly to the horse's head, pulling down on the harness and putting his hand over the panicked beast's rolling eyes, murmuring to it. The animal shivered but calmed, and the wagon came to a stop, the front wheel halting only a foot from where Alain lay. Pascal gave the harness to one of the men who had run up.

"Hold him steady—he'll be all right now," he said shortly. "And send someone to the village for the boy's parents. Quickly!"

He ran back to Alain, who writhed in agony between the two sets of wheels.

"Help me!" Alain cried, clutching at Pascal's shirt with one hand. "Help me, please! Don't let me die!"

"It will be all right, Alain," Pascal said in a calm, steadying voice, much like the one he had used on the horse. "I will help you, I promise, but first I have to move you to a place where I *can* help you. I'll try not to hurt you."

He took Alain under the arms and slowly, carefully pulled him out from under the wagon, then dropped to his knees and gently pried the boy's hands apart, speaking softly to him at the same time. "Let go, Alain. I can't help you unless I can see. Let go. Don't worry, I won't let anything happen to you."

Alain squeezed his eyes shut for a moment, but he did as he was told, and as Pascal gently examined him, Alain's eyes opened wide. He looked over his head at the silent crowd that had gathered a slight distance away, his eyes darting as if he might find solace there. But Lily noticed that no one met that pleading gaze. Instead, they looked away as if they were embarrassed—and then their eyes returned to Alain's gaping abdomen in morbid fascination.

Lily moved closer, wondering what Pascal could possibly do. Perhaps he just intended to offer solace while the boy died. She couldn't see how Alain could live, not with such a terrible wound. She swallowed hard.

Pascal looked up, and his eyes immediately found her.

"Lily," he said in the same voice he used to Bean when he expected absolute obedience. "Run to the house as if your life depended on it. Open the chest in the corner next to the barn door—the key is in the front pocket of my satchel next to it—and bring me the leather bag inside. I'll need blankets, too. Hurry!"

She ran, faster than she had ever run in her life. She paused just for a moment outside the house, realizing something astonishing. *Lily,* he'd called her, the name only a few people had ever used—and those the people who were fond of her. But there was no time to wonder about it now.

The key was where he had said, and with trembling fingers she fitted it into the lock and threw the lid of the chest open. She grabbed the square-shaped bag, pulled two blankets from the walnut armoire, and tore back out the door, ignoring Bean's frantic barks from the barn.

Alain lay in the same spread-out position, his face white, his lips blue, his body shivering violently. Pascal bent over him, doing something she couldn't see as a round man with a red face held Alain's shoulders down. From one side of the crowd she heard the sound of a woman softly weeping and a deeper voice trying to comfort her.

As she came closer she saw that Pascal had a bucket of water and a cup, and he was washing the coils of intestine with the water, then methodically replacing each coil back into the open cavity.

"Here is your bag, Pascal." She placed it down very carefully. She'd never seen anything like this in her life—and for some reason, instead of being shocked she was fascinated.

Pascal glanced up at her as if to assess her condition. "Good girl," he said. "You're doing beautifully. Put one of the blankets over Alain's chest and one over his legs, then open the bag. Inside you'll find a blue bottle. Pour the contents into the bucket of water."

She did as she was told, and he continued to wash the loops of bowel and tuck them away. She couldn't believe she was standing over Pascal's shoulder, watching him calmly replace someone's insides as if it were a normal thing to do. There was a radiance coming from his hands, a shimmer like the road on a hot day, but it had a pink tinge to it.

"Lily," he said, when nearly all the loops of intestine were back in place, "in my bag there is a small wooden box. Take out the needle and a piece of the thread. Thread the needle. It's an odd shape, but you should be able to manage."

She did manage, although it was no easy task—her fingers were shaking badly with nerves. She'd never been required to do anything so important before.

"Good," Pascal said when she held the threaded needle out to him. "Now, listen carefully. Take out the pads of linen, but don't put them on the ground. They need to stay as clean as possible. I'm going to sew Alain up, and I want you to blot any blood away so that I can see what I'm doing. If you don't think you can do it, tell me now, and I'll ask someone else. Can you manage?"

His eyes met hers, and somehow, from somewhere deep inside, Lily knew that he was asking something of her that was far more important than a strong stomach or mere courage. There was something in his eyes that insisted, but at the same time they offered her strength and confidence. She nodded.

"All right. Let's begin."

Pascal grasped the right side of the abdominal wall with his thumb and forefinger as his other hand forced the curved needle through the skin, careful not to nick the intestine. He then brought the needle up toward the left edge of the tear, pushing at the underside of the skin until the needle came through. He pulled the thread taut, forcing the edges of the skin together, tied a knot, and repeated the procedure.

The next half hour passed in a blur. Lily became so focused on what Pascal was doing that she almost forgot she was looking into someone's innards. Twice Pascal asked her to thread another needle and she did, then went back to blotting away the blood.

Alain didn't seem alert, nor did he react much, save to jerk once and elicit an oath from Pascal. She couldn't think of anything else to do, so she began to talk to the boy.

"It's really a lucky thing that my husband was here to help you—he's a most resourceful man," she said. "Just wait and see when the harvest comes in and you're dancing with everyone else. You can dance, can't you?"

His eyelids lowered.

"Good, because you're going to have to dance with me. I have to warn you, I'm a terrible dancer, but you'll have to dance with me nonetheless, since you will owe me a very great favor for not swooning directly on top of you while my husband practices his sewing."

Pascal's eyes flicked up at that.

"I'll have to find him something more suitable, I think," she continued. "It simply will not do, going about embroidering his laborers." Lily knew she was babbling, but she didn't care, not if it was helping Alain.

"Lily," Pascal said with a catch of laughter in his voice, "you can stop chattering now. I don't know whether it was shock, my stitching, or the idea of dancing with you, but Alain has mercifully fainted. I need some more thread."

Lily took the needle, threaded it yet again, and handed it back to Pascal. "Will he recover?" she asked anxiously.

"I hope so," he said in English, beginning the next set of sutures. "The immediate danger is past. Alain was damned lucky that the intestine itself wasn't ripped open or he wouldn't have stood a chance—not that it's fun to be eviscerated in any manner, but at least the bowel stayed intact." He inclined his head toward the bucket. "The biggest thing is to pray that infection doesn't set in, but the solution you put in the water should help with that."

He bent his head back to his task, and not much later he was finished. Alain's firm young belly had a long, slightly zigzagged line of stitching across it. The flesh around the stitching was puffy and angry-looking, but at least it resembled an abdomen again.

Pascal gently rubbed some ointment into Alain's flesh, then covered the wound with a linen bandage and wrapped some strips of linen around the boy's hips and waist to hold the pad in place. Alain began to stir, and Pascal smiled down at him. "Welcome back, my friend. It's all finished now."

Alain opened his eyes hazily and looked around as if surprised to find himself there. "Oh. Monsieur . . . I am still alive?"

"Indeed you are."

A spontaneous cheer went up from the workers, and the woman who had been crying throughout came forward and dropped to her knees, first kissing Pascal's hand, and then Alain's face, her tears liberally sprinkling both.

"Maman—" Alain said faintly. He looked down at himself as if not quite sure what he would discover, and saw only the large white bandage. "Ah . . ." he said on a shallow breath of acute relief. "Thank God!"

"And Monsieur LaMartine, Alain. He is a savior! How will we ever repay you, good monsieur? You delivered our only son from certain death!"

"I assure you, madame, I did nothing that any person with some water and a needle on hand could not have done. You might thank my wife for having produced that needle so quickly, or we would have been in a fix."

Alain's mother bestowed a beaming, if tearful, smile on Lily. "Forgive me, madame. Your speed and your courage in assisting the good monsieur are most appreciated, and permit me to say that you are very, very fortunate in your husband."

Lily bowed her head, confused but humbled by what she had just witnessed. She felt horribly guilty about the wicked thoughts she'd had about Pascal's mysterious locked chest, when it contained only books and the materials necessary to save a life.

Alain's father pounded Pascal on the back and vigorously shook his hand, then took his beret off and bowed to Lily. "Our eternal thanks, monsieur, madame. I don't know how we can ever repay you. I saw with my own eyes how it was and what you did. It is a miracle!"

"No miracle, monsieur, only common sense and a little training. As for repaying me, work as hard as you can in the fields and let us see a harvest in together." He dug in his bag. "Apply this salve to the wound three times a day, and keep the dressing clean. I'll be by daily to check on Alain. In ten days' time the stitches can come out, but Alain is not to do anything but rest between now and then."

"As you say, monsieur."

Lily thought that Alain's mother was going to kiss Pascal's feet any moment, and Pascal looked quite accustomed to such idolatry.

"Feed him only clear fluids for the first three days," he said. "White willow bark tea will help with the pain and keep the fever at bay. Have you any? No? Then I'll bring some over to you later this evening. For now, let's see to a litter on which to carry your son home." He looked down at Alain. "You're a brave boy to have withstood that. I'm sorry for any pain I caused you."

"I thank you, monsieur," Alain murmured. "I owe you my life."

"Get well and you'll owe me nothing. But should you fail me, I'll be mightily put out. Put all your mind and your energy to healing."

"I will, good monsieur. I swear it."

"It is all I ask." He chuckled. "Besides, you wouldn't want to miss out on all those exciting experiences life has yet to offer, would you?"

Pierre Marchand, who had been kneeling by Alain's head, gave a bark of laughter, and Alain managed a faint smile. "Indeed, no, monsieur."

"Good. Sleep now." He smoothed Alain's forehead with his fingers, then rose to his feet and turned to Lily about to say something. He stopped abruptly. "What is it? Are you all right, duchess? Here, sit down. Put your head between your knees—you look very pale. I asked too much of you. I shouldn't have expected you to—"

"I'm fine," she said quickly. Lily's head was spinning, but in shock rather than illness.

She had an absurd desire to burst into wild laughter. The truth—the real truth of the matter—had finally penetrated her brain. It was the word "miracle" that had set the thought off, not unlike it had the village priest.

There is a monk at St. Christophe with the ability to work wonders with living things, Father Chabot had said. *A maker of miracles, they call him.*

The only thing Father Chabot had gotten wrong was the part about the monk. Lily had, if she was not badly mistaken, literally fallen at the feet of the man she'd gone to find. Now, by a bizarre twist of fate, she was married to him.

She really didn't know whether to laugh or to cry.

14

"ALL right. Suppose you tell me what's going on in that convoluted brain of yours." Pascal paused in the middle of peeling a potato, aware that Lily had been staring at his hands as if they were something she'd never seen before. It was not that he was unaccustomed to people gaping at him, but the last thing he wanted was for Lily to think him a freak on top of everything else.

"I was thinking how extraordinary it was that your hands were inside someone's body a few hours ago," Lily said. "Now they're doing something as mundane as peeling a potato." She laid out a bunch of carrots and started to chop them.

"Well, that's honest," Pascal said carefully. "Does the thought disgust you?"

"No—just the opposite, although I admit that if you had asked me the same question this morning, I'm sure I would have said yes. Now . . . well, I suppose I'm curious. How did you know what to do?" The words came tumbling out all in a rush, as if she'd been waiting all afternoon to ask.

Pascal breathed a sigh of relief. Healthy curiosity was a far sight better than awestruck worship, or whispers of mystical powers. For the first time, he was almost glad Lily didn't believe in God, since he was thoroughly sick of being regarded as some sort of saint. In truth, certain aspects of life with Lily were refreshing, since she rarely treated him as anything other than a complete cad.

"Pascal? Shouldn't I ask?"

"What? Oh. No, of course you can ask. It's quite simple. I was taught." He picked up the potato and went back to peeling it with quick, deft strokes, feeling self-conscious. He wasn't about to tell Lily the full truth, but then, he hadn't done anything today that was truly unusual, only dramatic, so he felt fairly safe.

"Where were you taught?" Lily asked, her own chore of cutting up carrots forgotten. Instead, she propped her chin on her fist, her smoky eyes glittering with fascination.

"Here and there. It all started with Georgia, who is a skilled healer herself. I learned a tremendous amount from her over the years—she started me on gardening, too. Then in university I took some medical courses, and since then I've picked up what I could."

"Oh," Lily said. "What was in the blue bottle?"

"An infusion of St. John's wort," he said, surprised that she'd even asked.

"And the balm?"

"Lanolin and marigold mixed with comfrey. That will help the incision to heal."

"And the needle?"

"It was given to me in China. The curve is specially designed for suturing skin."

Lily nodded. "Yes. I saw that."

Pascal glanced up at her, then cut the potatoes into chunks and tossed them into the cast-iron pot. "You surprised me today. You kept your head, you didn't faint or even flinch. You were a great help."

Lily's flush extended from her cheeks all the way down her neck. "I was happy to help. You surprised me too. Not one person I know could have done what you did."

"No, probably not, because it wouldn't have crossed their minds to try."

"Well, it certainly wouldn't have crossed mine, but should it ever come to it again, I'll know what to do—well, a little bit, anyway. I wish I knew more."

He gave her a long look. "You really are interested, aren't you?"

She nodded shyly. "I don't know that I'd be any good— I've never been much good at anything, except making people cross. But today when I saw that poor boy dragged under that wheel and—and split open like that, I thought he was finished. I felt so helpless."

"Yes, I can imagine," he said more comfortably.

"I thought you were only being kind by pulling him out from under the wagon the way you did. It never occurred to me that you could fix him." She frowned. "Pascal . . ."

"Hmm?"

"Why would no one meet Alain's eyes? Why did they all

shy away like that, as if he were a stranger, when they must have known him perfectly well?''

''Accidents like this bring people too close to their own mortality. They need to distance themselves for fear of being overwhelmed,'' he said, glancing up at her, interested that she'd noticed.

''Then why didn't they go away altogether instead of standing around and staring like a herd of silly cows?'' Lily hacked at the poor carrots as if she meant them grievous harm.

Pascal smiled, watching her. Lily's finely etched eyebrows were pulled together in righteous indignation, her mouth in full pout. The beauty of it was that her indignation was over someone other than herself.

''You're right, you know,'' he said as he prepared the fire. ''Most people can no more keep themselves from standing about staring at those more unfortunate than themselves than they can keep themselves from breathing. It can be a nuisance when one is trying to get something done. I had to ask three separate people to bring a bucket of water before anyone actually went for it.''

''Oh, yes. The water. What was it for?''

''To clean the intestines, for one,'' he said, looking up over his shoulder. ''They also need to be kept moist while they're exposed to air. Thirsty things, intestines.''

''Yes, I noticed. They went all dry and tacky almost immediately. What were you looking for when you first examined Alain?''

''I was looking to see if any of his bowel had been pierced. I also wanted to be sure that there weren't other internal injuries.''

''Such as what?'' Lily asked.

Pascal stood and chucked her chin. ''You are a bloodthirsty thing, aren't you?''

''No,'' she said indignantly, pulling away and fumbling with the strings of her apron. ''I only want to learn. I don't see anything wrong with that.''

''There's not a thing wrong with it. In fact, I'm delighted that you want to learn. I'd be happy to teach you what I can.''

''You would?'' she said, her eyes lighting up. ''Truly? You don't mind?''

''Truly, and no, of course I don't mind. I could use the

help. I have a feeling that after this I'm going to be even busier.'' He smiled at her. ''There's a great deal to study, but I'll give you books to read if you like, and you can be helpful by learning to identify herbs and how to cull and blend them correctly. I always need to restock.''

Lily bit her lip. ''Why do you keep your chest locked?''

''There are all sorts of things in it that could be dangerous if not used correctly. Why?''

She hesitated for a moment, then gave him a lopsided smile. ''I thought there was a body in it. Or at least some very terrible secret you were hiding.''

Pascal stared at her for a moment, then howled with laughter, collapsing onto a chair. ''Oh, God, duchess, where do you come up with these things?''

Lily's smile widened. ''I'm not entirely sure myself. I think it comes from knowing what a fiend you are. It only follows that you would have something fiendish in your trunk.''

''Are you now convinced that I haven't and I'm not?'' he asked, straightening and regarding her intently.

''Well,'' Lily said slowly, ''we shall have to see. Perhaps if you stay on your best behavior and don't do anything fiendish for a week or two, I might consider the notion.''

''*Consider* the—'' He rose and lunged for her.

Lily squealed and vanished out the door in the direction of the garden.

Pascal dropped back into the chair and watched her go. Lily was one of a kind. But the smile slowly faded from his face. Was he ever going to rid her of the idea that he was a fiend, and what would happen if he did? What would happen when she discovered the truth about him? That might almost be worse. He knew it was inevitable—eventually something was bound to happen. It always did. Could he bear Lily's looking at him as if he were a saint? He doubted it. But how else would she treat him—what other choice would she have? She'd never understand how it really was. How could she?

The entire situation plagued him and he didn't have the first idea what to do about it.

He rubbed his stiff neck, then finished preparing supper.

Lily lowered the shirt she was mending and surreptitiously stole a glance at Pascal. He was doing the accounts at the table as he always did after supper, his head bent in concentration. He didn't seem to be aware that she was even in the room. Just as well.

Her head had been swimming with all sorts of speculation ever since her realization of who the wretch truly was. A botanist. She had brought her brother a botanist after all . . . and a physician of sorts, too.

It all made sense now—well, not all of it. She still didn't know what he'd been doing in the monastery, and she certainly didn't believe any of the nonsense about miracles. He was an educated man, a scientist, highly skilled.

Lily sighed with pleasure. The wretch was going to teach her about medicine. It almost made up for what he'd done to her—almost, but not quite. She couldn't change the circumstances of their first meeting, nor ignore all the dreadful things he'd done to her since then.

But to be given the chance to learn how to do what he had done this afternoon—that was worth a lessening of hostilities without its being a betrayal of her vow.

It wasn't going to be easy, of course, working in close quarters with him, as she would no doubt have to do. His physical presence never failed to make her feel flushed and agitated—and empty somehow, as if his touch was the only thing that would complete her.

How could she feel this way toward a man who had treated her so abominably? How could she feel this way about a man who resented her brother and his station so much that he had deliberately withheld funds Jean-Jacques so desperately needed? How could she feel desire for a man who resented her own station so much that he forced her to live like a peasant, to work her fingers to the bone and sleep on the floor like an animal?

She'd become no better than a beast, the most appallingly carnal thoughts constantly running through her mind, thoughts that no lady of breeding would ever have. It showed how low she had sunk—she was even beginning to think like a peasant. And it was all his fault.

Even now, she couldn't help but want him. He was so . . . so beautiful. So strong and well made, all superbly shaped muscle and bone and height and breadth. Her hands smoothed over the material of the shirt in her lap, as if by touching it she was touching a small part of him.

Even Jean-Jacques, whom Lily thought perfect in every

way, could not compare in physical splendor to the wretch. It wasn't fair that he should be so magnificent.

He looked up, his gaze locking with hers. Lily blushed fiercely, but she couldn't seem to tear her eyes away. Her breath involuntarily quickened at the expression on his face, naked, filled with need.

"Lily," he said. It came out a strangled whisper.

"What?" She ducked her head, fiddling with the shirt, trying to compose herself.

"You were giving me the strangest look. What were you thinking?" Pascal wore a pained expression, which she didn't understand at all.

"I was—I was thinking about Jean-Jacques," she said.

His face changed instantly, becoming cool and shuttered. "What about Jean-Jacques?"

"Just that I—I'm glad he's coming home." *Maybe seeing him will remind me of what's important,* she thought desperately.

"I'm sure you are delighted." He put his pen down. "Was that really all you were thinking?"

"I wish you wouldn't interrogate me," Lily said, terrified that he was going to get the truth out of her. She jumped up, the shirt spilling from her lap onto the floor. "I have the right to a little privacy, haven't I?"

"I'm sorry," he said. "It was just that I—never mind. Never mind, it isn't important." He picked up his pen again, then threw it down and rose. "I'm going to check on Alain. I'll see you tomorrow."

He collected his bag and left before she had a chance to speak. It was obvious that he was upset, and it was her fault.

"I'm sorry," she whispered miserably, going to the door and pressing her hands against it as if she could shut him out. "I'm so sorry. But I can't tell you the truth. Oh, God, why do I feel this way?"

She leaned her forehead on her hands and burst into tears.

Pascal saddled his horse, a dry, hot anger burning through him. He was not angry with Lily so much as with himself. He had no right to ask her what she was thinking. Her thoughts were her own affair. But like the idiot he was, he'd intruded upon them, only to discover she'd been thinking about her damned brother.

When she hadn't looked away, but met his gaze squarely,

her eyes wider and smokier than usual, her mouth slightly parted, he'd thought that she was feeling the same thing he was: pure, unadulterated desire. To discover it was Jean-Jacques she'd been thinking about—Pascal kicked the horse into a canter.

He probably deserved everything he was getting.

He opened the door to Alain's bedroom, his mind still half on Lily, but stopped short when he saw there was a priest in the room, sitting by the side of the bed with one of Alain's hands clasped between his own, saying prayers over the sleeping boy. The priest looked up when he heard the door open.

"Excuse me, Father," Pascal said. "I didn't mean to interrupt you. I've come to see to Alain, but it can wait."

The priest's mouth dropped open, his face draining of color. "Holy Mother of God," he whispered, making the sign of the cross.

Oh, please, not this again, Pascal thought wearily. "Shall I leave you?" he asked politely.

"No. No, my son. You . . . you are Pascal LaMartine?" the priest asked, making a visible attempt to recover himself.

"Yes, Father, I am." He put his bag down by the side of the bed. "And you are?"

"Michel Chabot. I am the Catholic priest for the village. This has been my parish for many years." He stood and made room for Pascal at the bedside.

"Has it? Then you must know quite a lot about the history of Saint-Simon," Pascal said, as he picked up Alain's wrist and felt for his pulse.

"Sometimes too much," the priest said cryptically. "Still, I go where I am needed." He continued to stare warily at Pascal.

"You need not worry, Father. I won't harm the boy."

"I realize that. Alain's parents told me about what you did today for their son. I am most grateful for your skill. The villagers are in a stir, naturally."

"Yes, and that I understand. But you, Father? You appear to be an educated man, and yet you look at me as if I were the devil himself."

The round little priest bowed his equally round and bald head. "I regret it. I do not think such a thing in the least. It is only that you have a look . . . forgive me, monsieur."

"Not at all." Pascal wondered if perhaps it was his halo that was showing rather than a set of horns.

The priest cleared his throat as if to change the subject. "I once knew a Henri LaMartine many years ago, here in Saint-Simon. He was a relative of yours, perhaps?"

Pascal shook his head. "Not to my knowledge. LaMartine is a common enough name. I confess, Father, I haven't missed your startled reaction to me. Is my surname the cause of it, or does it have to do with the events of this afternoon?"

The priest's face relaxed into a suggestion of a smile. "It is neither. You bear no resemblance to the LaMartine I knew. I was only curious. As for this afternoon, I am grateful for what you did for Alain, but I admit I am surprised. Is it true what they say, that you have married the duke's sister?"

"I hadn't realized that it was news among the village, as I haven't mentioned the fact to anyone. But yes, Elizabeth is my wife. She hasn't been out much since we arrived. I imagine people must have recognized her today."

"*Recognized* her? You understate the case. It was an extraordinary discovery." The priest scratched his shiny scalp in distraction. "Look here, you must understand this is all very peculiar for the people as it is. First a steward appears out of nowhere and takes charge on the duke's command, whereas the duke has shown no interest in his land before this. Further, this steward knows a great deal about growing grapes."

"I am a botanist by profession, Father."

"Ah, yes? Well, that is helpful. Nevertheless, all of this is already cause for talk. Then today it transpires that the woman the new steward is married to is the duke's sister, who was here not three months ago and, begging your pardon, behaving as if she were Marie Antoinette—not a popular personage among the peasants, as you know."

Pascal glanced up from examining Alain. "No, not very," he said dryly.

"Exactly. And yet today she was out in the fields helping her husband put a boy back together again without so much as the blink of an eye. This all seems preposterous, no?"

Pascal shrugged. "Yes, I suppose it does. However, Elizabeth is not the same person she was then."

"That must certainly be true," the priest said, scratching

his head again. "On top of all of that, monsieur, I learn that this same man, this mysterious steward—you must understand that I have been away on church business in Avignon for the month—I return this very day to learn that this mysterious man, now known to be the brother-in-law of the duke, has saved Alain Lascard from death."

"Yes, Father?" Pascal said without inflection. "What do you wish me to say? Everything you have said is true."

"Yes . . . I only wonder how it happens that this has transpired. The people were naturally curious about your wife, although it was assumed she was shy—and a person like yourself, of the bourgeoisie. But the duke's sister?" He frowned. "I have been told that you live in old Baumerd's cottage. This is correct?"

"Yes, we do, with his grace's permission."

"It was not in the best of condition when you took it on," the priest stated bluntly.

"No, Father, it was not," Pascal replied equally bluntly. "It was falling down about our ears and still is to a degree. I don't have the money at the moment to do much about it, and Monsieur le Duc does not seem inclined."

Father Chabot nodded rapidly, and Pascal, knowing that it could be some time before the priest gathered himself and his thoughts, turned his attention back to Alain, who appeared to be comfortable, considering his ordeal.

Pascal folded the sheets back and checked the dressing. He was pleased to see that it had remained clean, with almost no seepage. Alain's breathing was even and his skin cool to the touch. There was no point in disturbing him further until morning—he needed sleep more than he needed anything else. Pascal pulled the sheets back up and sat down on the corner of the bed, watching the priest.

Observing him, he decided he liked the man. Father Chabot appeared honest, and he obviously cared about his charges. Pascal thought it over and decided he could be trusted.

"I'd like to speak candidly with you," he said, "but it might be best if we went elsewhere. Alain is sleeping peacefully. There's no need to disturb him."

The priest nodded. "There is a room next door. Let us adjourn there."

They lit the lamps, and the break in conversation gave Pascal time to think.

"I understand why you would be confused," he said, turning to Father Chabot. "Yes, we live in Baumerd's cottage, since that's what Elizabeth's brother offered us. It hasn't been an easy time for her, but she has worked hard to adjust, despite her brother's attitude."

"I see." Father Chabot pulled up a hard-backed chair and lowered himself into it, planting his feet firmly on the floor. "And what attitude is this?"

Pascal's jaw tightened in sudden anger. "With the exception of one letter, Elizabeth's brother has ignored her since our arrival, most likely because of her marriage to me." He shrugged his shoulder. "I can only assume he considers her beneath him now. I don't believe she has yet come to that conclusion, thank God, for I'd hate to see her spirit broken. Elizabeth's spirit has become—ah, well . . ." Pascal hesitated.

"Yes, my son?" the priest said, gently prompting.

Pascal sighed. He was sorely in need of an ear to pour his troubles into, and he felt an affinity with this man. He'd explode if he didn't talk to someone.

"To be perfectly honest, she has become important to me," he said, groping for a way to explain the situation. "I'm not quite sure how, or even when it happened. All I know is that she has. But I—I haven't treated her very well."

"Do you wish to make confession?" the priest asked.

"No, thank you, Father, although I am Catholic and probably will soon be confessing for all I'm worth. No, what I need right now is someone to listen. I don't really have anyone else to whom I can speak, and this is a little delicate. I could use some advice."

"Anything you wish," the priest said, putting on a properly solemn expression, as befitted a man of the cloth. He then folded his plump hands together on his lap and fixed Pascal with a firm but sympathetic eye. "What is this matter that troubles you?"

Pascal walked over to the window and looked out on the night, his hands resting on the thick sill, the stone cool under his palms. "It's not easy to explain. You see, we were forced to marriage against our wills. We both felt acute dislike for each other." He turned around and spread out his hands. "But now here we are."

"Yes, my son? Here you are." He cleared his throat. "Just where is that?"

"Well, that's the problem. We're not one place or the other, and for the life of me, I don't know where it is we should be or even how to get there." He paused, shaking his head in bafflement. "I find that with each day that goes by everything changes—I never know from one minute to the next what to expect. That's typical of my wife, though."

"Ah, yes. I see. You are saying that your wife has a spontaneous nature."

"You could certainly call her spontaneous," Pascal said with a slight smile. "That's part of the problem, and the reason for much of my initial anger and resentment. I felt trapped by circumstances not of my making, and I was furious with Lily because she was responsible for both our predicaments."

"How is that?"

Pascal rubbed the corner of his mouth with one finger. "You will probably find this odd, even given her spontaneous nature, but Lily practically fell on top of me from a monastery wall."

Father Chabot's little eyes bulged half out of his head. "A monastery?" he asked shakily.

"Yes. God only knows what she was doing crawling about on the wall to begin with, or why she was hissing at me like a deranged reptile, for she's never bothered to say, other than that she climbed a tree to have a look inside."

"Oh. Oh, my. Oh, dear."

"Yes. Those were my feelings at the time. In any event, she fell off the wall, and then told the abbot that I'd assaulted her, when all I'd done was to see if she'd succeeded in killing herself. It was a physical examination, not an attempt at rape."

A strangled sound came from Father Chabot's throat, and he coughed vigorously to cover it. "Ah, what was it that you were doing in the monastery, my son? Were you a novice, perhaps?"

"No. I was restoring the gardens and acting as physician for the people of the area."

Father Chabot flushed. "Oh," he said, looking as if he'd just made off with the church plate. "Oh, dear. I see. Yes. How very difficult."

"In any case," Pascal continued, "Lily's father required us to marry to avoid any scandal—or so he said. Personally, I think he decided I'd make a convenient husband for his wayward daughter, and he knew I'd given my word to the abbot that I'd obey."

"And you did."

"I did, Lily had no choice, and it was a miserable business all the way around."

"And yet?" Father Chabot asked, looking hopeful.

"And yet . . . it's not so miserable anymore. It's not exactly wonderful, either. I'm not sure what it is, but I've come to care about Lily. I'm—I've grown fond of her."

"Why, that *is* wonderful!" the priest said, a smile lighting up his face.

"No. It's not. She still thinks I'm a black-hearted, lecherous devil who tried to ravish her, not to mention ravishing countless others before her, and nothing I do or say has disabused her of the notion." Pascal plowed his hand through his hair in frustration. "The irony of it is that I've never even been with a woman—not that I'm about to tell *her* that."

He turned back to the window. "I can't get anywhere near her—every time I try she pulls away, or looks as if I'm about to jump on her, or starts an argument. Right after we were married I told her in anger that I'd never go near her bed, and I haven't, which is just as she would have it. The trouble is, Lily's bed is beginning to be the only thing I think about."

"Oh?" Father Chabot said politely.

"Yes, and it's been driving me to distraction. She's my wife, for the love of God! Oh—I beg your pardon, Father. Only two months outside of a monastery and my language has gone to the dogs."

"Never mind your language. I'd like to know what you plan to do about the situation. A marriage is not a marriage in the eyes of God—or the laws of man—unless it has been consummated. Surely you know this?"

"Yes, of course I know, but I've never dealt with anything like this before. Maybe if I knew better what I was doing I could do it, but I don't." He turned around and leaned his hip against the sill, his arms folded across his chest.

"Er . . . had you chosen celibacy as a gift to God, my son?"

Pascal's cheeks could have lit up half the village. "No . . . not exactly," he said, feeling as if he'd like to drop through the floor. "It's just the way it's been. I mean—well, it's not as if I haven't kissed women before, or been interested in the rest of it."

"Yes, yes, perfectly normal. But to have remained celibate all this time, there must have been a reason."

Oh, there was a reason, all right, Pascal thought, *but how am I going to explain that?* He fumbled for words the priest might understand.

"It was just that I never felt . . . I didn't think that God meant for me to go about mindlessly rutting for my own pleasure with no thought to the sanctity of marriage. As I never intended to marry, I didn't pay much attention to the more subtle details—I didn't think I'd need them. So I put the whole thing out of my mind."

"If you are looking for advice in this quarter," the priest said wryly, "I'm afraid this is a case of the blind leading the blind."

Pascal's eyebrows shot up and a corner of his mouth lifted in genuine amusement. "Yes, I realize, Father. I wasn't asking for instruction. I imagine I can figure it out if given half a chance. It's getting the chance that worries me."

"Why is that? It seems a perfectly natural thing for two married people to do, especially if you are fond of your wife."

"Yes, but she is in no way fond of me. For one, I refused to live in the château, and I've forced Lily to live a life that she finds humiliating. She hates me for it." Pascal looked down at the floor, then back at the priest.

"Hate—that is quite a strong word. Perhaps she is only displeased with you."

"No," Pascal said adamantly. "She hates me. She hates me for any number of things, and I'm probably deserving of most of them." He pulled his transgressions from the list he'd made in his head on his way to the village. "I've been cold to her, and rude, and I've said a lot of nasty things, even if some of them were true at the time. I've lost my temper with her on countless occasions. I've been too proud to correct her on a number of false assumptions she's made about me."

"Oh? Why is that?"

"Mostly because I'd rather she aim her barbs at things that aren't true than things that are. Lily has an infuriating ability to crawl under my skin."

"Yes, so I gather," Father Chabot said thoughtfully, rubbing his chin.

"Then there's the matter of her brother," Pascal said, the whole thing pouring out like a dam suddenly unstopped. "Lily adores the blasted man—blindly, I assure you. He's her mission in life, and I'm the only thing standing in the way of his happiness, the way Lily chooses to see it."

"Hmm, yes. A difficult impediment to a marriage."

"Yes, and it doesn't seem to matter a bit to her that I'm doing everything I can to help him." Pascal banged his hand on the sill. "All Lily wants is for me to hand over her fortune to him so that he can throw it all away on God only knows what and ignore his responsibilities. But I won't touch her money and I'm certainly not giving it to Jean-Jacques. So she hates me for that, too."

Father Chabot's shiny head bobbed up and down. "Yes. Yes, I see. It is a bit of a problem."

"Yes, it bloody well is. I'd bed Lily in the blink of an eye, but I don't think that God intended for a man to bed a wife who hates him. *That's* the problem."

"I can understand your dilemma," Father Chabot said. "Elizabeth is as stubborn and determined as the day is long, and if she has made up her mind to despise you, it might be quite a job unmaking it."

"Oh, then you know my wife?" Pascal asked with surprise.

"Slightly," Father Chabot said uncomfortably.

"Do you know Lily's brother?" Pascal asked.

"Again, only slightly. I confess, I agree with your appraisal of the duke. He is not a bad man, only lazy and self-indulgent. He has not made himself popular in the area. Nor had your sister when she came the last time, but I think that her actions this afternoon will do much to turn that situation around."

"I hope so. It was brave of her to come out to the fields at all, feeling as she does about everything. But what she did once she was there is a good example of the person she is—the person no one knows, least of all Lily."

"Well, my son. As for advice, I think that your . . . ah . . . growing fondness for your wife should eventually make a difference. You cannot force her to an act she does not want, but perhaps with time and patience she will find a way to be fond of you in return."

"Considering that Lily has sworn to hate me for all eternity, it could be a long wait."

"Ah. Yes, eternity is a very long time indeed," the priest agreed.

"Too long for my liking." Pascal looked up at all those stars a good eternity away, and just as unreachable as Lily. "I can't go on like this."

The priest was silent for a few moments. "Does Elizabeth truly know you?"

It was Pascal's turn to be silent.

"It's a fair question," he said, thinking it over. "There are things she doesn't know about me, as I already told you. Correcting those false assumptions isn't much of a problem. There are things—other things—that I'd rather she didn't know. I don't really see how I'm going to be able to keep them from her in the course of living a lifetime together, though."

There was a long pause before Father Chabot spoke. "Do you not trust her to accept that God made you for a special purpose?" he asked quietly.

Pascal's head snapped around, his eyes sharp. "What do you mean by that?"

"I have heard of you," the priest said apologetically. "News travels quickly in certain circles, and the priesthood is no exception. I am correct in thinking that the monastery you were at was St. Christophe?"

Pascal blew out a long breath. "Yes," he said. "It was St. Christophe."

"And it was you I had heard of?"

"Yes," Pascal said, seeing no point in denying it. At least he now understood the priest's initial response to him, not that he liked the situation. "Yes, it was." He looked away.

"Then how very fortunate we are to have you among us," Father Chabot said simply. "However, by your reaction to my question, I am led to think that there is more than one reason that you chose life in a monastery. Gifts such as yours can be a burden, I would imagine."

"You are very astute, Father," Pascal said with considerable surprise. He hadn't expected this kind of easy acceptance.

"Ah, well," Father Chabot said. "I don't know about astute, but for forty years I've listened to people pour out their troubles. No wonder you were so annoyed with Elizabeth. She took you from your sanctuary."

Pascal managed a smile. "It is sometimes easier doing one's work in a place where people are accustomed to God's hand in things."

"Yes. And now you are here, and it begins again."

"It will," Pascal said with a heavy sigh. "It will."

"Alain will recover then?"

"Yes. Alain will recover, and he'll do it with no trouble, although I wouldn't say such a thing to anyone but yourself. I go out of my way to make people think I'm a run-of-the-mill healer."

"I understand," Father Chabot said, sympathy heavy in his voice. "But that won't last long, will it?"

Pascal shook his head. "The people will come to me, and after something happens that can't be explained away by simple medicine, those same people will start to cross themselves, or make the sign against the devil. I never know which. They'll smile and shake my hand, but they'll keep a certain distance. It's human nature to do that with people who are . . . different."

Father Chabot nodded. "And you do not want this to happen with your wife, now that you've begun to care for her."

"I'm beginning to wonder if God didn't give you the Sight," Pascal said, looking at the priest incisively.

"It's been said before," the priest replied, casting his eyes down modestly. "So. I think you must put your trust in God. He gave you Elizabeth, and He did it quite emphatically, did He not? I don't think He would have sent you a wife who would shy away from His other gift to you. Trust her. Tell her what you have told me."

"Lily," Pascal said, "would probably laugh in my face if I told her. She doesn't believe in God as it is."

"Then find a way to show her His face. She is going to need to know Him if she is to know you, my son."

Pascal rubbed his forehead. "That might be an even bigger challenge than taking Lily to bed."

"Oh, I begin to think that is not so far off. You gave the Lord your celibacy, and He gave you a wife in reply. I doubt He'd be so cruel as to make you wait too much longer."

That earned a laugh from Pascal. "You're an earthy man

for a priest, Father, and bless you for it. I'll think over what you said. And thank you—my heart is lighter for our talk.''

"I am pleased. Oh. About the vineyards . . .'' His voice held a note of hopeful question.

Pascal held up one hand with a smile. "Don't worry, Father. I have a green thumb, too. But you might say some fervent prayers. We're not out of the woods yet.''

As soon as Pascal left, the priest got down on his knees. He said a heartfelt prayer of thanks to the Good Lord. He was confident that young Alain would fully recover if Pascal LaMartine said he would. He had no reason to doubt that Pascal was blessed with the touch of God, and given what he'd said—and hadn't said—he was certain of it.

Then he said another, more fervent prayer asking for wisdom and guidance, for he also knew that he was going to be in hearty need of both.

He finally rose, knees creaking, wondering how long it would take for the rumors to start, almost surprised that they hadn't already. Odd. Pascal LaMartine did have a look of his father about him.

15

PASCAL left his pallet at dawn the next morning and climbed up to the meadow on top of the hill behind the cottage. From there one could see far over the countryside, over the Dordogne that glittered beyond, a wide silver thread that wound its way back and forth between the verdant fields and the vineyards that spread out in a vivid patchwork of color and life. Here there was a stretch covered in the scarlet red of poppies, there another, the brilliant yellow of mustard. Little clusters of villages were scattered about, Saint-Simon closest by, sleepy and still.

The château rose up on its own hill to the west, its fortified towers glimmering in the rosy light, the limestone softened into a pale ochre. It was a beautiful sight.

Very little moved at this hour when the sun was drifting up over the horizon, save for an occasional farmer or his wife out to milk the cows or tend to one of the various other chores that needed doing before the day's work really began. For Pascal, this time alone was precious, as peaceful and fulfilling as Matins had ever been.

He settled on the ground, drawing his legs up and crossing them, his feet placed against his thighs, his hands resting on his knees, then drew in a deep breath and let it out. He had a great deal on his mind, not the least of which was the talk he'd had with Father Chabot the night before. Chabot was a good man and brilliant at his calling, his intuition as sharp as anything Pascal had ever seen, his practicality sweetly gentled by humor.

The contrast to Father Mallet could not have been more extreme, and Pascal fervently wished that Lily had been brought up with Chabot's version of God rather than Mallet's.

Show her His face, Chabot had said. But how? Lily refused to admire something as simple as a sunrise. She was hardly likely to be any more receptive to its Maker. He couldn't imagine Lily being cordial to her Maker at all. No doubt when the time came and Lily was confronted with positive proof, she would tell Him off for not having been more scientific about His existence.

Pascal smiled, then closed his eyes and surrendered himself.

Something cold and wet pressed through the cloth of his trousers and nudged his knee. His eyes flew open to find Bean, her entire body wriggling with pleasure. Not far behind Bean was her mistress, holding a basket in one hand, her nose buried in the pages of a book on herbs he had given her the night before.

Lily had clearly taken it upon herself to learn all about their harvesting and was serious enough in intent to have dragged herself out of bed at this hour to gather the herbs before the heat of the sun drew out the oils. Unfortunately, she had missed the part about letting the dew dry first.

He pulled Bean's warm little body into the cradle made by his thighs and watched Lily with fascination as she poked her way along the ground, bending over various plants, very few of which were going to be of any use. She was concentrated on her task, her rosy mouth pulled together like a raspberry ripe for the plucking.

Pascal drew in a deep breath of longing. He may never have been with a woman, but there wasn't a thing wrong with his instincts. Lily in the wild, unfettered by a duchy, was a sight to behold. Her dresses had faded with constant washing and the help of the strong summer sun, and as she no longer bothered with layers of petticoats, he could see the outline of her long legs beneath the fabric. The nipples of her high breasts were equally visible, hard nubs pushing against the thin cloth.

Pascal broke into a cold sweat, painfully aware of the erection that would have impressed even Charlie. He wondered if he couldn't quietly slip away, but before he had a chance, Lily turned, calling for Bean, and saw him. He quickly reached for Bean and pulled her directly on top of his lap, hoping to hide the evidence of his arousal.

"Pascal? What are you doing here? You must be soaked through." She marched toward him, reminding Pascal once again of an avenging angel.

"I was meditating," he said, hoping his voice didn't sound as hoarse to her as it did to him.

"Meditating about what? Why?" She planted her hands on her hips in a familiar stance.

"It's something I do every morning. As for what it's about, I can't exactly say. It's, ah . . . it's a little like praying, I suppose, only without the litany. It all works out to be the same thing in the end." He prayed for his erection to subside, not an easy thing, for Bean was wiggling on it.

Lily rolled her eyes. "It sounds incredibly boring. I really can't see the attraction."

Bean, impatient with sitting in Pascal's lap, jumped down and trotted off to explore the edges of the wood, and Pascal realized with infinite relief that his body was back under his control—probably because of Lily's expression of withering disdain.

"It's not easy to explain," he said helplessly. "You have to experience it to understand the attraction."

And then inspiration struck. Without thinking about it further, he reached up and grabbed both of her wrists, pulling her down opposite him in a disordered heap.

"You brute! What do you think you're—"

"Hush, Lily."

"Lily . . . you called me Lily," she said suspiciously. "You called me that yesterday, too. Why?"

"It's your name isn't it? I shall call you much worse in another moment if you don't listen to me. For once just close your mouth and open your eyes. I want you to look."

"Look at what?" she said in confusion.

"Just look. Look out over the valley. Look at what's around you. Look at the mist shifting below, the brilliant green of the grass, the rooftops of the village."

Lily sighed impatiently. "I'm not blind, you know. I can see perfectly well."

"You said you wanted to learn, didn't you? Well, this is part of it. Half the art of healing is learning to pay attention. And if you're going to pay attention, the first thing you need to do is to learn how to look—and how to listen, and not just to me, but to yourself."

"All right," she said, biting her lip. "If you insist. But I think this is very silly."

"Never mind," he said, releasing her hands but maintaining a light touch on her fingertips, supporting them under his hands. "Now, close your eyes. Listen to everything around you. Listen to the sounds, listen to the silence, and when you've done that, take all of it into yourself. Let it sit inside of you like a great comfort, Lily. Let it speak to you in its own language. It will, you know. All you have to do is to let it."

Lily was sure that Pascal had gone mad, but she did want to learn about making people better. She tentatively closed her eyes.

"Breathe," he said softly, and she heard the catch of laughter in his voice. She realized that she'd been holding her breath, and she exhaled sharply, then took in a few quick breaths for good measure. Her breathing soon settled down as she concentrated on listening. At first she heard nothing at all except a few birds twittering, but gradually she noticed that the wind was sighing in the trees and she could hear the leaves rustle in response. She heard voices too, faint but still noticeable, floating up from the village far below. Much closer came the sound of Pascal's breathing, slow and even.

An extraordinary blanket of calm slowly began to drift over her, a lovely sense of peace and well-being, and it seemed to slip directly from Pascal's fingertips into her own. She felt the warmth of his hands under hers, and she realized that his hands were resting on his knees, and those knees were lightly pressed against her own.

She felt the breeze in her hair and the sun warming her back, and she felt as if there were a sun inside her as well, something that glowed in her center and spread out gently through her limbs, leaving her as open and soft and vulnerable as a new life experiencing sensation for the first time. Maybe this was what a newborn babe felt like after squeezing its way out of the dark and into open space, all raw and fresh and happy to be breathing air and seeing light.

She drifted for a time, safe and secure, but then she became aware of something insistent pulling at her through the warm haze, something she could no more resist than drawing breath. She sighed and slowly opened her eyes, obeying the silent call that sounded as loud as if it had been shouted. Pascal looked directly at her, a faint smile lifting the corners of his wide mouth, his dark eyes unwavering as they held hers in a steady grip, as steady and firm as the hands beneath her own.

She fell into the gaze that was and wasn't Pascal. There was a brilliant light all around the outer edge of her vision, all around him, whitish-gold and shimmering, yet all she could see was the endless depth of those dark eyes as the call touched her soul and led her toward something with a yearning beyond description. She was helpless to do anything but follow it. And so she went, and as she did, something sharp and painful rose in her, an open flame that grew steadily brighter until it shot through every vein, exploding into fire as it reached that soft open place just below her heart. She almost cried out, it hurt so much.

Yet it was not the unbearable, unceasing pain of emptiness that she'd felt when her mother had left and, later, Jean-Jacques. This was altogether different, a pain born of fullness and joy, too profound to fit into a single thought— or even a thousand. It went on and on in great rolling waves as if it would never stop, flowing ever fuller, filling her until she felt she could not contain it and would burst apart. Just as she thought she could bear no more, it gently began to release her, infinitely slowly, leaving her with nothing more tangible than the desire to burst into tears.

In that moment she realized that hot tears were coursing down her cheeks.

"Sweet Lily," Pascal murmured, and the brilliant, translucent light shivered and rippled around him, slowly fading until it became nothing more than simple sunlight.

"Pascal," she whispered shakily, "what was it?"

"Some people call it God," he said very, very quietly. "Others call it the touch of the soul."

"You know—you know, then, what I mean?"

"I know," he said, then reached out to her and wiped away the wet trails of tears with his thumbs.

"Where does it come from? How did you make it happen?"

"You made it happen," he said, smiling gently. "I think you must have been doing a very good job of listening."

"Were you there too? Did you feel it?"

His smile widened. "I was there too. And yes, I felt it."

Lily thought about this for a moment. "Can you make it happen again?"

Pascal burst into laughter. "Ah, Lily. You really are amazing."

"But can you?" she persisted, wanting nothing more, for she felt a sense of real loss.

"That depends entirely on you," he said, grinning, and he suddenly looked completely normal, quite like the wretch she was accustomed to.

She shook her head as if to throw off a spell. "Are you sure this is part of healing?" she asked doubtfully.

Pascal stretched out in the grass, resting his cheek on the palm of one hand. "It is if you believe that the body and the soul are connected," he said, tracing two interlocking rings in the grass with the other. "You can tell the body to heal until you're blue in the face, and use every medical trick you can think of, but it won't do much good if the other part isn't listening."

Lily's brow furrowed in concentration. "Yesterday . . . was Alain listening?"

"Yes," Pascal said in a matter-of-fact tone. "If Alain hadn't wanted to stay here, he could have gone easily enough. But he did want to stay, and he was listening very carefully indeed."

"You knew that?" Lily asked, fascinated.

"Yes, I knew that."

"How?" Lily demanded.

Pascal let out a deep breath, amazed at how quickly Lily had grasped the essentials—amazed at how quickly and sweetly she had opened herself to his touch—but he was now in the difficult position of deciding how much to tell her without frightening her away. Then again, no one had ever questioned him so forthrightly before, and in a way it was a relief.

His family and the monks had simply accepted his gift, as had Father Chabot. Doctors either ignored it or called him a charlatan. The people he'd treated over the years had been grateful, but behaved as if he were not altogether mortal.

Lily, on the other hand, was regarding him as if he were very mortal indeed, and she didn't look the least bit worried about it either way. If anything she looked slightly skeptical.

"Well?" she persisted.

"I can't really explain it in words," he said. "It's a feeling more than anything. You probe with that feeling just as you might probe a body with an instrument. Does that make sense to you?''

Lily stared at him. "Make *sense*? You wretch! *That's* what you did to me just now, isn't it? You went probing. I should cuff your ears for taking such liberties with my person.'' She pulled up a handful of grass and threw it at him.

"I didn't take a single liberty with your person,'' he said indignantly, deflecting the grassy shower with his forearm. "Only with your soul. That's quite a different matter.''

"So you admit it. I *knew* it.''

"There was a point to be proved,'' he said mildly. "I didn't think you'd mind.''

"Well, I think you're very presumptuous indeed, marching about in other people's souls without so much as a by-your-leave. You'd think you were Christ himself, the way you behave.''

"I see that your opinion of me has gone up by leaps and bounds,'' Pascal said, but he was relieved that she wasn't really angry. "As I last remember, you considered me no more than a common gardener. No, wait—an ill-bred, common guttersnipe variety of a gardener.''

"Well, not much has changed as far as that is concerned. The only difference is that you are an ill-bred *and* fiendish guttersnipe of a gardener with a penchant for poking about in people. Not that I don't think there isn't a scientific explanation for this probing of yours.''

"Oh?" he said, his eyes dancing. "What would that be?''

"How am I supposed to know? You're the scientist, not me.''

"Oh, so you finally noticed,'' he said dryly. "I confess, I'm surprised.''

She fell silent for a few minutes, and Pascal watched the emotions that chased across her face. There was pride and uncertainty, followed by true confusion, and finally, as if she'd won some sort of inner battle, there was resolution.

"Pascal?" she finally said, her cheeks flushing.

"What?" he asked softly, seeing that her flippancy had vanished. He wasn't surprised. He'd realized that she had initially needed it for protection, but she now looked as if she was ready to talk.

"What is it, duchess?'' He reached out one hand and took her slender fingers, comfortably enfolding them in his larger ones, rubbing the tips with his thumb.

"I'm sorry," she said, in a voice so low that it was barely audible.

"Sorry? Why? For what?"

"Because I didn't understand." Her head was bowed and he couldn't see her eyes.

"There are many things none of us understands," he said. "What particular lack of understanding has suddenly cast you into gloom?"

"You," she said bluntly, pushing her hair out of her face with her free hand and looking at him solemnly. "I really did think that you were a common gardener, and you're not."

Here it comes, Pascal thought. *Best face it head on.* "No?" he asked cautiously. "Then what am I?"

"You're a botanist," Lily said, looking at him as if he ought to have known that for himself.

Pascal opened his mouth and then closed it again, desperately trying to recover his equilibrium. This was the last thing he'd been expecting, and yet it was the antithesis of what he had been dreading. "Well—yes," he finally said. "That's true. I am."

"Then what were you doing shut away in that monastery? I mean, of all places that you might have been, why were you there? Were you doing penance or weren't you?"

"Penance? Whatever gave you that idea?"

"Isn't that why laypeople usually hide away in monasteries?"

"Rarely. Some go for a period of retreat, others because they're not sure they have a calling and want to test the waters. Some go to escape. There are a myriad of reasons why people are drawn to monasteries, a myriad of others why they stay."

"And yours?"

"I'd been asked," he said simply. "There was a problem with the gardens and they needed an expert. Dom Benetard knew I was accustomed to monastic life, having studied for a time at a monastery in Tibet, so it would be no hardship for me to live away from the world. But what has that to do with—why are you asking me this now?"

"Because I feel bad that I doubted your skill and your education, and I don't understand why you didn't enlighten me."

He smiled. "I didn't think you were interested in enlightenment. I'm not sure you would have heard me even if I had tried to tell you. It's not the first explanation you've closed your ears to."

"Well, you told me to listen, so I am trying."

She looked so earnest that it tore at Pascal's heart. There were a great many things about Lily that were suddenly tearing at his heart. There was always a risk involved when one went delving into another person, but he'd only ever done it before in the pursuit of healing. This had been different, and he'd known it in that moment of decision, the split second when he'd chosen to follow her. Still, it was one thing knowing it at the time and another thing dealing with the consequences.

He'd intended for Lily to look within herself, and he'd intended to help her on that journey. What he hadn't intended was to lose himself so completely in the process. But he had. He'd gone along with her, opening himself, opening her, urging her on. He'd traveled with her, feeling his way through the labyrinth of tight, dark places she struggled so hard against, the pain, the misery, the scars, experiencing for himself the truth of her life.

His heart had nearly broken for her then, but he had fought to keep her going, deeper and deeper into herself. He'd felt her softening, felt her vulnerability, felt the sweetness of her spirit as it quickened, approaching that place where all things became one. Home. He had never been there with another living being, not like this, not as if they were one soul, one heartbeat, one breath.

The light had been so bright, so clear, so filled with love, and with it had come a comprehension that had shaken him to his very foundation. He was in love with Lily—deeply, achingly, irrevocably in love with her.

He wondered how long he'd been keeping such a simple truth from himself. He wondered if it hadn't been out of sheer terror at what such a thing would mean to a person like himself. He'd never expected it, never even thought to ask for it, sure that this aspect of life was not intended for him.

And yet it had happened. Despite everything, it had happened. He ought to have realized as much when he had spoken to Father Chabot. It had never been in his nature to desire—not like this, not this burning, overwhelming physical need to join himself with a woman. The most he'd experienced was the usual curiosity of an adolescent—and those few brief forays had never given him any satisfaction, leaving only disgust and a sense of alienation. He had decided it wasn't for him, and ignored any further impulses he had.

But this was different. He had expressed his love for Lily without words, without anything but the touch of his soul on hers. Consummation was an interesting thing, he'd discovered, although he doubted that very many people went about it in quite such a way.

"Why do you look at me so?" Lily asked, her teeth nervously worrying her bottom lip, her eyes now more smoke than moss. She looked as soft and open on the outside as she'd felt on the inside. He was tempted to take her right there and then and do in body what he'd just finished doing in spirit.

"Pascal?" she asked uncertainly.

"I look at you like this because I daren't do anything else," he said, his voice hoarse. "If I follow my instincts, I don't know what you will do."

"What instincts?" she asked, equally hoarsely.

"This, for one," he said, unable to help himself. He shifted, lifting himself into a sitting position and wrapped his hand around the soft, fragile nape of her neck, pulling her toward him.

To his amazement her bones were soft and giving under his hands and she didn't flinch as he lowered his mouth to hers and took it. His heart pounded as hard as if he were a youth making his first attempt at a kiss. Lily's lips were so soft, so ripe, and they trembled beneath his own. He wanted her so badly that he didn't know what to do with himself.

Lily, true to form, took care of that, shattering his senses with a fist that socked into his unguarded stomach. He doubled over, gasping with pain.

"Just as I thought," she said furiously, shaking her hand hard. "You had no intention of anything but using me for your own gain, had you? You manipulative beast! You—you rakehell!"

"Lily—I swear to you, it wasn't like that. You must know it wasn't like that."

"Oh, and what was it, then? Explain yourself, you rutting cad!"

"I—I can't." Pascal was torn between fury and a treach-

erous desire to laugh. Laughter won out in the end, and he
shook with it, clutching his bruised belly at the same time.
"You have one hell of a fist, duchess," he said admiringly.
"And I thought your mouth was dangerous."

"Wretch."

He grabbed her wrists before she could do him any more
damage. "What are you so afraid of? All I did was kiss
you, and what harm was there in that? You are my wife,
after all."

"In name only."

He chose not to answer that. *Go slowly,* he told himself.
Go very, very slowly.

"And I'm not afraid," she added, belligerently adjusting
her skirts, but he felt the sudden fear release its grip on her.

"Lily," he said, releasing her hands and leaning back on
his elbows. "I must say, it is an odd name for a spitting
cat. I once knew a Lily. She was housemaid at the Close.
Actually, she was a good friend. She married happily and
went off to have half a dozen children, and I haven't seen
her in years."

"Oh, are you now comparing me to a housemaid? Why
am I not surprised?"

"Stop, duchess," he said quietly. "It's not necessary.
Not anymore."

She stuck her chin forward as if to argue, and then she
suddenly dropped her gaze, staring at her hands. "I'm
sorry," she whispered. "I don't mean to be so difficult. I
don't know how to be any different."

"But you do," he said, reaching out a hand and stroking
her hair. "You might be too frightened to behave any other
way just now, but I'm here, and I'll continue to be here.
I'm *not* going away, as much as you might wish it. Do you
wish it?"

She lifted her eyes to his, tears hovering on her lashes.
"I—I don't know anymore," she said.

"I love it when you're honest," he said, brushing his
thumb over the tears. "You weren't being honest with me
last night, were you?"

She bowed her head again. "I'm so confused."

"That I understand," he said with a smile. "Tell me
what you were thinking last night. Really."

Lily fiddled with her skirt. "I can't."

"All right," he said, picking up one of her hands and

rubbing his thumb over the palm. "I'll tell you what I was thinking. I was thinking that I wanted to kiss you, very badly."

Lily's eyes shot to his. "You were?"

"You know I was. Because you were thinking the same thing, weren't you?" He rubbed his thumb up and down the inside of her arm.

Blood began pounding in Lily's ears. She could hardly think over the noise. He raised her hand to his mouth and kissed the inside of her wrist where his thumb had just been, and she felt faint and yet vibrantly awake at the same time.

"Weren't you?" he persisted, his breath warm on her racing pulse.

Lily nodded, her head all heavy and dreamy. "But I shouldn't have been thinking that at all," she said thickly, her eyes half closed.

"Why not, sweetheart? Why ever not?" He kissed the tender inside of her elbow, causing a shock to race through her, snapping her out of her drugged stupor.

"Don't call me sweetheart." She pulled her hand away abruptly.

Pascal laughed, and Lily glared at him. He looked like the worst sort of rake, his grin flashing strong white teeth, his eyes lazy and dangerous, his powerful body relaxed, but ready to do all sorts of decadent things, she was quite sure.

"Why did you kiss me?" she demanded.

"It seemed the most natural thing to do just then. Why did you punch me?"

Lily couldn't help herself. She smiled broadly. "For the same reason."

He pushed his fingers through her hair, gently separating the strands. "Are you going to do me bodily damage every time I touch you? I'd better lay in a good supply of splints and arnica balm then. Breaks and severe bruising seem inevitable."

"Do you mean to touch me often?" Lily shivered. "You said you wouldn't—right after we were married. Don't you remember?"

"I remember very well, and I was an idiot," he said succinctly. "Although I truly thought I meant it at the time. But things have been changing between us for quite some time." He took her face between his hands, his eyes filled with a banked fire. "I want you, Lily."

She stared up at him, her eyes filled with tears of confusion and misery and longing.

"It's all right to want me too," he said quietly.

She shook her head furiously inside the cup of his hands. "It's not all right at all," she cried. "It's not! You are my enemy! How can I wish for such a thing—how can I wish for you with any conscience?"

Her voice rang with a clear honesty that cut Pascal to the core. He dropped his hands and looked down, his fingers clenching tightly in the grass. Inasmuch as he had opened Lily's heart and soul to him, he had opened his own to her, and was now discovering exactly how vulnerable that made him.

He released his fingers with an effort and forced himself to speak calmly. "I learned long ago that it's a waste of time to speak words that you refuse to hear. So I won't answer you now, save to say that I am not your enemy. One day you will hear me and know it to be the truth, but until then I won't touch you again, no matter how much I might want to. As God is my witness, I swear this to you."

She covered her face with her hands. He knew her heart was breaking and he knew why. Sweet, lovely Lily. Lily, the clean vessel, who drank in everything, and if she found it to be soured, spat it right back out.

She had just drunk of the finest, the headiest of wine served in the clearest of crystal. They had sipped of each other's souls in a communion that could only have been given by God. He knew it had no comparison to anything she had ever tasted before—everything before this was cheap and false, unripened grapes served in a tin cup. Lily knew it too.

But until she had tasted the false wine one more time, she wouldn't be able to judge it. Lily's palate needed a good cleansing before she could truly savor what she'd been given.

He suddenly couldn't wait for Jean-Jacques to come home.

"Lily," he said, taking her hands away from her tear-stained face. "Don't upset yourself like this. It will all come right in time." He rose to his feet in one swift movement. "I must go to the vineyards."

Lily nodded without lifting her head.

Pascal walked away, using all of his willpower to keep from looking back.

* * *

Lily clutched her hands around her waist and bent over as if she'd been brutally hit in a place far more painful than her stomach. "I can't feel this way," she whispered, rocking back and forth. "I can't!" And yet she did, and knew it to be the ultimate betrayal.

Only half an hour before she had let him walk into her very center as if she had been an open door. She had let him touch her with his fire as if he had been branding himself on her, and she had been helpless to fight. She hadn't wanted to fight. He had marked her, and when he had finished he had smiled at her, the very sun itself, and her heart had turned inside out.

Now she knew what it was she'd seen that day at the monastery when he had looked up over his shoulder and nearly toppled her. Now she knew why she'd thought him dangerous. She wondered how many women he had done this to before, first made their souls flame and then ignited their bodies.

A violent shiver ran through her in memory and her fingers crept to her mouth. When he'd kissed her, she'd thought she'd go up like straw. One more second and she would have lain down on the ground with him and let him do whatever he pleased to her. But she would not give in. *She would not.* Her self-respect and her loyalty to her brother were all she had left to her, and she would remain true to both.

Her eyes dry and her throat hot and constricted, Lily pulled herself together, called for Bean, and started home, only remembering her book and her basket at the last minute.

Just now life felt not worth living, and yet she had never felt so alive. It seemed an impossible paradox.

16

"LILY, hand me the balm of echinacea, would you?" Pascal extended his left hand as his right moved over the burned area of little Jeannie Moreau's arm. She'd been shrieking when she first came in, scalded by a spilt pot of water, her skin in some places violently red, in others covered in blisters. Pascal had immediately doused the arm in cold water mixed with an extract of chamomile, and now the blisters were subsiding along with Jeannie's pain.

Lily gave him the balm and he applied it, then covered the area with a fine linen cloth. "Jeannie will be fine in two or three days," he told Madame Moreau. "Keep the dressing clean and dry, and don't let her pull at it. If you have any worries, don't hesitate to come." He refused payment, as always, and after the door had closed behind them, he leaned back in his chair, stretching his back.

"I think that's it for the night," he said, looking over at the pot. "What's for supper? I'm starved."

"Plucked chicken," Lily said wickedly. "My specialty."

Pascal groaned. "Singed feathers again?"

"Not quite so many as the last time around. I *am* improving, Pascal, believe it or not." She cleaned up the table, put the soiled bandages aside to soak, ready for washing in the morning, then went outside to fetch a lettuce from the garden.

It was a beautiful evening, the sun barely topping the trees, casting a soft glow over the valley below. She cut a particularly nice lettuce, the leaves still soft green and tender. Her heart caught painfully as she straightened and her gaze was drawn to the turrets of the Château de Saint-Simon, shining mellow gold in the evening light. She tried to avoid looking at it, with its dark windows and deserted air. It had been well over a month since Jean-Jacques had written to say he'd be home within the week.

She missed him terribly and she wanted him to see his vineyards, bursting with fruit. She wanted to see him, to see his dear face, flushed with her own financial success. She just wanted to be near him, to be reminded of her family, to be reminded of the other world, the one in which someone called Elizabeth Bowes had lived a lifetime ago.

And yet . . . Lily closed her eyes, trying not to think about that qualifier. If she had a choice, she knew she'd choose that other life filled with beautiful dresses and parties, courtiers and laden tables, respectful servants bowing to her every need, and most especially a husband who allowed her to go her own way.

Or would she? What about Madame Moreau and her sweet little Jeannie? Or Alain, or the dozens of others who had visited their humble cottage with runny noses, aching bones, sore throats, and upset stomachs? What about Jean-Pierre Hubert, who had broken his arm so badly that the splintered bone had poked out of his skin?

What about tiny Marie-Claire, all of six months, who had been brought by her frantic mother, the baby's lips blue as her face. Pascal had cut a hole in her windpipe and inserted a tube, and the baby had begun breathing again. He'd then dislodged the stone of a plum from deep in her throat with a long skinny metal thing he called forceps. Lily had helped him, holding Marie-Claire down.

She loved it, her work alongside Pascal, the nights of studying, learning all she could, making ready the supplies, waiting for Pascal to open the door in the early evening as a sign that the people were welcome.

And in the end, what about Pascal?

Lily was more torn than she'd ever been in her life. Everything she'd been brought up to believe, to think important and worthy of respect, was disputed every day by her experience with the villagers, by Pascal himself, though he remained her single greatest fear.

Nothing made sense any more. She looked forward to each day, to each new challenge. But more than anything, she looked forward to Jean-Jacques's return. He would make sense out of everything. Seeing the château come to life with his presence would restore her sense of balance and order and put that old life that she missed so much into proper perspective. It had to.

Pascal paused in the act of rolling clean linen strips into neat bundles, arrested by the sight of Lily sitting in a chair by the fire, her hair shimmering in the last of the light as she bent over an English translation of the ancient *Pen Tsao Ching,* Shen Nung's classic book of herbal prescriptions, her feet tucked up underneath her. Open next to her on the table was Culpepper's *Complete Herbal and English Physician.* The pink tip of her tongue poked out of one corner of her mouth, worrying back and forth as she read, hypnotizing him. He could think of other ways for her to occupy her tongue.

His groin stiffened as he watched her, pushing painfully against the front of his trousers. That was nothing new—in fact, it was so old it was becoming second nature, but that didn't lessen the need for her that grew daily.

Lily flipped the page, stroking two tapered fingers over the paper as lightly, as intently, as he wished she would stroke him. His forehead broke out into a sweat, and he dragged his gaze away from the sight of Lily by the fire, trying to think of something other than how she would look and feel and taste if he walked over to her, took the book out of her hands, and pulled her to the ground.

Pascal swore under his breath as he fumbled and dropped the roll of linen. Keeping his hands and his heart to himself was driving him to distraction, and living inside of his own body was becoming sheer torture.

He found himself watching her all the time, taking simple pleasure in her natural sensuality, the easy grace with which she moved. He loved the slow smile that spread over her face and lit up her eyes when something pleased her, or the grin that came and went like a streak of quicksilver when she was amused but trying to hide it from him. She was good at that, hiding her feelings from him. He was just as good at chasing them down.

Lily had surprised him in the last month. She studied constantly, stood at his side when the patients came in, supporting, fetching, doing whatever was needed without question or complaint. She saved her questions until they were alone, listening carefully to his answers—and almost always retaining what he told her.

Best of all, Lily hadn't once looked at him oddly, nor even seemed to notice that he had an extraordinarily high success rate with his patients. She accepted everything that happened as a normal part of medicine.

He wasn't going to question her acceptance. He wasn't going to question anything at all. He was far too happy watching her coming to life, just as the land had been coming to life—at first starved for sustenance, then gradually warming, stretching, putting out the first shoots, then flowers, and now bearing healthy clusters of fruit. She had blossomed in the fresh air and sunshine, the satisfaction of hard work and the steady warmth of kindness and companionship—not that she would admit it.

He risked glancing up at her again. Her concentration was absolute, her breasts rising and falling with the rhythm of her breathing. There was a new beauty to Lily, something that had gradually grown in her as the weeks passed. She'd turned the cottage into a home, putting vases of flowers about, taking pride in keeping the place clean—she'd even made curtains out of some pretty material that Madame Lascard had given them after Alain had recovered.

Lily had become domestic . . . content.

And he continued to love her even as she kept him at a distance—or so she thought. She had no idea how very near he was to her, always. But he couldn't intrude, not until she opened the door herself. In the interim he wished there was a way to stop aching for her.

He wondered what she was thinking about. She hadn't turned the page in minutes, and her eyes were focused on some distant thought.

As if in response to that silent question, she looked up at him, her smoky eyes narrowed in thought. "Pascal?"

"Hmm?"

She tucked her chin on the heel of her palm. "What made you go to China and Japan and all those other places you said you'd been to?"

He put down the bandage on the clean sheet in front of him and picked up another. "I wanted to examine new types of plants, thinking to import them to Europe."

"How did you find out about Chinese medicine? It's different in so many ways, and you were a botanist, not a doctor."

"Well," he said, dodging the issue, "the two aren't so very far apart, being linked by plants."

"Yes . . . I suppose that's true." She closed the book on her lap. "But still, you seem to know a lot about it."

Pascal paused before carefully answering. "Certain aspects of Western medicine leave something to be desired, so in every country I visited, I learned what I could about the local healing methods. I discovered an interesting commonality among the Asian traditions."

"Really? Such as what?"

"Well, let's see. In India there are the Ayurvedic healers—also herbalists; in China, I found many of the formulas to be the same. I confess I still don't know much about the practice of Asian medicine, so if you're asking about the different pulses, the yin and yang, all the elements and functions and so on, I can't help you."

"What about the energy paths described here?"

Admiration surged in him for Lily, a swelling of pride in the way she absorbed knowledge, valued it as much as he did. "I suppose the most I ever saw of that put into actual practice was in the use of acupuncture," he said. "The results were impressive. I was fortunate to watch a difficult surgery conducted with needles placed to deaden the pain. The patient never blinked."

"Oh . . . yes, I've been reading about that," Lily said. "No, that's not what I meant. I don't understand why nothing is mentioned anywhere in these books about the colors." She rubbed her neck and yawned. "I suppose some of these books are so old that the authors weren't aware of the scientific value of certain descriptions. Or perhaps they took them for granted."

"The colors?" he asked, as casually as he could manage.

"Yes—you know, those very subtle colors that come from your hands when you're working." She frowned, looking uncertain. "You do know what I mean, don't you? It was blue just now when you were working on Jeannie's burn. I thought you must have learned how to do that in China. I'm not imagining it, am I?"

Pascal stared at her. Only one other person he'd known in his life had seen colors when he worked, and that had been a monk in Tibet. Yet here was Lily the scientist behaving as if the unexplained phenomenon was merely another fact to get straight. "No, you're not imagining it."

He suppressed a strong desire to pick her up and crush her to him, overwhelmed with relief and love and a feeling of kinship. Lily could see auras, and since no one had ever told her that she shouldn't, she didn't know that it wasn't a normal thing—that *he* wasn't normal.

"Pascal, why are you looking so self-satisfied?"

"Because you are a star pupil, Lily my love—a genius."

"I can't think why. It seemed an obvious enough remark."

Pascal grinned, still filled with elation. "Yes, but not everyone can see the way you do. It takes a special talent that very few people have."

Lily flushed with pleasure. "Really? Why?"

"It's not a physical talent so much as an inner one. What you are seeing is different energies. The colors change because each one has a different purpose, a different vibrancy. Usually there's a heat that goes along with them, although not always."

Lily's gaze became distant, thoughtful. "I think I understand. In the meadow, when you did that—that thing, there was light, clear and white, all around your body. It was . . . well, I don't know what it was, only that it was different from this. When you work on people, it's very focused. Is that right?"

"Yes. That's exactly right."

"Oh, good!" she said, looking extremely pleased with herself. "Maybe I will be competent at this someday."

"I think you're already competent. You're learning very quickly, and you're more help to me than you realize."

"I enjoy helping you. And I enjoy helping the people who come. They're always so grateful. It's nice to feel needed and appreciated."

She smiled mischievously, the sparkle in her eyes and the provocative curve of her mouth drawing his gaze, holding it. "I must admit I love opening the door and discovering the things left outside," she said. "Food is always nice, but my very favorite was Monsieur Lascard's bedstead. I thought I'd expire with delight."

"To this day I don't know how he knew we were without a proper bed," he said, the very mention of the damned thing driving him to distraction.

"I told him," Lily said, as if it were self-evident. "He kept going on and on to me about how he could repay you, since you refused to take his money, and since he is a carpenter, I told him that a bedstead would be greatly appreciated.''

He forced his gaze away from her mouth, willed his blood to flow smoothly instead of pulsing wildly through his veins. ''You can't ask people for things, duchess. That defeats the purpose.''

''Pascal, be sensible. Monsieur Lascard was miserable about not being able to show his appreciation, and he didn't feel that Madame's fabric was enough of a gesture. So I did what was practical, and now he's happy, because he knows his bedstead was something we needed, and he's repaid you for his son's life. You can be far too stubborn.''

''*Stubborn?* That, coming from you?''

She nodded. ''You are proud and impossible, especially when it comes to asking for things. It's a good thing that you have a wife to be sensible for you, or we'd be in a terrible pickle. Really, Pascal, you must try to understand people better.''

There was nothing to say to that, short of bursting into laughter at her assessment of herself. Pascal managed to control himself though, a discipline born of three months of life with Lily. He turned away to bottle the infusions that she had been steeping in the sink that day.

She'd already become accomplished at gathering and drying plants, and had recently begun making infusions and tinctures and balms. The cottage always smelled of something interesting, although he'd prefer to forget the day that Lily had inadvertently gathered great quantities of the wrong species of hawthorn and crushed the leaves. The entire place had smelled like the bubonic plague, and it had taken two days to air it out. She hadn't made that mistake again.

He was beginning to wonder if Lily didn't have something of the true healer in her, if perhaps that explained her quick grasp of medical knowledge, her lack of shock and revulsion at the more gruesome aspects of treatment. Perhaps it explained her ability to see auras . . .

''Lily,'' he asked, wiping the neck of the bottle and corking it, ''how long have you been seeing these colors? Has it been always, or just recently?''

''I really don't know. I was rarely in the hands of a doctor. But there was the time when I was ten and had the fever and a sore throat.'' Frowning, she wrapped her arms around her middle as if to protect herself. "It was the only time I ever did see a doctor. His hands were dirty, and there was a nasty brown light coming from them that had nothing to do with dirt. I remember now—it was murky, like mud, and I didn't want him to touch me."

She looked at Pascal sheepishly. "I threw a terrible tantrum, and he was forced to go away and take his lances and leeches with him. I was better almost instantly."

"I am glad you had the good sense to pitch a tantrum." So it was a natural thing, deeply ingrained in her. He ought to have known, considering what had happened in the meadow. *Lily, my love,* he thought with a longing so intense it physically hurt, *when are you going to let me back in?*

"I don't know," she said, her arms tightening around her waist. "It might have been more sensible to let him bleed me. Father Mallet took the cane to me in the worst way, for being ungrateful to those who knew better. I couldn't sit down for days."

Pascal's hand froze on the cloth he was using to wipe the bottles. "Did Father Mallet take the cane to you often?"

"Oh, yes. I think it was his favorite pastime—other than praying. Whenever I'd done something wrong his eyes would light up, and the next thing I knew, I was in the chapel, bent over the altar rail, my skirts over my head 'to blind my eyes and muffle my mouth so as not to offend God,' he said. He never bothered to mention that a cane on one's naked backside stung twenty times harder than it did when delivered through the layer of a petticoat, as my father did it. I don't think Father Mallet liked me very much. Why do you look so appalled? Jean-Jacques got much worse . . . surely you were caned?" she asked uncertainly.

"No. I wasn't," Pascal said, struggling against his rage. Had Father Mallet been in the room, Pascal would not have been accountable for his actions. "Go on," he said tightly.

"There's not much more to tell you. Father Mallet would always be much nicer to me afterward. He would give me a sweet, as if that helped, and pat me as if I were a dog, telling me that God would forgive me if I was a good girl. Well, he and I both knew that I was never going to be a good girl, but I'd pretend, because I knew that if I didn't pretend, I'd just get caned again. I'd learned that lesson. So I pretended humility. Then he'd smile—you know that horrible little smile of his?"

Pascal nodded stiffly as a bone-deep chill cut through him. He stared at the floor, not trusting himself to look at Lily, to let her see the outrage that gripped him. No wonder she had repudiated God if this was how one of His priests had treated her. "Is that all?" he asked harshly.

"No," Lily said. "Then came the worst part, although at least this time I had my dress to cover me. I had to turn back to the altar and bend over again in supplication to God for having sinned, and Father Mallet would say absolution over me and rub this dreadful hard thing over my sore backside while he said it."

Pascal's head snapped up. "He did *what*?"

Lily shivered as if she, too, were cold, and shrugged a shoulder, her posture one of misery and defeat. "He rubbed something hard over me. I think it was a crucifix, but I'm not sure. And then he'd put his hand on me where he'd hurt me and say a *Sanctus*. He always managed to shame me, no matter how hard I tried to pretend that it didn't matter."

"How long did this go on?" Pascal asked, his hands clenched so tightly on the bottle that the skin of his knuckles showed white against the bone.

"My father made him stop the canings when I turned fourteen. I think it really infuriated Father Mallet to have only bread and water and penances to punish me with. Coffey tried to keep me out of his way, but she didn't always succeed."

Lily looked down at the tears falling onto her hands, then touched her face and furiously wiped them away. "I don't know why I told you that," she said tightly. "You must think me ridiculous. I can see that you're angry."

Pascal didn't answer as he carefully put down the bottle, afraid he might break it. In three strides he crossed the room and dropped to his knees, pulling her against him, holding her close, saying nothing. He smoothed his hand over her hair as if she were a child, cradling her head on his shoulder, listening to the sobs she tried so hard to contain, feeling her tears sink into him, all the way to his soul.

Angry? Oh, yes, he was angry. But how could he tell her why? She was so damned innocent, and he could only be grateful for that innocence. It had saved her from realizing what Mallet had done to her. A crucifix? Not bloody likely, but Lily didn't need to know that. It was bad enough as it was.

He waited until there was nothing left in her body but shudders, then stroked her hair off her face. "Better?" he asked.

Lily lifted her head. His clear dark eyes looked into hers with sympathy, his expression so tender it made her want to burst into tears again. "I do feel better," she said, and it was true—there was a strange new peace in her mind, as if an open wound had closed up and the pain was finally gone. She sighed. "I still feel like an idiot for having told you."

"Don't," Pascal whispered as he cupped her face in his hands. "What Father Mallet did to you is unforgivable, the act of a sick man. It had nothing to do with God, Lily. You must realize that by now. If it's any comfort, I've never heard such a load of fanatic, deranged nonsense come from the mouth of a priest. Can you imagine Father Chabot spouting off like that?"

Lily rubbed her sleeve across her eyes and managed a trembling smile. She'd become fond of Father Chabot, who often dropped by in the evenings to ask about the villagers Pascal was treating, or simply to chat over dinner. He *never* droned on about theology.

"No," she admitted, taking the handkerchief Pascal offered her. "But then he's not really like a priest, more like a round little Friar Tuck, with the same sense of humor. He's awfully worldly, isn't he?"

"Yes, which is how it should be. How else could he attend to his worldly flock?"

"I like him," she said simply.

"He likes you too, very much. So do the villagers. Did you know that?"

Lily gave him a look of patent disbelief. "Are you trying to make me feel better?" she asked, disengaging herself from him.

"No, it's true, I swear it. Father Chabot wouldn't come around so often if he found you unpleasant company, would he? You make him laugh. And the villagers have nothing but nice things to say about you." Pascal rose to his feet, but remained in front of her, looking down at her as if he were willing her to listen to what he said, to really hear him and believe him. "They say you are down to earth and pleasant, and they marvel at how you calm the children when they're frightened about being treated. 'Where did Queen

Elizabeth go?' they ask me. I shrug and tell them that as far as I know, Queen Elizabeth died some years ago. I live with a simple woman who knows how to look after her house and her husband and is kind to those around her.''

Lily colored hotly, with a combination of pleasure and embarrassment. Pascal was not lavish with praise, but when he gave it, she knew he meant it.

He leaned over to squeeze her hands, then went back to filling and corking the bottles.

Lily picked up her book again, but the pages went unread. With every day it became harder to keep him at arm's length. She knew she had become far too vulnerable to withstand very much more from him. Eventually her last fragile walls would crumble, and she would crumble along with them. Just look at what he'd managed to pull out of her tonight, her deepest humiliation, and he'd done it without any effort.

Pascal made her feel safe, and that was the most terrifying thing of all. To feel safe was to trust, to trust was to love and think that one was safe in that love, only to learn it was not so.

And the hell of it was that it was already too late.

17

BEAN'S ears cocked up and she barked once, alerting Lily to the sound of carriage wheels rattling over the road leading up to the château. Lily glanced out the window to see a cloud of dust rising behind not just one, but at least five or six carriages.

"It's Jean-Jacques!" she exclaimed, running to the door and swinging it open. "He's home at last!"

"Timely," Pascal said dryly.

"Oh, don't start being horrible now," Lily said, her face shining with excitement. "I must go to see him."

She tossed aside the bundle of dirty bandages and ran out the door, ignoring Pascal's frantic call.

The château was alight as Lily ran over the bridge of the dry moat and into the courtyard, her throat pounding painfully. She stopped to catch her breath, her lungs heaving for oxygen. There were carriages everywhere, and liveried footmen, and people in fine dress milling about as their baggage was attended to. Lily blinked, dazzled by such a display. She looked desperately around for her brother, and finally, with a gasp of relief, she spotted him, over near the front door, laughing heartily with a large, florid-looking man with a gold tooth and gold braiding to match on his waistcoat.

She pushed her way through the crowd, ignoring the sounds of dismay as she went. Manners were not uppermost in her mind at the moment.

"Jean-Jacques!" she called, her voice a cracked whisper. "Jean-Jacques?" She pulled at his sleeve to get his attention.

He turned with annoyance, his eyes barely skimming over her. "Go away, woman," he said, flicking his hand as if to dismiss an irritating fly. "My God, home only a few minutes and already the scavengers are descending. Go on, away

with you or I shall have the law after you." He turned back
to the florid man with a grimace of distaste. "Beggars, the
lot of them."

Lily froze. "Jean-Jacques," she said again, her throat so
tight from his scorn that she could hardly speak at all. "Jean-
Jacques. It is Lily."

His body stiffened, then he slowly turned to face her. He
took her by both arms, his fingers biting into her flesh as he
looked her up and down, first in recognition and then in
dawning horror. "Lily? What is this? What in God's name
has become of you?" He dropped her arms as if she were
infested with lice.

"What do you mean?" she asked, then looked down at
herself, belatedly realizing that she still wore her dirty apron
and that her hair was in its usual braid down her back. "I
forgot to change. Pascal and I were lancing a boil." She
laughed. "It did make a mess, didn't it?"

Jean-Jacques's face paled, and he cast a quick glance over
his shoulder at his friend, who watched with keen interest.
Other people stared as they tittered behind their finely gloved
hands.

"For God's sake, what are you trying to do to me, Lily?"
he hissed, moving her well away from earshot. "You'll ruin
my reputation. You always were trouble and taking me with
you every chance you had. Go now, before you manage to
destroy everything I've worked so hard to accomplish.
Quickly, before anyone realizes who you are!"

Lily stood paralyzed by the distaste in his expression, the
cold rejection in his voice. "You cannot mean that?"

"I damn well do," he said desperately.

Lily reached out to him, but lowered her arm helplessly
at her side as he jerked away from her touch. She bowed
her head. "You will not acknowledge me, then?"

"I cannot," he said in an undertone. "Look at yourself.
How could I? That man must have a powerful influence over
you—and I, for one, will not be a part of it. Now, please,
leave before you cause me any further embarrassment. People are already talking. I would hate for them to know you
for my sister."

Lily clenched her hands at her sides and glared at him.
"Damn you, Jean-Jacques," she cried, her tears burning
angry trails that scalded her cheeks. "Damn you for a be-
trayer," she said, her voice dropping to a whisper, her throat

too choked for anything else. "Damn you for a fool, and damn you for turning away the *one* person who loved you more than anyone ever loved you. I wanted only the best for you—I wanted only happiness for you—"

But he had already turned away, dismissing her as if she were nothing more than a common whore.

Pascal found Lily standing on the small patch of lawn in front of the river, her arms crossed over her middle, her eyes fixed on the horizon, dull with pain.

He dropped his medical bag and enfolded her in his arms. "He hurt you," Pascal said bluntly, without trying to soften it in any way.

"Yes," she said in a ragged whisper. "I don't think he meant to, but he found me an embarrassment in front of his friends. I—I am an embarrassment . . . oh, God! What has become of me?" She buried her face in his shoulder, weeping as if her dearest friend had just died. In a way, he had.

He held her close for a few moments, wishing he could take her into himself, hold her fast and safe against all the cruelties of the world. And then he took her tear-soaked face between his hands and looked her directly in the eye, hating for the first time in his life the demands that same world placed on him.

"We'll talk about it later, sweetheart. Right now, I need you to help me. There's a baby to deliver. Monsieur Jamard's just been here to say that there's trouble with his granddaughter, Emelie. There's not much time to waste."

Lily drew in a deep, shaky breath and stepped away from him, her expression under tight control. "Yes, of course," she said. "Wait one minute. I need a clean apron." She started toward the house, then turned back in sudden alarm. "A baby? I've never seen this done before."

"There's no time to worry about that. Just follow my lead as you always have, and we'll all be fine."

Lily nodded, pushing Jean-Jacques and his betrayal out of her mind—she would have ample time to worry about that heartbreak in the morning.

If there was one thing she'd learned from Pascal, it was that medical matters always came first.

Emelie Claubert was in trouble.
Pascal pulled the sheet back and ran his hands lightly over

her abdomen, bunched into a position that was clearly abnormal. He'd met Madame Claubert many times before in the village, a pleasant woman with a ruby birthmark high over her left cheek and a cheerful attitude.

Now she lay hunched up, her hands clutching the tight, unnatural mound of her unborn child, her face pale and drawn, her body soaked with perspiration.

"Madame Claubert," Pascal said, taking her hand in his. "It is Pascal LaMartine. May I examine you?"

She nodded tersely, no spare strength left for conversation.

He washed his hands, then inserted his fingers into the birth canal and gently pressed over the swollen mound of her womb with the other hand. Emelie cried out in agony and he quickly removed his hands, waiting as she recovered.

"How long has she been like this?" he asked her husband, who was sweating as freely as his wife.

"Hours, monsieur. Three, more perhaps."

"But straining?" Pascal asked. "How long has she been straining like this?"

"As I said, monsieur. Three hours perhaps."

"Ah, no!" Pascal pounded a fist against his thigh in sheer frustration. At this late stage the baby was already badly compromised and there was little time left. "Why did no one call me?"

Charles Claubert hung his head. "I did not want another man touching my wife," he said with acute embarrassment. "I was waiting for the midwife."

"Who obviously is unable to come, Charles."

"I have called the priest," Charles said in a shaky whisper, blinking back tears. "I fear this is the will of God."

"Nonsense," Pascal said impatiently. "Your wife has a malpresentation—this is Emelie's third child?"

Claubert nodded soundlessly.

"Well, at the moment, Charles, your wife and unborn child are in far more need of immediate physical help than they are a priest, and if we get on with it, perhaps we'll be lucky. It's best if you leave now. You don't seem in any frame of mind to cope with this, and your wife will be better off without your nerves."

Charles left willingly enough, and Pascal turned instantly to his task the minute the door had closed.

"Emelie," he said, stroking her sweat-soaked hair. "I can help you. Will you let me?"

Emelie made a strangled sound of assent in her throat.

"It will soon be well, and you'll have your baby in your arms. Just bear with me and do your best to relax. I have to turn your child so that he can enter the world." As he talked he touched her gently on both sides of her head and held his hands there. She squeezed her eyes shut, but gradually her face began to soften into something almost akin to sleep.

Pascal immediately spread his hands over her abdomen. "Lily, come feel this." He put her hands beneath his. "Feel the hard head, the shape of the shoulders. Here, the soft bottom and the feet tucked under, yes? The child is lying sideways, so we need to turn him. It is done like this . . ."

He literally began to shift the baby around, working swiftly and surely, the mother unresisting, in a soporific state, her womb relaxed. "Look for the turn of the shoulder, always—make certain that the head is positioned with the back of the skull facing you. If the body resists one direction, then try the other way. Here, feel the head moving down, and the bottom going up around?"

Lily nodded, amazed.

"There," he said, positioning the head in the pelvis and releasing her hands. "Get towels—and scissors and thread from my bag."

She obeyed immediately. There was an urgency to him that she hadn't ever seen before, not even when Alain had been hurt.

He turned back to the mother. "All right, Emelie," he said, touching her forehead. "It's time."

Emelie opened her eyes as if from a deep sleep. She looked up at Pascal, dazed.

"Push," he ordered. "Push for all you're worth. Your baby must be born as quickly as you can manage."

She obliged, her eyes locked with his, seeming to gather strength from him, pushing hard, her eyes never leaving him as his hands gripped hers.

Lily watched in awe as Pascal did his work. His concentration was absolute, and there was an intensity about him, a sense that he was literally *with* Emelie.

She imagined that he probably was.

A knock came at the door, and she opened it to find

Father Chabot there, panting from the exertion of running all the way from his house.

"Hello, Elizabeth," he said, looking into the room with a worried frown. "How is Emelie?"

"She's exhausted," Lily said in a low voice. "Pascal is practically willing the baby out."

Pascal glanced over his shoulder as Emelie rested briefly between contractions. "Ah, Michel. Thank God you're here. Go down and give Charles a strong glass of something medicinal, will you? He's probably falling to pieces."

"He is," said Father Chabot, "and everyone else with him. What should I tell them?"

"Just say something religious and reassuring. You know the sort of thing. Then get back up here, quickly."

Father Chabot met Pascal's worried eyes, and he nodded with understanding. "I will be back directly," he said, and quietly shut the door after him.

Lily sponged Emelie's forehead as Pascal spoke to her, encouraging her in her efforts, willing strength into her. Father Chabot soon returned, taking his place against the wall without a word, making himself an invisible presence as he held his stole and a vial of holy water.

Lily rinsed out the cloth, telling herself that everything would be all right. It had to be. Pascal knew what he was doing. Pascal wouldn't allow life to slip from his hands.

He ignored everything but the laboring mother. "Take courage, take heart," he said to Emelie gently as she faltered. "Think of your child now. He's nearly here. Push again. Breathe. In. Out. Think of the rhythm of life. Push now, Emelie. Push!"

She gripped her thighs and groaned, and suddenly Lily saw the top of the baby's head, the dark hair filling the entrance to the birth canal. It was the most extraordinary, beautiful thing she'd ever seen.

Pascal cupped his hands beneath the baby's head, supporting it, encouraging Emelie even as his expression became more grim.

"All right, Emelie," he said. "One last time. You're almost there."

She cried out, a thready wail that spoke of lost strength and failing will. The child's head emerged into Pascal's hands, then one shoulder and the other. A small, still body slithered out all at once. It was a little boy.

But his flesh was a waxy blue, his limbs limp. He didn't move, didn't make a sound. Lily watched in heartbroken dismay as Pascal slapped him on the bottom of his feet, cleared his mouth, then breathed gently into it again and again and again. Nothing. The infant's chest remained still, his body lifeless.

"Oh, Pascal," she whispered. "Can't you do something? Oh, please . . . there must be something?"

Pascal raised his head, and the expression on his face was one she had never seen before, stark with anguish and desperation.

"God help me," he said, his voice breaking. "Lily, don't go from me—please, don't go from me."

"I'm here," she answered helplessly, feeling his pain in the depth of her being. Never before had she wanted—needed—to take another's anguish onto herself as she did now, but there was nothing she could do.

Pascal tied and cut the umbilical cord, then whispered a quick prayer under his breath as he gathered the lifeless child into his arms, supporting the infant's body with one arm, his large hand cupping the head. He placed his other hand over the tiny chest and closed his eyes.

"Come back, little one," he whispered. "We need you here. It's not your time."

A radiance Lily had never seen before shimmered around Pascal, a vibrant golden aura that slowly grew in brightness, spreading outward, veiling man and child in ethereal light that became life itself, sustaining them both. He stood as still as the infant in his arms, the light reaching into all corners of the room, turning the air to brilliant gold.

Lily felt an extraordinary swell of love for Pascal as she watched him, a love that seemed as clear and pure and holy as the light that surrounded him. He looked peaceful, as if he were in a place filled with a quiet joy, just him and the ageless child in his arms, two angels standing together in a farmhouse bedroom, separated from life yet a part of it still.

And then she noticed something else in that light, a tinge of silvery pink, and she realized that it was coming from around the baby's heart. The infant stirred and gave a sudden hiccup. His skin turned rosy, first around his chest, then spreading outward into his limbs until he was pink all over. His little hands and feet began to flail around in the air, and he gave out a loud and healthy cry.

Life, Lily thought, stunned by what she had just witnessed. *I've just seen life taken and given back again. And he did it. He did it with his love.*

Tears poured down her face, tears of gratitude and joy. She didn't understand any of it, but it didn't seem to matter.

Father Chabot dropped to his knees, his hands pressed together in prayer, his eyes closed, his lips moving soundlessly, an expression of profound gratitude on his face.

Pascal bent his head and kissed the child's brow. "Welcome to the world," he said softly, the golden light fading now, like ripples being absorbed into a pond. "Make good use of it. Be well and strong."

The baby stared into Pascal's eyes, long and hard without blinking, and Lily could have sworn that pursed little mouth turned up in a sweet smile.

Pascal smiled back. "You're on your own now, friend," he murmured, then handed the infant to his mother, who gazed at Pascal wide-eyed, tears streaking her face.

"Give him a strong name, Emelie," he said. "Your child is a worthy fighter. Be grateful for him and for the grace God has given him. He will do fine things." He caressed the infant's fragile cheek with the tip of his finger before stepping back. "Now put your warrior to your breast. We must finish things and nursing him will help."

Pascal showed Lily how to deliver a placenta, as if this had been a most usual birth with the usual sort of finish.

"Clean up here, would you, Lily?" he said quietly. "I'll see you later." He abruptly left the room, only briefly glancing at Father Chabot as he went, accepting the effusive thanks of the new father with distraction.

She stared after him, torn between doing as he asked and ministering to the need she sensed in him. Pascal was usually so warm and good with his patients, laughing with them, or reassuring them, never in a hurry. And he was always strong and in control, not like this—so obviously vulnerable, so weary and drained.

With a sigh of defeat she cleaned up mother and child and the room, packed the medical bag, and tried to make up for her husband's quick exit by admiring the baby, soothing the mother, complimenting the father on his forbearance, and settling everyone down. But the first moment she could, she said her farewells and left.

She was desperate to find Pascal, but no sooner was she out the door than Father Chabot was there behind her.

"Lily," he called, using her private name. It caught her attention as nothing else would have done, and she spun around.

"Father?"

He steered her away from the house. "You did very well. The child was truly a gift from God, was he not?"

Lily shook her head. "Father . . . I have no words for what happened. Did you see? Did you see what Pascal did?"

"Yes," Father Chabot said, smiling peacefully. "And I feel blessed to have been there."

Lily frowned. "I don't understand it. Such things aren't possible. That baby was dead. There wasn't a whisper of life in him. I don't think there had been for some time, if Pascal's expression was anything to go by. How did he *do* that?"

"Your husband is a special man, Lily—I may call you Lily?"

"Yes, of course," she said. "I like being called Lily."

"Good. I feel we are friends, and after this evening, we share an even more special bond. Given that, I thought it wise to speak to you tonight, before you go to him." He took her firmly by the elbow. "Shall we take a little stroll?"

Lily had no choice but to walk alongside him.

"Yes, indeed," he said conversationally, "your husband is a very special man, but you probably know that."

Lily didn't know what to say. It wasn't the first time she had heard Pascal described as special. Charlie had said the same thing months before, and she was beginning to wonder if there wasn't something to it.

"You realize, of course, that he is the man I told you of at St. Christophe?" he asked.

Lily nodded. "A maker of miracles, you called him. But I don't believe in miracles, Father. I don't even believe in God."

"No? Then what did you see tonight?" Father Chabot smiled at her, his eyes merry.

Lily's brow furrowed. What had she seen tonight in that bright, still room? Medicine hadn't brought a dead child back to life, she knew that. It had been Pascal. Pascal and that wondrous light that filled the air and felt like the touch of a heaven she hadn't believed in for a very long time.

"Are you saying that what I saw was God?" she asked. If that was God, He bore no resemblance to the God of her childhood, who punished without mercy and condemned rather than comforted. Father Mallet had never told her about a God of hope and love and life, a God who lived in light and joy rather than in a dark and cold stone chapel filled with the sound of tears.

"You saw your husband doing the Good Lord's work, child."

"Well, I don't know what Pascal is doing rubbing shoulders with the Good Lord," she said with a shrug, "but it worked when nothing else did. Father, I honestly don't know what to think . . ."

"You shouldn't think at all. What does your heart tell you?"

"My heart—my heart tells me that what I saw, what I felt, was a miracle. My head tells me that such things don't exist." She let out a long sigh. "But I felt so much love, so much joy and peace when Pascal was holding that little boy. It was as if a life force was going straight from Pascal into the baby. It was so beautiful, all brilliant gold." She gave the priest a sharp look, realizing he was regarding her with grave interest. "You did see the light, didn't you? It lit up the whole room."

He lifted a shoulder apologetically. "I saw something, yes, something faint around your husband's head. It made me think of a halo."

"Well, yes, I suppose you could call it that, only it's much bigger and brighter. I've seen it once before, all around him like that, but that was another sort of light, although it did have something of the same feel to it." Lily's mind raced, trying to put all the bits and pieces together. "There are usually colors when he works," she added, "healing energy, although he says not many people can see it."

Father Chabot nodded thoughtfully. "How very interesting that you do."

"It seems so obvious—though I have to admit at first I didn't see as clearly as I do now. Practice, I suppose."

"Did you see this—this light coming from him from the very start?" he asked, fascinated.

Heat climbed into Lily's face. "Oh, no. I had no idea

who Pascal was. It was an accident, finding him the way I did.''

Father Chabot chuckled. ''Yes, I heard about that. It didn't sound like the usual way to go about locating a botanist, climbing about on an abbey wall.''

''He told you?'' she said, glancing at him anxiously. ''You didn't tell him why I'd really gone to St. Christophe, did you? I mean, that I'd gone to find him? Well, not him, exactly, since I didn't know who he was.''

''That is your story to tell, Lily. To be honest, I felt guilty enough about my part in the matter. However, I have come to think that everything has happened just as it ought, bringing us right to this night, with a newborn baby whose life was given back to him, and a man who very badly needs his wife.''

''He—you think he needs me?'' Lily said, her hand clutching Father Chabot's sleeve. It was suddenly the most important question in the world and she desperately needed an answer. ''Why would he need someone like me? I'm odious!''

''You are not odious in the least,'' Father Chabot said. ''You are a sweet, warm, loving woman who has never been loved or appreciated as you ought, so you do not think yourself worthy. Yet the most worthy of men loves you with everything he has in him.''

She stopped dead in her tracks. ''That can't be,'' she said, her voice shaking.

''It is true. He has waited and waited for you. He is only half a man without you, alone in this world and frightened.''

''Pascal, frightened?'' she said with disbelief. ''That's ridiculous. He's the strongest, most forceful person I know.''

''Lily, my child. You saw him tonight. You saw that he is not as other men.''

She looked away. She didn't want Pascal to be different. How could he love her if he were, when more ordinary, flawed people found it so difficult?

''Can you not imagine how lonely he is? Can you not imagine his fear that you will not be able to love him for who he is, now that you have seen what he is?''

''He is just Pascal, a man like everyone else!'' she cried desperately.

Father Chabot took her hands between his. ''Child. You

know the truth. I suspect you have known it from the very beginning, which is why you convinced yourself that he was a depraved devil. It was far safer to think that than to acknowledge the other.''

"He—he told you that?''

"It has bothered him, Lily, this vow you made to hate him. I am not surprised that you have fought so hard against him. But it is time to acknowledge the truth.''

Father Chabot's gentle compassion broke through Lily's defenses and landed in that soft, vulnerable place in her breast, that place that Pascal had shown her, where only truth spoke.

Truth. Awful, wrenching, heartbreaking truth.

From the very beginning . . . Lily couldn't help thinking of that devastating moment when she had first seen Pascal's face, the haunted look of a fallen angel in his eyes. And she'd been right. Yet he was not like Satan, fallen from God's grace, but simply an angel fallen to earth, as if he'd misplaced his wings and tumbled out of heaven quite by mistake. Tonight he'd even had a halo. Tonight he'd made a miracle happen.

Oh, God. It really was true.

"Father, I can't,'' she wept, terrified. "I don't know how to do this. I've never seen his God.''

"Haven't you?'' Father Chabot asked softly.

"No! All I have seen are dark, damp walls and cold anger and ugliness. If such a God exists, He has not shown Himself to me.''

"He has shown you what few others have ever seen, Lily. He has shown you His light.''

Lily's scalp prickled. "Why?'' she whispered.

"I imagine for the same reason He sent you to Pascal.''

"Why would God have sent Pascal an atheist?'' She looked at Father Chabot, unblinking, needing to see the truth in his eyes.

"You are no more an atheist than I am,'' Father Chabot said with a gentle smile. "You've just had your head filled with nonsense.''

"But I drive Pascal to distraction—I'm impossible, and stubborn, and disgracefully spoiled—all of the things he has no use for.'' She trembled from head to toe.

"You are who he needs. You, just as you are, complete with shortcomings. You are the woman he loves, the only woman he has ever loved in this way.'' Father Chabot looked at her intently. ''Did you not hear what he begged you before he laid his hands on that child? He *needed* you. It took tremendous courage for him to do what he did tonight, knowing he might lose you once you witnessed the truth. Did you not see how he hesitated out of fear, for that very reason? But he could not deny God, even for you. That is the measure of his love.''

Lily turned away from the priest and stared toward the cottage she shared with Pascal. Pascal . . . a special man, touched by God. Chosen by God. Her heart felt as if it might be ripped from her chest any moment.

''What can I do?'' she asked, her voice no more than a faint whisper in the night.

''Love him, Lily.'' Father Chabot's voice came clear and strong behind her. ''Let him be the man he needs to be, in body as well as in soul. God has given you a great gift, child, and a great responsibility.''

Lily mutely shook her head, tears streaming down her face.

''Take good care of him, Lily.''

He said a quiet prayer behind her. When she next looked up, he was gone.

Lily took her time walking home. She had no idea what to say to Pascal when she got there, no idea of what he would say to her. But she understood why he had left so quickly. She understood the fear of rejection and the measures one took to avoid it. She'd been doing just that all of her life.

''Pascal?'' She pushed the door open. The house was dark. No noise. No lamps. No Pascal.

She opened the door to the barn, and Bean flew out, wildly leaping around in canine joy.

''Hello, little Bean,'' Lily said, bending down and scratching her ears, calming her. ''I'm happy to see you too, but I wish I hadn't, because it means Pascal hasn't been home, has he?'' Bean washed her face in reply.

Lily sighed. Wherever he'd gone, he'd gone alone.

''Oh, Bean, he shouldn't be alone, imagining all sorts of dire consequences, just because of what he did tonight. He ought to be with me, so that I can tell him that I'll never

go away from him. Never. I don't ever want him to feel
alone again.''

Bean wagged her tail and ran over to the door, asking to
be let out, and Lily opened it for her. The house felt oddly
empty and silent, and Lily lit the oil lamps, another gift
from a grateful patient. Looking around, she realized that
Pascal had finished cleaning up when she'd gone to see Jean-
Jacques.

Her hands clenched into fists. Her beloved brother. He
wasn't the person she'd loved and trusted all of her life. The
person she'd loved would have taken her into his arms, no
matter how she looked. He would have introduced her to
his friends and taken pleasure in her hard-earned accomp-
lishments. He would never have turned her away.

She looked up toward the château. Lights twinkled in the
windows, and the faint echo of raised voices and laughter
drifted down through the warm night. Jean-Jacques was
probably having yet another party for his precious friends,
celebrating his good fortune with not a care to what she
might be feeling, not a thought to his sister in the hovel he'd
given her.

''Damn you, Jean-Jacques!'' She turned away abruptly,
not wanting so vivid a reminder of what a fool she'd been.

All this time she had stayed loyal to him, thinking of his
vineyards, putting him and his happiness before anything
else. All this time she had fought against her feelings for
Pascal on her brother's behalf.

She had been blinded to real love by the thin, insubstan-
tial smoke of another, had suffered, and made Pascal suffer
too. Lily brushed away the tears that burned at her eyes.
God, how she'd made him suffer, not knowing how he felt.
And he'd told her—or tried to, that day in the meadow. He
was not her enemy.

He was anything but her enemy.

She let Bean in and sank into the chair by the cold hearth,
kicking off her shoes and settling down to wait for him.
Bean plopped down at her feet, her head on her paws, watching Lily with intelligent eyes, as if she felt Lily's anxiety
and was keeping watch over her until Pascal finally made
his way home.

Lily picked up the pair of trousers she'd been mending
before the evening surgery. This time Pascal had worn a
hole through the knee. She smiled tenderly. He was forever

coming home with torn clothes, but she didn't mind mending them.

She bent her head to the patch. "I've become quite good at mending, haven't I, Bean? In fact, I've become good at a number of things, things that high-born ladies would never think to do—scrubbing floors, growing vegetables, scouring pots." Lily scowled.

"I wonder what Jean-Jacques would make of that," she said, jabbing her needle up through the patch. "He'd probably be horrified. I wonder what he would say if he found me scouring a pot with my sleeves rolled up and my elbows black with grime?" She lowered her voice, mimicking her brother. "Lily, what in God's name has become of you? You're a disgrace!"

She leaned down and rubbed Bean's nose. "He's the disgrace, sending me to this falling-down cottage without so much as clean linens and a proper bed. What did he expect to happen?" she said indignantly, sitting back and picking up her sewing again. "Well, I don't care. Pascal's proud of me. He doesn't care how dirty I get—and he likes my hair down my back." The belligerence faded from her voice.

"Do you know the best thing of all, Bean?" She sighed deeply. "I love him with all my heart, and I need to tell him that, because something happened, and he has to know."

Bean's eyebrows moved up and down as Lily talked, her ears perking up at her name, the tempo of her tail changing with Lily's emotions. The last sentence inspired her to wash Lily's foot with adoration.

Lily smiled down at her. "I was at a birth tonight, and I saw a miracle happen."

Bean adored the other foot.

Lily drew in a deep breath and let it out again. "It's really quite a lot to absorb, the idea that Pascal is—well, that he is what he is."

She stared down at her hands, long, slim fingers pushing the needle through the fabric, a tracing of blue veins showing through the skin on the back. Perfectly normal. She thought of Pascal's hands, hands she'd watched so many times as they went about the business of stitching up skin or writing out accounts, or hammering wood or showing her how to prepare an unguent.

They looked perfectly normal too, a nice, masculine

shape with those long, square fingers and generous palms
and that scattering of soft dark hair across the back. Nice
hands. Comfortable hands. It was just that he could make
light come out of them. Holy light.

Lily chewed on her lip, thinking. "You know," she said
slowly, "I can understand what Father Chabot said about
feeling lonely, Bean. It would be horrible to have people
look at you as if you were different, treating you as if you
were some sort of saint, to be adored but not touched."

She poked the needle into the air as if to make a point.
"It would be terrible, as if you didn't have the same right
to be human as they did. I'll be very angry if people start
treating Pascal that way here, in the place that he's chosen
to make his home. They should consider themselves lucky
to have him."

She nodded vehemently and poked the needle in the air
again, Bean watching in fascination. "I'll give them a
proper piece of my mind, don't think I won't. I'll explain
that he's a perfectly ordinary man with an extraordinary
talent and they are very ungrateful to think anything else—
even if he really is a fallen angel."

Lily frowned. That possibility needed to be considered,
although she found it very difficult thinking of Pascal as an
angel. He certainly didn't behave like one.

He had a terrible temper, he was grumpy when he was
tired, and stubborn beyond belief when he'd made up his
mind about something. Angels didn't roar with laughter or
swear fluently or make rude jokes. Angels didn't frost over
and ignore you when they were annoyed. They certainly
didn't set one's body on fire with lust—she was absolutely
positive that one did not have lustful thoughts about angels.
Or saints either. And they didn't have lustful thoughts about
you.

"No," she said firmly, "Pascal really is a perfectly ordinary man, living a normal, productive life, working hard,
helping people who need it, laughing and talking and arguing with his perfectly ordinary wife."

Lily gave a start of surprise as she heard what she'd just
said. "I really *am* an ordinary wife, aren't I, Bean? I really
am—I'm just like every other wife in the village, looking
after my house and my husband, and do you know what? I
like it!"

She didn't have any idea how long she'd felt that way. She

must have gradually grown into it, because somewhere along the way she'd become happy. In fact, she *loved* her horrible hovel and her impossible husband and her miserable life.

It was an incredible revelation and it filled her with a sense of peace and warmth.

Her hands stilled and her gaze drifted around the home they'd made for themselves. Herbs hung from the rafters, drying. A bucket stood in the corner, soiled bandages soaking in it as they did nearly every night. Dishes gleamed on their shelf above the sink, neatly stacked, reminding her that they hadn't yet had dinner.

"Never mind, Bean," she said, "there's enough meat left on the joint I cooked last night—we can have it cold with a salad when Pascal comes home."

That decided, she went back to her perusal of her little house. Volumes of books were piled into the bookcase Pascal had made, most of them botanical or medical texts, although there was a well-thumbed cookbook Pascal had found for her. She'd made good use of that, enthusiastically trying out recipes, some with more success than others, but Pascal was extraordinarily tolerant. It was a good thing he had a sense of humor, too.

In the bookcase were also a Bible and a few other books on religious subjects ranging from Judaism to Buddhism. "Pascal isn't picky about where he finds God, is he?" she remarked to Bean. "He seems to find God in a variety of places. Monasteries, farmhouses, meadows, and—"

Meadows. Lily's gaze jerked to the window. "Of course! What an idiot I am!"

She jumped up, the sewing falling unnoticed to the floor. "Stay, Bean!" she commanded.

Lily flew out the door, not bothering with shoes, running toward Pascal as unerringly as an arrow to its target.

18

H E sat in the thick grass beneath the stars, his knees pulled up, his head resting on his arms. The meadow was silent, only the soft whisper of a breeze cooling the night. A full moon rose over the horizon, and a few birds stirred restlessly in its bright light. He didn't hear her approach.

She dropped to her knees in front of him. "Pascal?" she said tentatively, touching one of his hands.

His head shot up, and in the moonlight she saw streaks of moisture drying on his cheeks. In that one unguarded moment, she also saw raw, naked pain in his eyes before he shuttered them. Lily wanted to cry for him, understanding his desolation and his fear, and knowing his pride would not allow him to show either to her.

"I told you to go home," he said, drawing away from her touch. He frowned. "Are Emelie and her baby all right?"

"Yes."

"Good," he said, not meeting her eyes. "I'll check on them tomorrow."

"Emelie is very tired, but I imagine a good night's sleep will do wonders," Lily said as casually as she could manage.

"The labor was hard on her. I could strangle Charles Claubert for waiting so long." Pascal pulled up a stalk of grass and began stripping it with his fingers.

"Men," she said, "can be idiots."

That got his attention. "What's that supposed to mean?" he asked, his eyes narrowing.

"Just that. The only reason he didn't call you was because he didn't want you touching his wife so intimately, as if you'd be in any frame of mind to assault her—or she'd be in any frame of mind to let you."

Pascal shook his head. "Physicians generally do not assault their patients. Not even I, despite what you've accused me of in the past."

She flinched. "I just meant—"

"I know what you meant." He threw the shreds of grass away. "Look, Lily, my mood is foul and my patience is short, which is why I'm up here and why you should be at home."

She sat back on her heels and stared at him, willing him to look at her. "I wanted to be with you."

"Why?" he asked wearily. "So you could pester me with questions?"

"No. I just wanted to be with you. I'll pester you with questions tomorrow."

"No doubt." He rubbed his neck, looking cold and distant and miserable all at the same time.

She smiled at him, wishing she could wrap her arms around him, but knowing that he'd only pull away at this point. "It was beautiful tonight, seeing a baby born," she said. "Thank you for taking me along."

He shrugged. "I'm sure Monsieur Claubert found your presence reassuring, knowing I wouldn't rape his wife in front of my own."

"Pascal, will you stop this? Why are you being so difficult?"

"I told you before. I need to be alone."

"Don't be ridiculous. That's the last thing you need."

He gave her a long look. "You haven't the first idea of what I need."

Lily flushed. This was more difficult than she'd anticipated. It wasn't going to be a simple matter of telling Pascal that she didn't mind about his miracles. She had a number of things to make up for, and it was going to require some serious humility on her part—not her strong point.

She swallowed hard. "I'm sorry," she said in a small voice.

"Sorry for what?" he replied bitterly. "Sorry that you're married to me? Or perhaps what you're really sorry about is the life I've forced you to." He laughed, a harsh, grating sound that made her wince. "Well, I'm sorry too, Lily. Living with someone like me must be embarrassing for someone like you." He pushed himself to his feet, looking down at her. "I should have let you go your own way from the beginning instead of bringing you to this."

"Don't—oh, please don't," she cried miserably. "It's not like that—really it isn't."

"Oh?" he said coldly. "Then how is it? Tell me—how is it now that you know your husband is not only a rutting, lowborn cad, but he's a freak on top of it? You must be disgusted."

"No! Everything is all right." She reached up to him, but he grasped her wrists and pushed them sharply down, holding them tightly.

"Is it?" he said roughly. "How can it be?" He released her abruptly.

"Pascal . . ." she said, trying to find the right words, frightened by his distance and his anger. "I—I've said a lot of dreadful things to you, things I often didn't mean. I was afraid of you, and afraid of myself, and afraid of *feeling*. And I . . . I was wrong."

Tears ran down her cheeks. She, Lady Elizabeth Mary Bowes, was on her knees before a man, this man, her husband, and she deserved to be, as he deserved to see her. "Please, forgive me," she said brokenly. "Please forgive me." She took the back of his beautifully made hand between both of hers and kissed it.

"Lily, don't—" he said, his voice shattering on the last word. "For God's sake, get up. I'm not—oh, Lily," he groaned. "Not you, not you of all people." He dropped to his knees and took her hands in his. "Don't you see, this is exactly what I was afraid of when . . ." He swallowed hard and shook his head. "I don't want you to think this of me."

"To think what of you?" she said through her tears.

His jaw clenched as he raised his head and stared up at the sky. "Damn it, I won't have you seeing me as others do. I won't have you kneeling before me," he said tightly, forcing each word out as if it hurt to speak.

Lily wrenched her hands from his grasp as understanding dawned. "Pascal, no. I kneel before you because I owe you that much. I've been horrible to you—and you deserved very little of my behavior. I kneel here as your wife, asking for your forgiveness."

He frowned as he looked down at her, his body suddenly very still. "Why?" he asked softly.

She exhaled, a broken sound that seemed to echo around them. "I love you, Pascal." It was so hard to say it. Her mouth was dry with the old fear of being rejected and abandoned again. She had loved before, and it had never been enough. But she had to be as honest with him as he'd been with her—she had to show him her heart with the same trust with which he'd shown her his soul.

"Just like that?" he whispered, and still he didn't move, as if he were waiting . . . as if he were praying.

Lily whispered too, hoping that her answer might be the one he prayed for. "I've loved you for a very long time, but I've been too stupid and proud and frightened to admit it."

He slowly shook his head as if he couldn't believe what he was hearing.

"I know what you risked tonight when you brought that baby back," she said. "I saw, Pascal, I saw the incredible light that filled the room, what you did in spirit—reaching right into heaven for that little boy and bringing him back with you."

A deep shudder ran through his body. "You *saw* all that?"

"Yes."

Pascal squeezed his eyes shut for a moment. "Dear *God*, what must you think of me?"

"I think you're wonderful," she whispered.

"A proper sideshow," he said tightly. "Saint Pascal and his Incredible Healing Hands."

Lily heard the bitterness in his voice, felt his loneliness as he held himself away from her—so close, yet so very, very far away. Deliberately, she leaned forward and rested her forehead on his chest. "No, Pascal, my husband, the man I love so much it frightens me."

He let out a deep, jerky breath and grasped her shoulders, holding her away from him, examining her face. "Why, Lily? Why now? Is it because of that, because of what I did?"

Lily met his gaze without flinching, giving him her own truth as clearly as she knew how. "Not because of what you did. Because of who you are. I love *you*, Pascal, not your ability, although that's a part of you."

"Are you sure?" he asked, his voice so strained the words nearly didn't come out.

"Of course I'm sure. Do you think I'd risk saying such a thing to you on a whim?" She touched his face with her fingertips, felt the warmth of his skin, the scratch of his beard. *He is so human, so real,* she thought with an aching tightness in her chest.

"Lily—this, this ability I have. It's *difficult* for people."

"Some people have no imagination," she said with a sigh.

"It's no good making light of it," Pascal said, folding her hands in his and lowering them from his face, but this time gently. "It has always created a barrier, something that people can't get beyond."

"I'm not making light of it. But I don't feel a barrier. I'm fortunate, because it's not an invisible mystery to me. A miracle is much easier to accept if you can see it happening, all beautiful and golden, like the sun come down to earth. It gives what you do substance. Do you understand?"

He stared at her warily, his body stiff, as if he were afraid to believe her, afraid that she was merely trying to make him feel better.

"Pascal, don't you see? It makes perfect sense."

"Sense?" he said incredulously, the word ripped from his throat. "Where in God's name do you find *sense* in any of this?"

"Listen to me, you impossible man. A month ago, right here, you did something to me that changed me, when you took me with you to that place. You left your imprint on me, and you can't take that imprint away, not ever. You're a part of who I am now, as much as I'm a part of you."

He nodded. "That was different."

"Why? Because it was between you and me, instead of you and God and a baby? You gave me back my life that day as surely as you gave that child back his life tonight. You know you did—you practically told me so at the time, looking smug as could be, I might add."

The shadow of a smile crossed his face. "Surely not smug?" he said.

"Well . . . very pleased with yourself."

"I was very pleased with myself—and with you, too."

"Then be pleased with me now? I couldn't go with you where you went tonight, not all the way—I don't have your gift. But I could see some of it, and feel some of it, just as you taught me. You make heaven real, Pascal."

He groaned and bowed his dark head as if struggling for control.

Lily took one of his hands and turned it over, kissing the palm. "Why would something that beautiful do anything but bring me even closer to you?" she said softly.

Pascal looked up at her, and she saw the glimmer of moisture on his lashes. "I—I can't . . ." he started to say, then stopped, swallowing hard.

"I'm beginning to think you haven't much faith in me," she said. "You're behaving as if *you're* the skeptic."

Pascal reached out for her and pulled her against him, holding her tightly. "Lily," he whispered against her hair. "You are the extraordinary one. I should have realized—but I thought . . ."

"What? That I would suddenly find you repellent?"

"That, or even worse, that you'd be in awe of me. I couldn't bear the thought. I didn't know you had come so far. I didn't know it was possible."

Lily smiled against his shirt. "I love you, Pascal. You may be a stubborn wretch," she added, stroking his back, savoring the feel of hard muscle under her hands, "but at least you're my wretch."

"I certainly am that, duchess," he said quietly.

She leaned back and gave him a caustic look calculated to goad him. "As for awe—if you expect me to treat you any differently than I always have, you're going to be sadly disappointed. You may have fooled a great many people into thinking you're some kind of saint, but you haven't fooled me."

"Oh?" he said, raising an eyebrow.

"Yes. And anyway, I thought it through and decided it would be most improper for saints to have carnal desires—which you certainly have." She smiled wickedly. "That makes you a rogue, which I've known all along."

"Lily . . ." he said, suddenly looking dangerous.

Lily stroked the corner of his mouth with her finger. "You know, for a rogue you're awfully slow to take advantage."

That earned a reluctant grin from him. "Are you asking to be kissed?"

In answer she reached up and pulled his head toward hers, wrapping her arms about his neck, her hungry mouth waiting only for his response. He gave it to her in full measure. His mouth covered hers, his fingers caressing one side of her face and then the other, stroking her skin as his lips stroked her lips, and his mouth opened against hers. He groaned, grasping the back of her neck in his hand, his arm moving around her back, lowering her to the ground, kissing her until she gasped.

He raised his head and looked down at her. "Will that do?" he asked, breathing hard.

"No," she said. "Be a proper rogue, Pascal. I don't think I could bear it if you became saintly now."

Pascal laughed, and once he'd started he couldn't stop. It cleared the tension from him, grounded him, opened his heart so wide it felt it might burst. He wrapped his arms around Lily, his head resting on her soft breasts, his shoulders shaking with laughter as cleansing as tears.

Lily lay quietly beneath him, embracing him tightly, her mouth on his hair, her hands stroking his back. He felt such love for her and such gratitude and awe. She was truly extraordinary, as comfortable with miracles as she was with duchies, impressed by neither, and certainly not impressed with him.

Thank you, God. Thank you.

He also gave up a quick prayer of thanks to God for throwing Lily practically on top of him. How many women flung themselves off monastery walls for no good reason? Only Lily. God hadn't been so unkind after all. In fact, He'd been downright beneficent.

"Pascal?" his beneficence said, stroking his hair.

"Hmm?" He lifted himself onto his elbows and looked down at her sweet face, pushing the wisps of hair off her face.

"Will you make love to me?"

Pascal stared at her. "Here? Now?"

She nodded. "It seems right. After all, you made love to me here once before. Didn't you?"

Pascal's throat tightened. "Yes," he said. "I did. And you made love right back. But do you mean like that?" he asked, trying to hide his disappointment. "Is that how you want me?"

She shook her head. "Oh, no. I want . . . all of you. I love your heart and your soul too, Pascal, but I want your—" She blushed, her face the delicate color of the inside of a seashell.

"My body?" he finished for her, a devilish gleam in his eyes.

Lily licked her lower lip. "Yes. I know that carnal desire is supposed to be a sin, and I've tried not to feel it, but I haven't been able to stop thinking about it—with you, I mean.''

He closed his eyes for a moment, suppressing a stab of anger toward Father Mallet and his depraved teachings. He was determined to banish them as quickly and effectively as possible. "Ah, Lily," he murmured against her forehead. "Sweet, innocent Lily. My clean vessel. I want to fill you with the potent wine of love. I want you to know it for truth."

She closed her eyes and arched her neck, inviting a kiss in the hollow of her throat. "So wicked," she sighed.

"Feeling carnal desire for your husband is no sin, sweetheart," he said gently. "It's one of God's blessed gifts, that we can love each other and take pleasure in that love. Like this . . ."

He lowered his mouth onto hers, stroking her full lower lip with his tongue, drawing it between his teeth, taking her with his tongue in deep, leisurely thrusts, relishing the feel of her lithe body moving under his in response, the sound of the moan wrung from her throat.

"Oh, Pascal," she breathed. "Oh . . ."

"And like this," he said, brushing her throat with his lips, drinking in the sweet, natural fragrance of her warm skin, savoring her taste, her softness, as he'd wanted to do for so long. He smoothed his hand over her breast, molding its delicate shape, his fingers brushing over the erect bud of nipple. He bent his head and breathed onto that tight bud, touching it with his tongue through the thin material of her dress, taking it between his teeth and gently tugging until she whimpered low in her throat.

His body shook at her reaction. She was everything he'd ever wanted, ever needed to become whole and solid.

He raised his head, his life force an unleashed fire in his blood, searing at his veins. "I want you, Lily," he said hoarsely. "I've wanted you for so long. But you have to know that I never intended you harm that day in the garden."

Lily didn't answer. Instead, she moved away from him and stood.

For a terrible moment Pascal thought he had his answer.

Instead, she unwound her braid, combing her fingers through her hair until it streamed down her back in a river of burnished copper. She undid the buttons on her dress with visibly shaking fingers, opening it and letting it drift to the ground. Her simple gesture told him everything he needed to know.

She slipped her shift from her shoulders, standing still as it skimmed down her body and fell on top of her dress. She stepped out of her underthings and stood before him clothed only in the beauty God had given her.

God had not been stingy.

Her high breasts were creamy white, tipped by pale pink nipples, her waist and hips so slender, a lovely triangle of deep auburn curls at the juncture of her long, beautifully shaped legs. Everything that was woman—that was Lily, standing in the moonlight, staring shyly down at the ground, her hair spilling about her shoulders as the moon gilded her with silver light.

Pascal slowly rose to his feet.

"Lily . . ." he said, his voice thick. "Thank you." It was the last shackle unbound, the last tiny but infinitely important thing that had been holding him back. And it was gone, as if it had never been.

She lifted her head and met his gaze. "I'm sorry I ever thought it," she said in a small whisper.

"I'm not," he said, pulling off his half-boots. "If you hadn't thought me a reprobate, we wouldn't be here right now, would we?"

Lily bit her lip. "No, but I ought to have realized sooner."

"I thank God you've realized it now. I don't know how much longer I could have held out. There have been times I really have wanted to throw you to the ground and ravish you."

"Rogue," she said with a faint smile, as she watched him closely, nervously.

Inexperienced blockhead is more like it, he thought. He undid his shirt and pulled it over his head. A little moan escaped from Lily's throat at the sight of his bare chest. He grinned wickedly and undid the fastening of his trousers, then stripped them off and tossed them aside to stand as naked as she, his arousal seeming to reach for her. Well, he might be a virgin, but at least it was a good beginning.

He took in the rapid rise and fall of her breasts, the look of complete awe on her face, and with a rush of euphoria he knew it had nothing to do with his gift. All he could do

was stare at her—all of her—and wonder where to touch her
first . . . and how.

"Come to me?" he asked, reaching a hand out to her,
trusting instinct and hoping it was enough.

Tentatively, she lifted her hand, then dropped it back to
her side. Her gaze lowered to the center of his chest.

"Oh, God, what is it now?" he asked with a groan.

"I think I'm suddenly afraid."

He exhaled and closed the distance between them, his
arms wrapping, winding, enfolding her as he lowered his
head and kissed her, his mouth warm against hers, his lips
shaping her own, breathing in her breath, her heat, her life,
tasting her until her fear dissipated and she gasped with
pleasure, asking for more.

He explored the silk of her flesh, the generous curve of
breast pressed against his chest, the soft curl of feminine
hair brushing just under his aching arousal, her yielding
belly cushioning his length. It was the nicest thing he'd ever
felt, exactly right, just perfect.

He stroked her shoulders, down her arms, up again, his
fingertips outlining the shape of her breasts, around, underneath, up again, brushing his palms over her taut nipples.
He ran his hands down the smooth skin of her back, cupping
her buttocks, tracing the curve of her hips, up to her waist,
then buried his hands in her soft hair as she did the same to
him, smoothing her hands up and down, over, around, until
the trembling of his body matched hers.

"Lily," he sighed. "My sweet, sweet duchess."

She turned her face against his chest, sweeping her mouth
over his skin, opening it over one of his nipples and suck-
ling, drawing a groan from his throat.

He lowered her onto the soft, springy earth, his body
pressing over hers, more than ready to discover what God
had had in mind when he'd designed man and woman to
find pleasure in one another.

He pushed her shoulders back against the grass, moved
her arms up over her head, imprisoning her hands, lacing
his fingers through hers, and bent his head to her breast,
taking it into his mouth. She moved beneath him as desperate little noises came from her throat, sweet noises, Lily
noises.

A cool nighttime breeze danced over the flaming skin of
his back, his buttocks, his legs, cooling. Beneath him, Li-

ly's flesh scorched his as he explored her. Everything was
body, dense lovely body, hands and mouths and heat—soft
curves molding into hard ones, the different shapes of bone
and muscle, the insistent ache of desire pressed against that
which he so desperately needed.

He shifted slightly onto his side, taking her two wrists in
his one hand, her bones so fine, so small. His other hand
drew a line up and over her fragile rib cage, spanning her
back, trailing down her shoulder to cup her breast, to lift it
and mold it in his palm, bending to her erect nipple, pulling
it into his mouth, tasting her yet again.

"Pascal—oh, Pascal . . . I can't bear it . . ."

His senses swam at the sound of her heated whisper—he
definitely had to be doing something right. He lightly bit
down, and Lily cried out.

Yes, he was definitely doing something right.

"Duchess," he breathed, releasing her wrists, moving up
to her mouth, covering it with his own. "I love you," he
murmured, then kissed her until she moaned, having mas-
tered that art fairly early on.

It was an extraordinary sensation, being able to turn her
body to pure flame with his mouth and hands, mortal hands,
flesh and blood, and that blood pounding and racing in his
very mortal veins.

Lily, precious Lily, supplicant Lily, his love, his heart.

He could smell the heady feminine scent of her arousal,
as primal and rich as the earth she was lying on, her downy
curls now damp as the night-cooled grass. He bent his head
to her breasts, pulling on them as hungrily as the newborn
he was, reveling, like a newborn, in intense pleasure and
satisfaction, in Lily's cries, her hands clenched in his hair.
It was good. God, it was good. And there was more to
come. He was close now, so close to becoming one with
her.

He arched up to look at her and Lily's eyes opened, soft,
liquid, filled with love and heated desire. She smiled up at
him, a wobbly sort of smile.

"What?" he murmured, stroking his finger against the
corner of her mouth.

"Oh, Pascal," she whispered achingly, running her fingers through his hair. "I'm so sorry. How could I not have
known? I love you more than life itself. I love you so much
it hurts."

Pascal shuddered at hearing words he never thought he'd hear from anyone, words that were infinitely precious coming from Lily.

"You're so beautiful. God, how I want you, to be inside you. Do you want that too?"

Lily nodded, but he saw the small flicker of fear in her eyes, and he felt a stab of remorse for what he had to do. "I'll be careful, sweetheart. I swear I'll be careful." He stroked her hair off her smooth brow and kissed it. "Don't be afraid of me—please don't be afraid of me."

"I'm not afraid of *you*," she said softly, drawing her fingers down his back. "I just . . . I hadn't realized." She ran her tongue over her bottom lip, embarrassed. "What I mean is that no one mentioned anything about the male, umm . . . the male *organ* changing so—so drastically. What I really mean," she finished in a rush, "is that no one said anything about it standing up like that."

Pascal grinned down at her, loving her all the more for her forthrightness. "You saw a child born tonight, didn't you? I'd judge he was about seven pounds. Surely you can accommodate something as modest as myself?"

That drew a small smile from her. "Oh. I hadn't thought of that. But Pascal, I don't think you're modest in the least."

Pascal took her hand in his and kissed the palm, then put it between them, wrapping her fingers around his erection, although he had to squeeze his eyes shut and fight for control.

"There," he said after a moment, his breath coming in hard pants. "God made me for you, to give you pleasure. He wouldn't have been so inconsiderate as to make me the wrong size or shape, would He—not after everything else He's put us through?" Pascal hoped to heaven he was right. Such things were not unknown.

Lily tested his dimensions with a light skim of her fingers, and Pascal closed his eyes again.

"You're beautiful," she whispered. "You're so beautiful."

Pascal couldn't have spoken if he'd tried. He took her mouth in a fevered kiss, drinking of her until his senses swam and his heart hammered inside his chest.

"Lily," he said hoarsely, "it will hurt the first time, but just for a few moments." He hoped he was right about that, too.

"I know," she said.

"Then will you have me?" He stilled, waiting for her answer.

"Yes—oh, yes, Pascal."

She gasped as his hand moved down over her belly and his fingers slid into her warm damp curls.

"Good," he said. "Oh, that's so good." His fingers moved lower, finding the soft flesh of her womanhood. It was silky wet, and he knew that despite her fear she was ready for him.

He gently parted those delicate folds with his fingertips, petals like a rose all full and wet with dew, and eased two fingers into her—oh . . . she was hot, like the white molten heat of a fire. At the same time he could feel the warmth of her breath against his cheek, little gasps as he caressed the heart of her, gently stretched her to receive him, then ran his thumb over the nub of that other exquisitely sensitive place that made her quiver and moan.

"Lily," he said, and kissed her, his tongue thrusting in and out of her mouth in rhythm with his fingers, ruthlessly invading, plundering, taking what he wanted from her like a true rogue.

Lily liked rogues—he could tell by the way she writhed beneath him, by the way she opened wider for him and plundered right back with her own tongue.

Wave after wave of desire rolled through him, shaking him to his very core. He brushed his mouth down to the tender juncture of jawline and throat, his tongue stroking the rapid pulse there, as rapid and desperate as his own.

She shifted under him and her thighs opened to embrace his hips, asking for more, calling for him in the timeless way of women, her head tossing back and forth on the grass, her hands restlessly kneading the muscles of his back.

"Sweet duchess," he groaned, answering her. He rose over her, wondering where best to put his weight so as not to crush her. His forearms, he decided, but first he had to position himself correctly. It was an awkward business, having to use one arm to support his weight, then get his hips at the right angle, and finally to use his other hand to guide himself into her.

He managed it, and hoped he hadn't made *too* much of a fool of himself. He eased slowly into her, feeling those incredible folds opening, giving around his tip, wet satin against velvet, heat against heat. Oh, yes, the same, but so very different, hard against soft, male against female. God definitely had done it right, although why He had included a maidenhead, Pascal really couldn't understand, coming up hard against that barrier.

She cried out and dug her fingers into his back. He leaned his forehead against her neck for a moment, collecting himself, fighting for control against the surge of sensation that touching her had caused, feeling guilty for enjoying it while she suffered.

He lifted his head and looked into her smoky eyes, wanting her to know how much he loved her, how much this moment meant. "Lily, I'm sorry to hurt you. I'm so sorry." He moved his hips to put a very gentle pressure against her.

Lily put her hands on both sides of his face. "I *want* you to love me. It's our wedding night." She smiled bravely up at him as he stretched her as gently as he could.

"Our wedding night," he said, loving her more by the moment. "You're so right." He pushed a little harder as he spoke. "And I vow to you, I will be all the things I said I would be in that ghastly chapel and didn't mean. But I mean them now, Lily, as God is my witness."

Lily looked at him with all the love in the world and then some. "Then tell me," she whispered. "Tell me while you take me. Please. Do it now?"

He took a deep breath and steadied his voice with an effort, but the words came from his heart—solemn vows spoken reverently beneath the stars of heaven.

"I, Pascal, take thee, Lily, to my wedded wife." He pushed into her just a little more, feeling her stretch and give, but seeing her forehead furrow even more deeply. "To have and to hold from this day forward," he said, kissing her as he pulled his hips back and steeled himself to penetrate her fully. "For better for worse, for richer for poorer, in sickness and in health, to love and to cherish . . ." He thrust hard.

Lily's eyes widened and she gave a sharp cry as her flesh gave way to him.

"I'm sorry," he said with infinite regret, as he stilled inside her and gathered her to his arms. "I'm so sorry, sweetheart. But it's over now."

She took a few quick breaths. "Till death us do part," she finished with fierce determination, her eyes shut.

"Till death us do part," he said, his voice tender but shaking. "According to God's holy ordinance. God, how I love you."

Lily opened her eyes again, the pain that had marked her

brow clearing now. "How I love you, too. Oh, you really are a wretch." She smiled up at him.

He smiled in return, smoothing her hair. "My brave little duchess." He moved his hips again, this time no barrier to resist him, only soft, yielding flesh, enveloping him, cradling and inflaming him.

He buried his head between her breasts, drinking in her warm scent, feeling the rapid beating of her heart, the strength of her arms around his back. "Oh, Lily."

He pulled back and drove into her again and again, thrusting in earnest as her arms tightened and her hips arched up to meet him, and soft little woman cries filled the night.

Thank God, he thought, with real relief. *Lily likes it too.*

He felt powerful, omnipotent, humbled beyond belief, and overwhelmed by the incredible delicacy and heat and giving of Lily.

He felt as if he were going to erupt.

He put his hands on Lily's hips and pulled her toward him, pushing into her as deeply as he could, his jaw clenched and his head thrust back as passion swelled unbearably. He groaned as it burst within him, great waves pouring out, his seed, his life in Lily, a pleasure beyond imagining, a love beyond question.

She trembled beneath him, her calves locking around his hips, straining up to him, taking him, all of him, her body shaking with acceptance. He felt her flesh flutter like the wings of a young bird learning to take flight, a gentle little tremble that rippled around him, barely felt. And her sigh was the same, a small shiver of release breathed into him as he lowered his mouth to hers.

"I do love you, duchess," he whispered as he raised his head and met her gaze, his hands brushing strands of hair away from her face.

"I love you too, Pascal," she whispered back to him. "Beloved wretch."

He smiled into her hair.

Consummated. Doubly over. Three times, if you were really counting.

A trinity of love.

19

LILY came out of a deep sleep as dawn broke, slightly disoriented, knowing something was different, but not immediately sure what it was. It didn't take her long to work it out. A hard, well-muscled leg was pressed between her own, and one equally hard, well-muscled arm was thrown over her waist as if it belonged there. Lily shivered, remembering. It had been a long night.

They'd walked home, both silent. Lily had put dinner on the table, but they'd barely eaten. Then had come that silent moment when the dishes had been washed, Bean put out, and there'd been nothing left to do except go to bed. Pascal looked at her, his eyes full of question. And then he abandoned the question and simply picked her up and carried her up the stairs to bed. She shivered again, thinking of the things he had done to her.

Oh, no angel. No angel at all.

She carefully disentangled herself and rolled over onto her other side to look at Pascal, a heavy sensation rising deep in her belly as she studied his sleeping form, that powerful masculine body, the lean hips outlined beneath the sheet.

She'd never seen him asleep before. His hair was tousled, his face relaxed, serene, his breathing deep and even. He looked beautiful to her, strength and vulnerability mixed together. His lashes were so long, a thick black sweep against those high cheekbones. His mouth, so finely shaped—and so skilled, so adept at giving pleasure. And his hands, oh, his hands, and the wonderful, hot, abandoned things he'd done with them, things that had made her moan, things that had made her writhe like one possessed. She *had* been possessed, possessed with lust and heat and more abandon. He'd fed it, built it into fire as if he'd been taking little pieces of kindling and adding to them one by one until he'd created a conflagration worthy of the devil himself.

No, Pascal was definitely no angel.

Lily quietly got up and pulled on her robe, then went to heat water and put Bean out.

She heard his feet on the stairs and turned to look up at him, almost shy, not quite sure what he would think of her after last night's behavior. He wore only the sheet, wrapped around his hips, and his trousers and shirt dangled from one hand. She thought he looked a little tired—hardly surprising, considering.

"Up early, aren't you?" he asked with a smile. "I didn't manage to exhaust you?"

"Oh, you did that well enough," she said, relieved that he was behaving in so normal a fashion. "But there are things to be done around here, you know. Lounging about in bed won't clean the house or bring in the crop."

Pascal tossed his clothes over the chair and walked over to her, sliding his arms around her, strong, warm arms, a strong, warm, beautiful chest against her cheek.

"Oh?" he said. "It won't?" He nuzzled his mouth into her neck. "Are you quite sure?"

Lily found it hard to do anything other than nod.

"Feeling a bit upended, are you, duchess?" he asked with a muted laugh, his hands wandering up and down her back.

"Yes, I am," she said indignantly. "You would be too, if you were in my position."

"Would I? What position is that?"

"Well," she said, coloring, "it's not easy when one is not sure how to conduct oneself after—after doing . . . umm. After last night."

"I see," Pascal said, considering this. "Are you saying there should be rules for this sort of behavior?"

"I don't know," she said, wishing he'd stop stroking her back like that, for it made her feel weak at the knees. "No one ever said anything beyond losing my virginity. They certainly didn't say anything about . . . well, about—you know."

"Oh, yes," he said, that wicked note back in his voice. "I know—but then they wouldn't say anything, would they?" He smoothed one of his hands through her hair, the other continuing to stroke her back. "Not when they were busy telling you that carnal desire was a sin." He lowered his head and kissed her slowly, his tongue reminding her of what they'd been doing only a few short hours before.

"Oh, Pascal," she said shakily when he finally drew away from her. "I really don't think you ought to kiss me like that in the daylight."

"No?" he murmured, sliding his hands around her rib cage, cupping her breasts. "Why not?"

Lily's breath caught in her throat as the touch of his hands burned into her flesh through the thin material of her robe. She could feel him stiff and ready against her, and it was enough to make her head swim with renewed desire. Her legs threatened to cave in altogether.

"B-because it's improper," she stammered.

"Mmm," he replied, untying the sash of her robe and running his hands up and down her naked flesh. "It certainly is." He slipped the robe off her shoulders and dropped to his knees, his arms around her hips, his mouth doing all sorts of incredibly, wonderfully improper things, starting with her breasts and gliding lower, his tongue stroking a flaming trail down and down until he reached her nest of curls and—

"Pascal!" Lily gasped as he stroked her there too.

"Mmm," he murmured against her, kissing her most intimate place. "Nice."

Nice? Oh, he really was a rogue.

The next thing she knew he'd somehow pulled her down onto the floor, and his hand caressed her where his mouth had just been, unrelenting until she trembled all over with hot sensation, not caring that she was lying naked on the floor in the sunshine, letting him have his wicked way with her.

"You do make a nice wife," he said, dropping a kiss on one throbbing nipple. His hands slid under her thighs and pulled her knees up and apart as he looked down at her, his face taut with passion. "I've never felt anything so wonderful as you, Lily." He penetrated her in one smooth stroke, filling her completely with his length.

She moaned and arched up to him as his hands stroked her hips, holding her against his long, deep thrusts until she thought she was going to expire. He didn't stop, he kept going and going, his hips pushing her back against the floor, the wood hard against her spine, but she didn't care. Her hands traveled over the smooth, hard curve of his buttocks, tracing the hollow there, up to the valley of his spine, over the broad expanse of muscle that shifted under her hands as he moved.

Lily reveled in sensation, in the increasing tempo of his hard masculine penetration, his breathing rough and shallow against her ear. Something unbearable gathered deep within her, something just within her reach. She lifted toward it, her muscles tense with effort.

As he plunged again, Lily exploded. Her head fell back and she cried out again and again, throbbing deep in her body, where he was, around him, over him, waves of never-imagined pleasure fiercely milking him until he shuddered and pulled her as close to him as he could manage.

"Ah, God!" The cry was torn from his throat, harsh and jubilant. He thrust hard, spilling into her, liquid heat pouring into the neck of her womb, causing another swell of waves to break over her, just as powerful, just as overwhelming as the first, until she was drowning, gasping for air, clutching at Pascal as if he could save her.

He couldn't even save himself. He was gasping every bit as desperately as she was, holding on to her for dear life, consumed not by water but by flame.

Water . . . fire . . . eternity.

Lily opened her eyes to find that the world was restored. Her brow was wet, her hair damp. She lay tangled in Pascal's arms, his skin as wet as hers, his heart still pounding, his head bent, his forehead resting against her throat.

"Oh . . ." Lily said on a long, wondering sigh.

He opened his eyes and lifted his head, then groaned and collapsed onto his side, bringing her with him. He pulled her leg over his hip, still inside her. "Oh, dear God," he said raggedly.

She looked at him, her eyes enormous. "Pascal . . . what—what happened? Is it—was that usual?"

"I have no idea," he said. "I hope so."

"What do you mean, you have no idea?" she said, frowning. "Surely you must know, with all the experience you've had?"

He was quiet for a moment, and then he took in a little breath and blew it out, looking at her sideways, an abashed expression on his face.

"Pascal?"

"I haven't had any more experience at this than you have."

Lily's mouth opened in complete astonishment, but no sound came out. "No . . ." she finally said. "No, I don't believe it."

"Believe it. I was as much a virgin as you last night." He kissed her fingers one by one.

Lily stared at him. He really did look embarrassed, she realized, a faint blush staining his cheeks.

"*You?* But . . . but why?" she asked, dazed.

He looked at her over her fingers, those beautiful dark eyes filled with the honesty of his reply. "It never felt right before," he said softly. "I suppose I was waiting for you, duchess."

His words pierced straight through Lily, and tears started to her eyes. "Oh, Pascal, I've been such an idiot. All those things I said to you. You must have been enraged."

"Sometimes," he agreed, his finger stroking her throat. "I did have some nasty thoughts about this part of your anatomy." He paused. "Tell me something. Why did you assume I was such a reprobate? Was it because I touched you?"

Lily shook her head. "Oh, no. It was before that, when I first saw you. You were so handsome, and you looked so dangerous."

"*Dangerous?* Lily, I was meditating. How could I possibly have looked dangerous? If anything, I'd think I looked harmless."

"Well . . . actually, I first saw you when you were gardening. You turned to look at the sun, and I thought you were going to look like a hound, and you didn't."

The corner of Pascal's mouth twitched. "I don't think I'll ask."

"I think I must have been having carnal thoughts about you even then," she said, mortified by the realization.

"Really, Lily," he said with a wicked smile. "Carnal thoughts atop a monastery wall?"

"Don't tease. I mean it—I really did think you had to be thoroughly corrupt. My father warned me away from handsome men. All handsome men, no matter the circumstances. That's why when you touched me like that, I couldn't help but think the very worst. I'm sorry, I truly am."

"As I told you last night," he said gently, "don't be. Thank God for your carnal thoughts. If you hadn't had them then, I wouldn't be having them now."

"Now?" she asked, her eyes widening. "Now?"

"Now," he said lazily. "I may be inexperienced, but I do intend to take care of that. For example . . ."

He pulled her closer, stirring, growing hard inside her, and Lily, still exquisitely sensitive, closed her eyes and gave herself up to him, in complete, helpless, blissful surrender.

Pascal approached the south vineyard later that morning with trepidation, well deserved, as it turned out. Charles Claubert was there, and he'd been busy. The fields were humming with the news of what Pascal had done the night before.

He saw the heads turning as he came up the hill, heard the excited murmurs, and his heart sank, although he should have been accustomed to the reaction by now. There went the easy camaraderie, the pleasant days of being regarded as a normal human being and treated accordingly.

He smiled politely to everyone, said good morning in his usual fashion, and set to work, going down the rows of vines, carefully examining them as he did every morning. Charles Claubert wasted no time in running up to him, wringing his hand until it hurt.

"Monsieur—you left so quickly last night, I didn't have time to thank you properly. Emelie told me everything, how you gave our son his life back. What can I ever do to repay you?"

"Nothing at all, Charles," Pascal said. "Your son only needed a little encouragement. It was hard on him, your wife's labor. They are both well this morning?"

"They could not be better," Charles said, with glowing eyes. "A son! My first, you know. But for you, monsieur, he would have been buried today." He looked as if he were about to kiss Pascal's hand, and Pascal quickly pulled it away. "As I said, he needed a little encouragement. Have you named him?"

"Ah, but of course. We have named him Joseph-Jean, a fine, strong name after the saints. It seemed fitting, especially given what you did—and what you told my wife about him. It is true, monsieur?" he asked eagerly. "He has God's grace? He will do fine things? A warrior, my son?'' He recited what Pascal had said nearly word for word.

"Indeed, he is a fighter, although I don't think he'll end up razing cities. He is strong in soul, your Joseph-Jean.''

Pascal bent over one of the vines, examining the heavy cluster of cabernet grapes. They were setting, the color turning from green to black, well on its way. Best of all, they'd beaten the mildew.

"Look at that, Charles,'' he said, distracting the man from the litany that was bound to continue. "Not a single speck. That is as plump and healthy a bunch of grapes as one could hope to find. We'll have a nice strong vintage out of this lot if the weather continues to hold. The small planting of white should be decent too—nothing spectacular, a simple *vin de pays*, but decent nevertheless. But the red—that I have true hope for.''

"Ah, well, monsieur,'' Charles said happily, "you hit upon a piece of brilliance last month when you came up with the idea of stripping some of the leaves off each plant.''

"I can't think why I didn't think of it sooner. It only makes sense that more sun and air circulating on the skins of the grapes would chase away the mildew.'' He scratched his cheek. "Of course, I don't know what effect, if any, the added sun will have on the flavor, but it has to be an improvement over the flavor of fungus.''

"Any crop at all is an improvement, monsieur. That is for certain. They are saying that the land has finally turned, all thanks to you.''

"Any more thanks, Charles, and I shall have a raging fit of temper.''

"*You*, monsieur?'' Charles peered at him. "No. I do not think so. I have never seen the slightest sign of temper in you—except for a little last night, and that I deserved.''

"It's there,'' Pascal said with a small smile. "Ask my wife. She thinks I'm impossible.''

That brought a grin to Charles's face. Wives were safe subjects, unlike miracles. "All wives think their husbands impossible. At least yours listens to you.''

"I don't know what gives you that idea,'' Pascal said dryly. "When it comes to medical matters she listens to me, but only because I know more than she does. The rest of the time—listen to me?'' He laughed. "Only if I'm very lucky.''

Charles nodded. "You are fond of your wife."

"Oh, yes. Extremely fond. But we'd better get back to work. This entire slope needs weeding and trimming." He went back to examining the rows, checking for healthy growth.

He felt Charles's eyes on his back as he moved away, eyes that were not entirely sure of him.

So it went for the rest of the morning. Pascal moved along the vines, watching, instructing, pruning and tying. Everywhere he went it was the same. Watchful eyes, lowered voices, the inevitable signs of the cross as he passed along. He could only thank God that Lily hadn't had the same reaction; he didn't know what he would have done if she had.

He was speaking with Pierre Marchand, who was behaving in a painfully reserved fashion, when he heard Lily's voice, and his head jerked up in surprise. Lily came to the vineyards only if it was something important, and yet she had nothing more than a blanket over one arm, a basket on the other, and a smile on her face.

"*Bonjour, messieurs,*" she said as she strolled down the row toward him, hips swaying provocatively, briefly stopping to chat with one person or another along the way. She looked beautiful, her hair caught back in a ribbon, her dress simple, and save for her naturally regal bearing and the sculpted structure of her bones, she might have been any laborer's wife. She certainly didn't look like a duke's daughter—nor was she behaving like one.

"Lily," he said as she came up to him. "What is it?"

To his amazement she reached up and kissed him on the mouth in front of Pierre and the entire work force. "Do I need a reason to visit my husband?" she asked, swinging the basket in front of him. "I brought you a meal. You missed breakfast, and I thought you might be hungry. When I stopped in to see Madame Claubert, she pressed some of her famous *saucisson* on me." She spoke clearly, her voice carrying to listening ears.

"Come along, Pascal, you work too hard. It's a beautiful day and we're going to have a picnic. You don't mind, do you, monsieur?" she said to Pierre with a charming smile. "I won't keep him very long."

Pierre shook his head, as blinded by Lily's sensuality as all the other men who were staring at her.

Pascal suspected it had something to do with a collective masculine sense of a beautiful woman exuding an unconscious sexuality—or was it unconscious? He gave Lily an assessing look. "A picnic?" he asked suspiciously, speaking in English. "You've never brought me a picnic before. What are you up to?"

"Sheer brilliance," she replied in the same language. "Watch." She took him by the hand and switched back to French. "Excuse us, Monsieur Marchand. Do give my regards to your wife. Your children are now recovered?"

He nodded, his eyes round. "Yes, thank you, madame."

"I am happy to hear it. Chicken pox is such a trying thing." She pulled Pascal away, down to the shade of a walnut tree growing on the edge of the vineyard, in clear sight of the fields. She spread out the blanket and started putting out the various things in the basket.

"What are you doing?" he asked with a laugh in his voice.

"Feeding my husband," she said cheerfully. "You do need occasional feeding, you realize—especially after vigorous exercise." She slanted a very feminine glance up at him.

Pascal dropped down on his haunches. "As God is my witness, I haven't a clue what you're doing, but I have half a mind to take you here and now, the way you're behaving."

"Exactly," she said with a grin, putting a hand on his chest and pushing him so that he overbalanced and had no choice but to sit abruptly.

"*What?* You can't be that far gone? My God, I thought this morning would last you a few hours at least." His eyes lit up in amusement. "We have half the male population of Saint-Simon watching us with avid curiosity."

"I know," she said, cutting a piece of *saucisson*, "and what they are seeing is a besotted wife attending to her most satisfactory husband." She stroked her fingers through his hair. "You are a most satisfactory husband." She put the sausage to his lips.

"I'm happy to hear it," he said, obediently taking the piece into his mouth and chewing it. "But why must the village of Saint-Simon be made aware of the fact?"

Lily uncorked the bottle of wine. "Because," she said, pouring it into two glasses, "Madame Claubert seemed to be under the impression this morning that when you and I go to bed at night, I sleep adoringly at your feet—Mary Magdalene to your Christ.''

Pascal snorted. ''She's badly wrong on all three counts.''

''I didn't bother to tell her that there was no resemblance, since I didn't think she'd believe me. So instead I implied that you were—well, that you were . . .'' Lily trailed off.

''Yes?'' he asked, suddenly wary. ''That I was what?''

Lily fed him another piece of sausage. ''A lusty devil,'' she said mischievously, ''having your way with me day and night and every chance in between.''

Pascal nearly choked on the *saucisson*.

''I hope you don't mind,'' she continued blithely. ''I thought it would counteract this other silliness.''

''I'm not sure I understand your strategy,'' he said, recovering his voice. ''It doesn't change what happened.''

''Oh, yes it does. There's some use in having been brought up by zealots—I understand the Catholic mentality very well.''

''And I don't?''

''No, you're much too liberal in your thinking, and I don't think you care in the least about dogma. My strategy is really quite simple, Pascal. Madame Claubert has convinced herself that you're a holy man. She said as much.''

Pascal mutely shook his head, then cast a glance up at the fields. ''Her husband didn't waste any time spreading the word either. You'd have thought I was walking on water instead of terra firma when I went out today.''

''That's exactly what I expected, and that's why I had to think of something that would convince people you were not the least bit holy. So I came up with the perfect thing.'' Lily put up her hand and counted off on her fingers. ''First, holy men have no interest in earthly matters. You're up to your elbows in earth. Second, holy men may have the ear of God—but they're all priests or martyrs. You are neither. Third, no serious holy man would actually enjoy consorting with his wife, and you do. Constantly,'' she added with a little smile. ''Given all that, it only follows that you're a man just like everyone else, overflowing with carnal desire.''

Pascal gazed at her with fascination. ''You actually *told* Emelie all that?''

''Not in those exact words, but by the time I was finished,

she was most impressed with your virility.'' She stroked his thigh with the tip of her finger.

''I see. Well, I'm sure you thoroughly distracted Madame Claubert at my expense, but it still doesn't explain away last night.''

''Of course it does. God would never give a worldly, lustful sort of man like you the ability to work miracles, would he?'' Her finger moved a little higher.

Pascal quickly covered her hand with his own. ''Stop right there, Lily, or I really will take you here and now and more than prove your point to the men of Saint-Simon.'' He folded her fingers through his and rested his back against the tree, regarding her thoughtfully. ''That's exactly what you intended, isn't it? Having ensured that Madame Claubert will spread the word of my extraordinary physical prowess among the women, you thought you'd come out here and take care of the men's opinion.''

''Precisely,'' Lily said, looking very pleased with his acuity. ''As for the miracle, Emelie begins to doubt what she saw—I told her she was delirious at the time. Also, I expounded on your medical training.''

''What about the next time something like this happens, Lily? What then?''

''I shouldn't worry about that,'' she said, a smile hovering on her lips. ''After what I told madame, people are just as likely to stare at your groin as they are at your hands.''

Pascal burst into laughter. ''I ought to strangle you, you know. I really ought to.''

Lily shrugged nonchalantly. ''Which would you rather? Saint or stallion?''

''Oh—oh, stallion, by all means,'' he said, laughing even harder.

''Then that's settled,'' Lily said, grinning. ''I didn't lie to madame, you know.'' She gave him a piece of bread and cheese and bent her attention to cutting some for herself.

He watched her, one arm resting on his knee, thinking that she bore no resemblance to the hellfire child he'd met all those months ago. This Lily was enough to bring him to his knees with desire and love and immense gratitude that she was his. He was more fortunate than he'd ever thought possible.

She glanced up at him. ''What?''

"I was counting my blessings," he replied softly, "and being thankful for my wife."

"Oh . . . Pascal," she said, her voice catching. "I do love you." She leaned toward him, curving one hand around his neck, and kissed him fully, this time with no thought to who might be watching.

Pascal kissed her right back with even less of a care.

Monsieur Jamard climbed up to the south vineyard to bring a message from his granddaughter to her husband. He then stopped to speak to his great-nephew Pierre Marchand, whom he found leaning on a hoe, watching his employer and his wife down below with a great deal of interest.

"Eh, look at that, uncle," Pierre said, straightening as he approached and shaking his hand. He pointed down the hill. "Now that's a sight for you: LaMartine kissing the duke's sister under the walnut tree. Maybe he's not such a saint as Charles made out. By the way she looks at him, I'll bet he makes her moan in bed." Pierre gave a hearty laugh. "Uncle?" he said, puzzled, looking at the old man, who had gripped him by the shoulder.

"The duke," Monsieur Jamard whispered.

"What about him? He's up there playing in his castle as usual, while the rest of us slave for him."

"No—no," Monsieur Jamard whispered. "The old duke. I was there that day. I saw them together, kissing, just there, just like that . . . I *knew* there was something familiar about him! Didn't I say so from the first?"

Monsieur Jamard's hands had started to shake, and Pierre patted his shoulder. "Calm down, old man. What are you going on about, eh?"

Monsieur Jamard looked around the vineyard, bursting with grapes. "The legend, Pierre—the legend, boy!"

Pierre nodded his head in the direction of the château. "The duke's descendant is back and the land is beginning to thrive, just as it said, even if the nephew is a wastrel. We all decided that a good month ago. So what are you getting yourself worked up over?"

"Not that descendant, you young fool," Jamard said impatiently. He pointed at Pascal. "*That* one!"

Pierre looked at his great-uncle as if he'd finally gone senile. "Now, now, uncle," he said soothingly. "Are you imagining things? The old duke's been dead thirty years."

Christian Jamard looked at his great-nephew with acute disgust. "Expect me for dinner tonight. You and I are going to have a long talk about Monsieur Pascal LaMartine."

"Henri LaMartine," Pierre Marchand said again to his great-uncle, tapping his fingers against his full, contented belly. "You are quite sure this was the name of the *régisseur* at the château in the old duke's day?"

Christian Jamard nodded slowly. "Yes, I am certain of it. LaMartine left when the duke died, of course. But I have been puzzled about it for months now. The name seemed a coincidence at the time—this Pascal LaMartine said his people were from Paris. Why should he have reason to lie? But two LaMartines, *régisseurs* to the château?"

"Well, it is a common name," Pierre said reasonably. "You did say he looks nothing like Henri LaMartine."

"Exactly my point!" Monsieur Jamard said irritably. "I told you, he has a look of the old duke. Slight, it is true, but it is there. It would explain many things." He shook his head. "Why must you be so hardheaded, Pierre? Just like your father, you are, God rest his soul. If he were alive today, he would tell you the same thing I am telling you. He would remember well enough."

"I don't know, uncle," Pierre said, scratching his thick brown thatch of hair. "This idea of yours seems very far-fetched to me. A surname and a slight resemblance—what is that to base anything on?"

Monsieur Jamard struggled to his feet and went over to the window, pointing up at the hills. "You seem to be forgetting the business of the vines, Pierre. What about the vines?"

Pierre shrugged. "Monsieur LaMartine knows his work. You told me so yourself at the beginning, and I have seen it to be true."

Christian Jamard shook his head again and turned back to the window. "You think this is all coincidence, boy? What is wrong with you?"

"There's not a thing wrong with me," Pierre said, raising his voice. "I am not the one with these crazy ideas. I listen to Monsieur LaMartine, I do as I am told, and the vines come back. What is the surprise in that? If you ask me, I think bringing back dead infants is more interesting. What is that, eh?"

Pierre's wife turned from washing the dishes. "I'm not so sure about that. I sat with Emelie this afternoon, and she had a different story to tell. According to her, Monsieur LaMartine is no saint." She grinned and tapped the side of her nose as if she were keeping a particularly delectable secret.

"If you're referring to his behavior with his wife, I've seen it for myself." Pierre sucked on his teeth.

"Insatiable is what I hear," Marie said happily, going back to the dishes. "Poor madame."

"Poor madame, indeed. I don't think she minds at all."

"He's insatiable," Marie repeated. "Emelie had it from madame's own lips. He wears her out, but she loves him, so what is she to do? It's no wonder we saw nothing of her when they first arrived, wed only a week. It took a whole month before she could walk well enough to leave the house, that's what I think." She nodded wisely.

Pierre raised both his eyebrows, and Monsieur Jamard turned around with interest. Birth, death, sex, and scandal—they were the mainstay of village life and thoroughly pored over on a regular basis with no regard to anyone's sensibilities.

"He looks the kind," Pierre noted. "It's probably everything he can do to keep it tucked away when he's working. You should have seen him today, Marie, stiff as a board when his wife came along."

"It sounds like the old duke to me," Monsieur Jamard said. "He was as lusty as the day was long—but once married, faithful to his wife," he added loyally. "He was devoted to her."

"And there you are," Pierre said impatiently, giving up sucking his teeth and going to search for a toothpick. "If he was so faithful, uncle, then explain how he fathered a bastard child." He dug in a drawer.

Monsieur Jamard gazed up at the château. "Perhaps when the duchess was with child?" he said, shrugging. "A man needs his release, after all, especially a man like that, and the duke would have been considerate enough not to take it with his wife." He nodded in agreement with himself. "Yes, perhaps. Pascal LaMartine would be about the right age. And Henri LaMartine's wife was pretty enough, as I remember, not that she mixed with us."

"I don't see why your uncle's story is so farfetched,"

Marie said practically, drying her rough hands on a towel and handing her husband the toothpick he hadn't been able to find.

"Come, Pierre, the coincidences are too many. Children fathered on women by men not their husbands are everywhere. What would be the surprise in this?" She settled into a chair with a sigh, happy to take the weight off her feet. "A nice, handsome duke taking his pleasure with a pretty woman living right there under his own roof? It would only be natural. No, I begin to think your uncle's story might indeed be true."

"Marie!" her husband said in an injured tone.

She ignored him, having now made up her mind on the matter. "I wonder if Henri LaMartine ever knew the truth about the child? How many do, eh?" Marie gave her husband another one of those superior smiles.

Pierre leaned over and squeezed his wife's arm. "It had better not be the butcher I see in our children's faces," he said in mock threat.

Marie picked up a sock to darn out of her sewing basket and waved it at her husband. "Bah—Louis Valbert? Never. Now, Pascal LaMartine, he is another story," she added with a saucy toss of her head.

Pierre wagged his finger at her. "Monsieur LaMartine is too busy with his own wife to pay any mind to you, Marie, insatiable or not. You'll have to settle for what is in front of you."

Marie lifted her eyes to the ceiling. "I could be waiting all year for what is in front of me."

Monsieur Jamard ignored this marital byplay, deeply engrossed in solving the mystery before him. "Another glass of the wine, Pierre," he commanded. "I need to think."

Pierre obliged him, upending the bottle into his great-uncle's glass. "But let me say this—no matter what light either of you tries to put on the matter, we don't really know anything."

Monsieur Jamard took a deep swallow of the coarse red wine. "You might not know anything, Pierre, which is not surprising, but I know this much—base-born he might be, but that is the duke's son come back to the land, and it finally prospers."

* * *

Pascal was still laughing when he and Lily got home that evening after checking on Emelie and her infant.

"By God, you were right, duchess," he said, putting his medical bag by the door and greeting Bean. "It didn't take long, did it?"

"Emelie went red in the face the minute you walked in the door. I thought I was going to collapse, trying to keep a straight face."

"You didn't keep a straight face," he informed her. "Don't think I missed the look the two of you exchanged when I examined her."

"Well, can you imagine what she was thinking?" Lily said with an enormous smile.

"Far worse, I could see what her grandfather was thinking. I thought Jamard was going to stare me down when we arrived. You know, I noticed him up in the vineyard earlier, pointing down at us. I think our behavior shocked him." He walked next door and pulled his shirt off, washing thoroughly.

"The other men approved," Lily called, slicing tomatoes for a salad. "I saw the grins when I left."

Pascal stuck his head out of the door. "Didn't I tell you?" he said, drying himself with a towel. "I've become a hero. The envy of Saint-Simon. The Don Juan of the Périgord."

"Well, of the Côtes de Franc, at least," Lily said.

Pascal tossed the towel away and strode into the room. He slipped his arms around Lily's waist, drawing her back against his bare chest. "What?" he murmured against the tender hollow just behind her ear. "Are you saying that I'm not the greatest chevalier in all of France?"

Lily looked at him over her shoulder. "The Côtes de Franc is quite large enough. Your head is swelling, chevalier."

"Not my head, duchess," he said with a muffled laugh and pulled her even closer, pushing his hips against her buttocks. Lily sighed, and he cupped her breasts, stroking them with his thumbs, then slipped one hand down the front of her dress to the juncture of her legs, pressing against her with his fingers until she trembled and her legs relaxed. "I want you," he murmured against her ear, caressing her through her dress. "I've been thinking about you all day."

"What about dinner?" she asked, her voice suddenly all

smoky and soft, just as he knew her eyes would be. Good. She wanted him too.

"Dinner can wait," he said. "I can't—your chevalier is in a state of intense need, and you can hold yourself responsible—you didn't have to bring me a picnic and remind me."

Lily laughed deep in her throat—a womanly sound, full of promise.

He picked her up in his arms and carried her up the stairs like a victor with his prize, stopping only to kiss her midway. Depositing her on the bed, he proceeded to strip her, one piece of clothing at a time, stripping himself as he went, then fell onto the bed with her, kissing every available inch of skin. "Mmm, soft, sweet duchess," he said, nuzzling her breasts, slipping his fingers into her, trembling as Lily, bold Lily, took him in her hand and stroked him in the same rhythm.

They were both learning quickly. All sorts of possibilities were occurring to him.

He rolled onto his back, and sat her up over his hips. She looked down at him in question, her face soft and open, receptive. He reached up and undid the ribbon holding her hair back, spreading her lush hair over her shoulders, the curling ends brushing her breasts.

It was no effort to lift his head and take Lily's breast in his mouth, licking and pulling and nipping until she squirmed. He lifted her by the waist and fitted her over his erect shaft, sliding her down onto him.

Lily's eyes widened, and Pascal grinned up at her. "You wanted a stallion, duchess. Another time I'll figure out how to take you like one, don't think I won't, but now it's your turn. I'm all yours. Do with your stallion as you will."

She smiled then, the smile of a seductress. She tentatively moved on him, and he shut his eyes for a moment, handing himself over to her, relinquishing all control.

She put her hands on his chest, adjusting, testing her weight, finding her balance, and then she began to rock, slowly at first, then faster, her lip caught between her teeth as she concentrated, her eyes half closed, her full breasts shivering just over his face. He couldn't help taking advantage of that.

"Ah, Lily," he moaned, his breath coming in hard pants, trying to hold on for her. His hands circled her hips, holding her, steadying her as she moved up and down on him, driving him to the edge.

Her eyes shut and her brow furrowed, and she sank down on him all the way, crying out, sharp high little cries that matched the rhythm of her pulsing flesh. His hips jerked, and he thrust against her hard, pumping his seed into her, groaning against the exquisite agony of release, pulling her down against him full length and kissing her, rolling her onto her side, his hands twining in her hair, thinking for the hundredth time in twenty-four hours that he was the luckiest man alive.

Lily rested against him, silent, content. He drifted, equally content. But after ten minutes or so, she finally spoke.

"Well . . . maybe I'll grant you the Périgord," she said grudgingly. "But all of France is really going too far."

Pascal, who had gone in another direction entirely, laughed softly. "Don't draw any conclusions yet, sweetheart. Give me a little time and I'll be the best chevalier in all of Europe."

"Let me know when you take Asia," she said, smiling against his arm.

"I won't have to. You can take Asia for yourself. I've just conceded you a corner of Tibet, in fact. A very nice corner. Himalayan—lots of peaks and valleys."

Lily pulled him over on top of her. "You might as well try for the Swiss Alps, Monsieur Chevalier."

He did.

20

LILY'S strategy served its purpose. Over the next ten days Pascal noticed the return of bawdiness around him, himself the target on a few occasions. He was also treated with a new deference that he imagined was a holdover from Joseph-Jean's birth, but since the evening surgery sessions went as usual, he decided that no one was more skittish for the initial rumors. Privately he did his best to live up to the reputation Lily had established for him. It was no hardship.

Life was good, fulfilled, contented. Yet there was an issue that sorely aggravated him—that of Jean-Jacques. He'd had not one summons, not one word from the man. A continuous party had been raging up at the Château de Saint-Simon for over a week, carriages coming and going up and down the hill with monotonous regularity.

Lily had not heard a thing from her brother either—hardly surprising, given what the fool had said to her on her last ill-advised visit. Lily had told Pascal all about it, and it had been all he could do to keep from going up to the château and tearing Jean-Jacques apart.

Still, in many ways it was just as well that the man stayed away from Lily so as not to upset her further. It angered Pascal nevertheless. It also angered him that Jean-Jacques had given no thought to paying his debts.

He threw down his pen in frustration. Tomorrow was payday. The books were balanced properly, but money was owed everywhere. Pascal was down to the end of his own resources and would be hard-pressed to make this week's payroll. Money would be plentiful once the harvest came in, but there was another fortnight to go before that began, another two weeks after that before it was completed. There was a wine-maker to be hired, the winery to be scoured out, the vats made ready.

Pascal had had enough.

It was four in the afternoon, and he imagined that Jean-Jacques would have to be out of bed by now. There was always the possibility that he'd gone back to bed in order to prepare for the excesses of the evening. Pascal had heard all about those, via the local gossip. The daughters and wives who'd been employed at the château since Jean-Jacques's return had a good deal to say, most of it scandalous, and it went straight into the men's ears and back out into the vineyard.

Oh, yes, Pascal was well informed.

He picked up the books and glanced out the back door. Lily was in the vegetable garden, re-staking the tomato plants. They'd borne so much fruit that they were sagging under their own weight. She looked happy in her work.

"I'm going out for a while, duchess," he said, walking over to her and leaning on the fence with his free arm.

Lily stood and brushed off her hands. She had a streak of dirt on her nose, and little wisps of hair had escaped from her braid. "Will you be back for supper?"

He leaned a little further over and dropped a kiss on her lovely, ripe lips. "Long before, I should think. What are we having?"

"Oh, Monsieur Valbert dropped by a ham earlier." Lily brushed her hair off her face, leaving another streak of dirt on her cheek. "He said he's feeling much better."

"Hmm," Pascal said, thinking Lily looked utterly adorable, "I would imagine he is. But you wait and see—the minute he's recovered, he'll go straight back to butter and cream and all the things that made him sick in the first place."

"Monsieur's eating habits will keep us in meat for months," Lily said, smiling up at him.

"Probably." He kissed her again. "Where's Bean?"

"She went bounding off after a rabbit—tomorrow's dinner if she remembers to bring it back."

"Thank God for Bean. Better her than me," he said, smoothing her hair off her face.

"I wouldn't worry," Lily said dryly. "Between Bean and the butcher's gallbladder we're doing very well."

"We are indeed, duchess. We are indeed. I'll see you later." Pascal stole one more kiss, then headed up the hill, accounts in hand.

People waved to him as he passed, calling out greetings. He waved in reply, smiled, called back, but his mind was on his objective and his temper was rising with every step that he took toward the château.

A proper butler in full regalia opened the door. "Monsieur?" he said, looking Pascal up and down, taking in the shirtsleeves, the simple dress. Pascal hadn't bothered with a jacket.

"I have come to see the duke on his business. I am LaMartine, his *régisseur.*"

The butler looked surprised. "Ah, Monsieur La-Martine—yes, of course. However, the duke is busy. I do not know when—"

"Now!" Pascal demanded, his voice even enough but frigid with anger as he noticed that the hall had already been beautifully refurbished. "Now," he repeated.

The butler was no match for Pascal. He stood aside and let him in, crossing the hall to the library.

"Monsieur le Duc," he said, opening the door, and Pascal could see clearly inside.

Jean-Jacques lounged in a chair, his feet propped up on a stool, a glass of cognac in his hand. He was addressing a caustic comment about one of his guests to a portly, over-dressed gentleman, who snickered in return.

Pascal took in the gentleman with an instant, sick, and violent recognition. Unfortunately, from the look of things it appeared that Jean-Jacques had fallen under the unholy influence of Maurice, Comte de Passy. Pascal had met him on a visit Passy had made to England five years earlier, although he doubted the comte would remember him. He would have had little reason to.

Pascal, on the other hand, would never forget the man. He suppressed a shiver of distaste. A hundred years would be nowhere near long enough to erase that particular memory.

Passy was a man of strong influence, capable of making or destroying reputations—and equally capable of destroying souls. Looking into his history in the year that followed, Pascal had learned more about the man than he cared to know. None of it augured well for Jean-Jacques.

If this was the man Lily had described when she'd gone up to see her brother, it was little wonder Jean-Jacques had reacted as he had to her. Passy would have turned Jean-

Jacques into an object of ridicule in no time. His presence explained a great many things about Jean-Jacques's behavior.

"Monsieur le Duc," the butler said again, clearing his throat.

"What is it now?" Jean-Jacques said with irritation. "I told you I do not wish to be disturbed." He didn't bother turning around.

"But there is a gentleman . . ."

Pascal touched him on the shoulder and nodded toward the door. The butler backed away, and Pascal shut the door behind him.

"Monsieur le Duc," he said coolly. "I wish to speak with you. Privately, if you please."

Jean-Jacques's head snapped around. "You!" he said, dropping his feet to the floor with a thud. "How dare you come in here like this?"

"Your butler, being a sensible man, let me in. I explained that I was here on your own urgent business. He obviously has a better-developed sense for your business than you have."

"Who is this impertinent devil?" Passy demanded, his complexion turning even more florid than usual.

"LaMartine, my steward," Jean-Jacques replied, waving a lazy hand in Pascal's direction. "Forgive him. What he lacks in manners he makes up for with an overinflated sense of his own importance."

"Do I?" Pascal said indifferently. "Perhaps it's your underinflated sense of responsibility that's the cause for that. Someone needs to look after Saint-Simon, given that you've shown no interest."

"How *dare* you speak to the duke in such a manner?" Passy spluttered.

Pascal flicked a glance in his direction. "This is no affair of yours, monsieur."

"Monsieur LaMartine," Jean-Jacques snapped, "you address the Comte de Passy!"

"Good day." Pascal briefly inclined his head and turned back to his brother-in-law. "What I have to say to you regards your estate. It concerns no one else."

"You may speak in front of the comte. Get on with it, and let me get back to my conversation."

Pascal looked at Jean-Jacques more closely, and with

mounting concern as he noted his enlarged pupils, his lethargy. "Very well," he said, wondering how long Jean-Jacques had been imbibing opiated wine. "You and I had an agreement regarding your vineyards. You have not yet honored it."

"Things have changed," Jean-Jacques said with a shrug.

"You wrote me two months ago stating that you had acquired a large sum of money to put into the estate and that you were returning shortly. You did not."

"I was not aware that I had to answer to you, monsieur." Jean-Jacques took another sip of cognac, then dangled the glass between finger and thumb, looking down into it as if bored.

"As your steward, I have been acting on your behalf as you instructed me," Pascal said. "That was as of the third week of May. It is now the end of August, and the merchants have yet to be paid. You have been back for ten days, and still I have heard nothing from you. Why?"

Jean-Jacques shrugged again. "I have been busy."

"Have you?" Pascal said caustically. "Yes, I suppose that entertaining until all hours must be exhausting."

"What would you know about it, you—you peasant." He looked Pascal up and down, his eyes heavy with insult. "Can you not even dress properly when you come to see me? And speaking of that . . ."

"Yes, speaking of that," Pascal said, his eyes sparking with real anger, the subject of Lily hanging between them. "You were going to say?"

Jean-Jacques cast a look at Passy, who was listening carefully to every word. "Speaking of that," he said feebly, "how dare you come barging in here?"

"I dare because I have a job to do—a job I accepted on certain conditions, to which you agreed." Pascal walked over and tossed the books down on the desk. "You might look through these, and then I would appreciate a draft for the money outstanding. There are people who need to be paid, myself included."

"Oh?" Jean-Jacques said with a cynical smile.

Pascal looked down at the toe of his boot for a moment, thinking he'd like to take a hammer to Jean-Jacques's opiated head. "Yes," he said, when the immediate desire had passed. "I believe I explained my financial position to you when we first met? It has not changed, other than that my

pockets are even emptier than they were before. That is a
result of my paying your employees' salaries for you in your
absence.''

"More fool you," Jean-Jacques said. "I told you to use
credit.''

Pascal looked around the room, more finely appointed
than before, just as the huge hall had been. "Credit might
buy things, but it will not put food on the table at the end
of a hard day. I cannot pay men on credit.''

He was well aware that Passy's intense gaze was focused
solely on him. He hoped to God he looked like the peasant
Jean-Jacques had accused him of being.

"Very well," Jean-Jacques said, idly inspecting his fin-
gernails, "leave the books there. I will attend to them
later.''

"I think not. I think it would be best if you attended to
them immediately.''

Jean-Jacques half rose out of his chair. "*You* think? Who
do you think you are?''

Pascal rubbed his lower lip with his thumb, then gave
Jean-Jacques a half-smile, calculated to send him right back
into his chair. He'd learned a little more at Nicholas's knee
than how to swear. He was certain that Jean-Jacques didn't
want Passy to know that Lily was the woman Passy had seen
outside the château the previous week. He was also certain
that Jean-Jacques didn't want Passy to know that Pascal was
his brother-in-law.

Pascal felt exactly the same way. There was fuel there for
some seriously malicious mischief on Passy's part. He'd
rather that Lily be left out of Passy's regard altogether, but
Jean-Jacques didn't know that, and it made a fine bargaining
chip.

"I am a married man, responsible for my wife's welfare," he said. "My wife is only one among many who will
be happy for a meal on the table tomorrow night," Pascal
said. "Surely you wouldn't want her to go hungry?''

Passy's head turned from one to the other, his eyes narrowing as he picked up the subtle undercurrents running
between the two men.

"Very well," Jean-Jacques said, nervously rubbing a finger over the top of his glass. "I'll pay you. I'll pay you
what I owe you and the others up until now, but not a franc
more for those miserable vineyards.''

Pascal went very still. "What do you mean, not a franc more? Surely you intend to honor your commitment?"

"I made an agreement out of desperation," Jean-Jacques said, not meeting Pascal's eyes. "I am no longer desperate, and there is no point in throwing away good money after bad on a crop I won't see a decent profit from for years, if ever."

Pascal looked at him hard. "You need your crop for future income, no matter how much money you have on hand now. You can't afford to squander it."

"I don't need my crop in the least," Jean-Jacques said.

Pascal frowned. "Then how do you intend to pay back your loan?"

Passy laughed nastily. "Go on, tell him, Jean-Jacques. Put him out of his misery. Tell the arrogant fool, then throw him out into the streets."

Jean-Jacques smiled smugly and rested his feet back on the stool. "I didn't need the banks. I did it all on my own."

"Did what?" Pascal asked warily. "Just what—exactly—did you do?"

"I won a fortune," he replied, taking another sip of cognac from the snifter. "No interest to pay, no debt incurred. I am a rich man and have no further need of you or of anyone. I certainly have no need of these damned vineyards."

Jean-Jacques might just as well have delivered a blow to Pascal's stomach. The effect was the same. He sank into a chair uninvited, his head lowered, trying to catch his breath. "Saint-Simon?" he said, looking up after a minute, his voice shaking with an effort at control. "Your stake was Saint-Simon?"

Jean-Jacques shrugged. "What else? What else was there? It wasn't doing me any good as it was."

"You risked the entire estate on the toss of a coin or the roll of the dice—"

"No, it was cards," Jean-Jacques said, lolling back in his chair. "Lady Luck was watching over my shoulder. I couldn't go wrong."

It was too much for Pascal—control went straight out the window. "I don't give a damn what it was," he shouted, slamming his fist on the arm of the chair. "You risked everything without the first thought to anything but yourself! Did you once think of the people? They have a heritage, too, a history of their own, all wrapped up with this château and its dukes, and for the last thirty years their dukes have served them poorly indeed!''

"I really can't see why it's any concern of yours," Jean-Jacques said sulkily. "You're only here on my sufferance."

"I am here," Pascal said, his eyes snapping dangerously, "because I choose to be, *Monsieur le Duc*. I have much to report to you. Perhaps you will change your mind about your vineyards by the time I have finished."

"I will not," Jean-Jacques said with extreme annoyance, "but if the only way to get rid of you is to hear you out, then get on with it."

Pascal picked up the first ledger, glancing over at Passy. He looked back at Jean-Jacques. "It will take some time to go through all the figures," he said, then waited.

Jean-Jacques took the bait. "Oh, very well. There's no point in your staying to be put to sleep as well, Maurice. I'll find you later." Jean-Jacques waved toward the door. "If you see Violette, tell her that I haven't forgotten her."

Passy gave Pascal one last sharp look, then left without a word.

Jean-Jacques waited until he'd heard the door close. "Really, how you think you can speak—"

Pascal cut Jean-Jacques off abruptly. "Be still," he said curtly. "And pull yourself together—you're a dissipated wreck. You will listen to me now, Jean-Jacques, and I will not hear a word out of you until I'm finished." He tossed the ledger back onto the desk and looked down at him. "What you did to your sister when you returned home was unforgivable. What you did in putting this land up as a gambling stake was also unforgivable. But you are the duke. I imagine you feel invincible at the moment."

Jean-Jacques glared at him, his hands shaking violently on the other side of the desk. "You are quite right—*I am the duke*. You will not speak to me in such a way."

"Ah, but I will," Pascal said softly. "I will, because I refuse to watch you throw away generations of trust, of work, of devotion to the land and to the people. Have you any regard for the people entrusted to you, Jean-Jacques? Any at all?"

"Naturally," he said, fiddling with his glass.

"Well, then, prove it. Pay your bills." Pascal slapped open the ledgers. "It's all written out. All you need do is check my final figures and add them up for yourself. You can add, I assume?''

Jean-Jacques looked ready to go for his throat. "Yes," he said, his voice cold as steel, "I can add, damn you."

"Then do it. I'll wait."

"If it weren't for my sister," Jean-Jacques muttered, taking a pile of blank bank drafts from the drawer.

"If it weren't for your sister," Pascal said bitingly, "I'd have slammed you against the wall and throttled you." He took a deep breath. "But because I care for your sister, and because deep inside her she still cares for you in some small measure, I'll keep my hands to myself."

"You impudent scoundrel," Jean-Jacques spat. "What do you mean by saying that you care for my sister after the way you've treated her? I was sickened—sickened, do you hear me?—by what you have brought her to. I mistook her for a beggar, for God's sake."

"You wasted no time in making that clear to her," Pascal said, trying to keep a grip on himself. "You haven't the first idea about your sister, have you? I doubt you ever have had, just like the rest of her miserable family. It's a damned shame, Jean-Jacques. Lily's a remarkable woman. Ask the villagers if you're not inclined to take my word for it."

Jean-Jacques stared at him, his mouth hanging open. "Don't tell me you've gone and fallen in love with her?" He pounded a hand on his desk. "Unbelievable! So that's what this is about?"

"No. What this is about is paying your bills and honoring your commitments. If you withdraw your financial support now, there will be no harvest. There will be no one to weed or trim. There will be no one to pick the grapes, nor to crush them, nor to barrel them. Your crop will rot on the vine, Jean-Jacques."

He put both hands on the desk and leaned over them, his face only inches away from Jean-Jacques. "And you will rot with it, my friend. You're well on your way. Your precious Comte de Passy will see to the rest of it. Opiated wine and sexual diversions, social and political games—that's only the beginning. He'll weave you into his net and get precisely what he pleases from you, and he'll squeeze you dry in the process."

Jean-Jacques shrank back in his chair. "How—how dare you?" he stammered.

"I dare because I know, and someone needs to warn you. I know what he's capable of. God, I've *seen* what he's capable of." Pascal drew a shaky breath, remembering that dreadful day in every last detail.

"I don't know what you're talking about," Jean-Jacques said. "How would you know anything?" His mouth twisted. "You are no one, and yet you presume to speak of your betters like this?"

Pascal ignored the jibe. He straightened and pushed a hand through his hair, wishing he didn't have to get involved, knowing he had no choice, not if he was to save Saint-Simon from Jean-Jacques's idiocy.

"I don't presume anything," he said. "I once had to care for someone your friend had taken his pleasure with. He nearly died. He was only fifteen, a stable boy."

Jean-Jacques paled. "No . . . I don't believe it. Passy's not like that—he's all over the women. I've seen for myself, all of it."

"No doubt you have," Pascal said with disgust. "Passy thrives on perversion. He also doesn't limit himself to one sex."

"P-perhaps you had better tell me just what you mean," Jean-Jacques said, thoroughly shaken.

Pascal released a heavy breath. "It was a bad morning. I didn't know which was likely to kill Julien first, the internal injuries or the loss of blood. Fortunately, he survived, although he'd been robbed of the rest of his childhood and his innocence, and for a time, his sanity."

"The boy accused Passy of being his attacker?"

Pascal lifted a shoulder. "Not exactly."

"Aha!" Jean-Jacques said triumphantly. "I knew it!"

"He didn't say anything," Pascal replied tightly, "because Passy had taken precautions against that. Along with Julien's innocence Passy removed a good portion of the boy's tongue—after he'd used it to his service, of course. A knife can serve a double purpose." Pascal looked away. "In this case it did."

Jean-Jacques looked as if he might be sick at any moment. "No," he groaned. "Oh, God. No."

"Oh, yes. It didn't occur to Passy that Julien might be able to read or write. That, Jean-Jacques, is your friend. A charming man, wouldn't you say?"

"My . . . my God," Jean-Jacques said, his mouth white

and strained. "But where—when did this happen? What proof?"

"It happened in England. In Devon. Ask Passy if he's ever been to Haddington Hall. Five years ago the French met the English there to discuss trade routes to the Far East."

"What were you doing there? Perhaps you were a stable boy as well?" Jean-Jacques said snidely.

Pascal looked at him coolly. "No. I was there as an advisor to my adoptive father. I'd recently returned from Asia, having researched those routes for him."

"Oh," Jean-Jacques said uncertainly.

"The last evening Passy was in an argumentative mood, frustrated because he hadn't had his way as completely as he would have liked." Pascal rubbed his forehead, then sighed, dropping his hand. "I remember thinking that he looked dangerous. He left abruptly after dinner, saying that he was going to bed."

"B-but he didn't?"

"No. At least not immediately. He went to the stables, a reasonable distance from the house, and with the noise of the music and the conversation to cover him, he didn't have to worry about the screams of a defenseless young boy being heard."

Jean-Jacques swallowed hard. "You—you were summoned from the house? Why?"

Pascal sat down in the chair opposite. "Because the groom who found Julien the next morning was employed by my father. He knew I could help." He stared down at his hands.

He would never forget his first sight of Julien—sobbing in the deep woods where Passy had left him, his body folded up against itself, stiff with shock and pain. His poor mutilated mouth was filled with blood, and most of the lower half of his body was covered in the same as his life slowly ebbed away. It had been a horrible, heart-wrenching sight.

"I spent half the morning trying to stop the bleeding," he said dully, "and the other half stitching Julien up. All he could do was make dreadful guttural sobbing sounds. Of course, he never spoke again."

"This happened in England, you say?" Jean-Jacques leapt at the first straw he could find. "Well, that says everything.

You can't practice medicine in England—not without a license. You'd be thrown into jail.''

''I do have a license,'' Pascal said impatiently, ''and for that very reason. I don't advertise it, since I don't take money for my work—not that kind of work anyway.''

''What? Why not? You complain of being poor,'' Jean-Jacques said, desperately trying to ignore what he'd just been told as if it hadn't been spoken.

''I complain of no such thing. What difference does it make to you, Jean-Jacques, how I earn my way? When it comes to that, surely you must realize that the salary I have asked of you is absurd, given what I've just told you?''

The color rose in Jean-Jacques's cheeks. ''Then why do you work here at all?''

''As I said, because I choose to.''

''Then you are a fraud. You led my sister and myself to believe you were a gardener, and now you call yourself a physician?''

''I have a degree in medicine,'' Pascal said tightly. ''I call myself a botanist. I have a degree in that, too, Jean-Jacques, if you want to nit-pick.''

''Why should I believe anything you say?'' Jean-Jacques said stubbornly.

Pascal gave himself a moment, carefully feeling his way along an entirely new understanding of the man before him. It wasn't easy—it required the last of his patience. But then Lily hadn't been easy in the beginning either. There was Lily's father, he reminded himself, counting to ten. Father Mallet, that brought him to at least twenty. Then there was the mysterious mother, the one who had walked out on her children. That was worth another five seconds of counting.

''I've told you the truth about everything, including Passy,'' he said, when his temper was finally back under control.

''You have no proof,'' Jean-Jacques insisted.

''Julien was clear as day about everything that happened,'' Pascal replied.

''What happened to him then? Where is he now? Can you produce him?''

''I have no intention of producing him. I kept him by my side for a year while he went through the worst of his suffering, and then I took him to a monastery I'd been told of and left him there to finish his healing.'' He thought of the day that he'd handed Julien over to Dom Benetard, who had taken the boy under his wing and kept him firmly tucked there until Julien had been strong enough to manage on his own. "Julien will remain at St. Christophe for the rest of his life," he continued, "having recently taken vows. You may inquire of the abbot, if you do not wish to believe me."

Jean-Jacques sat frozen behind his desk. "Why didn't Passy recognize you, then?" he persisted. "Maurice prides himself on never forgetting a face."

"There were many, many people at Haddington. I was no one important, only an aide to my father—whom Passy would remember. He is the Earl of Raven, and not an easy man to forget."

Jean-Jacques stared at him as if he'd just grown another head. "The—the Earl of Raven?"

"Yes. He would also tell you that I speak the truth about Passy. Now the question is," Pascal said reflectively, "what is it that Passy wants from you?"

"But—but he doesn't want anything," Jean-Jacques said, attempting to recover his equilibrium. "We are friends."

"The Comte de Passy doesn't have friends, he has puppets. I wouldn't put it past him to have set up this gambling coup of yours. But why?" Pascal paced the room, thinking hard.

Jean-Jacques shook his head, little beads of sweat forming on his brow. "No. I cannot believe it."

Pascal looked up. "Why not, Jean-Jacques? Why not get at the truth? I could probably act out the entire scenario for you. It was he who approached you about the gambling, wasn't it?"

He nodded uncertainly.

Pascal smiled with satisfaction. "Yes. As I thought. He took you to his private club, where the stakes are nothing less than enormous."

"But how do you know all this?" Jean-Jacques asked in disbelief.

"It's a usual ploy. He probably heard about your plight from one of the banks he controls. Then he arranged for you to win more money than you ever hoped for."

"How could one arrange such a thing?" Jean-Jacques asked. "I won it fairly, and not without some frightening losses in the beginning."

"Of course," Pascal said. "It would be idiotic to have it

look any different. Was it your idea to gamble the estate or his?''

"His,'' Jean-Jacques admitted, looking more frightened by the moment. "He said it was the only way, that no bank would touch Saint-Simon because it had been losing money for so long. It was true, too—I couldn't get a loan anywhere. He said that I might as well take the risk, and either win a fortune or have the worry off my hands for good.''

Pascal nodded. "Thank you for being honest, at least. But again, the question is, Why would he bother? What do you have to offer him? He has estates and money enough of his own. You have no political connections, have you?''

Jean-Jacques frowned impatiently. "As I told you, it is a simple matter of friendship. I cannot see why you must find intrigue in every corner.''

"Can't you?'' Pascal shrugged. "Well, that's probably because you don't know as much about your friend as I do. After what happened to Julien, I made it my business to find out about him, and my father helped. He has a number of useful connections in the British government.''

"Lord Raven,'' Jean-Jacques said, clearing his throat.

"Yes, that's right,'' Pascal said, privately amused by the turnaround in Jean-Jacques's attitude. It was amazing what a little name-dropping could do—a practice he had always abhorred, but had just deliberately employed. It looked as if he was growing more human by the minute. "Anyway, we discovered that Passy had been watched by the British government for years.''

"But—but why?'' Jean-Jacques nervously flicked his tongue over his lips.

"Oh, all sorts of reasons,'' Pascal replied. "The French keep a close eye on him as well. He's loyal to no one but himself and his own interests. Which brings us back to you.''

"But I am no one—I mean, I have a title, and now I have money, but what use is that to him? As you just said, I have no political connections other than him and his friends.''

Pascal considered. "He must be planning to use you as a pawn in some game of his, and for that, he needs you to be wealthy and under his thumb.'' Pascal's eyes narrowed. "Wait—was this ongoing house party your idea or his?''

"His,'' Jean-Jacques said. "He knows I hate the country,

but he said that inviting people to Saint-Simon would create the right impression with the right people.''

''And the invited guests?''

''His suggestions. He said he wanted to help me into a small but influential circle, and this was the best way.''

''Their names?''

Jean-Jacques reeled off a list.

Pascal listened with dawning understanding. He might have retreated from the world for two years, but Nicholas had kept him well informed by letter. One of the things Nicholas had mentioned was the small and very quiet group of French who supported Bonapartism—although Passy's name had not been among their number.

Yet more than half the names Jean-Jacques had just mentioned were part of that select group. Louis-Napoléon, currently exiled in England, was probably planning another coup d'état against the Bourbon government, and Passy was somehow behind it.

''What is it?'' Jean-Jacques asked nervously. ''Why do you look at me in such a calculating manner?''

''You, Jean-Jacques, are being used as a front for a very dangerous game,'' Pascal said. ''I begin to see why Passy chose you. You've been out of the eye of society for three years, yes? Invisible. Now after a brief reappearance you're back out of the eye of society, but you have Saint-Simon and enough money to entertain lavishly.''

''Yes?'' Jean-Jacques said. ''What is that supposed to mean?''

''What it means is that Passy and his friends are up to no good. They've been conspiring right under your nose, knowing no one would look to you for political intrigue.''

''Conspiring? What about?'' Jean-Jacques asked, appalled.

''I'd rather not say. Not yet, anyway.'' Not until Passy was well out of the way and Jean-Jacques was off opiates— opiates that Passy had been feeding him to keep his wits dulled. It was diabolic—and worth every franc it had cost Passy to fund Jean-Jacques, for should King Louis-Philippe come to hear of a plot, they'd all be thrown into jail, if not executed for treason.

But in the state Jean-Jacques was in at the moment, Pascal could not trust him with such dangerous information.

''Listen to me, and listen very carefully,'' Pascal said,

measuring his words. "Passy is using you. He has exploited your vanity, your desire to be important, and he is now addicting you to opiates, so that he can control you completely. Eventually all he'll have to do is withhold the drugs from you, and you'll be on your knees, willing to do anything at all. Anything, Jean-Jacques.''

Jean-Jacques colored deeply, unable to disguise his embarrassment. "How did you know about the opiates?''

"A trained eye,'' Pascal said. He nodded toward the glass of cognac. "How long have you been drinking laced wine?''

"I—I'm not sure,'' Jean-Jacques said, trying to remember. "Two months, perhaps?''

"How much of it a day, then? One glass, five, ten?''

"Perhaps as many as five,'' he admitted.

Pascal assessed him, noting the pallor of his skin, the slight shake of his hands. "If you stop taking it now,'' he said, "I can give you something to make the withdrawal easier on you. I will guarantee that if you go on like this, it will become very much worse for you, and you'll never get out of Passy's clutches.''

Jean-Jacques nodded, looking acutely unhappy.

Pascal gazed out the window at the countryside. The vineyards ran down the hill, backlit in the deepening afternoon light. Here and there men moved among the rows, doing the work of every day. It was a simple and peaceful sight. Conspiracies had no place here, nor did filth like Passy.

"Speaking of Passy's clutches,'' Pascal said, "I'd make some plausible excuse to get rid of him and his friends as quickly as possible. You're in danger, and you could well end up being the lamb led to slaughter. Should something go wrong, Passy wouldn't hesitate to use you to save his own skin.''

"I—I feel like an idiot,'' Jean-Jacques whispered. "But it never occurred to me . . . I was flattered to be part of their inner circle.''

"Naturally you were, but you don't belong with people like that, Jean-Jacques. You never will, and thank God for it. You're a man who enjoys his pleasures and the company of his friends. These people—they know nothing about friendship.''

"I was never comfortable with them,'' Jean-Jacques said

shakily. "The opium helped with that. How do I make them go away?"

Pascal thought, then grinned as an idea occurred to him. "How would you feel about an outbreak of diphtheria? I'm sure it could be arranged."

Jean-Jacques stared at Pascal. "Really? How?"

"I have any number of friends who would be willing to oblige," Pascal said, thinking that he really had come to enjoy the world of men. Intrigue, counterintrigue; it was good fun. He began to understand why Nicholas derived such enormous pleasure from his work, which was rife with this sort of thing.

"I'll start the rumor," he said, "and word will spread up here fast enough through the servants. From the servants it will then go to the valets and the ladies' maids. And voilà. You will have a mass exodus by tomorrow afternoon—the following day at the very latest."

"Very clever," Jean-Jacques said.

"Thank you. And—this is important—when Passy comes to you tomorrow to find out if you know anything about the epidemic, tell him that you don't believe a word of it, even though I warned you of an outbreak today."

"Yes, all right, but Passy is hard to fool," Jean-Jacques said, looking nervous again.

"Nonsense," Pascal said. "Beat him at his own game. Pretend you are desolate at having your friends desert you. Then rub your throat, cough a little, and say you think you might go along to Paris with him."

Jean-Jacques nodded. "You are the one who is diabolic, I think."

"I begin to think I might be," Pascal said, "for here's another idea. You ought to be pale and sweating by tomorrow, maybe shaking a little. I'll come up in the morning with something to help you through the withdrawal, but I'll announce that I've come about your throat. If that doesn't alarm them, I'm useless."

"No, not useless. I don't know how to thank you for your help."

Pascal smiled. "That's simple. Be happy for your sister. Lily is in her element here, and well loved, not only by me. I think it's time you saw her in a new light—and offered her an apology, perhaps?"

Jean-Jacques reddened, but he nodded.

"Good. You are welcome at the cottage anytime, although I'd wait until your guests leave. You ought not be seen leaving your sickbed once you've taken to it."

He gestured toward the books. "You might write those bank drafts now. By the way, you will have a harvest this year, and a good one, if the weather holds. You will also have a profit, Jean-Jacques, and it should be substantial."

"What?" Jean-Jacques said, as if he couldn't believe his ears. "What are you talking about?"

"I suppose it shouldn't surprise me that you haven't had time to notice the vineyards. They're bursting with fruit, healthy fruit. It has taken a tremendous amount of work to get them that way, and you have nearly every able-bodied man in Saint-Simon to thank for that."

"Fruit? *Healthy* fruit?"

"Your vintage should be excellent, if everything continues as it has. You will definitely need a wine-maker, Jean-Jacques."

Jean-Jacques rose and walked over to the window, and Pascal came up behind him. "With a little time your red wines will become known again, admired and appreciated," he said.

"You truly think this is possible?" Jean-Jacques asked. He half turned to look at Pascal.

"Yes, I do. But first you must pay your bills."

Jean-Jacques went back to his desk and started to look the books over. But after a moment he passed his hand over his eyes. "I can't seem to concentrate on the figures . . ."

Pascal sat down opposite him. "If you will trust me this far, I'll fill everything out for you. All I need is your signature on the finished drafts." He quickly made out the necessary forms and handed Jean-Jacques his pen.

Jean-Jacques dipped it into the ink and signed everywhere he was told.

21

PASCAL was quiet that night, although in a fine enough humor. Lily knew that it was no good to try to make him talk when he was in a silent mood, and since there had been no patients, she put dinner on the table early. He ate it, his thoughts elsewhere.

Lily washed up the meal, while Pascal dealt with the daily books, but from the way he was going about it, it was obvious that his mind wasn't on his work. She walked up behind him and rested her hand on his warm cheek, and he absently covered it. That having failed to get his attention, she leaned down and kissed him.

He smiled, looking up at her. "Like that, is it, duchess?"

"Not necessarily," she said, stroking his hair. "I wouldn't want to distract you any more than you already are."

"Sorry," he said. "I know I haven't been the best of company tonight."

"It's all right, Pascal. I don't need to be entertained. I can tell that you have something on your mind. Is there anything I can do?"

"Yes, but not just at this moment. I've been formulating a plan to stop the nonsense up at the château. I spoke with your brother this afternoon."

"You did?" she said, surprised.

"Yes, and he paid the outstanding balance in full. He has also decided he no longer wishes to entertain his friends."

"He what?" She gave Pascal a suspicious look. "All right, what did you do? Did you go probing?"

"No," he said, all innocence. "We had a nice long talk, and I explained about his vines. He was very happy. He saw the sense in investing in them."

"I thought that was the plan all along," Lily said.

"It was, but Jean-Jacques had temporarily changed his mind. He has now decided that he needs to concentrate on business, and concentrating on business is difficult to do with a houseful of noisy, badly behaved people.''

Lily's lips twitched. ''Devil,'' she said, and Pascal pushed his chair out a little and drew her onto his lap. ''You must have done something to force his hand,'' she prompted.

''Well, I did use a little friendly persuasion,'' he said, nestling her against his chest. ''Actually, I was quite rude to start with, but then Jean-Jacques saw the light—''

''I knew it.''

''No, not that sort of light.'' He nuzzled her throat. ''It was the light of reason. Sweet, clear reason, presented by your very clever husband.''

''I see,'' Lily said, snuggling closer. ''What else did my very clever husband do?''

''I called up a diphtheria epidemic,'' he said.

''*What?*'' Lily sat bolt upright, just as a knock sounded at the door.

''That should be the beginning of it,'' he said with a grin and went to open the door. Father Chabot stood there, wearing a puzzled expression.

''Michel,'' Pascal said with satisfaction. ''Do come in.''

''I received your note,'' the little priest said, entering. ''What is all this about bringing down a coup?''

''May I first offer you a glass of wine?''

''I have a feeling I'm going to need it,'' Father Chabot said dryly.

Lily put out three glasses and opened a bottle, then sat down, just as mystified as Father Chabot. Pascal appeared to be very pleased with himself, like a small boy who was about to stir up some real mischief.

''All right,'' he said, when they were settled. ''I should start at the beginning, although it's a miserable story.''

He began with Julien and the Comte de Passy and worked all the way to the end of his conversation with Jean-Jacques, leaving out nothing.

Lily listened in appalled silence, but she didn't interrupt and neither did Father Chabot.

''And so,'' Pascal said, ''I'm going to run the lot of them away, and both of you are going to help me do it. Now, Michel.'' He pulled a list from his pocket and handed it to the priest. ''I need you to visit the houses of the supposed victims starting first thing in the morning and continuing throughout the day—or for as long as it takes the château to empty. I've spoken to Pierre, and Charles, and the others on the list, of course. They've all agreed with enthusiasm.''

Lily propped her chin on her fist, regarding Pascal with amusement. "Just how are you going to go about this?"

"Marie is to succumb during the night. Emelie is already in a state of terrible illness, as of late this afternoon. I made sure I was seen going in and out of the house with my bag. Naturally, tiny Joseph-Jean will be next to fall. So there must be a quarantine on all of these houses, and you, Michel, have to be seen going to offer comfort.''

"It is not often I am called to God's more solemn services in complete jest," Father Chabot said, "but a finer cause I cannot think of.''

"Excellent," Pascal replied. "I'm sorry to have to alarm those people not in our confidence, but we can't take the chance that Passy will work out the truth of the matter. That would compromise Jean-Jacques.''

"About Passy," Father Chabot said with a frown of concern. "Does he happen to be a large, red-faced gentleman, imperious of manner?''

"Yes," Pascal said, surprised. "Why?"

"He was poking about the fields late this afternoon, asking questions of the men—questions about you, Pascal, and also about Lily. I've had three people come to me already this evening, troubled.''

Lily looked at Pascal with worry. "He can't have remembered you from before?''

"No," Pascal said. "I don't think so. He was probably more concerned with my lack of respect toward the sacred duke. My mistake, but I was so angry with Jean-Jacques that I didn't stop to think. I'm sure Passy only wanted to find out if I had any influence over your brother. Did anyone answer his questions, Michel?''

Father Chabot blew out his cheeks. "I'm sorry to say one loose-lipped fool did, but I'll decline to mention his name. Passy now knows your wife is Jean-Jacques's sister. He knows how and where you live, and he knows about the rumor. I worry that he might try to find a way to use it against you.''

Pascal shook his head. "If you're talking about little Joseph-Jean, that rumor has long since been dispelled." He looked over at Lily with a smile. "My wife took care of that.''

"No, I don't refer to that. I'm afraid this one is a bit more awkward," Father Chabot said uncomfortably.

"What could possibly be more awkward than counteracting talk of miracles?" Pascal asked cheerfully, but abruptly sobered. "What is it, Michel? You look unusually serious."

"You really haven't heard, then? Or you, Lily?"

Lily frowned. "I have no idea what you're talking about."

Father Chabot rubbed a hand over his shiny scalp. "I thought you must have heard and dismissed it as nonsense."

"Michel," Pascal said impatiently, "will you get on with it? Rumors run rife through the village. What is it now?"

"It will sound odd to you, no doubt. It's about your parentage."

"My *parentage*?" Pascal said, perplexed. "What about my parentage? Do you mean that I was adopted by an English family? Who would care—who would even know?"

Father Chabot raised his eyebrows. "I certainly didn't. When—ah, when was that? I thought you said you lived in Paris?"

"I did. My parents died when I was ten. For the love of God, Michel, why are you fumbling about like this? Whatever it is can't be that bad."

Father Chabot pinched the bridge of his nose. "I don't know what you will make of this, but they are saying . . . they are saying you are the sixth duke's bastard son."

Pascal stared at him. "You can't be serious."

"I am very serious."

"No—that has to exceed the limits of even these people's superstitions." He met Lily's puzzled gaze and shrugged. "I suppose it has to do with the land coming back."

"Yes," Father Chabot agreed. "That has something to do with it."

"Ah, well, it's not the first time someone's called me a bastard," Pascal said, grinning at Lily. "Although a duke's bastard—now there's a step up in the world. I suppose I should be complimented. I imagine they attached my name to those past LaMartines and cooked up an affair between the duke and madame?"

"For your information, Henri LaMartine was the last *régisseur* at Saint-Simon," Father Chabot said, rubbing his finger on the table.

"Was he? How interesting. Yes . . . I suppose I can see why they might have put the pieces together, although it's ridiculous.'' Pascal laughed. "Stop looking so serious, Michel. Let them think what they will. It doesn't matter to me—why should it?''

"I'm pleased you find this so diverting," Father Chabot said.

"Why not? After this, they'll be disappointed to find out that my parents were ordinary working people like themselves. Anyway, I'm afraid that my mother was devoted to my father. She would never have looked at another man. I'm certain of it.''

"Tell me," Father Chabot said, "what happened to your parents? If you don't mind talking about it, that is.''

"I don't mind. They died during the influenza epidemic that swept through Paris during the winter of 1819," he said grimly. "I was ten.''

Father Chabot looked down. "How dreadful. What happened to you?''

"The authorities put me in an orphanage, but I escaped after a month." He glanced over at Lily. "You were right about the sewers of Paris, duchess.''

"Oh, Pascal—I'm so sorry," Lily said with true remorse, her hand slipping to her mouth. "I was just being horrible when I said that.''

"I know," he replied. "You hit your mark, not that I was going to let you see it.''

Lily gently touched his arm. "How did you survive?''

"Oh, a little begging, a little thieving. It wasn't all bad, and there were a number of other street urchins. We banded together. We had some good times too, mostly at the expense of the police." He shook his head.

"Did they catch you in the end?" she asked, her imagination sketching pictures of a miniature Pascal evading the entire *gendarmerie* of Paris.

"Certainly not," Pascal said disdainfully. "But by the time the next winter rolled around, I decided that I needed proper shelter and steady food. I signed on with a British merchant vessel. I couldn't cook, but I figured the position would keep me close to the food supplies.''

Father Chabot chuckled. "Very resourceful.''

"Too resourceful," Pascal said ruefully. "It was nearly my undoing.''

"Did they catch you stealing food?" Lily asked.

"No." He twisted his glass back and forth, his eyes hazy with memory. "The ship went down.''

"Oh . . ." Lily said, dismayed. "Oh, how awful for you."

"It was," he agreed, glancing up at her. "The captain misread the strength of a storm blowing in off the coast of Sussex, and we were caught right in the middle of the worst of it. It swept us onto the jagged rocks off Pevensy and smashed the ship into bits."

He shuddered. He would never forget the noise—the howling wind, people screaming and shouting, the sound of wood splintering against stone, the furious, unrelenting pounding of the huge waves.

"I was so scared," he whispered. "So damned scared." He covered his eyes with his hand for one brief moment, then shook his head as if to dispel the memory.

Lily's eyes filled with tears. "You don't have to go on, Pascal—not if it's too painful to remember."

"No, it's all right. You once asked me how I met Nicholas. I couldn't answer you then for a number of reasons, but this seems like a good time to tell you about it."

An enormous knot formed in Lily's throat. *Maybe someday when there is trust between us, I'll be able to speak of it with you . . .* "Thank you," she whispered.

Pascal looked at her, his dark eyes filled with love, and she knew he too was remembering that night.

"Would you like me to leave?" Father Chabot asked tactfully.

Pascal glanced over at him. "No, Michel, that's not necessary. Anyway, it's a story you might be interested in hearing, given the line of work you're in. You've been so tolerant about everything else that I don't think you'll have trouble with this. I admit, I've only ever told the full story to three other people, Nicholas and Georgia being two of them. They're my adoptive parents, by the way. The third person was Dom Benetard."

Father Chabot nodded, his face solemn. "Then I am deeply honored."

"Please, don't be that," Pascal said lightly. "I'm in a storytelling mood, and I consider you my friend."

Despite Pascal's easy words, Father Chabot appeared shaken. Lily had the strong feeling that Pascal was about to say something that was going to shock the good priest to the depths of his soul, and Pascal was carefully laying the groundwork to prepare him. He didn't seem at all worried about her, but then he knew that she wasn't prone to being shocked—at least not by him.

"What happened next, Pascal?" she asked, resting her chin on her fist.

"Well," Pascal said, pushing that untrainable lock of hair off his forehead, "we all went overboard. Unlike many other poor souls, I was fortunate enough to avoid the rocks and was swept out to sea."

"Could you swim?" Lily asked.

"Yes, but it made no difference, not in that sea, duchess. All I remember is being on the deck one minute, high up in the air the next, and then pounded down on the surface of the water so hard that the breath was knocked out of my body."

He ran a thumb over his lower lip in a gesture Lily had come to know well, a sign that he was thinking, collecting himself.

She waited. The room was hushed, filled only with the ticking of the clock and the snuffle of Bean's little snores coming from under Pascal's feet. Father Chabot sat with his hands folded together on the table, his head bent as if he were in prayer.

"The water was very cold," Pascal said softly into the silence. "After a few minutes of freezing and being unmercifully pounded around, I gave up fighting. It was nice—I felt as if I'd gone to sleep. Everything was suddenly peaceful and quiet, and there was the most beautiful light—brilliant white, much more appealing than the heaving sea. I went straight into it."

He met Lily's eyes and held them. "Do you remember how you felt when you watched Joseph-Jean coming back?"

Lily nodded.

"It was like that, only more powerful. It was like *being* the light. Well, not exactly, but that's the closest I can come to describing it. My mother and my father were there in that light, although they were too far away for me to reach. There were others, too. I wasn't sure who they were, because I could hardly see through the brightness, but I knew they loved me. It was wonderful—I wanted to run toward them as fast as I could."

"What stopped you?" Lily asked, her eyes shining.

"An angel," he said. "She was so incredibly beautiful . . . do you know the classic image one has?"

Lily thought. "Yes, I suppose. Perfect features, blond, flowing hair, white robes, huge wings, all of that?"

"All of that and more," Pascal said, his gaze far away. "The sight of her made my heart ache. But then she said that I couldn't come any farther. I was terribly disappointed."

"Of course," Lily said, fascinated.

"She told me that I had to go back, that I had things yet to do. The last thing I wanted was to wake up in that dreadful water again, but being a good little urchin, I did as I was told."

"I doubt you were a good little urchin, but if they weren't going to let you into heaven, what were you going to do?"

Pascal smiled. "Exactly. You are quick to take a point, duchess. Still, she let me stay for a while longer, wrapping me up in her love as if it were bunting, preparing me for the return journey. Then the most extraordinary thing happened."

"Oh?" Lily said, straight-faced.

"Yes. I looked down—well, not exactly down, but never mind—and there was another angel. But this one was different. He looked like an angel, but somehow I knew he wasn't."

"Then what was he if he wasn't an angel?"

"He was a man," Pascal said quietly. "He was the bravest, most magnificent man I'd ever seen, and I knew he'd come to bring me out of that godforsaken sea at the risk of his own life."

"Nicholas?" Lily whispered. "Was it Nicholas?"

"It was. I don't remember much after that except a sense of timelessness and of moving toward something that was calling me. It hurt having to leave the angel and all that wonderful light, but she promised me I'd be able to go back one day. She knew just how to appeal to an eleven-year-old boy. Bribe him."

Lily chuckled.

"The next thing I knew," Pascal said, "I was waking up in a bed, being told by Binkley that I'd drowned and had been rescued by Nicholas—and that Georgia had spent an extraordinary amount of time on the beach trying to resuscitate me. It turned out that I'd been delirious with fever for three days, which to most people would explain everything—I dreamed the entire thing."

"Nonsense," Lily said disdainfully. "Oh, Pascal, what a wonderful story. Thank you so much for telling it."

He gave her a brief smile, then pushed back his chair and stood. Lily immediately forgot the image of the small, scraggly, drowned child in favor of this substantially built and very handsome man, whom she loved to distraction. *Oh, thank you, Nicholas and Georgia. Thank you. And thank you, God and Angel, for not letting him entirely into heaven.*

"So, Michel," Pascal said to the silent priest. "What do you think of that? Grist for the mill?"

Father Chabot slowly shook his head as if coming out of a daze. "I—I don't know what to say. It is a fascinating account indeed, and one I shall have to mull over carefully. I have never heard such a story before." He pressed his hands flat on the table before him and stared down at them.

"As I said, I haven't told it often, and for good reason." Pascal's voice gentled and he spoke carefully. "I don't mean to test your faith in any way, Michel. If anything, I told you this story to reinforce it."

Father Chabot gave him an odd look. "Your very presence here reinforces my faith, Pascal. The gift God gave you reinforces my faith. Of course, the Holy Diocese would probably be on its knees if it ever heard your story."

"As I have no intention of telling the Holy Diocese anything that would unduly disturb it," Pascal said calmly, "there's nothing to worry about." He regarded Father Chabot with a thoroughly wicked gleam in his eye.

"Do you know," Father Chabot said, "I have never come across two such irreverent people as you and your wife. If I were doing my job, I'd read you a stern lecture about not honoring the mysteries of Our Lord. Yet you are the only people I know who see such mysteries and take them for granted—you most especially, Pascal." He scratched his head again. "Angels, holy light, miracles," he said with a sigh. "I suppose as you live with this sort of thing every day, it must seem perfectly normal to you."

"Normal?" Pascal said, raising an eyebrow. "No. I'm not that deluded. But Lily has taught me a great deal about acceptance, and for that I can only be grateful. Lily," he added, as he rested his hands on her shoulders, "is extraordinary."

"Yes, I've noticed," Father Chabot said with a smile.

"Nothing gets in her way, Michel, including angels—certainly nothing so humble as a man like myself. I think I could tell her I was the reincarnation of Ramses and she'd fail to be amazed—or impressed."

Lily looked up at him, a saucy smile curving her mouth. "You're absolutely right. The only thing I'm interested in is you, Pascal LaMartine. Start playing Ramses with me and there really will be trouble."

"Do you see?" Pascal asked, but then his smile faded. "Michel. I only want you to understand that as much as God made me different, he made me the same. I've struggled for years to find that sameness, and I finally stumbled across it—here in Saint-Simon. The villagers accept me for what they see. You and Lily have no quarrel with what I do. I need nothing more."

He ran his fingers through his hair. "It's why I don't care if they think me a duke's bastard. They could think me the village idiot's bastard and I wouldn't care. All I ask is that they see me as a man."

Father Chabot had no answer.

Pascal waited until they were readying for bed before he broached the subject again. He sat under the sheets, his knees pulled up, watching Lily brush out her hair, giving it her usual thorough strokes, no doubt a regimen drilled into her by Coffey. He wondered if Coffey had been the one to teach her to rinse it in rosemary. But then who else would there have been?

"Come," he said, growing impatient, holding out his arms.

Lily put down the brush and moved into his embrace.

"Now tell me," he said, turning her soft body against him, his mouth burrowing into that mass of sweet-smelling, well-brushed hair. "What did you really think of what I told you tonight?"

"I thought," she said, touching her mouth to the warm flesh of his chest and kissing it, "that your angel was absolutely right. If she hadn't had the sense to turn you back, you wouldn't be here right now with me, about to do very wonderful things. Very human things. Very, very magnificent things."

Pascal gave a low laugh. "Magnificent? I must be improving."

Lily slanted a look up at him. "Is that Ramses speaking?"

"No," he said, brushing her full lips with his finger. "Only a poor, ignorant man doing his best to please his wife." He bent his head to Lily's mouth and concentrated in earnest.

An hour later, Lily lay sleepy and prostrate in his arms. "There's something I didn't tell you," he murmured against the curve of her ear. "I didn't want to say anything in front of Michel, but you should know."

She shifted to face him, and her eyes changed from drowsy satisfaction to sharp attention at the expression on his face. "I can't think what you might have left out," she said.

"It wasn't to do with me. It was to do with Nicholas." Pascal took in a deep breath and released it. "Lily, when I said Nicholas was brave, I didn't come close to describing what he did for me."

"What he *did* for you? He risked his life for you! What more is there than that?"

"The man risked not only his life, he also risked his sanity for me—and nearly lost it." Pascal's arm tightened around her for a moment, then released her. He sat up and wrapped his arms around his knees.

"What do you mean?" Lily asked, pushing herself up to face him.

"I mean that he'd been in the same situation himself as a child. He'd nearly drowned. He'd lost his parents. He'd been plagued by the experience, dreaming of it over and over again, a vicious nightmare that never left him. Nicholas was terrified of water. Placid lakes were enough to give him the shakes."

"Oh, dear Lord. But he went in after you?"

"He went in after a number of people," Pascal said, staring down at the sheet. "But he went back for me at the end, when no one believed there was anyone left to save. He was injured and exhausted and frozen half to death, but he still went back into that water for me."

Lily bit her lip. "Oh, Pascal."

He turned his head away. "He brought me in, and he broke as if he were a twig someone had carelessly snapped in two." Pascal's voice broke at the same time. "He thought he'd been too late," he whispered hoarsely.

"What happened?" she asked quietly.

Pascal was silent for a long moment. When he spoke again his voice was steadier. "He vanished into himself. His pain was too much, so he simply went away. His body was there, but nothing else. Six weeks it lasted. Six damned weeks of his own private hell. I remember almost every minute of it.''

''And you couldn't help him?''

''At eleven years of age? I did what I could. I talked to him incessantly. If anything, I probably drove him out of it because he couldn't bear my infernal chattering anymore. Thank God, Nicholas came out of the experience a whole man.''

Lily thought for a moment. ''Is that when it happened, Pascal? Your gift, I mean? Do you think your angel gave it to you? Or maybe you already had it, and it was the reason they sent you back?''

Pascal leaned back against the pillows. ''I think it must have started after I came back, something I gradually grew aware of. By the time I was fourteen, I was fully conscious of what it was and exactly how to use it.''

''Like Charlie and the boar?'' she asked softly.

''Yes,'' he said. ''Like Charlie and the boar. And hearing Charlie telling you about that put the fear of God into me, sweetheart. I thought my heart would stop. But you were so blissfully disdainful, I soon realized I had nothing to worry about.'' He chuckled.

''I've just realized why you won't eat anything with proper wings,'' Lily said with a little smile.

Pascal gazed at her. He opened his mouth, then closed it again. ''Have I ever told you,'' he finally said, with a gleam of unholy amusement in his eyes, ''that I have a total aversion to mutton?''

Lily stared at him. ''What?''

''It's true,'' he said unsteadily. ''I suppose it must have something to do with being named after a sacrificial lamb.''

She burst into laughter. ''Pascal, what am I going to do with you?''

''Well,'' he said, grinning wickedly and reaching for her, ''I have a few ideas. For example,'' he said, moving her hand under the sheet, ''you might take this poor lamb and start right here . . .''

Lily was happy to oblige.

22

PASCAL'S plan worked beautifully. Lily sat on the stoop, watching the last carriage rattle down the hill. "Look, Bean," she said to the puppy dozing in the late-afternoon sunshine. "It's the Comte de Passy. He must have held out until the last possible minute and finally succumbed to panic." Bean opened one eye and shut it again.

Lily smiled, thinking that Pascal was brilliant, and went back to sorting herbs. Her head snapped up as she heard the carriage turn down their own little road. It could only mean trouble.

Passy had been asking questions yesterday about Pascal, obviously searching for a trick. She prayed for quick wits, then put down the bundle of herbs and slowly rose to her feet as the carriage pulled up in front of the cottage.

Passy descended. "Good evening, madame," he said. "I believe you are Monsieur LaMartine's wife?"

"I am," Lily said carefully, trying not to show her revulsion.

"Is your husband at home?" He held a scented handkerchief over his nose and mouth as he spoke. Lily wondered if he was worried about infection or if it was the possible stench he was protecting himself from.

"He is not, monsieur. He's tending to the sick in the village." She looked down at Bean, who was growling ominously, her fur bristling. "Bean, stop that. Lie down!" Bean reluctantly obeyed, but her lip stayed curled. "Forgive my dog. She is protective of me when I am alone."

Passy gave the dog a look of distaste, then looked Lily up and down. "Should your husband not be up at the château tending to the duke?"

"The duke will have to wait, monsieur. There are three in the village near death, including a newborn."

"You do not appear to be overly concerned that your own

brother might have contracted diphtheria." He watched her closely.

"My brother and I are not on speaking terms," she said indifferently. "I am surprised he even acknowledged my existence to you. He made it clear to me that I am to be ostracized. In fact, I believe you witnessed my brother ordering me away the night that he returned. Neither his health nor his welfare is any longer my concern."

Passy nodded. "It is a sad thing, what has become of you." He looked about him with disgust.

"I know what you must think, but what can I do?" Lily said with a shrug. "I am now nothing more than a common laborer's wife. I have no rights and must do as I'm told." Lily hoped she looked downtrodden.

"Yes," he said. "It is a sad thing indeed, madame. I assume you must have been forced to this marriage?"

"I was, monsieur." Lily stared at the ground for a moment, then lifted her head and met his piggy eyes. "To be honest, it was my own fault, but I never expected this to happen. I thought Jean-Jacques would come to my aid."

Passy coughed delicately. "Forgive me, but perhaps you were a little indiscreet to have ended up in such a situation?"

Lily paused. "My husband is a handsome man . . . I made a bad mistake." That was true enough.

Passy eyed her with interest. "Ah, well, you are an attractive woman. It is not hard to understand, but to be forced to marry so far beneath you . . . this is the tragedy."

Lily wanted to slap his smug face. "Yes, monsieur. My father assumed I would have my fortune to protect me, but my husband is a proud man. He will not touch it." She sighed heavily.

Passy's lips thinned. "I met him yesterday. He is proud indeed, too proud for his own good, I think."

"You understand? Oh, such a relief. So you see why I must live in a hovel like this." Lily gestured at her beloved cottage, its shutters painted green, flowers growing in the upstairs window box, more flowers by the front door.

Passy shuddered. "I cannot think how distressing it must be for you. Why does your brother not help you? This I cannot understand."

"He says that I made my bed and now I must lie in it." Lily turned to the side and pretended to wipe away a tear.

"Ah, madame. What a touching story," Passy said. "I cannot help but feel that your brother is a fool."

"You are kind to be concerned," Lily replied, forcing her voice to tremble. "No one from my old life speaks to me anymore. You have no idea what it means to me, your taking the time to stop."

Passy slowly shook his head, and his jowls swung back and forth with the motion. "I confess I was shocked when I learned of your predicament."

Lily sank down onto the stoop. "There is nothing to be done, so I am determined to make the best of my situation. I quickly realized that rebelling only made things worse."

"How dreadful for you." He shook his head again, and with a sick fascination, Lily watched his jowls swing again.

"Well . . ." she said coyly, "it is not *all* bad. As I said, my husband is a handsome man."

Passy smirked, and Lily knew he'd heard that rumor too. "Ah," he said. "At least you have some comfort. Still, a woman of your refinement married to this man—it is a true shame," he said. "You know, of course, what they say about your husband?"

Lily silently thanked Father Chabot for having forewarned them. She decided to turn the rumor to advantage. "That he is the old duke's bastard?" she said indifferently. "Yes, I know. He was never acknowledged, you understand, and for the sake of his mother's memory, he does not speak of it."

Passy's eyes glinted. "They say that your husband and your brother do not get along."

"Get along? They despise each other, monsieur. My brother despises my husband for what he has brought me to. My husband despises my brother for his irresponsible attitude." She shrugged. "At least my husband cares about the land and the people. It's in his blood to care. He watches everything that goes on up at the château, every coming and going. It sickens him to see."

Lily was pleased with that touch. Passy was bound to realize that Pascal was there to stay, ever vigilant—not a good situation for a group of clandestine plotters.

"Yes, I heard them arguing yesterday," Passy said, passing his tongue over his lips, and Lily really did want to be sick. It made her think of poor, scarred Brother Julien.

"Then you'll know," she said tightly, "that Pascal wishes

for money to be put into the land and Jean-Jacques wants only to fritter his newfound fortune away on his own pleasures.''

''Yes, it is true that your brother cares nothing for things of a rustic nature.'' Passy flicked at a speck of dust on the front of his jacket with his handkerchief, then clapped it back to his face.

''He never has cared,'' Lily said disdainfully. ''Jean-Jacques thinks only of himself, which is why he ignored my husband's warning about the diphtheria outbreak yesterday and put all of you at the château at risk.'' She feigned an expression of concern. ''If I might give you a word of advice, monsieur, I should not linger here. My husband is deeply concerned about the contagion.'' She frowned. ''You must know that half the people of Saint-Simon died in a typhoid epidemic thirty years ago? My husband is afraid that the diphtheria might do the same thing.''

That did it. If Passy hadn't been convinced before, he was convinced now.

''Yes. Well, I really must be on my way. I hope your brother recovers from his illness. Good evening, madame.''

''Good evening. Thank you for your kind concern—and do take the road to the west, away from the village. It is better to stay clear.''

Passy nodded and quickly climbed back into his carriage. It disappeared in no time at all.

Lily started to laugh. Pascal really was a clever, clever man. And she wasn't so stupid herself.

The entire village had a good laugh about Pascal's deception, then quickly settled back to business. The time for harvest was fast approaching and anxious workers watched the skies, looking for any sign of rain that could ruin the crop. Prayers were said and candles lit. The oak *cuves* were readied, the winery scrubbed down, the presses checked and double-checked. The fermenting vats were filled with water to swell the wood. It had been thirty long years since Saint-Simon had had any real harvest, and excitement hummed in the air.

The weather held. The grapes continued to ripen. One hundred days after the vines had first flowered, Pascal stood up from his examination of the fruit.

Eager faces watched him. Fingers made crosses on chests.

Baskets were at the ready, and great oak casks stood at the end of the rows to receive the crop.

Pascal grinned and raised his arms above his head. *"Vendange!"* he shouted.

The cry went through the fields, passed from vineyard to vineyard, and suddenly there was a frenzy of activity. Men, women, children, people from other villages, they had all turned out, ready to help.

For two long weeks the grapes were picked. Cattle dragged the wagons containing the casks back to the winery, where the grapes were sorted, stemmed, and crushed. Though the days were long, filled with backbreaking work, not one person complained. They were all too happy.

By the end of the last day everyone was exhausted, but not too exhausted to celebrate. An enormous fête had been planned for that night, and everyone who had participated in the *vendange* was invited. Pigs were roasted and long tables set up in the village square. The women had been cooking all day to produce food for a good two hundred people. It was going to be a fine night, Pascal thought, approaching the winery to check on progress before closing it down for the night. He stopped dead in his tracks, taking in the sight before him.

Lily was in one of the troughs, stomping grapes with a group of village women. Her skirts were pulled high above her knees, and her head was thrown back as she laughed with pure delight. She took his breath away. With strands of auburn hair escaping her ribbon and her calves stained purple with juice, Lily looked like a nymph as she danced among the grapes in a scene worthy of Bacchus.

The vision of Lily among the crushed grapes raised the most urgent of needs in him, a need that was straining for release. "Lily!" he called.

She looked up and waved a hand, smiling in a way that threatened to undo him.

"Lily, come here, will you?" *Quickly,* he was thinking. *Now, Lily.*

"Just a minute." She climbed out of the trough and wiped off her legs with a cloth, then lightly ran over to him, shoes and stockings in one hand. "What is it?" she asked. "Trouble?"

"Not trouble," he said, taking her by the hand. "Just the opposite. Come with me." He pulled her away, moving fast, heading toward the deserted south-facing vineyard. Lily followed him without question.

When they'd reached the top of the hill he stepped behind her and held her by the shoulders. The setting sun washed the sky with a light violet. Above them the turrets and windows of the château caught the last golden rays. Below them stretched row after row of vines, thick with leaf, no longer burdened by fruit, dark, rich green rising from the deep brown earth.

"Look, duchess. All around us. It's a completed harvest. Done," he said with deep satisfaction. "We made it happen." He was so hard that he hurt.

Lily turned to face him and laced her arms around his neck. "You made it happen."

"God made it happen," he answered against her mouth as he crushed her against his chest. "I need you, Lily. Here. Now." Without waiting for an answer, he pulled up her skirts and pushed her underclothes aside, sliding his fingers into her as he took her mouth in a hard kiss.

Lily reached down and pressed her hand against his, urging his fingers to touch her more deeply. "Yes," she whispered, pushing her hips forward. "Yes, Pascal."

He groaned and sank to the ground, taking her with him as he opened the flap of his trousers, freeing himself. He didn't bother with preliminaries but drove into her in powerful thrusts, drawing a gasp from her throat. He took her with primitive urgency and she accepted him as if she were the earth and he her reaper.

"Ah, that's good," he said hoarsely, watching her the whole time, thrusting ruthlessly, drawing a frenzied response from her that was as alive and vital and powerful as he felt.

She arched beneath him, grasping him by his buttocks, pulling him to her as she nurtured his need in the deepest well of her body. He sank into her, surrendering to her the last of his strength as she took his seed with warmth and welcome and joy.

Lily's lips turned up in a satisfied smile, a high flush on her cheeks. "I feel like Demeter," she murmured. "Mother-goddess of earth. Goodness, Pascal, for a Catholic, you certainly do behave like a heathen."

"Do you mind?" he asked, nuzzling her neck.

"I like being heathen," she said, wriggling with pleasure as he licked the delicate fold of her ear. "It's so enriching."

He tasted her lips once more, lingering in her heat, then rolled to his side as he readjusted his trousers and arranged her skirts over her legs. "It is, isn't it? God, I needed you, duchess."

She cupped his face in her hands, running her thumb over his mouth. "I needed you too, just like that, fast and furious. I was having the most disgraceful thoughts about you while I was treading grapes. You just made them all come true."

He laughed and nipped the pad of her thumb. Then he stood and held out his hand. "Let's go and have a wonderfully heathen evening. I doubt there will be much restraint in the village tonight."

He was right, Lily thought, watching Pascal as he danced with Madame Marchand, whirling the stocky woman around as if she were a young girl. She almost looked like one, all flushed and breathless with pleasure. Lily had already claimed her turn with Alain Lascard, who blushed beet-red but gamely took her on. She'd taken a particular pleasure in that dance.

Pascal was unbearably handsome, with his shirt open at the collar, his shirtsleeves rolled up to his forearms, that ungovernable lock of dark hair falling across his forehead, his teeth flashing white against the bronze of his skin. She admired his figure, his broad chest tapering to narrow waist and lean hips, the strength of his thighs apparent through the cloth of his trousers.

She shifted, still tender from Pascal's assault earlier that evening. A stab of renewed desire shot through her and hot moisture flowed between her thighs. She could hardly wait to get home.

Lily took a sip of wine, wondering what was going through Marie Marchand's head at that moment, fairly certain she knew the answer, given the sparkle in her eye and her flirtatious manner. The bawdiness had increased in direct proportion to the consumption of wine, and with stomachs well fed and spirits high, the village was definitely *en fête*.

Pascal gave Marie Marchand back to her beaming husband and returned to sit at Lily's side.

"What was madame whispering in your ear?" Lily asked.

"She was telling me about her corns," Pascal said. "Poor woman, how she suffers."

"Why?" Lily asked dryly. "Did you step on one of them?"

Pascal laughed. "Jealous, duchess?"

"Hungry," she murmured.

Monsieur Thenon from the neighboring village leaned across the table before he had a chance to reply and shook Pascal's hand enthusiastically, as people had been doing all evening. Pascal replied graciously and fell into conversation, but he claimed Lily's hand under the table and put it on his lap, beneath his napkin.

She had to struggle to keep a straight face. Pascal was hard as a rock, fully standing. Lily rested her chin on her free hand and gazed at him as he talked with Monsieur Thenon. She couldn't help herself. She idly squeezed, smiling innocently as Pascal's thighs stiffened, though he didn't betray himself by so much as a flicker. Monsieur Thenon went on and on, and Pascal politely answered him. Lily squeezed again, this time a little harder, rubbing up and down at the same time. The veins in Pascal's neck stood out, and his jaw tightened. He took Lily's hand and forcefully put it back in her lap, but this time his hand stayed with her.

Lily nearly fainted as his fingers unerringly found her cleft through the double material of her dress and petticoat and began to stroke her. She eased her thighs slightly apart, and he took full advantage, his skilled fingers pressing exactly on the point he knew gave her the most pleasure.

". . . Indeed, monsieur, I feel the *Bouillie Bordelaise* was of vital importance in the restoration of the vines . . ." He moved his finger in a little circle. Lily grew dizzy as a slow hum started at the tips of her toes and raced through her veins to center directly between her legs. If she could have pulled her dress up and spread her legs for him then and there she would have done it.

"No, monsieur," Pascal said, slowly increasing the pressure, "we really won't know until the secondary fermentation . . ." Pascal pushed his entire palm down, his fingers cupping her. Fire leapt deep into Lily's belly and erupted, obliterating all reason, as she came violently into his hand. She swallowed the cry that rose in her throat, closing her eyes as a tiny sigh escaped her.

"We hope the wine-maker arrives any day," Pascal said, as if oblivious. "It will be an enormous release—I mean relief . . . Thank you, monsieur. We are all very pleased." They shook hands again, and Monsieur Thenon finally left.

"Why, duchess," Pascal said, turning to her, all innocence. "You're flushed. Too much wine, perhaps?"

Lily put her forehead into her hands. "I should murder you," she said. "I really should."

Pascal laughed softly. "Don't think I won't finish the job properly later. But the next time you attempt to bring me off in public, be warned of the consequences."

"You asked for it," she said with a mischievous smile.

"So did you. God only knows what Monsieur Thenon thought. I don't think I was making much sense." His expression sharpened with interest. "Look, sweetheart, your brother's just arrived."

Lily shrugged. "Oh. He waited long enough, didn't he?" She was still annoyed with Jean-Jacques, even though he had apologized to her in full. She would never again see him as the wonderful brother she'd doted on for all the shining qualities she'd imagined in him. She saw him now in all of his truth, and it wasn't a particularly admirable one.

"Lily, don't be so hard on him," Pascal said. "He's worked hard to make amends to you. It doesn't happen overnight. Think back to how you were when you first arrived here."

"Don't remind me," Lily said uncomfortably. Pascal had an annoying way of making his point. Still, she resolved to try to be nicer to her brother.

As Jean-Jacques approached the square, the crowd parted, people bowing and curtsying without enthusiasm. Pascal shook Jean-Jacques's hand as a gesture of respect before the villagers. "Put them at their ease," he prompted under his breath. "This is their night."

Jean-Jacques nodded and cleared his throat. "Ah—do carry on," he said awkwardly. "Enjoy yourselves—the night is yet young."

The people took him at his word and went straight back to their revelry.

Eventually Pascal stood up on the bench, clinking on his glass with a knife. It was almost five minutes before people had quieted enough for his voice to be heard.

"It is time for a toast," he said. "Raise your glasses, messieurs, 'dames. We drink first to the harvest."

A great cry went up, and the people drank heartily.

"We drink secondly to you, the people of Saint-Simon, who worked so hard to see the harvest in."

Another cry went up and another deep drink was taken.

"And thirdly, we drink to your duke, who made the harvest possible."

There was a lukewarm response, but the people drank anyway. Jean-Jacques had the grace to look embarrassed.

"Now, if you will all indulge me," he said, looking down at Lily, "I would like to make a final toast to my wife, who has given me unending help and encouragement. I'm a lucky man. Come here, Lily."

He reached down and pulled her up next to him on the bench. "To Lily!" he said, raising his glass high, then turned to her and drew her into his arms. He kissed her lightly, to the delight and roars of approbation from the villagers. "I love you, duchess," he whispered, drawing her closer. "God, I love you." He kissed her again, this time thoroughly, without reservation.

It nearly brought the village down, that kiss. The music started up again, and almost everyone took to the streets, dancing with complete abandon.

Pascal lifted his head. His eyes smiled into Lily's, then swept over the crowd in satisfaction. Father Chabot was dancing with Madame Dupont, looking like an aged cherub. Charles and Emelie Claubert were in a corner, behaving like newlyweds. There was an air of fecundity, of renewal, in the village tonight. Monsieur Jamard sat at the end of one of the tables, watching Pascal. Their eyes met, and Monsieur Jamard inclined his head in silent acknowledgment.

Lily leaned back against Pascal, and he wrapped his arms around her waist. "Look at them," he said against her cheek. "Those are happy people." His arms tightened around her. "Good God," he said softly.

"What?" she asked, twisting to look up at him. "What, Pascal?" She followed the direction of his gaze and froze in disbelief.

Standing off to one side of the square just in front of the church, her face lit by the torches, was Coffey. And behind her, a woman Lily had not seen for fifteen years.

Her mother.

23

"**H**OW did—" Pascal cut himself off. "Never mind. Who is the woman with Miss Mc-Cofferty, Lily? She looks as if she's just seen a ghost." He glanced down at her.

"That," Lily replied sharply, "is the Duchess of Mont-crieff. In a way she has seen a ghost—her daughter."

The happy glow she'd had only a moment earlier had faded, replaced by a panicked expression. Pascal had long before discovered that Lily's mother was a forbidden subject, although he knew more about Lily's feelings than she realized. Probing had its uses.

He jumped off the bench and took Lily by the waist, lifting her down. "What do you want to do, sweetheart?" he asked, stroking her back. "Do you want me to take you over to her?"

"No," she said, her voice as stiff as her body. "I want to speak to Jean-Jacques. He must be responsible for this." Lily walked over to where her brother sat and leaned toward him, speaking in English. "Jean-Jacques, I have a little surprise for you."

"A surprise?" Jean-Jacques said with pleasure, looking up at her, unsuspecting. "What?"

Lily straightened. "Our mother. You remember our mother, don't you? Well, she's here."

He started. "What?" he said, as if he hadn't heard her correctly.

"Our mother is here," Lily repeated. "Standing by the church steps." She put her hands on her hips. "What do you know about this?" she demanded.

He blinked, looking just as alarmed as Lily. "But what's she doing here? She's never left the convent before, has she? Are you sure? You haven't seen her since you were a small child."

"I'm sure," Lily hissed. "She's with Coffey, and I'm not likely to forget my own mother's face. She's obviously here for a reason. I want to know what that reason is."

He stood up and took a quick look. "Holy Mother Mary," he whispered. "You're right."

"Of course I'm right, you idiot. And since she has Coffey with her, she must be looking for me. There's only one way she could possibly know that I'm here. From you." Lily glared at him.

"Well," Jean-Jacques said slowly, "I did reply to a letter she wrote me when I first returned, regarding you . . . I'd forgotten all about it." He rubbed his narrow chin, looking guilty as could be. "She wanted to know if I'd heard anything from you or knew where you were. Coffey had told her about some trouble or other. I assumed she was referring to your marriage."

"So you told her all about it, I suppose? You told her everything and painted it in the worst light possible, didn't you, bringing her right down on my head."

"I told her what I thought to be the truth," he replied defensively.

"The *truth*? What would you know of the truth? You never bothered to find out—you just assumed!"

Jean-Jacques flushed. "I told you I was sorry about that. Are you going to hold a grudge for the rest of your life? I don't know what your problem is, Lily. Why are you making such a fuss over a simple visit, anyway?"

"*Why?*" Lily repeated, her eyes narrowing dangerously. "My mother walked out the door when I was eight years old, and I haven't seen her or heard a word from her since. I'd say that was reason enough."

"Well, it's not my fault," Jean-Jacques hissed, his nose only two inches from Lily's. "It was *your* father who drove her away, not mine. And she walked out on me too, you know."

"You were sixteen when she left—you didn't need a mother."

"You don't suddenly stop needing a mother," he said furiously. "I have just as much reason to be angry as you. She left me in the hands of your blasted father!"

Pascal rested his hands on Lily's tense shoulders. "If the two of you would stop arguing," he said reasonably, "maybe we could find out why your mother has come. Someone ought to welcome her, don't you think?"

Lily scowled. "I don't want to speak to her. Why should I?"

"Lily," he said gently, "it seems obvious that she cares about you, or she wouldn't have written to your brother and she wouldn't be here now. I can't imagine it's easy for her, coming back out into the world. Trust me, I know."

With a stubborn set to her chin, Lily glared at him.

"Your mother's been in a convent for what—fifteen years, now?" he continued. "It must be doubly difficult, returning to a place where she was so unhappy."

"How do you know she was unhappy?" Lily asked tightly.

"Because both Monsieur Jamard and Michel Chabot have told me. Having to face the two of you must be terrifying. You're already at each other's throats. What are you going to do to her—tear her limb from limb?"

They both scowled at him, and Pascal shook his head. It was as if all the influences of their childhood had reasserted themselves at the first reminder. "Fine," he said. "The two of you can stay here squabbling, but I'm going to greet your mother and Miss McCofferty. They can't be left standing there on their own."

"No," Lily said reluctantly, looking up at him. "That wouldn't be right, Pascal. I'll come with you. I suppose I should at least acknowledge my mother. Not that I like it," she added belligerently.

"No one said you had to like it, duchess." Pascal dropped a kiss on her head. "I'm proud of you—I know this is very difficult. Jean-Jacques?"

"Naturally I will come," he said, drawing himself up. "I am the duke, after all."

Pascal nodded. "As the duke you can clear a path, which would be useful in this crowd."

Flushed with annoyance, Jean-Jacques strode toward the church.

Pascal tucked his hand under Lily's elbow. "I'll be right here beside you." He hoped it would be enough. He sensed Lily's fragility and it troubled him.

Lily didn't know what to say or do. She was overjoyed to see Coffey, of course, but her mother? They were strangers.

What did you say to someone who had left her children without a backward look? *Good evening, Mama. How delightful to see you again.* Lily thought not.

She met Coffey's concerned gaze and quickly looked away. Coffey had betrayed her. Coffey *knew* how she felt about her mother, yet with Jean-Jacques's help she had brought her straight to Lily.

What was it about her that caused people to abandon her? What terrible thing had she done to make her mother leave her, her father hand her away without a thought to her happiness, her brother push her aside in disgust? Lily swallowed against the hot, painful knot in her throat, watching Jean-Jacques kiss his mother's cheeks as if he were perfectly happy to see her.

Liar, she thought viciously. *You're a liar on top of everything else, Jean-Jacques.* Her entire body trembled with inarticulate rage.

Her mother turned to her, and Lily noticed new streaks of gray in her auburn hair, lines on her face that Lily didn't remember. But her eyes were the same, and so was the smile that had so often soothed and reassured Lily as a child but now made her heart hurt. Fifteen years hadn't done a thing to numb the pain that knifed through her, nor had the sharpness of rejection dulled with time. And yet she had a terrible, treacherous desire to throw herself into her mother's arms and weep a child's tears, to beg for an explanation. Lily hardened with a fresh rush of anger.

"Mama," she said, dropping a curtsy. "This is a surprise."

"Lily," her mother said uncertainly. "How—how wonderful to see you . . . you have no idea."

"No, I don't suppose I have," Lily said coldly. "How could I?"

Her mother's eyes pinched at the corner. "You couldn't, of course. I have so much to tell you, but not now, Lily. Let me just take pleasure in seeing you again. Coffey wrote, of course, describing you, but it is nothing like seeing you with my own eyes. You have turned into a beautiful woman."

Lily ignored the compliment. "I gather Jean-Jacques wrote and told you I am married," she said tersely. "That must be why you're here?"

The duchess's face clouded and she glanced at Pascal,

then immediately looked away as if the sight of him was too distressing for her to bear. "Yes . . . it is. Lily—I do not know what to say. Perhaps we could speak privately?"

"I think not, Mama. May I present my husband, Pascal LaMartine?"

"Monsieur LaMartine," the duchess said coldly. She did not offer him her hand, nor do more than cast him another curt glance.

"I hope the news of our marriage didn't come as too much of a shock, your grace." Pascal's tone was gracious despite the insult.

"Life is never what one expects," she said.

Pascal inclined his head. "Never." He turned to Coffey. "Miss McCofferty. I hadn't thought to see you again. It is a pleasure."

Coffey regarded him with heavy suspicion. "I would wonder about that, Monsieur LaMartine, considering the circumstances of our last meeting. I also find it odd that you have suddenly learned to speak English."

Pascal smiled. "I'd like to say I'm a fast learner, but I confess that I've been speaking English all my life."

"But I thought—oh, this is all most peculiar, not what I expected, not at all," Coffey said fretfully.

"I couldn't agree more," the duchess said, turning to glare at her son. "I come to France to help my daughter out of a disastrous marriage forced upon her, and what do I find? I find Elizabeth kissing this man—*kissing* him—in front of the entire village of Saint-Simon, and you, Jean-Jacques, looking on as if such behavior was perfectly appropriate. Have both of you lost your minds?"

It seemed to Lily as if every absurdity possible had come together in this one statement. She began to laugh, and once she'd started, she couldn't stop.

"You—you don't understand anything at all!" she said, tears of hilarity streaming down her cheeks, tears that suddenly weren't rooted in hilarity at all, but in a deep, subterranean pain that threatened to overwhelm her. "You don't understand anything," she repeated, her voice strangled.

Pascal gathered her close, steadied her against his chest, his hand cupping her head, soothing her, protecting her. "I think this conversation should be continued in the morning," he said. "Jean-Jacques, why don't you take your mother and Miss McCofferty to the château now? I'm sure it's been a tiring day for them. I'll bring Lily up tomorrow.''

Lily only vaguely remembered the next half hour. Pascal was obliged to say his farewells, and she remained by his side, smiling and shaking hands and saying the right things. But she felt as if Pascal were her only fixed point of reference, as if she were walking through a dream.

She remembered climbing the hill to the cottage, and Pascal undressing her as if she were a child, putting her into bed, enfolding her cold body with his own, warming her.

He didn't speak, and she was grateful. She felt as if there were wads of cotton stuffed in each ear, blocking out sound. She didn't want to hear, or to think, or to feel, for if she did, she knew she'd shatter.

Lily drifted off to sleep, wrapped in the safety of Pascal's arms, her head tucked against his chest. Sometime during the night she awakened, dimly aware that Pascal had slipped inside her.

"Oh . . ." she whispered. He was very still, and she felt him as much in her heart as she did in her body.

He kissed her softly, his mouth warm and relaxed on hers, demanding nothing, giving everything. One of his hands slid up to cup her breast, not to excite, only to cherish. "Lily," he said, the word a mere breath against hers. "Lily, sweetheart, she's here because she loves you."

"No." Lily's breath caught on a sudden sob, wrenched from her soul.

"Yes." He moved gently inside her as he stroked the hair off her face. "Think, Lily. Should we have a child together, created by love, born from it and into it, do you think we'd be able to stop loving that child? Ever?"

Lily swallowed her tears.

"I saw it in your mother's eyes tonight. She hasn't stopped loving you. You need to discover the truth of what happened. As God is my witness, that woman didn't walk away from you. She was forced away." He brushed his lips against hers.

Lily's brow knotted in pain, and he kissed that too. His hips rocked, stroking, soothing, the most tender of caresses, the deepest of touches.

"Don't leave me, Pascal."

"Never, beloved. Never."

The tight knot in her chest began to ease, and as it slowly

dissolved, an overwhelming peace washed through her. She knew it came from Pascal, as if with each sweet stroke he gave her his very being and held her own just as close.

Lily sobbed and shuddered, holding him inside herself as deeply as she could, keeping him there as if she could really make them one. He came with her in silent pulses, as simple and perfect in their joining as God had made them.

The butler directed Lily to the library. She had promised Pascal that she would at least try to listen to her mother, but she wasn't sure it was a promise she could keep. Her heart hurt, as if her chest were squeezing on a bruise. She put her hand on the knob and slowly turned it, feeling that she was opening not just a door but Pandora's box. She could only pray that she'd find a little piece of hope at the bottom. It seemed highly unlikely.

Her mother sat on the sofa talking with Jean-Jacques, who lounged by the window. Coffey was primly arranged in an armchair near the cold fireplace, her hands resting on the handle of her cane. They'd been discussing her—she knew by the guilty expression on Coffey's face as she walked in.

"Good morning, Mama," she started to say, but Jean-Jacques cut her off, a picture of outrage.

"Lily, why didn't you tell me about LaMartine molesting you in that monastery? The man's a damned pervert!"

Lily gave him a biting look, in no mood to deal with her brother. She was almost as angry with him as she was with her mother. "Haven't you learned anything about jumping to conclusions?" she said curtly. "Pascal didn't do anything to me in the monastery other than use his medical skills. Why don't *you* use your *head*?"

"But Lily," Coffey said, bewildered. "You insisted . . . you swore to the abbot that Mr. LaMartine assaulted you, child. Now you are saying it was not so?"

Lily shrugged. "I made a mistake."

"I think you had better explain," her mother said. "Coffey was certain about what happened."

"I don't think I owe an explanation to anyone," Lily said brusquely. "Especially not to you, Mama. However, since Pascal is not deserving of your contempt, I will tell you this, since you weren't around during my childhood to disabuse me. Both my father *and* Coffey told me that men wanted only one thing, so I assumed that Pascal was helping himself.''

"He is a licensed physician, Mama," Jean-Jacques said uncertainly. "He told me so himself."

Lily shot Jean-Jacques a look of surprise, but she didn't have time to wonder why Pascal hadn't mentioned it. Her mother was pursuing her line of questioning with a single-minded purpose.

"I see," the duchess said. "Yet your father, knowing that, still thought you'd been compromised?"

"No," Lily answered tightly. "He believed Pascal. Not surprising, considering he's never listened to a word I had to say. He saw an opportunity to marry me off, and he took it. Father Mallet was only too thrilled to encourage Papa. He couldn't wait to see the last of me.''

"Yes," the duchess said bitterly. "I know how that is."

Lily gave her mother a long look. *Here come the excuses and the lies. Don't bother, Mama. I already know the truth.*

The duchess patted the sofa. "Come, sit here, Lily. You must have wondered all these years why I left, why you have heard nothing from me.''

"Yes, I wondered. I gave up wondering, though, a long time ago." Lily stood proudly, her head held high. "I have no wish for anything from you now, including explanations.''

Her mother blanched. "Lily—I tried to write, but my letters never reached you. They were always intercepted."

"Really? How dramatic. Tell me, Mama. Who intercepted them? A jealous God, perhaps? After all, you did choose Him over us.''

"No—no, that wasn't how it was," her mother said, close to tears. "Please let me tell you what happened?"

"Why?" Lily asked, her throat burning, wanting to lash out and hurt as deeply as she'd been hurt. "Why? It doesn't matter anymore. It's over, finished. You can't take back the past, or change it. You left us without so much as a word. That is statement enough." Lily clenched her fists at her sides, her stomach churning. "Don't you understand? *I don't care.*"

Her mother's face crumpled and her erect shoulders slumped. She turned her face away and covered it with her hand. Lily felt satisfaction, but it was a hollow victory.

A sharp tapping noise interrupted the heavy silence, and

Lily realized it was the familiar sound of Coffey's cane descending hard on the ground in rebuke. "You will listen to your mother, Elizabeth," she commanded. "I did not raise you to break the heart of the woman who gave you life twenty-three years ago and has loved you every moment since. You are behaving like a spoiled, ungrateful child, and it is little wonder, given that dreadful man you married. Where have your manners gone?"

It was the mention of Pascal that made shame sweep through Lily. He would never have countenanced deliberate cruelty, no matter how justified her anger. "I beg your pardon," she whispered.

"That's better, child. Now hear your mother out, for she has a story to tell you and it's long past time for you to hear it. I back up every word, for I was there."

"Very well," Lily said, pulling up a chair and folding her hands into her lap, "I will listen. But don't expect any more than that."

"Thank you," her mother said gratefully, but her face was still badly strained. "I will try to be as brief as possible. I didn't want to leave Sutherby, Lily. I had no choice."

"Why?" Lily asked cynically. "If you didn't leave for God, then it must have been because you couldn't give my father a son. A daughter wasn't good enough for either of you?"

"Oh, no—that wasn't the reason. I adored having a little girl to love."

"Oh? You surprise me. Mothers don't generally abandon their children, especially not ones they love. Maybe you were bored? I suppose that's what happens when you haven't anything better to do." Lily stared hard at the weave of the oriental carpet. If she was ever lucky enough to have a child, she would never abandon it—no matter what. She'd love it and nurture it and give it every last bit of love she had. She'd never make it feel worthless and unloved as her mother had made her feel.

"Lily, please listen," her mother pleaded. "You have to understand, it started with Father Mallet. He despised me."

Her head snapped up. That, at least, was believable.

"He didn't like women to begin with," her mother said, fiddling with the cross around her neck. "Worse, he knew that your father and I loved each other, and he thought that I had too much influence over your father. So he came up with a plan, something he knew would break your father's heart and force him to send me away.''

"What kind of plan?" Lily said warily. "What could possibly have forced my father to send you away?"

Lily's mother had the same fair skin as her daughter and she flushed just as easily. "Do you remember the butler at the time?"

"Roberts?" Lily said in surprise. "Yes, of course. I thought he was terribly handsome."

Her mother nodded. "He was. It served to Father Mallet's advantage." She cleared her throat. "He told your father that he—that he found us together. He must have paid Roberts a large sum of money, because Roberts admitted to something that never happened."

"But surely Papa wouldn't have believed such a thing of you?" Lily asked, deeply shocked.

"He didn't want to, but no matter what I said, Father Mallet swore he'd seen us with his own eyes, and Roberts corroborated the story. He was fired, and I was sent to the convent and forbidden any contact with you ever again." She lowered her gaze to her lap, her expression withdrawn, now that she'd told her story.

Lily felt as if she were judge—and executioner. She put her face in her hands, unable to catch her breath.

It had all been lies. More smoke, more of the fabric of her life twisted from what she'd believed it to be into something else entirely. She might have had her mother all of these years if it hadn't been for Father Mallet and her father's willingness to believe him. But it wasn't all her father's fault. If her mother had been brave enough or strong enough to stand up to Father Mallet, the truth would have come out.

Now she understood why her father had filled the house with ugly men and constantly warned her about carnal desire. And yet he hadn't seen the darkest side of carnal desire living right under his nose. He hadn't been able to protect her from it.

Lily wanted to lash out at somebody, anybody. It wasn't fair, being robbed of love. It wasn't fair, what had happened to her.

"Lily?" her mother asked tentatively.

She lifted her head with an effort, a cold sweat covering her brow, and she stifled a rush of nausea with a strong effort. "Telling me your story still doesn't make it right," she said, swallowing the bile rising in her throat.

"I realize the truth must come as a terrible shock to you, Lily," her mother said gently.

"A terrible shock?" Lily repeated dully. "No, it doesn't come as a shock, Mama. It only serves as a reminder. You left us, knowing the hands you were leaving us in. You knew what sort of man Father Mallet was, and yet you left your children under his control. Do you know what he did to me, Mama? I suppose you have no idea." Lily trembled, finally realizing with a cruel, sickening certainty what had really happened all those times she'd been forced to bend over the altar rail, just what that hard thing was that had rubbed back and forth against her. Lily pressed the back of her hand against her mouth and bit hard into the flesh. She tasted blood.

"Lily? What is it? What are you saying?" her mother asked, bewildered.

"Never mind," Lily said. "Oh, God. Never mind." She wanted Pascal. She wanted him to hold her, to reassure her, to make it better. She needed to feel cleansed.

"I am so sorry," her mother said. "I wish I could have been there to help you, to support you. But at least I am here now, Lily. Won't you let me help you? Perhaps we can petition the church for an annulment? A marriage made against your will—"

"I don't want an annulment!" Lily said furiously. "Why can't you understand that I'm finally happy?"

Her mother gave her a puzzled frown. "How can you be happy when you were forced to marry a man you despised?"

"I may have been forced to marry him, but Pascal is a wonderful husband, and I couldn't love him more." Lily's eyes flashed. "I'd thank you to stay out of my business, Mama. You have no right to interfere. I'm sorry you wasted your time coming down."

The duchess stared at her daughter. Then she smoothed her skirts and her hair as if to collect herself. "You are saying that you have fallen in love with a commoner?"

"Pascal is the finest of men, no matter what his birth. You might try getting to know him a little before you judge him, Mama."

The duchess considered all of this. "Then will you explain to me why this wonderful husband of yours forces you to live in squalor when you have one of the larger fortunes in Great Britain?''

Lily thrust her chin forward. ''We're not living in squalor, despite what Jean-Jacques told you. We're living in a sweet little cottage. It wasn't so sweet when Jean-Jacques first gave it to us,'' she added, giving him a dirty look. ''It was falling down about our ears—and whose fault was that?''

Jean-Jacques straightened defensively. ''Your husband refused to live at the château. What else was I supposed to do?''

''You might have sent supplies,'' she snapped. ''You might once have come to see how I was, Jean-Jacques.'' She turned back to her mother. ''But despite that, it's a proper home now.''

''But Lily, you can afford nearly anything, yet Jean-Jacques says your husband won't touch your money. I don't understand. If he loves you, surely he would want to see you comfortable?''

Lily glared at her mother. ''I am comfortable. More comfortable than I've ever been in my life. Can't you understand? I have everything I need. A home, a husband who loves me, a purpose to my life. Pascal works hard and I work hard, and we're accepted for who we are.'' Her face softened slightly. ''The people truly love Pascal. You must have seen that for yourself last night.''

Her mother nodded. ''To be fair, I did see an affectionate response when he addressed the crowd. It made me think of a time long ago when Saint-Simon was still a happy place, before the epidemic.''

''You're not the only one who's thinking that,'' Jean-Jacques said with irritation. ''You ought to hear what they whisper about the man.''

''Just what do you mean by that?'' Lily asked sharply.

''Haven't you heard? They're saying he's my uncle's bastard.'' Jean-Jacques laughed harshly. ''What a joke.''

''Oh, that,'' Lily said with relief. ''Yes, I know. It's not true, of course.''

''I know that,'' Jean-Jacques said, thoroughly annoyed. ''It's because of the harvest. You'd think the villagers would be a little more scientific instead of falling back on old legends. What do they think all those expensive materials that went into the soil were for?''

"Superstition dies hard," Lily said, coming to the villagers' defense.

"What are you two talking about?" the duchess asked, confused.

"It's just a stupid old story." Jean-Jacques quickly explained.

"Oh," the duchess said, waving a hand as if to dismiss the matter, "how perfectly absurd. Serge was devoted to Christine. They were such a happy couple. I used to envy them . . ." Her fingers played at the severe neckline of her dress. "Never mind that. You're right, Lily. I think I should become acquainted with your husband before I pass judgment. I cannot be easy in my mind about the life you are living, but you do look happy."

"Well, if you claim to love me as you do," Lily said caustically, "then that should be all that matters, shouldn't it?"

Her mother cleared her throat and sat up very straight. "Blood is important, despite what you might think," she said. "You come from generations of the finest breeding on both sides of your family. This man is no one, yet he will sire your children. Have you thought of that?"

Lily shrugged. "I'm not a brood mare, I'm a woman. Pascal is a man. We love each other. It seems to me that should be what counts."

"Yes, and that brings me to another point. No matter how you might feel about your husband, I do wish you would cease these public displays of affection. He might not know any better, but you certainly should. I was shocked."

Lily couldn't find a single thing to say.

"Still," her mother continued, "if I'm to become acquainted with your husband, then I think you ought to join us for dinner this evening."

"Thank you," Lily replied. "That's an excellent idea. And you needn't worry," she added. "Pascal does know how to use a knife and fork."

That comment drew a look of disapproval from her mother and a snort of laughter from Jean-Jacques.

"Don't worry, Lily," he said, walking her out a few minutes later. "I'll explain about Pascal. It's my fault for having created the wrong impression with Mama."

"It won't make any difference. She's a snob," Lily said.

"We're all snobs. Your husband will knock her down a peg or two in no time. He has a knack for it."

Lily agreed, unbending a little more toward her brother. It was far more than she was prepared to do with her mother.

Dinner was not easy. Lily knew Pascal was as aware of her mother's steady observation as she was, but he was doing a good job of appearing not to notice—a talent he'd developed long ago. Still, he had to be irritated. If she were in his position, she'd be furious. She was furious for him. Here her mother was, posing as the arbiter of correctness, yet staring down one of her own dinner guests, never mind that he was her son-in-law. He might have been a mouse she was eyeing. Lily waited for the pounce.

It came during the dessert course at a natural break in the conversation. "My son tells me that you were adopted by the Earl of Raven," the duchess said.

Oh, of course, the research into Pascal's pedigree—or lack of one—is the first order of business, Lily thought with annoyance.

"I was, your grace," Pascal replied, "although my father didn't succeed to the title until seven years ago."

"Yes, I am aware of that. Where were you born, Monsieur LaMartine?" Lily's mother delicately spooned lemon pudding into her mouth. Lily would have liked to spoon it all over her mother's face.

"I've already been interrogated by your husband," Pascal said, meeting her gaze steadily. "Need we repeat it?"

Yes, Lily thought. *Pascal is definitely irritated.*

Her mother didn't blink. "I am not privy to my husband's conversations," she said. "But as Elizabeth is my only daughter, surely you must realize that I am curious about the man she has married?"

"I beg your pardon," Pascal said, not looking the least bit repentant. "I thought Lily had told you about me. I was born in Montreuil into a very ordinary family, your grace." He released a little breath, and from that Lily could tell just how annoyed he really was and how hard he was trying to control his temper.

"Oh?" she said. "Were they from Montreuil, then?"

"My father was. He'd met my mother in Paris three years before, and they were married in Montreuil a respectable fourteen months before my birth."

"Monsieur LaMartine, I did not mean to imply . . ." the duchess said, at least having the grace to look embarrassed.

Lily wanted to strangle her.

"We moved to Paris in the summer of 1810, when I was a year old," Pascal said, ignoring her protest. "My parents died nine years later. Being without other family, I was adopted. There's nothing more to say."

Her mother fell silent for a moment and Lily wondered what was going through her mind. *Common, common, common,* no doubt.

But instead she smiled. "Oh, what a pity. I thought that perhaps you might have been related to some people I once knew," she said. "They lived here in Saint-Simon. I've been puzzling over the name all afternoon—I knew I'd remembered it from somewhere."

Pascal nodded. "I've been told there was a Henri LaMartine who worked here as steward. You're not the first person to ask."

"No, I suppose not. It does seem an incredible coincidence, though, doesn't it? I didn't know Henri very well. His wife was more of a friend; she was secretary to my sister-in-law, Christine. They left during the epidemic."

"Typhoid is very difficult to control once it takes hold," Pascal said. "They were wise to leave, considering what happened here."

"Yes," the duchess agreed sadly. "It was tragic, losing our family as we did. My husband and I were fortunate to be living in Paris then." She shivered with memory. "Jean-Jacques was only a year old—he might easily have gone the way of the others. We were careful to wait until the epidemic had run its course before coming down to take over Serge's affairs."

"It must have been a difficult task with the steward's having left," Pascal observed.

"It was nearly impossible," the duchess replied. "Henri was the only one who knew the inside workings of the estate, and Anne had managed the domestic side. We were all at sixes and sevens."

Pascal carefully placed his spoon on the side of his plate. "Did you say Anne?"

"Yes, she was delightful," the duchess replied. "I enjoyed her particularly because she was British, and I often felt so alone among the French. Anne was such good company. We'd talk the hours away when my husband, Hubert, brought me down to visit.''

''Would you describe these two people for me?'' he asked. ''I begin to wonder if I didn't know them.''

Lily shot him a look of alarm. She knew that note in his voice, although she hadn't heard it since the day they'd been married and had that miserable fight in the carriage, when she accused him of all sorts of terrible things. His face looked as strained and white as it had then.

''Well, let's see,'' her mother said. ''It's been so long since I've thought of them. Henri was fairly nondescript, although pleasant enough and certainly intelligent. He was slight in build, I remember that, with thinning brown hair. But Anne, she was such a pretty thing . . .'' She looked away, thinking. ''Small. Everything about her was small. She had dark hair and a round face and the prettiest blue eyes—''

''And a mole near the left side of her chin?'' Pascal asked.

''Yes! Yes, that's right. A mole near the left side of her chin! You *did* know her.''

''Yes. I knew her. Anne LaMartine was my mother. If you'll excuse me, your grace, I need some air.''

24

A stunned silence fell over the dining room, the only sound the echo of Pascal's quick footsteps on the stone floor of the entrance hall as he left. Lily's first impulse was to jump up and run after him, but she reconsidered, thinking that he might need a few minutes to himself. He'd obviously had a bad shock.

Besides, she might be able to do more good by discovering what she could about the LaMartines from her mother, since nothing at the moment made any sense.

"Mama," she asked, "did Anne LaMartine have any children when you knew her?"

"No. No, she didn't," her mother said, looking as bewildered as Lily felt. "I suppose she might have been pregnant when she left."

"Yes, perhaps," Lily said. "But that doesn't explain why Pascal's parents told him a completely different story . . . or maybe it does. When was the epidemic? Thirty years ago, I know, but when, exactly?"

"It was the spring of 1809," her mother replied.

"And Pascal was born on the ninth of June, that year. I know, because he turned thirty this summer. So she *must* have been with child when she left," Lily said thoughtfully, "and if it wasn't with Henri LaMartine's child, there's only one other man who comes to mind."

The duchess soundlessly shook her head.

Jean-Jacques sat at his end of the table, his mouth hanging half open. "What the devil are you talking about?" he said. "What makes you think the child wasn't LaMartine's?"

Lily looked at her brother in disgust, thinking his brains were not all that they might be. Pascal had certainly grasped the essential point quickly enough. "You described Henri

LaMartine, Mama. Pascal doesn't look the least like him, does he?''

"No," the duchess said faintly. "Not at all."

"But the sixth duke, Mama? Serge, I mean? Does he resemble him?"

"I—I cannot say. Serge was tall like your husband. And his hair was dark." She grew more pale and disturbed by the moment.

"My God, Lily," Jean-Jacques said in disbelief, "do you honestly think there's some truth to the rumors?"

"I don't know, but I intend to find out for Pascal's peace of mind."

"Lily . . ." her mother said imploringly, "don't you think it's best left alone? What good will it do to dredge up the past now?"

"It's no fun to have your life suddenly ripped apart, Mama, to have believed one thing for so long and then to discover that none of it was true. I know. I've just been through it."

"I'm very sorry about that," her mother said tightly. "But in this case, there's no proof of anything, is there, except that the LaMartines told your husband that they had been elsewhere before he was born. It might have been for any reason."

"Nevertheless, I'm determined to get to the bottom of the matter. If you'll excuse me, I'm going to find Pascal."

She went straight out into the night, wondering where he might have gone. She didn't have to look far. She spotted him leaning against the château's fortified west wall, his forehead against his arms, his chest heaving for air.

"Pascal?" she said tentatively. "Pascal?"

He turned, and she saw that his face was covered in cold sweat. "Lily," he said hoarsely, passing his arm over his mouth. He was trembling, and she realized that he'd been sick.

"I'm here," she said, putting her arms around him. "I'm here."

"They lied to me," he said, his voice filled with anguish. "They lied to me."

"Yes," she said straightforwardly, releasing him and looking him in the eye. "I think they must have been protecting you from the truth."

"Oh, God. There's only one possible explanation." He

slid down to the grass, resting his head on his knees, his hands clenched on the back of his neck.

"Yes," she said again. "The villagers were right. You are Serge's child."

"Bastard," he said, spitting out the word with disgust.

"Bastard, then. And I don't care. You're my Pascal, no matter who fathered you, and I love you."

He looked up, his expression bleak. "Well, it's a damned good thing, since I can't change things back to the way they were. You're stuck with me—with this whole blasted mess."

"It isn't a mess," she said in what she hoped was a reassuring voice. "We still don't really know anything. It might be one enormous coincidence."

"My whole damned life has been one enormous coincidence," Pascal said bitterly. "Now I find out that it's also been one enormous lie. God, if there's one thing I can't stomach, it's lies and the people who tell them. My own parents, Lily—why? Why couldn't they have told me the truth?" Tears sparkled in his eyes and he angrily wiped at them.

"I'm sure they had their reasons," she said.

"How can you be so damned calm about this? You're behaving as if it's a perfectly normal course of events, that everyone's parents lie to them about something as essential as their birth."

"What do you want me to do? Rant and rage? It's enough to have one of us badly upset. As I said before, we don't know the truth yet."

"Don't we? There are a number of points that I find confusing—my father's name was Paul, for God's sake, not Henri, and he was *not* the sort of man who would have taken well to being cuckolded." He clenched his fists on his knees. "Further, I never thought my mother was the sort of woman to make a cuckold of him. Apparently I was wrong."

Anger, confusion, deep pain, they all marked his face. Lily dropped to her knees and took his hand between both of hers, desperately wanting to comfort him, knowing there was little comfort she could offer. "Maybe it was just one of those things that happened, a terrible mistake, instantly regretted," she said.

"It doesn't make any damned sense! Even if it is true that I'm Serge's bastard, why would my parents have kept their past such a secret? No one in Paris would have thought me

anything but Paul LaMartine's son. There was never an ink-
ling of anything else, so why the lies?''

"I don't know that either," she said. "Maybe they didn't
mention Saint-Simon because they didn't want you to come
here and guess the truth."

"Well, I'm here," he said, his eyes blazing. "And as far
as I'm concerned, that's the biggest damned coincidence of
all."

Lily bit her lip. It was all her fault that this had happened.
If she hadn't gone after him, he never would have come to
Saint-Simon. But she didn't think he needed to know that
just then. He was upset enough.

"Let's go home," she said gently. "There's no point sitting here worrying over something we can't do anything
about."

"This isn't going to go away, Lily."

"No," she said, putting his hand on her cheek. "But do
you remember what you said to Father Chabot the night he
first told you about the rumor?"

He shook his head.

"You said that you didn't care who people thought your
father was, as long as they accepted you. Well, they have
accepted you. That won't change, will it? They already think
you're the duke's bastard. What difference will this make to
anyone but yourself?"

Pascal wearily pushed a hand through his hair, then nodded. "I suppose you're right."

"You also said you had finally found the sameness you'd
been looking for all of your life, here in Saint-Simon. You've
had an affinity for the land and the people ever since you set
foot on this soil. Maybe you are where you truly belong, and
for good reason."

Pascal managed a faint smile. "Thank you, sweetheart,
for trying to cheer me up. I can't talk about this anymore,
not tonight." He gently brushed her cheek with his knuckles. "I do thank God I have you, though, or I don't know
where I'd be." He stood and helped her up, folding her
hand into his.

"Let's go home, duchess."

Pascal didn't sleep that night. He couldn't even toss and
turn. His muscles were too tense, and his brain wouldn't
stop working. There were too many disturbing things run-

ning through it, too many questions and inconsistencies that couldn't be answered.

He had become a man with virtually no past to cling to, a man who didn't even know who had fathered him. Pascal stared at the ceiling, anger burning in his chest. What heritage would he pass down to his children? That of La-Martine? Or was it going to be the legacy of a bastard?

He clenched his teeth and turned his head to the side, looking at Lily. She was so beautiful asleep, so peaceful. He'd made desperate love to her earlier, taking her fiercely, as if he could bury himself, his pain, his confusion in her. She accepted him, responding just as fiercely as she wrapped her legs around his hips and led him to oblivion until there was nothing but the pounding of their hearts, his groans mingling with her cries.

Generous Lily, who said it didn't matter. But it did, God, it did. It mattered so much it was tearing him into small, raw, ugly pieces. Lily had a right to know whose blood ran in his veins—*he* had a right to know.

Pascal watched dawn break, gradually easing darkness into light. He wished to God that his life might be illuminated as easily as the world was every morning. When it came to it, he wished God would stop holding out a hand in offering and then snatching it back again. Pascal felt as if he was always being tested. What would God expect next? The sacrifice of his firstborn son?

He decided it was time to take matters into his own hands. He knew that Wednesday was Michel Chabot's morning to clean the church plate, and he always began early.

Pascal walked into the vestry just as Father Chabot was pouring himself a cup of coffee before starting the chore.

"Michel. Good morning."

Father Chabot looked around in surprise. "Pascal—what are you doing in my quarters at this hour?" His eyes twinkled. "Have you nothing better to do, now that the harvest is in?" He cleared a place for him at the table. "May I give you some coffee?"

"No, thank you. I'm here to ask you if this bastard rumor might be true," Pascal said concisely, nearly causing Father Chabot to spill coffee all over himself.

"I'm sorry, I didn't mean to startle you," he said. "There's some fairly compelling evidence that has come to my attention."

"You think I can help?" Father Chabot said, rubbing a hand over his scalp.

"Yes," Pascal said. "I do. I've learned that my parents lived here before the epidemic, Henri LaMartine and his wife, Anne. You mentioned my father once when we first met, although he later went by the name of Paul."

"I see," Father Chabot said quite calmly, now that he'd recovered from his surprise.

"You see?" Pascal said impatiently. "I wish to hell I did! My parents made it very clear to me that they'd met in Paris in 1805 and married in Montreuil in 1808, where they continued to live until 1810. Yet I have it on the best authority that they were here in Saint-Simon until the spring of 1809."

"Yes, that is true, and they most certainly did not marry in Montreuil. They were married here in Saint-Simon in this very church. I performed the ceremony. That was—let me see, it was in the autumn of 1805."

Pascal stared at him. "Good God," he said softly. "This gets stranger by the moment."

"Yes," Father Chabot said, "it is interesting, isn't it? I can see that such a discovery would come as a shock."

Pascal smiled tightly. "Yes, you could say that. But why would they have gone to such elaborate lengths to keep the truth from me?"

Father Chabot picked up the chalice and began to polish it in careful circles. "I can't say."

Pascal slapped his hands down on the table in frustration. "You can't say, or you won't say? My mother was a devout Catholic, Michel. She would have made her confession to you. Surely you must know who my father is."

Father Chabot looked up and met his gaze evenly. "You of all people should know that I cannot break the sanctity of the confessional. Not even for you."

Pascal colored. "I'm sorry. I didn't mean to ask you to do that. But the only explanation I can think of is that my mother became pregnant by Serge de Saint-Simon, and she and my—she and LaMartine left to protect her reputation— or to protect me."

"I think it would be safe to say that they both cared very much about protecting you." Father Chabot put the Communion cup down. "They were good people, Henri and Anne. They raised you well in the years that they had."

Pascal raked his hand through his hair. "All right. I can

see I'm not going to get another word out of you, but I think you've told me everything I need to know. Michel, if you married them . . . may I at least see the church records?"

"Certainly." Father Chabot pulled a key from his pocket and went to the cupboard where he kept the books. He found the one for the year 1805 and opened it to October, then set it down on the table, pointing at the pertinent line.

Pascal bent over and read: *Anne Elizabeth, née Storme, married Henri Paul LaMartine, October 5, 1805.* Both of their signatures were there and also those of Michel Chabot and two witnesses.

He let out a long breath. Proof positive. "Well," he said, closing the book and handing it back to Father Chabot, "that clears up one mystery, anyway. Henri LaMartine's second name was Paul."

"As I remember, that was what Anne called him," Father Chabot agreed, locking the register away again. "She said it sounded more English to her ear."

Pascal rubbed the back of his neck. "I suppose that's it, then. I'd better get to work. Thank you for telling me what you could."

"I'm sorry I couldn't tell you more," Father Chabot said.

"We can't have you explaining to God why you broke your vows over the small matter of a bastard child," Pascal said stiffly.

"I never said that," Father Chabot admonished.

"No," Pascal replied with a shrug. "In the end, you really didn't have to."

He went out the same way he'd come in, but more despondent than ever for finally knowing the truth.

Father Chabot's morning was not spent in the usual happy contemplations that came when he polished the church plate, but rather in troubled thought. He'd known all along, of course, that Anne and Henri LaMartine had not told Pascal the truth about his parentage. He dearly wished he could sit the man down and explain it all to him, but that was out of the question.

There seemed to be no answer to his dilemma. No matter how many prayers he said, no answer was forthcoming.

He was about to set the Cross on the altar when he heard someone come in through the front, and he looked up to see who it was. He nearly dropped the Cross in his surprise.

He had known Frances Dambier, later the Duchesse de Saint-Simon, years before, when she'd been deeply unhappy, married to a man who was both cruel and ruthless, and he had often counseled her. Her undisguised relief when her husband had accidentally been shot and killed had been evident. It was one funeral service he had actually enjoyed conducting and he felt no remorse over his enjoyment.

She had left the day after the funeral, and he hadn't seen her since. Her beauty had not faded with age. Instead, it had matured, the bones of her face stronger, more sculpted now. She still moved with the same regal grace, had the same noble presence. But he also noted the added lines of suffering. He could see that Frances had not had an easy life since her departure from Saint-Simon.

"Frances," he said, carefully putting his treasure down and quickly wiping his hands. He hurried down the nave toward her, his hand held out in greeting. "Goodness gracious, is it really you? I was under the impression that you had retired to a convent."

"I am pleased to see you are still the priest for Saint-Simon," she said softly. "You haven't changed much, have you?"

"Oh, I'm older, fatter, a little wiser, one hopes. What a very pleasant surprise."

"I am not sure you will think so after we speak, Michel. I have passed a disturbing night."

His face instantly sobered. "Have you come to make confession?"

"I'm not certain. I need to speak with you in absolute confidence, but I don't know that I need to confess—yet."

The duchess appeared sorely troubled, and he knew that any number of things might be the cause. But he had a strong suspicion of what was on her mind, given Pascal's earlier visit. It occurred to him that maybe God had heard his prayers, after all.

"Please, come up to the front. We will pray together, and then we will speak, yes?"

When they had dispensed with the prayers, he settled the duchess on one of the benches and sat down next to her in the deep silence of the church. "You have come to visit your children?" he asked, trying to ease her into conversation.

"Yes," she said, her hands clutched in her lap. "I haven't seen them for a very long time . . ."

She quickly explained, and Father Chabot began to understand the pain etched onto her face.

"How tragic," he said sympathetically. "I hadn't realized. But now you are reunited. Your children must be overjoyed."

"I don't know if 'overjoyed' is the word I would use," she said. "We are slowly learning to know each other again, although Lily is the most difficult. She carries such anger toward me, toward her father. But never mind that now." Her expression grew even more troubled. "Oh, Michel—I am in a terrible dilemma." The words came out in a rush. "If I help one child, I will hurt the other terribly."

Father Chabot took her hand. "Tell me what has happened," he said quietly.

She shook her head, tears welling up in the corners of her eyes. "Last night I met Lily's husband, Pascal La-Martine."

Father Chabot went very still. *Finally, here it is. The reckoning.*

"I met him the night before," she said, "but only briefly, and the light was poor, and in any case I was expecting something quite different." Her words tumbled over each other. "Yesterday afternoon I started thinking about the name, and that's when I realized."

"Realized what, exactly?" Father Chabot said carefully.

"About Henri and Anne LaMartine. I thought about the rumor that Jean-Jacques had spoken of, about Lily's husband being Serge's bastard, which of course I dismissed. You must remember how they were together, Serge and Christine?"

"Of course," Father Chabot replied.

"We all knew that Anne LaMartine was barren, so it seemed ridiculous that she might have had a child with Serge. Then this Pascal LaMartine came to dinner last night and told me about his family living somewhere else entirely, so I thought I was being silly, seeing a resemblance. But it was there—oh, it was there, Michel, far more than I ever expected, once I started looking for it. When he told me his mother's name was Anne and the description matched perfectly, I finally understood."

"What was it that you understood?" he asked gently.

"I don't know what I could have been thinking, not to have realized from the first moment I saw him, standing up there on the bench, addressing the people with such confidence, so like his father." She trembled from head to foot, and he took her other hand and held them both steady.

"He has not just his father's height and coloring and his distinctive nose," she said, "but he has her mouth—it is more masculine, of course, but that full lower lip, the smile? And the way the eyes look at one, so directly, solemn one moment and then the laugh that suddenly lights them up the next. Surely you've seen it, Michel?"

"Yes. I've seen it," he said.

"I am not imagining things, then?"

"No, Frances. You are not. I saw it the first moment I met him. But I suppose that I had the benefit of knowing that one day I might."

She jerked in a sharp breath and pulled her hands from his. "So . . ." she whispered. "I am right."

He nodded. "You are right."

"Anne was barren after all," she said, looking away.

"Yes," he said. "Anne was barren. But she raised a child, who otherwise would not have survived under the care of your husband."

Frances was silent for a long moment, her head bowed. And then she looked up, tears streaming freely down her cheeks. "I thought that must be it," she said shakily, taking out a handkerchief and dabbing at her eyes. "Christine certainly knew what Hubert was capable of, how badly he coveted the dukedom. He would not have let an infant get in his way."

"That's right. As long as Serge was alive, their child was safe. The moment Serge died, Christine knew her infant's life was in danger—and not just from typhoid. She did what she had to. She was dying herself."

"It seems such a drastic measure to take, pretending a child's death." Frances twisted her handkerchief around and around in her hands.

"Perhaps," Father Chabot said quietly, "but she knew that sending Alexandre away with Anne and Henri would not be enough. Don't you think Hubert would have done everything he could to track them down?"

Frances wiped her eyes again. "Yes. I suppose he would have."

"So you see, she did the right thing. I have never before breathed a word of this, having been sworn to secrecy. But since you guessed the truth, I feel I have not broken my oath. Tell me, what do you intend to do, now that you know?"

"I—I don't know," she cried. "Perhaps it would be best if I did nothing."

"You must realize that Jean-Jacques is not the rightful heir?"

"Yes, but how can I go upsetting so many lives at this late date? Christine sent her son away, after all. The world believes he is dead."

Father Chabot's gaze traveled up to the altar. "Christine intended for Anne and Henri to tell the boy the truth when he reached his majority."

"How can you know that?"

"Because I witnessed her instructions shortly before she died. I wrote them in a letter that she signed and gave to Anne along with her husband's signet ring—sadly, both must have been lost when the LaMartines died. Christine wanted her son to know, Frances. The LaMartines never had a chance to tell him. You have."

"But he is content, not knowing the truth—and Lily will be a duchess in her own right, or their son a duke. Why should I rob Jean-Jacques of the only thing he has by dredging up the past now? Jean-Jacques would be left with nothing. Surely you can understand my dilemma, Michel?"

"Do you think it is right to leave the man we know as Pascal LaMartine wondering if he might be a bastard?" Father Chabot asked her. "He has no proof of anything anymore—not of his true parents, nor the people who raised him for the first part of his life. Don't you think he deserves to know of his birthright, to know where he belongs?"

Frances shook her head. "I don't know. I just don't know. He likes to live like a peasant. He doesn't care about the finer things. What good is a dukedom to a man like that? And Lily is happy, whereas this news might well destroy my son. Why should I overturn Jean-Jacques's life? Or Lily's? Or even Pascal's? No one would be happy for it."

Father Chabot stood. "I think you need to make a careful examination of your conscience, Frances. I understand your concerns. But you are the only one who can correct this situation. You know I can say nothing."

"Thank you for listening," she said, also rising. "I will let you know when I have reached a decision."

"Do not let it be too long," he cautioned. "Damage could be done that you might forever regret."

"Damage will be done either way," she said. "I must decide which will be at the least cost."

Pascal found the note Lily had left for him when he returned to the cottage at midday, saying that she'd gone up to visit her mother and see what more she could discover.

"You needn't have bothered," he murmured. "There's nothing more she can tell you, sweetheart."

He crumpled the note and tossed it in the fireplace, deciding to go up to the château to find her. He needed to be with her, needed to hold her, his constant in a world that had turned inside out.

He let Bean out and walked with her for a few minutes, then started back to the cottage. Lily's fishing pole leaned at the ready against the outside wall, and he smiled. Lily had become a fine fisherman over the course of the summer, and she didn't share his inclination to toss the fish back in. They'd made many a good meal from Lily's catch, and it looked as if she planned another for this evening.

He sat on the cottage steps, waiting for Bean to finish her run. Everything looked so normal, so typical of the life he and Lily had built together. Yet it all felt different. He was not the man he'd thought he was. His parents had not been the people he'd thought they were. Nothing was the same, nothing ever would be again.

He had been born into the world in the most ignoble of ways. The next ten years of his life had been built on a lie, and the following twenty had perpetuated it. Since he couldn't change the past, he could only try to live with it— and hope that Lily wouldn't eventually come to despise him for being the bastard she'd once called him.

Pascal walked upstairs to the salon at the butler's direction. Lily's voice echoed clearly down the hall as he approached, her mother's lower tones answering in response. He was about to knock on the half-open door, when Lily's words stopped him cold.

"No, Mama, you don't understand. You see, I *deliberately* went to St. Christophe to find Pascal, because I thought he could bring the land back, and Jean-Jacques was in such trouble.''

Pascal's hand fell from the door and he stiffened with shock. Lily? Lily had deliberately sought him out? She had *known*? Oh, God, it wasn't possible—it just wasn't. But her next words confirmed the fact.

"That's why I feel so guilty. I've never told Pascal the truth, and I don't know how to. It will sound so awful to him. I mean, tracking him down and falling off the wall and making false accusations, that's all bad enough. But the forced marriage—and my bringing him here, only to have him discover who he really is? How do you think he'll feel?''

"I don't understand,'' Pascal heard the duchess ask through the horrible pounding in his ears. "How did you hear about him in the first place?''

"Oh, it was something Father Chabot said last spring. He told me where to find him, so I went immediately,'' Lily replied.

It was enough for Pascal. It was more than enough. No wonder she had called him base-born in the carriage when they'd gone back to England, thinking he couldn't understand. No wonder she'd been so disdainful of him. And no wonder she'd accused him of assault. How else would she have dragged him down to Saint-Simon? He would never have left St. Christophe of his own accord.

Lily had planned the entire thing to get the bastard son back to the land.

He leaned back against the wall, his arms wrapped around his chest as if they could protect him. He felt as if cold water were sucking at him, and if he let go for an instant it would drag him down into its terrible depths. He'd been there once before when he'd drowned.

He was about to drown again, but this time his body was safe. It was his spirit that was in mortal danger. And this time there was no heaven waiting for him, only the echo of Lily's words—words that spoke of more lies and betrayal. He had to get away as quickly as possible before he heard anything more and was pulled completely under.

It was one thing being lied to by parents twenty years dead. It was another having been lied to by the priest he'd called his friend. But to have been lied to and manipulated by the woman he loved more than life itself—that was more than he could bear.

He somehow managed to get himself out of the château and down the hill. He somehow managed to write a brief letter to Lily telling her his intentions. And he somehow managed to pack his satchel and saddle the horse.

Pascal left Saint-Simon without a backward look. He couldn't afford one—not unless he was willing to stare into the depths of hell and know it for his own.

25

L ILY felt better about having unburdened herself to
her mother, not that they were on easier terms. But
who else was there who was so familiar with the Saint-
Simon history? On the whole, she thought her mother had
handled the prospect of Pascal's being Jean-Jacques's base-
born cousin rather well, even if she had been upset over the
matter.

"I honestly thought she was going to be much more
shocked, Bean," Lily said, filling the puppy's water bowl
and setting it on the floor, "especially since she was so
close to Serge's wife."

Lily cocked her head. "What's the matter with you?
You're not looking very cheerful. It's not that bad. Pascal
will grow accustomed to the idea with time."

The puppy miserably rested her head on her paws.

"Don't you want to go fishing? You love fishing. Come
on, little dog."

Bean didn't move.

Lily bent down and felt her little nose. It was cold and wet.
She didn't look ill, but maybe she'd eaten something to upset
her stomach, Lily decided. She straightened, intending to make
some chamomile tea just in case. As she put the water on to
heat she noticed a folded paper on the table, addressed to her
in Pascal's clear hand.

Pascal didn't usually bother to address things to her; he
just wrote them and casually tossed the paper on the table.
She picked it up and unfolded it, and her knees buckled in
shock. She had to grasp the corner of the table to steady
herself.

*Lily. I overheard you speaking to your mother today. I
wish to God I hadn't. I can't remain in a marriage that has
been based on a lie from the very beginning. Whatever other*

*truth there has been between us, this will always be in the
way.*

*I've taken one of the horses, but I've left you the other
and the carriage. I'll write to Nicholas and ask him to release your dowry to you, so that you will have plenty to live
on.*

*I'm going back to St. Christophe. Don't come after me.
Let me go, Lily. For God's sake, if you care for me at all,
let me go.*

He hadn't signed it.

Lily doubled over, her entire world crumbling. She sank
to her knees, shaking her head back and forth, back and
forth, as if she could deny what she'd read. It couldn't be.
He couldn't be gone. Not Pascal, not her love, her life.

Don't leave me, Pascal.

Never, beloved. Never.

But he had.

Lily cried every day and every night for the next ten
weeks, her pain too acute to deal with in any other way.
She felt stripped bare, as if everything that had ever been
her essence, everything that Pascal had found to love—and
in the end found lacking—had disappeared along with him.
She was nothing more than a wraith who woke and moved
through the gray place that her life had become, as insub-
stantial as she. She lived as a shadow in a shadow-world,
unable to bear the invasion of the real world beyond. It was
too vivid, too deafening, too acute.

She refused her mother's offer of refuge at the château.
She held her little cottage to her, a silent reminder of Pascal, and kept to herself. It was an effort just to do her chores,
to cook the food that continued to appear outside the door,
although it tasted like sawdust and she could keep little of
it down.

Everywhere she looked, there were echoes of Pascal. His
medicine chest sat where he'd left it, although he'd taken
his bag with him. Books. A shirt that had been drying on
the line. So many little things that tore at her, that only
made the silence more absolute.

The letters that she wrote to him were returned unread,
and as each bleak day passed with no word, she began to
understand that he really wasn't coming back. He had well
and truly cut himself off.

She knew she shouldn't be surprised. One way or another every person she'd ever loved in her life had left her. She should have realized that Pascal would eventually do the same. She ought to have prepared herself for the inevitable. Instead she'd allowed herself to bask in the glory of his love, to believe it was as infinite as her own for him, that nothing could ever mar it. She'd been wrong. She'd been wrong about so many things, most especially about the depth of Pascal's love for her.

Lily woke one November morning to her usual misery. She hated the moment when she surfaced to consciousness and the terrible jolt of realization that she was alone. At night, in her dreams, she felt him with her in that place he'd made, that part of her that *was* Pascal. She drifted with him, held safe and close, her soul bound to his. Then came daylight, and the sick ache began all over again.

She answered the knock at the door with no enthusiasm. Coffey stood there, as she did every morning, her wizened face filled with concern.

"I'm fine, Coffey," Lily said colorlessly before Coffey could start on her daily litany. "Thank you for coming by, but no thank you, I do not wish to speak to my mother, or my brother, or Father Chabot, nor do I wish to take a stroll."

Coffey looked her up and down. "Lily, I've had quite enough of this attitude, and I won't hold my peace a minute longer. Every couple has disagreements, but this has become ridiculous. Look at you, so deeply unhappy. It must stop."

"Is that what you advised my parents when they separated?" Lily asked caustically. "Did you write to my mother and tell her to pull herself together, to forget her unhappiness? It's ironic, isn't it, Coffey? First my mother locked herself away in a convent, and now my husband has decided he prefers a monastery to me. I don't seem to hold the same appeal as God."

"Don't blaspheme," Coffey said tartly. "And as for your husband, I wonder how long he will stay in his monastery once you tell him you're with child. He doesn't strike me as a man who neglects his obligations."

Lily stared at her nurse. "Are you mad? Do you think I'd lie to him, just to make him come home? I'm not that stupid—not to mention immoral."

"Maybe not, but you're as bad-mannered as ever. You might at least offer an old woman a seat." Coffey pushed past her and abruptly pulled out a chair at the table. "Now, see here," she said, gingerly settling herself. "I've had enough of this nonsense."

Lily furiously rounded on her. "What do you mean, *nonsense*? You really are heartless, Coffey. Can't you see I'm suffering? I've lost Pascal, and it's my own fault. Why can't you leave me alone?" Lily sank into a chair and covered her forehead with her hand, choking back tears.

Coffey's eyes softened. "You really don't realize, do you?"

"Realize what?" Lily asked bleakly, looking up.

"Think, Lily," her old nurse said. "How long has it been since your last courses?"

Lily hadn't thought about it at all. Time had ceased to have meaning, and her monthly flow had been the least of her worries.

"I don't know," she said honestly. "Before the harvest?"

"Just as I thought," Coffey said with satisfaction. "That was September. You realize it is coming up to December? You have the look of a woman with child—you've had it for some time, at least to my eye. But then, I've known you from the day you were born."

Lily looked down at herself in disbelief. "You really think I might be with child? I—I haven't been able to keep very much down . . ."

"A little dry bread in the morning will help with that. You need to think about your coming child, Lily. All this grieving you've been doing isn't good for either of you. You might better spend your energy thinking about what you're going to do to bring your husband home where he belongs." She planted her stick on the floor and stumped out without another word.

Lily impatiently waited for the door to close behind Coffey, then immediately smoothed shaking hands over her abdomen. Yes, it was more rounded than usual—and her breasts had been sore too. She had been so caught up in her own misery that the idea she might be pregnant had not occurred to her.

She went straight to the bookshelf and pulled out one of Pascal's medical books, leafing through it until she came to the section on childbearing, reading everything about the early stages of pregnancy. She closed the book and sat down again. A happiness she hadn't felt in months took hold of her, singing in every part of her being, throwing sharply pulsating color into the gray confines of her soul.

Pascal's child was growing inside of her, tiny, safe, and secure, a living part of him. She reverently cupped her hands over the swell of her abdomen. She had a strong feeling that she knew when their baby had been conceived, and she thought about the words Pascal had spoken so tenderly to her that night, the night of the harvest.

Should we have a child together, created by love, born from it and into it, do you think we'd ever be able to stop loving that child?

"Oh, Pascal," she said fiercely, "I swear to you I'll love this child with every breath I take. I won't ever abandon him to someone else's care. I'll be here for him from this moment to my very last, protecting him with everything I have in me." She released a deep breath of despair. "I only wish you could do the same," she whispered. "Pascal . . . won't you please come home?"

Lily leaned her cheek on her fist, her happiness tainted with a deep misery. How was she supposed to provide her child with a father if he insisted on locking himself away in a monastery? How was she supposed to tell him he was going to be a father if he wouldn't even read her letters? She slumped back in her chair, feeling utterly alone and helpless.

And then the most extraordinary idea began to occur to her. Lily's mouth slowly lifted in a smile, the first since Pascal had left her. Pascal might be able to refuse her and her letters, but he'd never refuse his own child. It was perfect.

Oh, she did feel pleased with herself.

Pascal looked up as a scratch sounded at the door. He supposed it was dinnertime, not that he had any appetite. Julien was persistent, bringing him trays of food whether he wanted them or not. He was equally persistent. He wanted only to be left alone. He divided his days between the gardens and his room, and spent much of the night in the church in solitary prayer.

Julien understood, naturally, knowing all about the far

reaches of hell. Pascal still didn't believe in a hell beyond mortal life, but he reckoned that man more than made up for it with his infinite capacity for pain. If God protected one's soul from hellfire, He didn't protect it from immolation on the altar of one's own humanity.

Pascal waited until he was sure Julien had gone away, then opened the door and took the tray, looking at it with disinterest. Soup. Bread. Wine. And a letter from Saint-Simon.

Just the sight of it tore at him like predatory teeth viciously ripping at the guts of a helpless animal. He groaned, wondering why Julien had not sent it the way of all the others, and then he looked again. It was addressed not in Lily's writing but in an unfamiliar yet distinctly feminine hand. It could only be the duchess's, which explained the letter's presence on the tray. He'd never thought to instruct Julien to return a letter from the duchess, since it hadn't occurred to him that she would write. Why would she? She must have been thrilled to see the last of him.

He thought about it for a moment. The duchess wouldn't have written without serious reason, and he refused to believe she would petition on Lily's behalf, or that Lily would allow it. The only thing he could think was that something had happened to Lily. The very idea compelled him to pick up the letter in panic and unseal it.

His eyes scanned the page, first in dread, and then in disbelief. It was disjointed, rambling to a degree, but it made its point with sickening clarity.

My dear Mr. LaMartine,
This is a very difficult letter to write. I have struggled long and hard with my conscience, but I have also seen how the people grieve for you. They are right to do so, and I have been wrong to keep you from them.

There is a reason that the land returned to life under your care. By all rights it belongs to you. You are the legitimate son of Serge and Christine de Saint-Simon, and by the laws of succession, the seventh duke.

I am sure this seems preposterous, but it is the truth, and Michel Chabot will swear to it. He took your mother's deathbed confession and saw you into the LaMartines' safekeeping to protect you from my husband. I knew nothing of this until the day you left, when I guessed the truth and

went to Michel Chabot for confirmation. He could not tell
you himself, but urged me to speak with you.

Forgive me for not writing before. I thought I could keep my
silence, but it became impossible. Jean-Jacques's father did not
love Saint-Simon, nor did he care about its people, not as your
father did, with all his heart and soul. Jean-Jacques doesn't
care either, not really, not as he should. But you do. I should
not have tried to hold on to Saint-Simon for the sake of my son.
If you can find it in your heart to forgive me, I will be grateful.
But I pray most especially that you will find it in your heart to
forgive my daughter. She suffers.

> *Yours in Christ,*
> *Frances Montcrieff*

He sank onto his hard bed, his hands clutching the paper as
if he were trying to grasp reality. He read it one more time,
then dropped it. It fluttered to the floor as he lowered his
head to his knees, trying to catch his breath, to ease the
stabbing pain that cut through his shredded gut and sliced
directly up into his already savaged heart.

When he lifted his head again, the early-evening light had
dimmed into the darkness of night, and he had come to a
decision. He might rightfully be the Duc de Saint-Simon, but
he would never go home to claim his birthright.

"I'm sorry, Elizabeth," Dom Benetard said once again.
"I wish I could help you, but I cannot. Your husband has
chosen seclusion and silence. It would be wrong of me to
disturb him."

"But why?" Lily repeated. "I must speak with him. He
refuses my letters. How else am I meant to communicate
with him? Please, Father—it is a matter of the greatest urgency. I know if I had the chance to see him for even a few
minutes I could make everything right."

"Elizabeth. When your husband is ready to speak about
what troubles him, he will come to me. At that time I will
tell him of your visit. For now it would be best if you returned home."

Lily had been so certain that Pascal would see her that
the pain of rejection hit her twice as hard. She walked
through the abbey arch, fighting back tears, her head bowed.

"Don't upset yourself too much, Lily," Father Chabot

said gently, patting her arm. "The abbot did say that Pascal will come to him when he is ready."

"But why wouldn't he at least tell Pascal we were here?" Lily said miserably.

"Dom Benetard explained that this is Pascal's way of dealing with his pain."

"What about my pain?" Lily said furiously. "How is either of us supposed to feel better if we can't even talk to each other and work the problem out? The abbot should have realized that and gone to Pascal."

"When Pascal said that he would see no one, most especially not you?" Father Chabot pointed out.

"That was nearly three months ago. Pascal is so stubborn it's ridiculous. There has to be some way of getting through to him." Lily glared at the high wall that kept her from her husband. If she knew anything about it, Pascal was on the other side, working in the garden. He wasn't the type to sit around and be idle, pain or no.

All that stone just to shut the world out—it was maddening.

Her step slowed. The wall! She had scaled it once before. Why not again? It was risky, perhaps—but Pascal was worth any risk. And she'd be very, very careful.

"Umm, Father?" she said, trying to think how to phrase what she needed to say without actually lying. "I—I think I need some time alone."

"Yes, of course," he said sympathetically.

"I thought I'd walk. I'll stay near the wall."

Father Chabot looked at her long and hard, then nodded. "Take your time. I'll go to the church; I've heard the stonework is very beautiful."

Lily waited until he had disappeared around the corner. She looked quickly around, then went straight over to the elm tree, hitched up her cloak and skirts, and reached for the first branch. She was far more careful on this ascent than she'd been the first time she'd scaled the tree. She hadn't been carrying Pascal's child inside her then. Her world hadn't included Pascal at all. She'd had nothing more to think about than Jean-Jacques's vines—a trivial mission in comparison to this one. Now her entire future and her child's future depended on her success.

She ignored the scrapes on the palms of her hands, ignored the crushing fear that grabbed at the pit of her belly.

The only thing she could allow to be important was finding Pascal and somehow convincing him to come home. A few minutes later she'd managed to climb high enough to see over the wall. She gingerly shifted on the branch and peered down into the gardens.

They were empty.

She scanned the grounds, but not a soul stirred anywhere. Lily closed her eyes against a stab of disappointment so acute that it hurt. It was three o'clock. If he wasn't outside by now, he wouldn't be coming out at all. She leaned her forehead against the cold bark of the tree. This had been her last chance, and it had failed.

It finally began to sink in—Pascal had disappeared into the bowels of the monastery, and he had no intention of ever coming out. He'd made sure that she would never be able to see him or touch him—or hurt him—again. He had slipped through her hands like dust, and all she had left of him were memories and dreams.

Lily thought in that moment that she might die of grief.

And then her head snapped up at the sound of a nearby door opening and closing. Her gaze flew to the shed, only twenty yards away, and the man who had just come out of it.

She clutched at the branch for balance as a wave of infinite relief swept over her. Pascal. Not a mirage, not a dream, but really Pascal. She felt as overwhelmed as she had the first time, when he'd turned to look over his shoulder and she'd seen a fallen angel, not completely of this world. But his eyes now held something else, something far more earthly. Raw, savage pain.

Lily recognized it for her own and knew it was in her power to change it for both of them. He was there, so close, almost within reach. She closed her eyes and prayed, as she had never prayed before—with real hope that she would be heard. *Oh, God, please? Please help me? You gave him to me once. It's not fair to take him back. I love him as much as You do, I swear it.*

Pascal stopped suddenly and looked around, then shook his head as if he'd been dreaming and shrugged into his jacket.

She squeezed her eyes shut against the sudden burn of tears. He could still feel her presence, her love. He hadn't gone that far away, not yet. She'd been given her chance back, and with a sudden and complete clarity, she knew what she had to do. Now she could only pray for the chance to do it. He walked toward her, and Lily held her breath, hoping he would stick to ritual.

Pascal obliged her. He sat down on the stone bench, pulling his legs up, his back to her. Lily knew he'd closed his eyes, because his breathing had slowed.

She very carefully lowered herself onto the wall and slowly crept along it until she was directly behind him. Then it was only a matter of arranging herself in a sitting position and tucking her legs up. She closed her eyes and slowed her breathing as he'd taught her, drifting . . . searching for the link between them to form a perfect circle. And then with every bit of love she had, she reached for him.

Pascal tried hard to clear his mind. It had become an obstacle course, trying to get to a peaceful place without running into thoughts of Lily. He had thought the pain would ease after a time, but it only grew worse. He'd begun to wonder how many more pieces of himself he'd have to amputate before he stopped feeling. His heart? His soul? Neither was a sensible solution, but both were attractive ones. It was either that or break apart.

He shook the thought away and concentrated on the light. Clear. Pure. Holy. *Heal me. Please, God, heal me. I can't take much more of this.*

A rush of love answered him, enfolded him, bright and reassuring, unique in its timbre, nothing remotely resembling the peace of his Heavenly Father. His eyes shot open and he leapt to his feet, turning to stare at the wall. A hum ran through him that was unmistakable, that resonance of Lily's that set off a corresponding resonance in him, a vibration that happens only when harmony is perfectly achieved. His gaze slowly traveled up the stone and he froze in shock.

"Lily," he whispered. "Oh, God. Lily."

Her eyes opened and she looked down at him, a little smile lifting the corners of her mouth.

"Hello, gardener," she said casually. "Nice day, isn't it?"

"Nice . . . *nice day*?" he croaked, his voice rusty from lack of use—except for the time that he called out for her in his sleep, his agony unbearable. Now the reason for that agony was blithely sitting on the abbey wall as if she had every right to be there.

Fury erupted in him. "Are you out of your mind? What in the name of God do you think you're doing?"

Lily leaned slightly forward. "It was the only way I could think of to see you."

"Can you not spare me anything? I told you not to come after me!"

"I had to see you," she said softly.

"Why? Do you plan to fling yourself at my feet again and cry attempted rape? It won't work—I'm already married to you. What could they possibly do to me now?"

"Throw you out?" she said hopefully.

"The bastard son you came to fetch the first time around has already brought your blasted land back," he replied savagely. "What more do you want of me? The damned duchy?"

Lily looked at him in puzzlement. "What are you talking about?"

"I'm talking about the lies you told. I'm talking about the way you manipulated me to get what you wanted."

Her smoky eyes flashed in sudden fury. "*That's* what you think? You think I originally came to find you because I knew you were Serge's bastard? You're insane!"

"Ah, God!" he cried in frustration. "Don't try to change your story now—I heard you confessing to your mother, every last miserable word."

"You may have heard every last miserable word, but you got it all wrong. What's the matter with you? I thought you knew me—inside out. Literally!"

"I thought I did too," he said, fiercely pushing the pain away. "Until I heard you say that you felt guilty about everything you'd done, that it had all been deliberate."

"Aargh!" She slammed her fists down on the wall. "Do you think I would be so stupid as to throw myself off a fifteen-foot wall and hope I survived on the slim chance that you might be foolish enough to assault me?"

"No, you threw yourself off the wall because you knew I'd be forced to see if you were hurt, and *then* you could cry assault," he said bitingly. "It's no wonder you took my medical training for granted later on."

"You've truly lost your mind!"

"Have I, Lily? I don't think so. You knew that the abbot

would feel responsible toward your father—*and* you knew what your father would do.''

Lily shook her head in disbelief. ''You think that I deliberately plotted to marry you, just to bring back Jean-Jacques's vines, all on the basis of a mere *superstition*? How stupid do you think I am? How can you even think me so wicked? You insult me, Pascal!''

''What other explanation is there? You can't deny it. We both know exactly how it happened.''

''I didn't throw myself at your feet, I fell,'' she said, incensed. ''And I didn't come to fetch someone's bastard. How could I? I didn't even know your name!''

''Then why *did* you bloody well come? It seems one hell of a coincidence to me.''

''Oh, stuff your coincidences. Hold God responsible, not me. I didn't even realize I'd found the right person until months later. I thought I was looking for a blasted monk!''

''Then explain why you went to such lengths to get my attention. Do I look like a monk to you?'' he demanded.

''No, you don't look like a monk,'' she shot back, ''and that's exactly the point. I thought since you weren't a monk, you might be willing to talk to me, to tell me who the botanist was, since the porter wouldn't help.''

''How had you come to hear about this botanist, then? Don't tell me Michel knew about that, too?''

''He *did* know that,'' Lily said with exasperation. ''He didn't know your name, but he'd heard about you and your talents. He put them down to God. I put them down to science.''

Pascal knew that much to be true, but he wasn't about to give Lily an edge, not if it meant being sucked into false hope. ''You're telling me Michel had no idea I had any connection to Serge de Saint-Simon? How do you expect me to believe that?''

She looked down at him with pure disgust. ''Some friend of Father Chabot's wrote him a letter about you,'' she said. ''He told me about it, and I thought you might be useful, since nothing else was working for the vines.''

''So you're telling me that everything else was coincidence?'' he asked, a treacherous, seductive thread of uncertainty creeping into his mind.

''Yes, it was coincidence—how could it have been anything but? If you know anything about me, you know I would never scheme in such a way and then lie to you." The anger left her face, leaving stark unhappiness. "For all my faults, if I've been anything, at least I've always been honest," she said simply. "I thought you understood that."

It hit him like a blow. Lily was honest to her very core, and it had often been to her detriment, especially in the early days. She never had been any good at pretending, most especially not in the midst of a full-blown rage.

She couldn't know about his parentage. Guilt would be written all over her face, not the desolate pain that marked it now. She couldn't have heard the original rumor, either; he would have seen that too, the night Michel had first mentioned it to them. And surely he would have felt the lie in her from the moment of their first communion?

"Oh, God, Lily," he said, when he finally found his voice, "that's the truth, isn't it?" He felt as if his knees might give out. The black, hopeless, endless hell he'd been living in had been blasted wide open, and light and love flowed into him in a great, life-giving stream. He drank of it as a man starved for oxygen might gulp at air.

"I can't believe you ever thought anything else," Lily said tightly. "That really hurts me, Pascal, and it's hard to forgive."

"I'm sorry," he said, wishing he could take back the three interminable months of agony they'd both been forced to live through. "I truly am sorry, but I do wish you'd told me all of this long before. You would have spared us both a great deal of pain." He looked at her, puzzled. Her crime was so small a transgression, it translated into none at all. "Why didn't you, Lily? I probably would have laughed my head off. It is a little ridiculous, isn't it?"

"Yes . . . but I wasn't sure you'd understand," she said, biting her lip, in that sweet gesture of confusion he'd missed so deeply.

"Why?" he asked quietly.

She released a quick breath. "In the beginning I didn't want my father to know why I'd really been at St. Christophe, because of Jean-Jacques. Later, I was embarrassed that I'd been so stupid. I planned to tell you, but I never found the right moment."

"All right," he said. "I can understand that. But you have to understand that what I overheard you say to your mother was damning. There was only one way I had to interpret it.'' He rubbed the back of his aching neck.

"You haven't much faith in me, have you?'' she said bitterly. "I know I've made some mistakes, but so have you. You might have stayed around to ask me about what you'd heard, instead of disappearing, leaving nothing more than a note. Do you have any idea what a shock that was? And you went after telling me you wouldn't ever leave me. How am I supposed to forgive you that?''

"It was finished as far as I was concerned.''

"Then the least you could have done was to read my letters!''

"I—I couldn't,'' he said hoarsely. "I honestly couldn't. It was hard enough trying to survive.''

"I know how that feels. I thought I'd never see you again, ever in my life, and I couldn't bear it.'' Her voice began to tremble, and she wiped her hand across her eyes.

"I'm sorry,'' he said, his heart hurting for her, for both of them. "I'm so sorry, sweetheart. I do know.''

"Well, you might know, but at least you had some control over your decision. I had nothing but a short note and the rest of my life ahead of me that I didn't want to live at all, not until I found out about the baby. But to come all the way here and be turned away just because you didn't feel like talking to anyone—''

"What?'' Pascal thought he might keel over in shock. "What—what did you say, duchess?''

"I said we're going to have a baby.''

He stared up at her, trying to absorb the news. A sudden, sharp joy seized him as it finally penetrated. "My God, Lily—you're pregnant?''

"Yes,'' she said simply. "I had no idea until four days ago. Coffey had to point it out to me. *I* thought I was suffering from grief.''

"Oh, Lily—sweetheart—this is wonderful! A baby . . .''

"I'm pleased to see that you're so happy about it, but I must say, to have to tell you from a monastery wall just because you were too stubborn to hear it any other way—''

His heart slammed against his ribs. "The wall! Oh, God, we have to get you down from there. It's dangerous. Don't move. I'm getting a ladder. Don't move. Please, don't move.''

He took off, found the ladder, badly barking his shin in

his haste, and made his way back to her, infinitely relieved to see she was still sitting in the same place. Lily. Impetuous, amazing Lily. Impetuous, *pregnant* Lily. The thought of her falling was enough to make the sweat break out on his brow. Lily did not have a reliable history on that wall.

"Don't move," he said again, solidly positioning the ladder. He climbed at lightning speed.

"It took you long enough," she said when he reached the top. "Now what do you intend to do?"

"I intend to get you safely down," he answered, scooping her up and putting her over one shoulder. Lily made only one token squeak of protest, which indicated to him that she didn't mind at all being removed from such a height. He very carefully made his way back down again and deposited her on firm ground, then looked at her for precisely one heartbeat and did what the moment demanded. He took her into his arms and kissed her so hard that it left them both shaking.

"Don't you ever, ever do this to me again," he said. "Ever."

"Don't you ever leave me again," she murmured against his neck.

"My God, duchess, do you think I wanted to? Do you have any idea? I thought I was—I truly thought I wasn't going to survive. I felt as if I'd been severed in half." He grasped her by the shoulders. "You and I, this connection we have, it's so damned strong it's frightening."

"Then why didn't you know the truth?" she asked in a very small voice.

"Because," he said, his own voice choked, "I'm only a man, Lily. I'm not omniscient." He pulled her against him and held her tightly, length against length, savoring the feel of her. It seemed an eternity had passed since he'd last had her in his arms.

"You were with me at night," she said, resting her head against his chest. "Always at night."

"I know," he replied, his arms tightening around her back. "I tried not to sleep. It didn't work. I tried to push you away. That didn't work either. But I didn't dare to truly look. I knew that if I did and found what I thought I'd find, it would finish me off." He sighed. "I suppose if I had, I would have known you were with child and spared us both a lot of misery. Lily?" he asked tentatively.

"What?" she replied, gazing lovingly into his eyes.

"The baby? May I feel it?"

A little sob escaped from her throat. She parted her cloak and pressed his hand against her. He gently covered the slight swell with his palm and closed his eyes. He was quiet for a moment, concentrating. And then he opened his eyes, smiling, his entire being filled with joy. "A boy," he said. "Oh, Lily! We're going to have a son, a fine little soul. Do you sense him?"

Lily shook her head, her eyes bright with tears. "Not the way you do. I feel love, and tenderness, and a need to nurture him, but I don't know him yet. I only know he's part of you and me, and that's enough. I—I thought he might be the only real thing I had left of you."

She gave a hiccup against his jacket, and he cupped her head tenderly. "I love you, duchess."

"I love you too," she murmured, and turned her face up for his kiss.

Oh, to have Lily's lips under his again, her sweet body real and firmly pressed against his, to have the unceasing torment vanish as if it had been a bad dream instead of a lifelong sentence. He felt like a condemned man being given a reprieve.

He was about to tell her that when he spotted Dom Benetard coming across the lawn toward them. He winced. "Ah, Lily. The abbot's caught us. Again."

"Oh, no," she murmured, trying to hide her smile. "These monks have such a prurient interest. I'm sure it comes from all that celibacy."

Pascal gave her a severe look, then turned to meet the abbot. "Father," he said, "forgive me. I—There was an unexpected, um . . . my wife appeared."

To his surprise, Dom Benetard laughed. "Never mind, Pascal. I'm happy to see you have worked through your troubles. Father Chabot alerted me that your wife might have done something unorthodox to command your attention, and we both thought we knew what it was. It seems we were correct."

"Forgive me, Father," Lily said, embarrassed. "I must be a terrible trial to you, but I could think of no other way."

"I do understand, Elizabeth. You love your husband with a great devotion. He is a fortunate man."

"Extremely fortunate, Father," Pascal said with a grin. "And doubly blessed. Lily is with child."

"Yes," the abbot said, smiling at her. "So I understand. I had a most elucidating talk with Father Chabot in the church while we waited for you to resolve your differences. I learned many interesting things." He regarded Pascal with an expression that clearly asked whether Pascal knew what he was referring to.

Pascal sighed. He hadn't given much thought to the repercussions of his birthright, not ever intending to act on it. "I had a letter a week ago, if you refer to the change in my worldly status, Father."

"What are you talking about?" Lily asked, perplexed.

Pascal rubbed his thumb over his mouth, wondering what Lily was going to do with this piece of news. "It seems, sweetheart," he said after a moment, "that I'm not Serge's bastard after all."

"No? Oh, Pascal . . . how wonderful! So Henri LaMartine *was* your father."

"No," Pascal said with a rueful smile. "He wasn't."

Lily regarded him as if the last three months in the monastery had affected his reason. "I know you have some unusual talents, Pascal, but *someone* has to have fathered you."

Dom Benetard chuckled, and Lily colored fiercely. "I'm sorry, Father, I didn't mean . . ."

"It's quite all right, child," the abbot said, his eyes sparkling with amusement. "I begin to see for myself why Father Chabot said you were meant for each other."

Lily smiled softly. "I do think God intended for us to be together; he certainly went to a great deal of trouble to see that we married and ended up in Saint-Simon. But speaking of that," she said, turning back to Pascal, "if you're not Serge's bastard, and you're not Henri's son, then who are you?"

"I'm ah . . . I'm a legitimate duke, Lily. Serge and Christine de Saint-Simon were my parents."

Her mouth dropped open.

"Your mother wrote to tell me. She is certain of it. Apparently Michel has known all along, but couldn't speak."

Lily drew in a shaky breath, then let it out again, and he couldn't for the life of him tell what she was thinking.

"Lily? Sweetheart?" he asked uncomfortably. "You don't

look very happy. It's not such a bad legacy to hand down to our child, is it?''

She looked up at him, a sparkle of tears in her eyes. ''Does this mean that we have to move out of our cottage?'' she asked with real sorrow.

Pascal gave a choked laugh. ''Oh, sweet duchess, only you. But yes, I suppose we will. Never mind. We'll need something larger anyway, with all the children I plan to give you.''

''Oh . . .'' she said, her hand creeping to her mouth. ''But Pascal, what about Jean-Jacques? I know he hasn't been a good duke, and the people will be thrilled to have you instead, but still—what will happen to him?'' She gazed at him gravely.

''I promise you, Lily, he will not suffer for this,'' Pascal said. ''He is family, flesh and blood, and I will see to his welfare.'' *I actually have a flesh-and-blood relative,* he thought with amazement as he heard his own words. With an inward groan he finished the thought. *But oh, God, why did it have to be Jean-Jacques?*

''What will he do? Where will he go?'' Lily said, her brow knotted with worry.

Pascal considered the problem. ''I think I might have a solution,'' he said, as an idea began to take shape. ''It's one that Jean-Jacques might well be happier for in the end. I'll tell you about it later.''

''Oh, good,'' she said with relief. ''You do have a talent for making everything work out, Pascal.''

He looked down into her sweet, trusting face. ''I'll do my very best,'' he said, hoping he could live up to her expectations. He was going to spend a lifetime trying.

Dom Benetard smiled at them both. ''I think it would be wise,'' he said tactfully, ''if we left the grounds before you're seen, Elizabeth. Why don't we repair through the back of the church to where Father Chabot awaits us? Now that the duchess has told you the truth, Pascal, he is finally free to speak, and he has things to explain to you.''

''As you wish, Father.'' Pascal took Lily's hand and started after the abbot, wondering why, when it came to the details of his life, he was always the last to know.

26

WORD spread quickly of their approach, and people lined the road even before they'd reached the village. Since the three of them sat up on the box, they received the full roar of approbation.

"The duke has returned!"

"I think the people approve, Monsieur le Duc," Lily said.

Pascal could only take her hand in his, speechless. He had been dreading his return, thinking that once the people knew the truth, they would be confused, perhaps a little resentful that a duke had moved among them as one of their own, and was now much grander than they. He certainly hadn't expected such a warm reception.

It hadn't been an easy thing, learning the truth, as gentle as Michel Chabot had been with it. He was shaken to his very foundation, and yet it was an enormous relief to have answers to so many questions. There were times that he still felt as if he were moving through a dream. He'd spent so many dark hours away from everything and everyone he'd come to love—now it was as though he was emerging into a daylight that was blinding, even more so for what it signified.

No, it was not an easy thing suddenly becoming a duke. But it was far easier than being set apart. It was infinitely easier than being severed from Lily. And in the end, being with Lily was everything.

He embraced her with his free arm. She'd been amazingly relaxed about everything that had happened, quietly listening as Michel had told him the heart-wrenching story of his mother's last hours, holding him close to her that same night in the inn, taking him into her body with gentle acceptance and love, allowing him to heal himself in her. Later, after they'd spoken the words that helped to soothe the painful breach of their separation, he had taken her again, this time a fierce act of reclamation. The third had been for simple joy.

Lily looked up at him, happiness glowing in her eyes. "They're so excited, Pascal. It's as if they're declaring you their very own."

He shook his head, his throat too choked for speech.

"You're more like your father than you realize," Father Chabot said, giving him a sidelong glance. "The people always turned out like this to welcome him home." He pointed ahead to the thronging village.

"How did they know?" Pascal asked in wonderment.

Father Chabot glanced at Lily. "I told your mother about your coming child just before we left," he said apologetically. "It seemed only fair that she be given the opportunity to do the right thing."

"You did well," Lily said softly. "My husband deserves a proper welcome home."

"Amazing, isn't it?" Pascal said hoarsely. "They really do look pleased." He skipped the turning to the château and headed straight into the village square. People swarmed around them, the cheers deafening.

Pascal leaned over and shouted to a beaming Alain Lascard to hold the horses' heads. And then he stood up and waved his arms, signaling for silence. It fell, a sudden, expectant hush.

"Friends," he said, thinking how true it was. They were all there, Pierre, Charles, their wives, old Monsieur Jamard, so many people he'd come to care for. "I . . ." His voice broke, and he had to swallow hard, for suddenly he couldn't speak at all.

Lily saw his dilemma and stood up next to him, taking his hand. "Friends," she said clearly, "my husband is so happy to be back among you that he is at a loss for words. It's not often that it happens to him, mind you, but at least it gives me a chance to get a word in edgewise."

That received a roar of laughter, and Pascal blessed Lily for her tact and for giving him the moment he'd needed to collect himself. He cleared his throat. "I did want to say a few words. This news has come as much of a surprise to me as it has to you." He smiled. "Probably more of a surprise to me—I understand you'd all had me named as Serge's son, anyway. I'm pleased to say that I'm proof my father was an honorable man."

More laughter and a few ribald comments, which pleased

him. He might be a duke, but apparently they still intended to treat him like a great, rutting commoner.

He gestured for silence again, his expression now serious. "As my father's son I have a pledge to make to you. As long as I live, I will see that you are cared for and that the land is looked after, and after me, my son will do the same." Pascal gave up trying to speak. He couldn't hear himself think over the uproar.

"And when can we expect this son, eh?" Pierre Marchand called out when the noise died down.

"According to my wife you can expect him next June," Pascal said, smiling down at Lily.

The villagers went wild. They would have picked Pascal up and carried him away if he'd let them. Instead, he climbed down and accepted handshakes and congratulations and words of encouragement. And then he returned to the carriage, leaving Michel Chabot to answer the countless questions.

Well, Pascal thought as he turned the horses toward the château, *it probably feels good to Michel after keeping his silence for thirty long years*. Now it was his turn to deal with the consequences of that silence.

He looked up toward the château. He would never forget the first time he'd seen it, all those months ago, perched on its rock, the limestone of the outer walls and turrets softly glowing in the evening light. Even then he had felt called to it, called to the land without knowing why. Now it made perfect sense.

He'd been born to it.

He'd been born to love it, to protect it, born to perpetuate it. And he would. As God was his witness, he would.

He let out a long breath against the aching twist in his chest, then turned the horses' heads for home.

"Large, isn't it?" Pascal said, poking his head into yet another room.

"After the cottage, it seems immense," she said.

"Drafty too," he noted. "We'll have to do something about that. I can't have my pregnant duchess running around in a draft."

Lily grinned. "I really am your duchess, aren't I? It's funny, that."

Pascal chucked her under the chin. "Not what you expected when you married me, was it?"

"Pascal, nothing about you has been what I expected. I've had one shock after another from the moment I first saw you, never mind married you. First I thought you were a gardener with a wife and a few children. Then I saw your face and decided you were a fallen angel.''

"Oh, yes, the hellish rake with no moral scruples.''

"Well, how was I supposed to know you were a virgin? You didn't look like one.''

"Oh?'' he said with a huge grin. "And how does a virgin look, duchess?''

"Not like you,'' Lily said adamantly. "Virgins are supposed to look innocent. You looked as if you had all the knowledge in the world and then some.''

"You just assumed in the wrong direction,'' he said, amused.

"And you accused *me* of keeping secrets? I didn't hide anything nearly so important as being able to produce miracles out of thin air. Can you imagine my astonishment when you brought Joseph-Jean back with no warning?''

Pascal kissed her nose. "Oh, all right,'' he said. "Maybe I should have told you first.''

"Yes, although I should have guessed something was up after that time you plastered yourself all over my soul.''

"I've paid the consequences for that in full measure,'' he said. "You don't have to worry about my ever leaving you again. I have a healthy respect for my sanity.''

"Good,'' Lily said, "because I intend to keep you right here next to me, Monsieur le Duc. For someone who was supposed to be born into the bourgeoisie, you've come quite a way in the world.''

"I do have a well-rounded background, haven't I?''

Lily smiled. "Comfortable in cottage or castle? I wasn't very pleased about *that* when you first installed me in the hovel down the road.''

"I just wanted you to be as well rounded as I was,'' he said, putting his arms around her. "I was successful, wasn't I?''

"I'll never be as well rounded as you, Pascal. I'm a simple duchess. You're a duke, a botanist, a physician—speaking of which, why didn't you tell me you had a medical license when I first asked about your training? I learned about it from Jean-Jacques. You made it sound as if you'd only taken a few courses here and there.''

"I didn't want you to think me *too* well rounded,'' he said with a smile. "No, to be honest, I didn't tell you because I didn't want to have to explain why I couldn't take money for my work. You believed exactly what I wanted you to—that I couldn't because of the law." He chuckled. "I took the medical degree because it seemed practical, and I didn't want any legal questions arising. But I had to become a botanist to support myself."

"Well, now that you have all these vineyards, be grateful you are a botanist—and that you're handy at carpentry. You have a large house to keep up, monsieur. Look, here's the duke's bedroom."

"I feel a little strange, Lily . . ." he said, as they approached it. "After all, I've just displaced Jean-Jacques."

"Nonsense," she replied briskly. "You were very diplomatic with him outside. I think your idea of having Jean-Jacques manage Saint-Simon's wine trade is brilliant."

"He'll enjoy himself in Paris, but his loss of position will still be a wrench," Pascal said tightly.

"Actually, I thought he looked relieved in an odd way. He never enjoyed the responsibility of the dukedom, and you did let him keep the fortune he won, after all. I thought that was *very* generous." She smiled mischievously. "Of course, I suppose you don't really need it, now that you've finally backed off your pride and agreed to use my dowry to support us . . ."

"Saint-Simon is worth far more to me than a small piece of my pride," Pascal said, reluctantly returning her smile. "It's Jean-Jacques's pride that I'm concerned about. I may have left him his blasted fortune, but I also took the profits from the crop away. I don't think he was very happy about that."

"It was only fair. Without you there wouldn't have been a profit. It's no good feeling guilty, Pascal. You can't change anything."

"No, I can't, but Jean-Jacques's anger was obvious, and he has every right to it. He's spent years in this role, only to have it snatched away from him through no fault of his own. What else has he ever had?"

Lily lightly touched Pascal's cheek. "He's always had himself. Maybe it's time he discovered who that person really is. Maybe this is even a blessing in disguise for Jean-Jacques. It seems to me that there have been rather a lot of blessings handed out lately, and perhaps this is just one more. How are we to know?"

"How indeed?" Pascal answered with a smile. He covered Lily's fingers with his own. "You are becoming positively wise, Lily."

Lily smiled. "Wiser than when you found me, anyway. Wise enough to know that you should let it be and accept your destiny.

Oh—and speaking of that, thank you for your graciousness toward my mother. I could see it meant a great deal to her.''

Pascal shrugged a shoulder. ''I don't envy her the battle she had to wage with her conscience. At least she won it, and in the end that will be a comfort to her. As for me . . . well, I suppose you're right. I will just have to learn about dukedoms.''

''And no better place to start than here,'' Lily said, opening the bedroom door.

Jean-Jacques had already moved out, and the room was empty of any personal belongings. Pascal stuck his head in, looking over the huge bed, the canopy worked in rich embroidery. The ceiling was painted with improbable scenes of heaven, discreetly draped men and women floating about on puffs of clouds, with an occasional cup of wine being offered to them.

Pascal gave a snort of laughter. ''Not very accurate,'' he said, ''but we'll let it go.'' He walked over to the bed and looked down at it, then up at Lily. ''I wonder,'' he asked with a little smile, ''if I was conceived here.''

''If your father was anything like you,'' Lily replied dryly, ''you might have been conceived anywhere at all.''

Pascal's smile faded. ''I wish I'd known them, Lily. I know they loved me, but it feels odd not having any memory of the people who brought me into this world. My mother carried me for nine months under her heart, yet I have no sense of her—or of my father.''

''You know they were good people and well loved,'' Lily said, thinking how inadequate that sounded.

''Yes, I do know that,'' Pascal said, ''and it was good of Michel to try to describe them, but that's not what I mean. I feel empty, somehow, as if a part of me is missing. I don't even know what they looked like.''

Lily's face lit up. ''I have an idea, Pascal. Let's go to the gallery. There are bound to be portraits of them in there.'' She grabbed his hand and dragged him out of the bedroom, down the hall, and down a flight of steps. The portrait gallery was in another wing. Lily knew; she'd been in it once before, although she hadn't been paying much attention at the time. Had she known she would later be married to the seventh Duc de Saint-Simon, she would have looked a good deal more closely.

The gallery was as cold as the rest of the house, and Lily shivered when she opened the door. ''Meet your family,'' she said.

''Good God,'' Pascal exclaimed, walking into the long room, whose walls were covered with portraits of varying sizes and shapes, from miniatures to life-size renditions. "Look at them all—and here I've gone through my life thinking that I had no relatives."

Lily looked at him with amusement. "Well, you are the only person I know who can lay claim to three separate sets of parents, but these people do share your blood. Goodness, who's this dreadful-looking old crone?"

She peered at a woman with an enormous powdered wig and a high-bridged nose. It was Pascal's nose, but far more attractive on him—and Jean-Jacques's nose too, she realized with surprise. She wondered that she'd never noticed the resemblance before.

"Lisette Marie de Saint-Simon," he read from the plaque underneath. "Painted in 1604. She looks a real battle-ax, doesn't she?"

"Awful," Lily agreed, straightening and turning to scan the room. And then she saw it. There, at the end of the far wall, was a portrait of a man, dressed in the clothes of thirty years before. He had been painted standing, a tall man, powerful in build. A slight smile turned up the corners of his mouth, and his eyes reflected the same gentle humor.

She knew him immediately for Pascal's father, not for any strong physical resemblance but more for a similar quality. She walked over to the painting and looked up at it.

Serge Alexandre, 6th Duc de Saint-Simon, the plaque read. The portrait had been painted in 1808, a year before his death.

"Pascal," she said simply, "I've found your father."

He came across the room without a word. Nor did he say anything as he looked upon his father's image for the first time. His face reflected his feelings far more eloquently than words ever could. Sorrow, regret, love, they were all there.

"I don't look much like him, do I?" he eventually said.

"You do in a way," Lily said, considering. "But Father Chabot did say that he thought you resembled your mother more than your father."

Lily noticed a portrait hung only a few feet away of a beautiful, fair-haired woman in a high-waisted blue dress. Her eyes were the same shape as Pascal's, and she had a sweet, wide mouth, the lower lip full and squared. "Look, Pascal, I wonder if this isn't your mother over here. You do have a similar expression, and it's the right period." She pointed.

Pascal's reaction stunned her.

"Dear God," he whispered. "Dear, dear God." He stared at the portrait as if he'd just seen a ghost. "It's her . . ."

"Who?" Lily asked, wondering why he'd gone pale. "Who, Pascal?"

He didn't answer. He walked over to the portrait and reached out a trembling hand, touching the painted surface very gently. "My mother," he said, his voice thick, barely audible. "All this time. My mother. I never knew."

"You never knew what?" Lily asked in confusion.

He turned to her, his face alight with a joy so profound that it took Lily's breath away.

"Do you remember when I told you about the shipwreck and what happened in the light?"

Lily nodded.

He looked back at the painting. "She was my angel."

The chapel sat on the west side of the château's boundaries, its back built into the fortifying wall. Pascal pushed the heavy oak door open. Although the sun was setting, it took a moment for his eyes to adjust to the dimness inside.

It was a peaceful place; he felt that instantly. It was also beautiful, a transverse arch suspending the dome, various elaborately carved tombs lining the walls leading up to the chancel.

It didn't take long to find the ones he was looking for.

Serge Alexandre. Christine Véronique. Their dates of birth and death were engraved alongside.

He ran his finger over the inscriptions. "Thank you," he whispered. "Papa, thank you for giving me life and this land. But oh, thank you, Mama, for looking after me when I was so badly in need. Thank you for loving me so well."

And then he traced his own name, the name that he'd been given at birth. *Alexandre Andre Philippe. Born April 9th, 1809* . . . No wonder the LaMartines had named him Pascal. He'd been born at Eastertide. *Died April 30th, 1809.*

But he hadn't died, Pascal thought with tremendous gratitude. *He'd been allowed to live, to find Lily, to find his place on earth.*

He dropped to his knees and gave thanks to God, who had finally seen fit to bring him home.

Epilogue

FATHER Chabot cupped his hand and dipped it into the baptismal font, pouring water over the back of the infant's head. He drew the sign of the cross in oil on his little forehead. "I baptize thee Andre Nicholas Serge," he said solemnly, "in the name of the Father, the Son, and the Holy Ghost."

Andre's face screwed up and his lower lip began to tremble in indignation. Lily had to suppress a laugh as he burst into tears. She glanced over at Pascal, who appeared to be relieved to have it over and done with. For someone as relaxed about the Kingdom of Heaven as he was, he'd been surprisingly anxious to see his son baptized.

"I'll have you know that Pascal was just as vocal when I baptized him," Father Chabot said, as Georgia wrapped Andre up and handed him back to Lily. "He howled for a good five minutes before he let himself be consoled."

Pascal looked down at their son, who had ceased crying and fallen into hiccups. "We're sensible people. Neither of us likes having his head soaked."

Georgia ran an adoring finger over the dark down on Andre's head. "He does look like you, Pascal, I must say."

"I certainly hope so, madame," Pascal said with a straight face. "It would be disconcerting if he looked like someone else."

Nicholas nodded. "A sentiment any father could understand." He looked around him. "It's a handsome chapel. Early sixteenth century, is it?"

"You have not lost your eye, monsieur. It is, indeed." He began to point out some of the more interesting architectural features, Father Chabot adding his comments.

Lily felt a tug of happiness as she watched Pascal with Nicholas and Georgia, who had arrived from England only an hour before and been dragged off to Andre's baptism as soon as Father Chabot could be fetched. Pascal had written them the day of Andre's birth, asking them both to be god-parents, for reasons he felt would be immediately evident. He'd been waiting impatiently ever since and had finally been rewarded.

"Your husband has a look of true contentment about him, don't you think?" Father Chabot spoke from behind her.

"He does, Father," she said, turning. "I was just think-ing that the last time he saw Nicholas and Georgia he looked very different. Of course, he was unhappy and angry, and being Pascal, naturally he'd bottled everything up. Thank goodness he doesn't do that anymore. But it's more than that, isn't it? He's changed, even over the last few months."

Father Chabot considered. "Knowing where he belongs has helped, and having a son has given him great happiness. But it seems to me, Lily, that what has made the most dif-ference is how well you have loved him. God must be pleased indeed."

"Father . . ."

"I must get back to the village. Tell Pascal that when he has a moment, Maurice Latvier has taken to his bed with another attack of boils." He smoothed a hand over Andre's head, gave her a swift smile and left, pretending not to notice the tears in her eyes.

Lily observed Pascal over dinner that evening, thinking about what Father Chabot had said. It was true. Pascal looked happy, fulfilled, very much at ease. He had grown naturally into his role of duke over the last seven months, intuitively finding his way. For a man who had always had the simplest of needs, she thought he'd done very well.

The people adored him, of course. They were more def-erential toward him, but he understood that it was a neces-sary part of his position, that he had an obligation to live up to expectations. Still, the deference didn't go so far as to separate him from his people in any way, and he'd been amusing about it.

"It's very difficult for people to be overly deferential when you have them at their most vulnerable," he'd said to her. "Monsieur Perotte never remembers to call me anything other than torturer when I have his backside bent over a chair."

Pascal did enjoy his life.

But she knew that the moment of his greatest joy, the same moment that had set the church bells to wild ringing and the villagers to mad celebration, had been Andre's birth.

"Brave, clever duchess," he'd said, love shining in his eyes as he received his son into his hands after a tedious but unexceptional labor. "Brilliant, beautiful duchess. He's perfect—just perfect." Lily had been so dazzled by the golden light surrounding them that she thought she might float away. And in that light, she could have sworn she saw the image of a lovely angelic being, remarkably similar to the portrait of Pascal's mother.

Lily rested her chin on her fist, gazing at Pascal with a dreamy smile, thinking what a lucky, lucky woman she was.

He met her eyes and smiled in return, a smile that spoke of warm, private things and made her desperately wish she didn't have to wait to do something about it. Pascal hadn't worried for one minute about restraining himself before Andre's birth, but he'd been adamant about keeping himself away for the month since. It really was a nuisance—she desperately wanted to be with him, to have him with her, inside her, in more than just spirit.

Pascal read her mind. She knew by his swiftly lowered eyes and the sudden tightening of his hands on his fork and knife.

"How is your brother, Lily?" Nicholas asked with an amused expression that Lily knew meant he'd intercepted their silent exchange. "I understand he's been very successful in promoting Saint-Simon's wines."

"He's well, thank you," she said, trying to suppress a blush. "Jean-Jacques loves Paris."

"A Paris cleansed of the Comte de Passy, thanks to you, monsieur," Pascal added. "I'm not sure Jean-Jacques would ever have gone back if it hadn't been for Passy's going to prison."

"Arranging for Passy to be turned over to the Bourbons," Nicholas said with satisfaction, "was an extreme pleasure. And thank you again, Pascal, for the list of conspirators. That really was a stroke of good fortune. We think that Bonaparte will try another coup in August, but he is now guaranteed to fail miserably." He looked back at Lily. "Your brother was far more useful than he'll ever know."

"Well, I'm happy he was good for something," Lily said. "I was very annoyed with Jean-Jacques for having brought

Passy here in the first place.'' She didn't think it worth
bringing up Passy's role in bringing her father and his priest
down to Saint-Simon—any mention of Father Mallet only
made Pascal's blood boil. But to her surprise, Pascal brought
the subject up himself.

He put down the apple he'd been about to peel. ''I don't
think I ever told you,'' he said, idly testing the edge of his
knife with his thumb, ''that Passy wrote a letter to Lily's
father, in which he accused both Jean-Jacques and myself
of mistreating Lily. I imagine he was angry that we'd foiled
his plan to use Saint-Simon for his meeting place.''

''I did like your diphtheria epidemic,'' Georgia said. ''It
was a masterly touch.''

''Thank you, madame. I was quite pleased with it myself.
Passy, however, was not, so he took his revenge.''

''I don't know what he thought a vitriolic letter was going
to accomplish,'' Lily said. ''There wasn't much my father
could have done even if the things Passy wrote had been
true.''

Pascal glanced down the table at her. ''Oh, I imagine
your father could have found a way to stir up some trouble
for me and embarrass Jean-Jacques if he had decided to put
some effort into it.''

''How very interesting,'' Nicholas said. ''A typically un-
derhanded Passy maneuver. What happened? Did Montcrieff come roaring straight down?''

''He did,'' Pascal replied, ''and he brought his priest
with him. Of course, by then I'd found out the truth about
my parents, and we were living here.''

Nicholas sat back and folded his arms across his chest.
''I must say, Pascal, when you decide to do something, you
don't hold back. First you marry the heiress to a duchy,
then you become a duke yourself, and finally you produce
a son who will eventually be a duke twice over—and all in
the space of a year. Impressive work.''

''Thank you, monsieur,'' Pascal said with a grin, ''although the only part I can really take credit for is the last.
Everything else was sheer accident. At least my title helped
placate Montcrieff, as did Lily's pregnancy, but Montcrieff
wasn't very happy to find Lily's mother in residence, poor
man. That gave him quite a shock. Father Mallet was even
unhappier.''

''Why is that?'' Nicholas asked, watching Pascal play

with his knife as if he intended to do some serious damage with it.

Pascal didn't answer for a moment, and Lily knew exactly what he was thinking.

Because he was finally caught out on every filthy point of his lies and perversions. Because I nearly put my hands around his neck and strangled him.

That had been a formidable moment, when Pascal had confronted Father Mallet about the awful things he'd done to her. Yes, better the entire truth remain between them. It was not a subject she wished to address either. They had put it to rest, and that was where it would stay.

Pascal put his knife down. "Because he was a miserable, corrupt excuse for a priest," he said mildly enough, his tone belying the anger in his eyes. "He'd interfered between husband and wife and succeeded in destroying a happy marriage. Once Montcrieff realized the damage Mallet had done, he expelled him."

"My goodness," Georgia said. "That must have been interesting."

"You've always been a master of the understatement, madame." Pascal let out a sigh. "Ah, well. It was too late for Lily's parents, but maybe Sutherby will be a happier place now that Mallet is gone. At least Lily's mother is happier for having her children back, and she and Coffey seem to be enjoying their travels. But never mind that. Tell me about Charlie. How do you think he's doing in Bombay? I had an enthusiastic letter from him, saying that he's having a wonderful time, but I don't know how well that bodes for the business."

Nicholas chuckled. "Let me tell you about Charlie and Bombay." He soon had them all in fits of laughter.

Pascal refilled Nicholas's glass and put the crystal decanter back on the table. "I'm pleased that you approve of my cognac, monsieur. You have very discriminating taste."

"I approve of your wife, too, and I have discriminating taste in that area as well. Lily has come a long way since we last met her. You seem very happy together." He leaned down and rubbed Bean's ears.

"We are very happy together. I love Lily with all my heart." Pascal returned to the armchair and picked up his own glass. "A year ago I never would have thought it possible. Now, I can't imagine life without her. Actually, I discovered that I don't have any life without her.''

''Oh, you mean that last sojourn you made to St. Christophe?'' Nicholas casually held his glass up to the light, examining the clear amber liquid. ''Yes, that sounded bloody awful. Well, at least it finally penetrated that stubborn head of yours that you weren't meant to be a monk.''

''No,'' Pascal said ruefully, ''I most certainly wasn't. Keeping my hands to myself this last month has been next to impossible.''

Nicholas grinned. ''I'm happy to hear it. I always did wonder how you managed those long stretches locked away from the world.''

''You can't miss something you know nothing about,'' Pascal said, amused by Nicholas's incredulous expression.

''No . . .'' Nicholas said on a long exhale. ''I don't believe it.'' He rubbed his neck. ''Then again, maybe I do.''

''It was worth waiting for,'' Pascal said with a smile. ''Lily was worth waiting for. It was . . . it was important that we came to each other virgins.''

''Why, if you don't mind my asking? It's not the usual state of affairs for men to go to their marriage beds inexperienced.''

Pascal thought. It was hard finding the right words. ''I suppose,'' he said slowly, ''that it had to do with claiming each other. We'd done that in spirit in a place where we were both pure. To take each other in body—we needed to be the same.'' He frowned. ''Am I making any sense at all?''

''Pascal, you've been places and done things that most of us can't even begin to understand,'' Nicholas said. ''Nothing you say surprises me, not really. For you to approach the sexual aspect of life from a spiritual level makes perfect sense. But tell me something. Does Lily understand about you, about your gift?''

''Oh, yes,'' Pascal said quietly. ''She thinks I'm perfectly ordinary. You see, that was God's real gift to me. Lily sees heaven too.''

Later that night Pascal turned the handle to the bedroom door and eased it open. Lily lay curled on her side, her hands tucked under one cheek. She was asleep.

He slipped into the room and quietly undressed, carefully sliding under the sheets. The look in her eyes tonight had told him she was ready for him. Very, very ready. He couldn't wait another moment.

He rolled toward her and gently dropped a kiss on her mouth, molding her lips to his. Her eyes opened halfway and her arms wrapped around him, pulling him close.

"Pascal," she murmured. And then her eyes opened wider. "Pascal . . . you're not in the dressing room. You're in bed."

"You're so observant," he said, kissing her neck, warm and sweet-smelling.

Lily twined her fingers in his hair and kept them there as he raised his head and kissed her soft mouth.

"Does this mean we don't have to wait any longer?" she asked happily.

"Not if you'll have me, duchess." He stroked his hand over her full breast.

"Always," she murmured, moving onto her back and reaching for him. "Oh, always, Pascal. I've missed you so much."

"I've missed you too, sweetheart." Pascal bent his head and began to love her in earnest.

Later, as Lily slept in his arms, Pascal looked up at the ceiling of the bedroom, painted with all those absurd clouds and cavorting angels. He smiled every time he saw it, thinking how little it resembled the real thing.

"Well, Lord," he whispered, "you may have made me different, and I honestly don't mind reaching into heaven to do a miracle here and there for You. But as an ordinary man, I have to say that there's nothing sweeter than the heaven I've found right here in my own home and my own bed."

He released a contented sigh, pulled Lily a little closer, and closed his eyes.